THE
PEACEABLE
KINGDOM

THE
PEACEABLE
KINGDOM

19 49

by Ardyth Kennelly

HOUGHTON MIFFLIN COMPANY · BOSTON

The Riverside Press Cambridge

To Mother

THE
PEACEABLE
KINGDOM

CHAPTER 1

IT WAS SAID that Sigrid cried for three solid days and nights when Olaf gave Linnea the big Home Comfort range with six lids and a reservoir on the side that said in handsome raised letters: "Both dampers up to bake, upper damper up, lower damper down to heat reservoir." The children at once memorized these directions and went about proudly repeating them like poetry. With the stove came a whole set of blue granite-iron cooking utensils—these were free, but Sigrid was mad about them too. She had a good kitchen range at the time, however, and all Olaf could do was buy her a gilt wicker-and-bamboo center table for the parlor and a hanging lamp with prisms.

When Linnea heard what Olaf had done, *she* got mad. "Here I haven't even got a album and have to keep the family photographs in a pasteboard box," she said, "till I'm ashamed to bring them out and show them. And Sigrid lays down and bawls and what does she get!"

It took quite a while for Olaf to have a little something extra so he could make this up to Linnea, but he managed it finally—he always made up to them both the best he could—with curtain rods, this time, and new lace curtains. These couldn't have come at a better time, right after fall housecleaning, and they were beautiful. The rods were something unique; they looked like long crooked branches with the knots showing, and the twigs sawed off. They were mounted across the window like gilded antlers, and had shiny brass curtain rings. The curtains were white lace, scalloped, as heavy as lead, and they were so long they lay out on the ingrain carpet in fan shapes which Linnea was long in arranging.

Linnea thought that Sigrid had so many drawbacks because she was of Norwegian descent. Sigrid thought that being Swedish on both sides was the main trouble with Linnea. The truth was, they only had the one husband, and their pique made them find fault with each other. One husband was really not quite enough.

Olaf Ecklund, the American-born son of Norwegian parents, a tailor by trade and a convert for some ten years to a large religious group called Mormons or Latter-Day Saints, living in Salt Lake City, to which he had come from Minnesota because it was this church's Zion, had been married (whether happily or unhappily he never was heard to say) eight years. He had a girl, seven, and a boy, four, to show for it when, at thirty years of age, he took a notion to cleave unto another helpmeet. He would go on cleaving to Sigrid, the wife he already had, of course. This was polygamy, highly extolled, and he decided he would try it. Sigrid gave her free consent as she was a still more pious convert than her husband. Besides, his second wife, though eight years younger than herself—Linnea was barely twenty at the time—couldn't hold a candle to her for looks. Sigrid was extremely pretty.

It nearly knocked Sigrid off her perch, therefore, when Linnea got her licks in anyway and in no time was such a favorite of Olaf's that it was alarming. But she claimed it was because he had to sneak around to get to see Linnea those first years. The United States Government was up in arms about polygamy and there were federal agents all over, trying to catch the polygamists. A man couldn't go from one wife to another. He had to be pretty sly and careful. Sigrid claimed that was why Olaf got to be such a fool over Linnea. "Forbidden fruit always tastes the sweetest," she said. "Just wait till the Church settles with the Government this polygamy business. Then you'll see the difference. It won't be the same thing at all."

Linnea, for one reason or another, couldn't stay put like Sigrid. She was always moving around. She liked the two back rooms she found down on Fourth East the time Bertha was three and Gertrude a year old, but then, she always liked whatever house she moved into. Her friend Ingeborg said it was because she liked moving so well, but Linnea denied this. She said, just let her own a house once and she'd stay as put as Brigham in his burying place. It was circumstances, she said, kept her on the go.

In that Fourth East house, for the first time in her life Linnea was afraid of somebody. She was afraid of her landlady. Mrs. Buller was a middle-aged woman who must have been lovely once, though always of the fat type. The only thing that wasn't nice about her was her cat's eyes, too round, with a queer elongation to the pupils. Three or four beautiful long white teeth showed that once upon a time her set of thirty-two must have been something to brag about. Her greasy gray hair, full of dandruff, untidily piled up on top of her head and precariously fastened with bone hairpins that always looked as if they were going to fall out, was still thick and full of vitality. She had a great many dimples, in her cheeks, her elbows and across the backs of her large babyish hands. A nice woman, Linnea thought. It was only when Linnea got moved in that she began to suspect there was something wrong with her head. She would, for instance, start to laugh nervously about something and couldn't stop. Her friend Mrs. Golightly told Linnea about a man in New York, found dead in a park, who had starved to death—she read it in the papers. Somehow or other the doctors got hold of this poor man and did a post-mortem on him (that meant an operation to see what he had died of) and when they cut his stomach open, they found it was full of grass! He couldn't get anything to do and the times were so bad, and here he went to work and browsed and nibbled on the grass like an animal, trying to keep alive. But he died. Linnea happened to mention this to Mrs. Buller, her landlady, right after Mrs. Golightly told her. To her astonishment, Mrs. Buller tittered and tittered and then laughed outright. She couldn't seem to stop. She laughed so much she had to brush the tears out of her eyes. Over a man starving to death with green grass in his stomach! Linnea thought it peculiar of her.

Then, she had a way of whispering to herself. Or staring at a person without once blinking. Or maybe she would take a notion at three o'clock in the morning and hang out a wash, or sweep the parlor.

Linnea thought Mrs. Buller lived alone in the house, not having seen or heard anybody else, until the night she woke from a sound sleep and heard a scream. She sat up in bed with her heart in her mouth, and heard it again, and heard a whistling thump, thump, thump, like a lash or a whip brought down hard through the air and landing on the floor. She got up and ran across the room to see if her two little girls were all right. They were sound asleep, curled into round balls. Moonlight made the room as bright as day but when she pushed open the door into the hallway she found it pitch dark. Feeling her way, she crept over to the foot of the stairs and looked upwards, but it was too dark for her to see anything. She listened, holding her breath. Now, there wasn't a sound. She strained her ears. All she could hear was her own ticking clock through her open door, and the creak of a bedspring as one of her babies stirred. "Mrs. Buller," she called softly. "Mrs. Buller." No sound. Oh, dear, maybe the woman was murdered upstairs. What in the world should she do? Go for somebody? And how could she leave Bertha and Gertrude?

But Mrs. Buller was not murdered. She was standing at the top of the stairs. All Linnea could perceive of her in the blackness was her voice. This floated eerily down the stair well. "Go to bed," she said. "What you up for? Go to bed. Ain't nothing wrong."

"But I thought I heard a scream," Linnea said. "I thought I did, just as plain. It woke me up."

"Me," Mrs. Buller said. "Hollering in my sleep. Guess I had a nightmare. Go back to bed."

Linnea went back to bed but she kept thinking of that scream and cold shivers kept running down her back. "I must of been dreaming," she decided.

When she heard it in the daytime one day about a week after she moved in she knew she was not dreaming and that Mrs. Buller was a liar. She went right out and started up the stairway but Mrs. Buller was at the top of the stairs coming slowly downwards, so Linnea backed up and stood by the newelpost looking upwards and waiting.

"What's wrong with you?" Mrs. Buller asked, beginning to laugh. She had been chewing on some cinnamon drops. The smell of cinnamon was plain and her lips and tongue were stained a bluish-pink. She still chewed reminiscently though the candy was gone, between titters.

"Nothing's wrong with me," Linnea said. "I thought I heard somebody screaming up there, is all."

"You got screaming on the brain," Mrs. Buller said, laughing roseredly.

Linnea went into her apartment and at once bundled up the children and took them to her friend Ingeborg's. "She gets the funniest look in her eyes you ever seen," she said, "and her eyes is peculiar to start with. The least little thing, she starts in with the giggles. It always makes me nervous to hear her, she can't seem to quit. I know I heard somebody holler. Maybe she's got a animal up there or something. It don't sound like either a man or a woman. I don't know what it sounds like."

"Maybe you just imagine it," Ingeborg said.

"No, I don't," Linnea said, "and you ought to know me well enough. That woman's out of her head as sure as I'm a foot high. And here I was so glad to get rooms with such a nice lady."

"She belongs to the church, don't she?" Ingeborg asked.

"What's that got to do with it?"

"Well—"

"That don't prevent her from being crazy, does it? There's crazy Latter-Day Saints just like there's crazy other people," Jensen, Ingeborg's husband, said.

"I dread to go back," Linnea said, sighing.

"Why not stay here?" Ingeborg asked.

"I believe I will," Linnea said. "At least a day or two, till I get my bearings, and thanks to you for the offer. She's a regular loon."

A few days later she found a place with an English convert whose husband was on a two-year mission in Finland. This was where Stellie was born, her third daughter. She often mentioned Mrs. Buller and wondered what that scream had meant and those whipping sounds, but nothing more was heard of her until a year later. The missionary husband came home from Finland and the English convert didn't have room for her any more, so Linnea moved again.

It was when she lived in Mr. Hudson's house that the news came of

Mrs. Buller's bad end, and Linnea talked about it for weeks afterwards. But then, everybody did. She said it didn't surprise her one bit—she knew something terrible like that was going on—she felt it in her bones.

Mrs. Buller had continued to rent her two rooms, always to polygamous wives, no doubt considering they were the least likely to cause any fuss, but eventually one of them brought the police to the house with a warrant and had them search it. They found an old man weighing eighty-five pounds chained to a massive bed in a small upstairs bedroom, with festering wounds across his back. Crying like a baby, he said he was Mrs. Buller's brother. He said he and his wife took her in when Mr. Buller died, whenever that was. He imagined it was quite a long while ago. And now his sister was always trying to persuade him to sign this property over to her and give her his money, too. He wouldn't do it, though, he said, because he didn't think she'd ought to chain him up and beat him like that. That wasn't no way to do. He thought it was mean of her. Sometimes he'd scream. The reason he didn't scream more often was because his sister said if he screamed and carried on, his wife wouldn't never come back. But she'd been gone such a long time. To save his soul he didn't know *how* long, he'd kind of lost track. His sister said if he'd sign the property over to her, and not make no noise, his wife would come back. His wife had gone to Cincinnati and wanted him to do that, his sister said. He didn't know, though. He couldn't quite make up his mind why she'd take such a notion. And anyway, why would she want to go to Cincinnati? It was very confusing. He would go there himself, and bring her back, only he was dwindling away so and his sister had such a bad disposition and kept him chained up. She was just like their father's family, onry and mean. All he could do was lay there and wait for his wife to come home. His story was in all the papers.

His wife, poor woman, was as helpless as himself, for she lay buried in the back yard in a rotting peignoir with her knees drawn up under her chin like an Indian. That is, if her chin had been in the proper place. But it wasn't, for her head was cut off and wrapped in a fringed bath towel and lay in her lap. Linnea had walked over her several times when she hung out diapers, for her grave was under the clothesline, and whenever she thought about it, the hair raised up along the back of her neck.

She used to tell the children about this in after years and say it was lucky they were not murdered in their beds. That is, it was lucky Bertha and Gertrude were not murdered in their beds. However, even the children who were not born at the time breathed a sigh of relief whenever they heard about it. They always felt that they had had a terrible narrow escape and that *they* might have been murdered in their beds, too.

The rooms Linnea rented at Mr. Hudson's were really very nice. Rudie was born there. It was a large old-fashioned house and Mr. Hudson, who didn't seem to have to work for a living, occupied it with three women. One of them was supposed to be his wife and the other two were either sisters-in-law or cousins, sometimes one and sometimes the other. Even Linnea, a polygamous wife herself, was never entirely let in on the secret. But it didn't make any difference, everybody knew perfectly well they were his three wives. It was a good thing he had them, Linnea told her intimates, for one of the women, the oldest and prettiest, never did anything but cook, one, the middle one, never did anything but clean, and one, the youngest and ugliest, never did anything but sit around and do fancy work and doll herself up—so he really needed three, in order to get one! In fact, maybe he needed more than that, for he hadn't a chick nor a child.

When Rudie, Linnea's first boy, was nine months old, the federal men got hold of Olaf and arrested him for unlawful cohabitation, which didn't mean *that*, exactly, but meant that he had two wives. They sent him to the penitentiary. Just before, there was quite a scare. At the time, the whole neighborhood was up in the air because so many polygamists were being taken up. Babies were the best evidence in the world, so Linnea, the alarm having been given that there were deputies in the vicinity, took Rudie to Mrs. Hansen's until the danger was past. Mrs. Hansen, however, got scared and sent her biggest girl with him to Mrs. Lundgren's. Mrs. Lundgren thought better of it and handed him to Mrs. Olsen for safekeeping. Mrs. Olsen stopped to consider the danger of his being found in her own ambiguous household and fobbed him off on Mrs. Peterson.

When the scare was over and Linnea went to get her baby, it was no easy matter to find him. From Mrs. Hansen's to Mrs. Lundgren's to Mrs. Olsen's to Mrs. Peterson's to Mrs. Williamson's to Mrs. Anderson's she walked twenty-two killing Salt Lake City blocks only to find him sleeping like an angel practically next door, at Mrs. Crawford's, who had the blinds all pulled down and had to peek out to see who it was before she opened the door.

Since he did not wake even to whimper before ten o'clock the next morning, Linnea suspected that someone had given him a good stiff dose of paregoric somewhere along the line. He might have had more than one, as a matter of fact, but except for being a little crosser than usual that afternoon, which might in any case be laid to his teething, he suffered no ill effects.

Gertrude, who was going on five at the time, always remembered her visit to the penitentiary because Mamma got her a white eiderdown "toboggan," a little bonnet-like cap with a curling pale-blue feather, and the warden took her up on his lap and gave her a horehound stick.

She only went once, because they let Papa out in six months. Mamma said not to blab around how well she remembered it; it wasn't any particular honor to have a father in the penitentiary even if he wasn't a regular criminal. It was just as well to keep kind of mum about the matter.

Some author, not perhaps considering the thing from all sides and from every angle, wrote smugly of woman and of her labor, creation, mothering, and homemaking, "She should . . . live a long time in one place. What sort of tree can you plant afresh every few years?" Well, but good trees marched away for Orpheus, whose music was so sweet and coerced them into it. The tree that Linnea was, could march and move, too, not the less shading and succoring those beneath her branches, when circumstances, not spell-weaving music, told her it was time to make a change.

She told Olaf, when she packed up and left the Hudson's, that now she had four children, one a babe in arms, she would be much better off in rooms on Second South with Miss Reese and her mother. She happened to pass the house and saw the For Rent sign and inquired within. It was a snugger apartment and the pump was closer.

Miss Reese was long past her time of power and prestige in the outside world though she still ruled her home with an iron hand. She used to have a very fine voice and was often asked to sing at funerals, she said. This voice had mysteriously left her, along with her eighteen-inch waist, number five glove and number two shoe. Almost everything about her was much larger now, except her hopes. These had grown small and humble as the knot of hair on top of her head, since love had dealt her such a wound. A man she knew, a piano salesman at the Daynes-Beebe Music Store, had up and married a widow woman who merely came onto the premises to buy a piano for her daughter's thirteenth birthday. That his intentions had been in earnest toward herself, she had no doubt whatsoever, for reasons she could speak of, and those such as tender glances and fond pressings of the hand which she would not reveal but would keep forever locked within her heart. For instance, the man (not to name any names) had not only paid several calls upon her but had escorted her out to Lagoon on Pioneer Day and had even taken her to the Salt Lake Theatre to see Edwin Booth in *The Great Moral Drama, A Warning to Youth, or, The Six Degrees of Crime: Wine, Women, Gambling, Theft, Murder, The Scaffold,* which was surely compromising enough if anything ever was.

Her hope box, already a collection of consequence at the time the perfidious piano salesman (and tuner, one perhaps ought to add) began his wooing, had now grown to breathtaking proportions. She had seventy-eight crocheted doilies alone, of all sizes, mostly of the pineapple pattern for which she had an almost unreasonable fondness, a crocheted piano scarf with tassels a foot long hanging six inches apart all across the front and sides for a nonexistent piano (thank God, she had not let herself be so far carried away as to actually purchase one from him—she could never have looked herself straight in the face again, if she had), sixteen bureau scarves, a pile of pillow shams that said *Good Morning,* a pile of pillowcases that said *Good Night,* twenty-three centerpieces and other items too numerous to mention.

Her mother, a frail mournful old lady who, in contrast with her daughter, had once been large and was now small, made two of the centerpieces and was said to have contributed an embroidered night-gown case that said in blue forget-me-nots *Don't Peek!*

Linnea always said she might have stayed permanently in the other half of Miss Reese's house (there wasn't any law against her saying it) for it was easy to heat in winter and was cool in summer and she and the children were really as snug as a bug in a rug there. Something very surprising happened, however, that not only necessitated her moving but called a halt on the hope box. Miss Reese died. She was only fifty-one years old at the time and had been as hale as anybody. It was almost more than a person could grasp. Old Mrs. Reese had had the doctor too, and been up day and night and done everything in her power to save her child. Linnea did everything in *her* power to save her landlady, but all to no avail, though at the last she didn't take her clothes off for thirty-six hours or even so much as shut her eyes.

And that summer, after Miss Reese died, what did Old Mrs. Reese do but get married? Her groom, a widower, whom she had met at a band concert in Liberty Park, an appetizing old man with a "little something laid by," had a married daughter. This married daughter had a married daughter now callously deserted, who lived with her and was *enceinte.* The married daughter also had three sons of various ages. They would be glad to move into the other half of Old Mrs. Reese's house, so the old lady, who was really only sixty-eight, asked Linnea politely if she would mind moving. Linnea said obligingly that no, of course she would not.

And she did not. For the first time in her life she had a whole house, all of four rooms and a pantry, so there was space and to spare for her to set aside that *sacrarium,* Holy of Holies, a real parlor . . . and it was for this Olaf supplied her with the gilt curtain rods and long lace curtains to make up for the center table and hanging lamp he had given Sigrid to make up for the Home Comfort range he had given Linnea to make up for—but the list could go on and on. No, she did not mind moving.

In fact, it was rather a good thing in a way, perhaps, that poor Miss Reese died. At least, somebody got some good out of her hope box. And if you want to know who—it was her mother, of course. Who else? She dipped into it freely and made lavish use of it, even of the seventy-eight doilies, and never a day but her own modest nightgown lay folded in the case that said *Don't Peek!* And when, after ten long years of wedded bliss, her husband gave up the ghost, it was upon Miss Reese's pillowcase sweetly embellished with the words *Good Night.*

As Linnea said to Ingeborg, "Honestly to goodness, a person has no idea, have they?"

Sigrid said Linnea just naturally didn't have it in her to stay put. She spoke of her own accomplishment, that of living in the same house ever since the day she was married, as a kind of talent, like an ear for music. Linnea just didn't have it, she said.

Linnea never happened to hear her say it. She would have told her a thing or two if she had!

CHAPTER 2

IN UNLAWFUL COHABITATION, otherwise known as polygamy, there were many problems to work out. For instance, what about holidays? Olaf did the following: If he spent Thanksgiving with Sigrid one year, the next Thanksgiving found him at Linnea's spending the day with her. The same with Easter or New Year's eve. He spent two Pioneer Days straight hand running, however, with Linnea, Sigrid being at home in bed getting over a miscarriage, and although she didn't say boo at the time, on later occasions—even years after—and in fact starting the very next day, she threw it up to him until he wished he had never heard of Pioneer Day or Lagoon or anything else. It was Sigrid's turn, there was no doubt of that, but on July 20 she came down with the miscarriage, so naturally she was in bed when the holiday rolled around. What she claimed was that it being her turn, the least Olaf could do was to spend the day with her, whether he forewent the celebration at Lagoon or not. He claimed she said that as long as he had tickets and everything and all his plans made to see the pageant and everything, there was no sense in wasting them. Anyhow, he went, and took Linnea, who had packed a big picnic basket and was wearing pearl-gray toile with a ribbon sash. One of Sigrid's lady friends who ran into Olaf and Linnea told her about that sash and how Linnea was laughing fit to kill and had curled bangs under a hat all weighed down with lilacs. Sigrid said she had little to do to wear a sash tied around her waist in a big bow in back like she thought she was sixteen years old or something. Also, that was bound to be a new hat.

"It's a mystery to me," Sigrid said, "how she always manages to sashay around in new clothes. Or rather," she added, glaring at him, "it ain't no mystery. Even somebody as blind as a bat wouldn't have to look around very hard to see who she makes putty of. You, that's who. Why, you're her regular *tool*," she said.

She cried and carried on terribly over Pioneer Day, but Olaf laid it
to her miscarriage and Linnea did, too, when she heard about it, but
all the same she wouldn't give Sigrid the following Thanksgiving, to
make up to her. "We'll go right on like we been going on," she said,
"otherwise there'll never be no end to it and we won't know *where*
we're at." So Olaf had to spend Thanksgiving with Linnea just as
though nothing had ever happened, because it was her turn and perfectly legal. Sigrid had her husband for Christmas.

Usually, when alone, Linnea went to Ingeborg's for the day, or
Ingeborg came to her, but that year Mrs. Orbit got her bid in very early
and would not take no for an answer. Linnea had to give her solemn
promise she would bring the children and eat Christmas dinner with the
Orbit family. Mrs. Orbit said that if it had not been for Linnea she would
be dead (she was not a Christian Scientist at the time and that made all
the difference in the world). Not only that, her youngest daughter
Juanita, at whose birth Linnea had officiated, would be dead, too. The
child got seriously tangled in the cord and nearly choked to death,
embarrassing and dangerous complications also arose, all of which
Linnea coped with brilliantly, so Mrs. Orbit felt that if ever she wanted
to do anything for anybody in her life, she wanted to do it for Linnea.
She had been after her for three Christmases now, and this time it was
either do or die.

Linnea had a great fondness for Mrs. Orbit but at the same time she
accepted the invitation with misgivings.

Mrs. Orbit was the only woman Linnea ever knew who read books.
Not only did she buy the paper-backed kind, but she actually went to
the library and drew books out, two at a time and read them all through.
The beds would not be made, the ironing close to mildew, the cold dishwater not thrown out the back door, the leftovers moldering in the
pantry, but Mrs. Orbit had to get through those books to see how they
turned out. The stove would not be blacked, the ashes showering down
upon the hearth, the house cold, the children as free as birds, herself in
a morning sack with an unkempt head of witch's hair, but the books
had to be read. For her neighbors Mrs. Orbit was that thing to be
mysteriously whispered about, like the drinker or hermaphrodite, the
Novel Reader. They pointed out her house to strangers: A Novel
Reader lives in there.

Linnea had misgivings about spending Christmas with the Orbits and
wished she had not had to promise. Everybody knew Mrs. Orbit did not
even set a Christian table for her own family, but let them help themselves at any hour of the day or night to bakery bread, eggs, coffee,
cheese or whatever they could find. Not only that, she was renowned
for her poor housekeeping, and when all the other ladies were in the
midst of Spring Housecleaning or Fall Housecleaning, Mrs. Orbit

wasn't in the midst of anything except a book called *Ethelyn's Mistake* or *The Lost Heir of Linlithgow* or *Spectre Lover*.

It would be pretty poor pickings, Linnea feared, in an untidy house, but she couldn't get out of it another year. She had to go, but she wasn't looking forward to it. She dressed the girls in more flannel petticoats than usual under their red-and-blue-plaid linsey-woolseys. She took an extra shawl for Rudie, too, in his long white baby dress, already smothered in shawls, and wore more under her own best silk than usual, in case the rooms were unheated and they'd all be wide open to the danger of catching their death of pneumonia.

Dinner was set for two-thirty, but she started out in plenty of time so that she, carrying Rudie, and the three girls walking in single file like ducks or little Indians, could cover the few blocks and arrive not out of breath at two twenty-five or even two-twenty, for politeness' sake. That morning when the children squealed over their orange apiece, and their new suits of underwear and new shoelaces, and she herself was holding out Olaf's mosaic brooch at arm's length and looking at it (wondering what he had got for Sigrid) and thinking what a pretty thing it was, the sun was out and shining for all it was worth. By noon it was gone, however, and now it was a bitter and biting iron-gray afternoon, that clanked like armor and was as cold as a frosty axehead. People had lamps lit in their windows all along the way, as though it were twilight, and Linnea looked for lights in the front part of Mrs. Orbit's house, for the cheeriness of the thing, but there were none.

At the gate she stopped and called for attention. "I don't want a one of you kids to even so much as hint that you're hungry. Mrs. Orbit'll put the dinner on, and she'll invite you to eat, when and how she wants, and if I hear so much as a whine or a hint or one single word beforehand, I just don't know what I'll do. Have you got that clear?" They all had it clear except Rudie. He, half-smothered by the shawls, was sound asleep against her left shoulder. She opened the gate and led the way up the walk and groped ahead up the stairs and onto the dark porch. She felt for the center panel of the door and knocked briskly.

"But I really am hungry," Bertha whispered behind her.

"I'm starved, Mamma," Gertrude whined softly.

"Remember what I said. One word out of any one of you and I just don't know what I'll do! All I can promise is, you'll be sorry." She had been in a quandary. Should she fill them up, so that in case they were not offered much, hunger wouldn't precipitate any crises? Or, should she bring them as ravenous as a bunch of famished Armenians, in case they had plenty set in front of them but most of it practically inedible? How could one forejudge with a Novel Reader, who had never been known to invite anybody for dinner before? She decided, thinking of Mrs. Orbit's goodheartedness and the urgency of her invitation, on the hunger method. Nobody, therefore, had had a bite since eight o'clock that morning so it didn't much matter what Mrs. Orbit served. Even a piece of old shoe leather would taste good. Her own mouth watered a little as she knocked again. Mrs. Orbit took quite a while getting to the door, but no doubt she was busy in the kitchen. She leaned as well as she could with Rudie in her arms over the porch railing and tried to peer in at the parlor window but it was all dark, with the blind pulled down.

It surprised her and she gave a little jump when the door flew open with a bang and either Gloriana, Guinevere, Rosabella or Juanita—well, perhaps not Juanita, for she was, after all, only a little past three—but they all looked so much alike and were so nearly of an age that it was hard to tell one from the other—stood dressed in white like a small-sized ghost haunting a large-sized doorway and cavernous dark hall beyond. "Well, hello!" Linnea said. "Merry Christmas."

> Dear Mrs. Ecklund, and family, come inside,
> On this happy Yuletide,
> You will find all warmth and cheer
> In your honor waiting here,

the little ghost cleared her throat and recited.

Linnea, hearing the words inside, tide, cheer, here, suspected she was being greeted with poetry and smiled tenderly. "Well, what do you know," she said. "Poertry for Christmas. Did your mamma make it up?" The little white figure backed up and Linnea pressed her brood firmly into the narrow dark hall.

"Yes, ma'am," said the child. In the faint light, by straining the eyes, it could be dimly seen that she was wearing something like a white shroud, with a pillow stuck in behind and amorphous curls, lumps of hair in rag curlers, like knots on a club.

> Please to leave your coats and wraps
> Here, good friends, with shawls and caps,

she recited,

> Then into the parlor go.
> YOUWILLBESURPRISEDIKNOW.

"Very nice," Linnea said. "Very nice, Gloriana."

"Guinevere," said the child.

"Why, of course," Linnea said. "Guinevere! Anyhow, you're letter perfect in the poertry, ain't you?" Somehow they all managed to get out of their coats and caps and mittens and shawls and mufflers and rubbers, and by some miracle managed to pile everything (except the rubbers which were neatly ranged along the wall) over the bannister and newelpost without anything falling down, Linnea hanging onto Rudie who had drowsily wakened and was now wondering, with batting eyes and motions of the head like a chicken just out of the shell, whether or not they were in an alarming situation. He decided they were and let out a little cry, but Linnea soothed him and reassured him and he stopped.

"Which way did you say we was supposed to go?" she asked the little guide.

This conjured up out of the shadows another small white shape, wearing a similar shroud-like garment and lumpily crowned by the wreath of rag curls. She was guarding the parlor door, which she now pushed open with a squeak. Beckoning theatrically she recited:

> *Enter here our portal gay*
> *On this merry Christmas day.*
> *In the shining candlelight*
> *'NeathbranchesofourChristmastreesobright*
> *One and all must now make merry*
> *Before our Christmas fire SO CHEERY.*

"Well, what do you know," Linnea said. "Are we supposed to go in the parlor? My, that sounded pretty. Did your mamma make it up?" She pushed her brood forward, the first little guide giving ground and backing up toward her sister.

"Yes, ma'am," both children said. "She made it up."

"What'll you bet it could go in the paper?" Linnea said. Her eyes were adjusted to the dimness now and she could see quite clearly. She would have thought her little lodestars were still running around in their nightgowns if she had not known they didn't have any and slept in their long underwear. "What you kids got on anyway?" she asked.

"We're angels," they announced. "These here is costumes."

"Of course!" Linnea said, smiting her brow. "I must be rumdum."

So they were. They even had wings! rudimentary and disconsolate, contrived of wire and gauze, fluttering down from the bony little shoulders. It was plain to see, as they led the way through the "portal gay" into the parlor, that they were angels indeed.

"Ain't you cold?" she asked worriedly.

"Oh, no," Guinevere said.

"We're hot," Gloriana (for it was she) announced.

It was almost too dark to see, but Linnea knew by the smell of stove blacking and furniture polish and the penetrating chill that they had been ushered into the parlor. It was more of a surprise that Mrs. Orbit did not step out of the gloom and greet them with more Christmas poetry, than if she had. "Where's your mamma?" she inquired, peering all around.

"She's upstairs throwing up," Gloriana said.

"All over everything," Guinevere added.

"Throwing up all over everything? Why, for heaven's sake," Linnea said. "What's the matter with her?"

From somewhere came the rumble of a man's voice. It rumbled louder. It was accompanied by a beam of yellow lamplight and came in and was small-sized Mr. Orbit all dressed up in his Sunday clothes and an embarrassed face, carrying a parlor lamp that livened up the scene immediately. It lit up all their eyes as a hunter's ray lights up the eyes of shy animals in a brake.

He walked across and set the lamp down on the center table. "If you please to sit down, Mrs. Ecklund," he said. "I'll get the fire rustled up. I don't know what a man could do, but I tell you something and I ain't lying a bit. I have got the damnedest wife a man ever had, and that's the God's truth. I don't know what else to say."

He was not, apparently, reciting poetry composed by Mrs. Orbit for the occasion. Linnea's heart went out to him. "Well, goodness," she said, "there ain't nothing so bad it couldn't be wor—"

"I'm a good provider," he said, "not that I mean to brag. I ain't one of these men that lays off, every little thing. I *provide*. My worst enemy will tell you I provide for my family. I do everything it's in my power to do and what happens? Here it is Christmas and company coming for dinner, and here are the damn kids running around in halloween costumes, and all it's been is writing pieces and speaking pieces like a damn program for the last week—"

"She cleaned the parlor, that much I see," Linnea said. "You got to give the devil his due." Her glance took in the cold pot-bellied stove shining like anthracite, the slightly over-blued lace curtains as stiff as a board with starch, the carpet that had been put over the clothesline and beat within an inch of its life, also the forgotten scrub bucket in the corner by the horsehair settle and the forgotten tin dish of lye soap on the taboret. "Why, there ain't a woman in town with a cleaner parlor. Not only that," she said, "just look at these pretty decorations of hers! That took time, cleaning, and then decorating so nice!"

Mrs. Orbit had tacked twisted red and green streamers of paper at intervals all around the picture molding and drawn them together in the middle of the ceiling, with just the right and artistic pendency, and hung there a honeycombed red paper bell. Red paper bows perched like feverish butterflies upon every picture frame. The fragrant Christmas tree, now seen to be standing in the corner tastefully trimmed with popcorn strings, gilded walnuts, pasteboard cutouts and numerous candles, could hold its own with any tree in Zion. And what was this innovation? Mrs. Orbit had used soap and drawn with it in grand style upon the mirror a ghostly holly wreath and the head of St. Nicholas. Also she had printed M E R R Y X M A S.

"All I can say is," Linnea said, "any woman that can clean up a parlor as nice as this, and decorate so beautiful, is somebody that ain't no numskull. Not only ain't she no numskull, anybody that done a job like this, but she's as smart as a whip and as bright as a dollar. That's what *she* is. And I ain't the only one would say so."

Mr. Orbit's small face brightened momentarily, but then humiliation and vexation tarnished it again. "Wait till you see the rest of the house," he said. "It could get right up and walk away. Sail, that's what it could. I been doing what I could out in the kitchen but if it sailed right out through the door I wouldn't be surprised. And here the fire's just been built up good and the roast put in the oven, when it should of been in hours ago and just coming out to be et. Not only that, not a damn kid with a decent breakfast. Nothing fixed. Every damn kid I look at saying pieces till they're blue in the face. And her upstairs throwing up. Throwing up, mind you, on Christmas. Honest to God, Mrs. Ecklund, if you'll pardon my English, sometimes I don't know whether I'm walking or riding and that's the honest to God truth."

"Did she eat something upset her?" Linnea asked. "Or what?"

"How do you mean?"

"What's she throwing up for?"

"Well, she was throwing up but now it ain't so much throwing up as gagging. Won't you set, Mrs. Ecklund?" His face as red as the paper bell with a blush, he gave her a gentle little shove into the rocking chair and she sat, with surprised Rudie in her arms. "Things maybe ain't going to pop right on schedule. There may be a kind of a wait."

All the children were silent, the two angels and Linnea's uneasy trio by the tree, carefully listening to the dire news. The cleanliness, the beauty, the decorations meant nothing. They never took their eyes off Mamma's face.

"It ain't so much throwing up as gagging with her," the unhappy man repeated. "She gets over it though. She'll be down to take holt. In the meantime . . . I'll get a fire going in here and warm you folks up. I was out rustling up some—I should of seen to things myself—" he broke off miserably.

"Does she have spells like this every once in a while?" Linnea inquired.

He avoided her eyes. "Well, she's kind of been gagging for the last two weeks or so."

"Oh."

"The least little thing and her stomach gets turned. Bingo, she'll take a notion to gag or maybe she'll take a notion to throw up her heels."

"Tchk, tchk," Linnea said, shaking her head, her concerned eyes on his face, "did you ever hear the like?"

"The least little thing," he said again. "Bingo." He meticulously examined the red roses in the carpet, his face matching them in hue.

So that's how it was with Mrs. Orbit. The most natural thing in the world. Linnea breathed a sigh of relief. "Well, there's lots of stomach trouble around," she said reassuringly. "She ain't the only one."

Mr. Orbit was perfectly miserable. He didn't know what to do. "It's a hell of a proposition," he said, "no matter how you look at it! Company coming! And what does she do but rig the kids up in halloween costumes and compose pieces to speak! What's a man supposed to *do,* that's all I want to know. What's a man supposed to do?"

Linnea opened her mouth to speak.

"These ain't halloween costumes," Gloriana said sternly. "We keep telling you and telling you."

"We're angels," Guinevere said. "We keep telling you."

He put his two hands up to his face and made some up and down motions as though he had a towel and was wiping it dry after shaving. Then he dropped them to his sides and blinked, drawing a deep sigh. "Well, anyway," he said. "I'll get a fire started in here. And she'll be down to take holt. And you just—sit there in the rocker and make yourself at home. And you kids—well, you kids," he looked at the three small visitors and his own pathetic angels, "you just go ahead and start in to—to play. That would be the ticket for you. Here we go round the mulberry bush and all like that."

Her daughters continued to look at Linnea and she saw they weren't going to be able to contain themselves much longer. They were cold. They were bewildered. Not only that, they were hungry enough to eat a sawmill and it a-running. She was going to have something on her hands if she wasn't careful. She leaned over and set Rudie on the floor, took off her Christmas brooch and fastened it firmly into her handkerchief. Then she dangled this before him. His eyes were beginning to squeeze shut, his mouth to pucker, but the sight of this fascinating toy —to his amazement when he reached out for it Mamma actually let him possess it—was enough to avert the gathering storm. Two more little angels with hosannahless faces, one very small indeed, had meanwhile crept in to join the others. Linnea stood up. "Now listen here, Mr. Orbit," she said. "Let's us get this straight right this minute. I ain't company and my kids ain't company. I'm just your old friend Linnea Ecklund that was here when Juanita was born and a hard old time your wife had of it, too, that night, if you'll remember. So when I say I ain't going to sit around rocking in the parlor when there ain't nothing I enjoy better than wading in and fixing a big Christmas dinner, why, I know you're going to take it in the spirit in which it's meant and ain't going to put no obstacles in my way."

She was going to have something on her hands with the girls, and possibly with the four little angels, too, but maybe she could get to the kitchen quick enough. She went out and went swiftly down the hall, Mr. Orbit following protestingly along behind her. The children began to mill about and make twittering sounds and then one by one they straggled out and followed too.

Mr. Orbit protested every step of the way that that was a hell of a way to do no matter what anybody said. Gagging was one thing but mismanagement was another. And in case anybody wanted to know, he was letting it be understood right here and now that he was either going to put his foot down and have somebody sit up and take notice or he was going to know the reason why. Nobody could accuse him of being one of them men that laid off, every little thing. Not him, they couldn't. He *provided*. Anybody that said he didn't was a bald-faced liar. But what did he get for it? It looked to him like a woman that didn't have a blessed thing to do but stay home could keep things going, at least, meals on, house warm, kids took care of, but no, read, read, read, nose stuck in some damn novel all day long and half the night. Where he made his mistake was, he should of sat down on that young lady years ago. Ma warned him, Ma said, Alvin, I tell you something, she said. Izola's all right, she said, but I tell you something, Alvin, she ain't just anchored right, she kind of wants to soar off into space. She had a head on her shoulders, Ma had, she knowed what she was talking about. He should of listened to Ma, and when Izola started soaring, he should of give her a good big yank. That would of showed her where to head in at and no fooling about it. She was a pretty girl when he married her, and a smart girl, and not only that, she had a good disposition—so far as that went, she had a good disposition now if you come right down to it, never said a cross word to anybody, never had, never been cross or mean in her life—but where he made his mistake was, he should of sat down on her long ago. That goddamn laziness. That read, read, read. When Izola soared off into space, he should of been ready with a yank that would of made her head swim. Not that he was blaming her for throwing up, but throwing up was one thing and mismanagement was another!

While the poor embarrassed man complained Linnea made little soothing noises and surveyed the kitchen. She had to take stock before she knew which way to enter the fray. There seemed to be great numbers of pots and pans that had been put to soak and stood here, there and everywhere half-full of discolored water. Linnea was glad Ingeborg didn't have a chance to see the cupboard. She would have fainted dead away. The tumbled oilcloth-covered table had on it not only unwashed dishes marked prominently with hardened egg yolk, but beads of honey strung in a row like a necklace, half-emptied jam bottles and a frying pan a third full of cold bacon grease. A stack of newspapers, a small gaiter, *Demorest's Monthly,* a green book entitled *The Bride of Llewellyn* or, *Cruel as the Grave,* and a clean but unironed corset cover also decorated the table. There was, however, a roaring fire in the capacious stove. That made up for a lot of things. So did the sight of various buckets, baskets and sacks, on pantry shelves, warming oven, kitchen dresser and even on the floor, full of sweet potatoes, cranberries, parsnips, Idaho potatoes, two monstrous fresh cabbages, flour, sugar, butter and apples—the makings of a Christmas dinner fit for the President of the United States. Not only that, there was a huge pork roast in the oven. Linnea looked at it. Its thick coating of fat was unmelted except for a transparent layer the thickness of tissue paper and it was not warmed through, but when it was done it was going to be a pork roast of pure white and golden brown, full of juices and flavor (plenty of salt, plenty of black pepper), that started the saliva running at full blast even to think of it! Linnea beamed happily, rolling up her sleeves and tying a small plaid tablecloth found hanging over the back of a chair, around her waist for an apron.

Shyly Mr. Orbit, much comforted by her words and manner, twitched back a fringed paisley couch cover and revealed, on the foot of the lounge on a large platter under a dishtowel, a huge cake sparkling with hard white frosting. "She went to work and made it this last week. Receipt Ma had." He tried to say it like it didn't amount to much but his eyes gave him away. "Dark fruit cake. Like we always had a saying about hash, Everything in it but the kitchen stove. Don't look like she made much of a bobble of it, either, does it?"

"Bobble!" Linnea said, "I should think not! Why, I never seen a prettier sight in my life!"

"Receipt Ma had," he repeated.

"You see!" Linnea said triumphantly. "What she can do when she puts her mind to it! Anybody that can clean up and doll up a parlor like that, and anybody that can bake such a cake, why, I tell you something, Mr. Orbit, if she'd take a notion, why, there wouldn't be a woman alive that could outdo her!"

He beamed. "Ma used to say to me, Alvin, she'd say, Izola's all right," he said, "the only trouble with Izola is, she ain't just anchored like she should be, she kind of wants to soar off into space. You keep her from soaring off into space, Alvin, she used to say to me, and you got something."

"You have, too," Linnea said. "She wasn't soaring far when she baked that cake."

"Izola's all right, Ma used to say. Ma liked Izola and Izola liked Ma. The only thing about Izola, Ma used to say, is, she kind of wants to so—"

"I think I'll fix the kids a little something to eat before I do anything else, if you don't mind, Mr. Orbit." Linnea broke in. "When they get filled up, they'll go play. Otherwise they'll stand around like they're doing with big sad eyes and long faces like a bunch of orphans that ain't got a friend in the world. Their appetite won't be hurt none for the big meal."

In no time, the table was cleared, wiped off with a damp dishcloth and places were laid. Bertha, Gertrude and Stellie, Linnea's girls, and Gloriana, Guinevere, Rosabella and Juanita, the Orbit angels, sat up to it to eat comfortable bowls of cornmeal mush with plenty of whole milk and sugar. They were too hungry to say much at first—Linnea used this breathing-space to nurse Rudie, joggle him to sleep and lay him on the kitchen lounge with a shawl over him, as far toward the head and away from the fruitcake at the foot as possible, where he took a long snooze from which he woke in seraphim wit and beauty—but by the time they were through they were talking as lightly and familiarly as ravens.

Bertha and Gloriana, being the oldest, had the task of shepherding their five assorted little sisters, angels and human, into the parlor. There never was a more inviting place than it now, for Mr. Orbit had built a loud and lively fire in the stove, and the reflections of it through the open grate danced redly upon everything, while the lamplight was yellow as a peach. Red and yellow, full of the blue-green odor of fir, the room was, delicious and warm yet coolly glistening. The heavenly hosts had been made to show they had on shoes, stockings, underwear, pants and flannel petticoats under their obvolute togas and adventurous wings. Whatever items were missing (and there were several) had to be fetched and put on under Linnea's watchful eye. All they had to do in the delightful parlor, before they started to play, was to see that all the rags were out of the Elysian hair and the celestial curls combed out. Only Juanita cried under this trial, but she soon stopped when everybody told her she looked the prettiest of all. She still had some snarls left at the nape of her neck, but nobody dared get into them with the comb so all they could do was let her be. There were a few toys in the Orbit household, if they could ever be found, but none of them were recalled to be in very good shape. Nobody had seen any of them for a long time. For Christmas they had received not much more than the Ecklund sisters. Toys, however, did not much signify, and well equipped with next to nothing but far-reaching imagination they began to play.

As the steam runs the steamboat and folly runs the perpetual motion machine, a bubbling song runs the game of pretending. It starts *Let's us play like* and ripples anywhere.

> *We're rich!*
> *I'm the Papa, you're the Mamma!*
> *Here's our house!*
> *Here's our back yard!*
> *Lookut us!*
> *I'm a old lady thirty-six years old!*
> *You're a old man with whiskers clear down to here!*
> *I got a silk dress hiked up in the back!*
> *Here's our kids!*
> *Johnny! Bessie! Mary! Nephi! Pearl!*
> *Here's our table!*
> *Here's our house, our boat, our sleigh, our wagon!*
> *Lookut our things!*
> *We found a sack of diamonds lost downtown!*
> *Lost!*
> *Wouldn't give um back!*
> *Kept um!*
> *Lookut us!*

It flows and meanders anywhere, any tiger, any crown, any sharpshooting gun, any necklace, any blue satin, any France, any scope, any face, has only to be reached out for and plucked as it grows down-hanging and full of flowers, its leaves in the water. . . .

Linnea and Mr. Orbit decided that Mrs. Orbit must have dropped off upstairs and they hoped so. They were conspirators now, conspiring how to please and bless Mrs. Orbit, and they hoped she would nap along until the feast they were preparing was on the table. Mr. Orbit did a lot. He kept the fire going, and peeled potatoes and dried the dishes, while Linnea went ahead and worked the miracle. She brought about perfect order in the topsy-turvy kitchen. She made apple pies, raised biscuits, cranberry sauce and never left a dirty dish behind her. At intervals she turned practised Apician eyes upon the pork roast popping and snapping with juice and turning more and more golden brown. She set the table for ten and in the exact center placed that more than decorative piece, the frosted fruitcake.

The dinner would not be ready to sit down to and eat until six-thirty, but at a little after five Mrs. Orbit appeared with the shamed strained eye-swollen miserable look of the man who has crept in the house at broad daylight with his shoes in his hand after having been out all night drinking and squandering his salary and doing God knows what else besides.

"Merry Christmas," Linnea said with twinkling eyes through the steam of the potatoes. She had just taken the lid off the kettle and was sticking a fork into them to see how much longer they had to cook.

Mrs. Orbit's face worked. She saw, not in detail but panoramically, that electrifying changes had been made in her kitchen. It looked beautiful, it smelled beautiful. Best of all, it was working, perking, running, a going concern. There was light to it, life to it, snap to it. It had a beating heart and a reaching soul. "Merry Christmas," she said brokenly. Then she put her hands up before her embarrassed face and she bawled.

"Why, say," Linnea said, dropping the lid back on the potatoes and going swiftly to her weeping hostess. She put her arms around her and began patting her gently on the back as though she were a baby with the hiccups. "Why, goodness sakes alive, why, say," she said.

Mr. Orbit edged over close, too, and looked sympathetically at his wife and said "There ain't a thing in the world—" and changed it to "Well, there's no need to—" and changed it to "There, there, honey," and didn't know what to do.

"I got one of my sick spells—"

"Your hubby told me." Linnea kept on gently patting.

"Got to throwing up—"

"I know."

"Got to gagging—"

"There, there, honey," Mr. Orbit murmured.

"Got to feeling better." She paused, sniffing and swallowing and drawing a deep breath, while her tears flowed like wine. "No dinner! company coming!"

"That's all right. Why, we—"

"Instead of coming down like I ought to!"

"There, there."

"Dropped off to sleep—imagine, imagine—"

Deftly Linnea turned the heartbroken Mrs. Orbit over to her husband, and he embraced her and got his handkerchief out and wiped her eyes and clumsily patted her cheek. They smoothened and comforted Mrs. Orbit and after a while she stopped crying and smiled and began to take an interest in everything and look around, never giving up offering an apology for all her shortcomings. Not a thing had they done but what she saw it and praised it. Linnea was the best friend in the world. Mr. Orbit was the best husband in the world. Nobody could say that she didn't know and appreciate what she had in Mr. Orbit. He fairly swelled up and had a face like a sunbeam when she talked like that about him, but he either went out of the kitchen (coming right back in) or said Oh, now, honey, or, Oh, no, that's going a little *too* far and tried to hush her up, when she said he was so kind and so patient, so clever, and took after the good-looking Plover side of the family, his mother's side, and not the Orbit side, that were nice enough people but honestly to goodness ugly enough to stop a clock, his own father included, dear old man though he was. And here she was lucky enough to have a husband like Mr. Orbit and what did she do? She never took hold like she'd ought to, that's what she never did! But from now on, things were going to be different! They'd never believe it was the same person! What they had done! Wonderful Mr. Orbit! Wonderful Linnea!

The two cast glance after glance at each other, beaming. Mrs. Orbit was blessed and pleased far beyond their fondest dreams.

"I tell you," Mr. Orbit offered confidently when Mrs. Orbit paused for breath. "All you got to do is lay off them novels for a while and you can lick the world!"

"Novels?" She was perfectly astounded.

"Sure, them novels. I tell you, Izola, you won't know yourself."

"Novels! Why, anybody's got to have a little breathing space," she said, her large myopic blue eyes appealing to Linnea. Her lower lip began trembling. "Why, even the mules in the mines got to be allowed to have a little breathing space *sometimes* and if I use mine—" she said, "if I use mine to pick up a nice elevating book once in a while . . ."

It was time to open the oven and see about the roast, and the brilliant sight and the brilliant smell of it stopped all the flurry. "Ain't that a sight for sore eyes?" Linnea said, pressing her finger down and instantly removing it to find a flake of brown crusty fat glued to it. She put her tongue out and took the morsel upon it. "Ain't that a sight?" she said, smacking her lips.

"Ain't it?" Mr. and Mrs. Orbit said, smacking their lips too.

Before they began to eat, when they all got settled in their chairs and stopped squirming and scraping and hitching upwards or shoving backwards, and just sat there, Mrs. Orbit said, "If a one of us has any sense, we'll just sit here and admire this dinner for a minute. It had ought to be framed."

It ought, too. Anybody would be proud to hang it up and admire it! They all said so. If ever there was a sight for sore eyes, it was that dinner.

When things started to circle around and be passed and the mothers began to fix two or three plates besides their own for the littlest ones who could not do the jobs themselves, Juanita started to tug on her mother's arm to try to get her attention. Mrs. Orbit, busy and happy, with a flushed face and bright eyes (Linnea's was the same, and Mr. Orbit's was the same, and so were all the girls') kept unconsciously flicking her off as one flicks off the winged company of sticky summer nights. She kept coming back, pawing and whispering. Finally, she let out a howl.

"What's the matter with Juanita?" everybody said.

"It's her piece," Gloriana elucidated.

"Oh, my God," Mr. Orbit said mildly, chewing, with a look of glazed beatitude on his face and a loaded forkful poised beneath his nose, ready to go into his mouth when he should be able to receive it.

"Hush," Mrs. Orbit said. "That ain't no way to do at the table. Bawl." She looked bewildered at her child. "What's wrong with your head?"

Juanita howled louder.

"Don't you remember?" Gloriana said. "Her piece!"

The two other angels joined in, nodding their heads vigorously. "Her piece! She gets to speak one, too."

Mrs. Orbit leaned down and in a stage whisper informed her daughter: "It's all changed now, Juanita. You don't really need to speak your piece. It don't fit in so good no more, see, honey? Why don't you just eat and forget about it? Next Christmas you can speak a piece!"

Juanita was more than hurt, she was heartbroken.

"Why don't you let her go ahead and speak it?" Linnea said. "We'd just love to hear her. I think them pomes you made up was just too cute for words. Like I was saying to one of the kids, Gloriana, I guess it was, I was saying I bet you could get them printed in the papers. We all enjoyed it. Let her go ahead."

"Well—" said Mrs. Orbit doubtfully. "It don't fit in so good any more. . . ."

Juanita could hear by the leniency in her voice that all was well, so she scrambled to a standing position on the seat of her chair, taking a deep gasp, throwing out her stomach and reaching back to scratch the spot where a wing sprouted. She opened her mouth. No sound came. She opened it again.

"Eat hearty and with good appetite," Gloriana prompted her.

"All the things on our festive board," Guinevere added softly.

EATheartyandwithgoodappetite
ALLthingsonourfestiveboard,

the three-and-a-half-year-old angel repeated hastily so as not to forget it. Then she opened her mouth again, and shut it, and didn't know what came next.

Mrs. Orbit used the pause to whisper, "Leave the part out about the turk. Turk, I say in the poem," she explained to Linnea. "Turk, you know, instead of turkey."

"Oh," Linnea said, as though that were the most usual thing in the world.

"It turned out we didn't get turkey. Your father brought home a roast of pork," Mrs. Orbit said.

"I done my best," Mr. Orbit said.

"Sure you did!" his wife told him. "Only the way I composed it—"

"Delicious," Linnea put in tactfully. "There's nothing better than a nice roast of pork."

Juanita was staring blankly down at her mother, twisting her raiment in one of her little claws.

> *Eatheartyandwithgoodappetite*
> *ALLthingsonourfestiveboard,*

she began again and repeated prestissimo.

None of the angels had any idea how to leave out the part about the turk so they all, helping Juanita, put it in. The piece in its entirety went as follows:

> *Eat hearty and with good appetite*
> *All things on our festive board.*
> *Take the cup and quaff it up:*
> *Drink to the bottom of the gourd!*

(Nobody had the faintest idea what this meant, but it made Linnea thirsty and she noticed they forgot to put any water on the table. She made a mental note to get up and get some as soon as the piece was recited.)

> *Nobody on their way will ever lurk*
> *If they know when they arrive they are going to get a turk!*

(That accounted for the turk, then, instead of turkey. Mr. Orbit tried out, "If they know when they arrive they are going to get a pork," but everybody shook their heads. Pork wouldn't do at all.)

> *Oh, what, oh, what is oh, so jolly,*
> *As the Christmas feast beneath the holly?*

(There wasn't a square inch of holly, but it sounded very pretty anyway.)

"My," Linnea said, "that was such a hard verse, that it looks like it'd be too hard for the littlest one to speak. How come you didn't have Gloriana or Guinevere speak it and leave one of the easier ones for Juanita, her being the smallest?"

Juanita had sat back down with a thud. Now she was busy shining, while they spoke of her.

"She liked that part about the turk, see," Mrs. Orbit said.

"All she liked was the verse with the turk in it," all the little angels explained.

Juanita kept on shining.

"Well, I don't blame her," Linnea said. "I don't blame her a-tall."

It was going on for twelve when Linnea bundle͟
her stuffed and drowsy daughters into their complicat͟
and, with Mr. Orbit carrying dead-to-the-world Rudie ͟
his shawls and with an added coverlet Mrs. Orbit had in͟
ing—for there had been another fall of snow in the evening͟
him into a bundle the size of a half-grown calf, started for ho͟

It had been one of the merriest Christmases anybody ever ha͟

About the dinner Mrs. Orbit's words were as good a descriptio͟
could be found: It should have been framed and hung upon the wall to
admire—and it tasted as good or better than it looked. But the hours in
the parlor afterwards, when, the dishes done and the kitchen left spick
and span, they all retired there, were scarcely less enjoyable. There was
such a roaring fire that Linnea, tucking up a strand of hair and finding
it damp with sweat, wished she had not put so many petticoats and other
clothing on herself and everybody, thinking the house might be chilly.
She had better taken a chance the other way!

They ate nuts and apples. Mrs. Orbit brought out a brown paper sack
of chocolate drops which she passed around. This act of hospitality
nearly precipitated a misventure, however, for the smell of chocolate
brought, as good as brought, that is, one of her spells upon her. She
flushed and paled and flushed and paled, and then she laid the sack
down on the marble-topped center table and gagged. Only the quick
thinking of Linnea saved the day. She made Mrs. Orbit sit right down
in a chair with her feet up. Then she rushed to the kitchen and poured
out a cup of hot water from the steaming teakettle. She brought it back
and had Mrs. Orbit quietly sip it, spoonful by spoonful, as though it had
been tea. That brought her around all right. In no time she picked up
her mandolin from the corner where it was leaning against the wall with
a red ribbon about its neck like a petted dog, and had it in her lap and
was plinking and planking the tunes of "Willie, We Have Missed You,"
"Murmur, Gentle Lyre," "Then You'll Remember Me," "Alice, Where
Art Thou?" "Polly Wolly Doodle," "We Three Kings of Orient Are,"
"I Traced Her Little Footprints in the Snow" and other songs too numerous to mention, while all joined in and sang. In the yellow lamplight, in
and among the dancing red firelight they sang and talked and laughed
and played games. It was a Christmas scene to be drawn by hand, by an
artist, to illustrate a book about yuletide. Even the four little angels, once
pathetic and ridiculous in their costumes, skipping around in cold and
chaos with their draperies held up, or stumbling over them, were now
idoneous and relevant, real Christmas angels, settled on the roses of the
ingrain like doves upon a bower.

When it was time to go, Rosabella had her inning. She didn't need
any help from anybody. She knew her piece as Joseph Smith knew his
pieces from the Lord. All the guests had their coats on and were ready

go; they were only milling around and the adults were saying a last word to each other. Mamma didn't even have to give her the high sign. She ran four or five steps up the steep staircase. Mamma held the lamp up high and cast its beams upon her. She hitched up her robe and her wings fluttered. Then she recited gloriously:

> Dear friends, good night, the day is o'er,
> The happy Christmas is no more.
> We hope you have enjoyed yourselfs and had a happy time
> Here in our house in this snowy clime.
> Good wishes go with you out through the door,

She pointed first to the guests and then to it, significantly,

GOODNIGHTDEARFRIENDSTHEDAYISO'ER!

"It could be printed in the papers," Linnea declared. "Honestly to goodness, if it couldn't."

In a flood of moonlight they walked home. The children were automatons more dead than alive with sleep, but Bertha and Gertrude made it across the hard-crusted snow, scarcely knowing the function they were performing. Stellie was too little and too tired to try it. She took half a dozen steps down the walk and then sat down hard. Linnea had to pick her up and carry her. Mr. Orbit wanted to trade Rudie for her, saying she was twice as big and heavy, but Linnea said Rudie was weighed down with so many covers. The truth was, she felt she should carry the bigger child because she was quite a lot larger than Mr. Orbit. She did it easily, in her left arm, leaving her right hand free to keep the two drooping sleepwalkers headed the right way in the shoveled path out of the drifts.

Mr. Orbit was still glowing from hospitality richly fulfilled, an experience rare to him. "Take the cake, for instance," he said. "Would you say she had made such a bobble of it?"

"Bobble!" Linnea repeated staunchly. "Why, that cake would of won a prize! It was just simply delicious!"

"It's the damn reading," he said, "mainly. And letting things go by the board. If it wasn't for that, Izola wouldn't have to take a back seat to anybody."

"Well, now I'll put in my two cents worth and tell you what I think, Mr. Orbit," Linnea said, making a grab for Bertha to keep her walking straight ahead. "A good housekeeper's fine. Nobody can have anything against a good housekeeper. But I tell you something, Mr. Orbit. A good woman's better. And if I had my choice between a fanatic on scrubbing and throwing out the garbage, and a loving mother with a sweet disposition and a pair of pretty blue eyes, that can laugh with the kids and play a game with them once in a while, and play the mandolin like a expert, and make up little verses, why, I tell you, Mr. Orbit, I'd let the fanatic go jump in the lake. Why, everybody knows, some of the miserablest homes in the world is the homes of A number one housekeepers. No, sir," she said, "you be tickled you got the woman you got and ain't got worse, Mr. Orbit."

"Yes, but some women is both," he said, not to argue but just to keep the conversation going and listen and be reassured the way people are when they listen to the music of Schubert.

"Some women is the devil's wife on wheels, and that's the truth of it," Linnea said. "You've picked about as near a daisy as a man can pick. You ought to pinch yourself."

He gave a deep peaceful sigh and she could see the smile that wanted to break out on his face in the bright moonlight. "Well, but—" he began, to keep the music playing.

"But nothing. You got to look at it this way. Take today, for instance," she said. "This Christmas was a day that'll stick in my mind till I die. Them little angels with their wings! Them little angel costumes! Them little pieces they spoke! I'll remember all that when I'm a old lady. My kids'll remember it when they're old ladies. They'll never forget it. Why, stuff like that—stuff like that, Mr. Orbit—" she groped for words. "Somebody that ain't like nobody else, that's as different as a blue moon's different from a regular moon, that goes at things in a way out of the ordinary—what I'm trying to say is, that gives you something out of the ordinary to think about and something out of the ordinary to remember, why, they're important, Mr. Orbit," she said, "they're awful important. Whenever the world gets so there's nobody out of the ordinary in it no more, it'll be a pretty sad old world, that's all I can say! A pretty sad old world!"

They all climbed the steps, scattering the pillows of coarse feathery snow that lay along each one. Linnea turned the knob and pushed the door open. She stood Stellie down inside the dark kitchen and turned and reached for Rudie. "I sure appreciate the day. We all sure do," she said.

"It ain't been so bad," he said, wiping away a clear droplet from the end of his nose with the back of his ungloved hand.

"The way it happened, it ended *happy ever after,*" Gertrude piped up and said, hanging onto her mother's skirts and afraid to step foot inside without her. She had been deciding this.

They laughed.

"Merry Christmas!" Linnea called when Mr. Orbit started down the steps.

"Merry Christmas yourself," he said. He paused at the bottom and turned, looking upwards. "She don't mean no harm," he said. "Izola. Reading them books. It's like Ma said."

"She wasn't soaring far when she baked that cake," Linnea reminded him.

He paused, thinking. The smile broke out all over his face, giving off a light of its own like a star. "Well, don't let the bedbugs bite," he said.

"Don't you," Linnea said.

He whistled "There is a Happy Land" all the way to the corner.

CHAPTER 3

FOR THE FIRST TIME in her married life, Linnea moved into a whole house where she could have a *parlor*. She had had a long old wait. Bertha was eight, Gertrude six, Stellie four and Rudie two. The way he celebrated was, on the memorable day they moved, to run off and get clear down to F Street before the girls found him. He was broke long ago but here he had his pants full. Bertha took one arm and Gertrude took the other and they carried him home that way, his feet swinging above the ground. He cried, anybody would have thought he was being killed. He certainly didn't smell like a rose, either. Mamma said that would be the way they would remember the day they moved into the house—August the twenty-fifth. It didn't seem like much of a way but it stamped it on their minds. A family has to have a few historical dates to go by.

It was a fine little house—not so little, unless you call four rooms, a pantry and a deep cellar underneath it all, little. It was made of adobe brick in a nice bisque shade, with a cupola on top for pure decoration and a gingerbread porch that was big enough for two or three ladies and a bunch of children (if they perched all over the steps like jackdaws) to sit on of a summer evening. The parlor had dark red wallpaper and the dining room, across the narrow hallway, had dark green wallpaper. These two rooms were at the front of the house. The dark-green paper was so ugly that Linnea took a great dislike to that room. She decided that she could get along very well without it and would rent it. She told everyone jokingly that she was renting it out because she couldn't stand the wallpaper, but the truth was it seemed a pretty big, extravagant house for her to have all by herself with only four children, and she thought it wouldn't hurt anything to have a little help with the rent.

When Linnea first laid eyes on Mrs. Dancey holding her little boy

Horace by the hand, she said, "Now there is a real lady," and was glad to have the chance to rent the room to her. But afterwards she said, "You can't always tell by the way a person looks."

Mrs. Dancey was not tall, but she was so overly thin that she looked as if she were. She had long small bones. Her hands were about average length, but since they were only about two inches wide they looked extremely long. Her feet were the same way, about two inches wide. When they were buttoned into tight kid shoes they looked as sharp as swords. She had an undersized face with everything about it undersized, though regular. Her teeth alone were of the usual size, which they had no business being as there was not nearly enough room for them and they had to lap over each other all the way around. Her small coiffure, surprisingly intricate when examined closely, was of khaki color and she had eyes to match.

Horace, three years old, looked just like a miniature Mrs. Dancey in bangs and a velveteen suit. Anybody who tried to play with Horace had better watch out. He would take a chunk out of them before they knew what happened. Horace bit. Worse than that, he would holler bloody murder over the least little thing. So the children would have given him a pretty wide berth anyway, even if Mrs. Dancey had allowed him to play with them, which she did not except on very rare occasions which always ended in a hullabaloo. Mostly Mrs. Dancey kept him in the poison-green room where she and he carried on a homogeneous existence as regular as clockwork.

Mrs. Dancey had a way of concealing all the vulgar equipment of life, even in her small quarters, so that no one would suspect that she and Horace had piles of winter underwear and a whole long list of unmentionables, besides other necessities like pots and pans, a chamber pot, a whiskbroom, clothesbasket and flatiron, also supplies like potatoes, onions and flour. Most of her waking hours were spent in concealing these vulgar things in clothespress, trunk, behind curtains and under the bed. What was left out had the pure excellence and virtue of inutility— a Bible about the size and weight of a marble tombstone, a china shepherdess looking to the right and a china shepherd looking to the left, a hand-painted vase of gilded cattails, a pin tray made of a pink seashell with no pins in it, a jewel case standing up on its hind legs with nothing at all lying under its ornate roof against its white satin lining (she wouldn't be such a fool as to keep her jewelry *there*), an unemployed paperweight that stood upon the taboret. It was of mere glass but it was heavy enough to mash a toe flatter than a pancake. Of green, its watery rays of green reflected by the sun were lost upon the greener wallpaper. Everything that was of use, Mrs. Dancey hid away. Anything that was of no use to anybody, she proudly displayed. That was another reason Linnea knew she was a lady.

Although she was a polygamous wife herself, it was about a week before Linnea knew that Mrs. Dancey was one too.

Mrs. Dancey kept this hidden the way she kept her corset out of sight when not in use. Her grievous dolor, her woe and dejection over the situation and her status, however, she plainly brandished. Linnea had wondered what was wrong with her. She told Ingeborg it was just like having one of the martyred saints in the house.

"I've seen some miserable people in my life," she said, "but I never seen anything to equal her. Her whole life is just like a funeral. When you talk to her she gives you that look like she was doing her best to bear up under a terrible sorrow."

"What's wrong with her?" Ingeborg wanted to know.

"Be blamed if I know," Linnea said.

They really had to laugh when they found out it was only polygamy. She was merely the third wife of Mr. Flodden Dancey, the cabinet-maker down on Second South, that was all that was the matter. Being Mr. Flodden Dancey's third wife was all the cross she had to bear! Ingeborg and Linnea really had to laugh, but it was a very serious matter with Mrs. Dancey.

She stayed around home as if she were a criminal, strictly within her room, and on the occasions when she had to take Horace and go out, she used to go heavily veiled.

"Mr. Dancey makes good money, too," Linnea said, marveling, "and he keeps her well supplied, her and Horace don't seem to want for anything although what they eat is a mystery to me—there ain't even a smell coming out through the keyhole—and they got decent clothes. She don't even have to take in a little sewing or go out on a baby case once in a while like I do, to make ends meet. I don't know what more a woman would want. What do you suppose she's so put out about and so sad?"

"She looks to me like her stomach ain't worth a darn," Ingeborg said.

They decided later that maybe one reason she took it so hard was because she was a convert, of English parentage. Not that there was anything wrong with converts. Olaf was one, and you couldn't have told him from a born member of the Church, but he was the exception rather than the rule.

Linnea explained it this way, and Ingeborg agreed with her. "Take me now," Linnea said. "I was born in the Church. Can I give you chapter and verse for everthing? No, I can't. Do I prophet this and prophet that? No, I don't. I just take it easy and natural. But take a convert now," she said. "You can't let a little wind but what they can give you chapter and verse for it. They prophet this and they prophet that. I feel sorry for converts, any kind of converts, converts to anything. They're people that goes *at* things so hard—they can't be easy and natural and not think about things, the way people can that's *born* to something."

"I guess you're right," Ingeborg said. "They always got to worry their heads over things. You and me and people like us don't need to, born in the Church."

"They got no leeway for nothing," Linnea said, "always having to rack their brains over the Word of Wisdom and everything. Will they drink a cup of coffee?"

"Never," Ingeborg said, "but then, it's against the Word of Wisdom. We shouldn't either."

"Joseph Smith never meant the Scandinavians," Linnea said.

"I never thought so myself," Ingeborg agreed.

"And if you say a word about the Romneys or Nesbits or Richards or Grants or Kimballs feathering their nests, just in fun, not meaning nothing by it, why, they bristle all up, like you was talking against the Church or something! They watch you like a hawk!"

"I wouldn't give you two cents for a convert," Ingeborg said, "as a general thing. Would you?"

"They go *at* things too hard. They don't take things easy and natural," Linnea repeated.

Mrs. Dancey didn't, certainly. Linnea happened to have a little discussion with her on polygamy one day. That was before the water trouble came up and while it was still possible for them to have an occasional conversation together. The water trouble did not make them bad friends where they had been good friends, for they had never become friends at all. Linnea had such a plenty of everything, she was good measure, pressed down and running over, she was all she was and then some, Linnea galore. Mrs. Dancey was just the opposite: she didn't have much of anything, she was pittance, half-rations; she was all she was, too, but so sparingly it was like being cheated out of at least half a woman, maybe more. Not that another such half as Mrs. Dancey was now would have done anybody any good whatsoever. Anyway, Linnea was large and locust, Mrs. Dancey was tiny and grub. They never would have been real friends if they had lived to be a thousand.

Linnea tried to lend her a sympathetic ear, however, that first week and second week before the trouble about the water came up. By that time, she knew about Mrs. Dancey's status, that she was a polygamous wife. "But that can't be her trouble," she told Ingeborg, "that she looks like she's so sorry and sad she can't hold her head up, and like she's just ready to bury her whole immediate family and half her cousins. She's got something really serious to contend with or I'll eat my hat. Nobody looks that miserable for nothing."

Mrs. Dancey had never invited her in, but impulsively one day she went down the hall and rapped at the lady's door.

Instantly Mrs. Dancey opened it a crack at first and then wider, for Horace, at her knee, thrust his head and shoulders through it. He craned his neck and stared upwards.

"Hello, Horace," Linnea said, glancing down at him. With no particular animosity he stuck out his tongue as far as it would go and instantly drew it back. It was about a half an inch wide. "I declare you'd ought to see that child's tongue sometime," she told Olaf later. "It ain't the width of a beetle."

"Yes, Mrs. Ecklund?" his mother said.

"I thought maybe you would like to come in and set down and have a cup of coffee with me," Linnea said impulsively. "It's about time for me to put it on. And I baked coffeecake this morning. It ain't still warm but you might like a piece."

"I follow the Word of Wisdom," Mrs. Dancey said. "I don't deviate."

Linnea smiled. "Well, I deviate," she said. "It seems like it's harder for a Scandinavian not to deviate when it comes to coffee than it is for other people. When it comes four o'clock I guess I'd just wither on the vine if it wasn't for a good cup of coffee." The big green glass paperweight on the stand by the window sent out rays as the sun struck it that made the ugly green wallpaper look as though it had a ripple in it like a pond.

They looked at each other. Horace at his mother's knee stuck his uncommon tongue out again but Linnea didn't notice. Mrs. Dancey did not make a move to invite her landlady in but only repeated, "I follow the Word of Wisdom."

Linnea drew a deep breath. "Well, I tell you," she said. "I thought maybe—I been thinking about you, Mrs. Dancey. You look so—well, you know, sorrowful, and I thought maybe you had you some deep trouble that you need help with. I thought maybe—well, I don't want to be a buttinsky or anything, you know—but I thought maybe I could help you someway. Sometimes just getting something off a person's chest is all a person needs, you know!"

"You should be the last one," Mrs. Dancey said gently. It wasn't, perhaps, that her face was so small, as that the regular and not unlovely features were all too close together in the middle. The close-set khaki eyes rebuked her. A lath-narrow hand went up and stroked back the prim khaki hair.

"The last one for what?" Linnea asked in astonishment.

"You are in polygamy. I knew before I rented the room here. That should be enough," Mrs. Dancey said.

"Enough for what?"

"For anybody," Mrs. Dancey said. "*You* ought to know what a woman goes through."

"Ain't there nothing else wrong with you?" Linnea asked. "I mean, you look like you never had a thing to live for, like you'd lost the last soul that was dear to you in the whole world. Ain't there something *serious* the matter?" she begged.

"I'd like to be told what's serious, if you please."

"Why, *serious*, you know—like a terrible sickness there ain't no cure for, like not having a dime in the world—" she broke off.

"You don't call this difficult proclamation serious then, which God's children must abide by?"

"What difficult proclamation is that?" Linnea inquired with the light tone she used for the children when she thought they were putting on airs.

"Why, that of multiple marriages, of course."

"You mean polygamy?"

Mrs. Dancey put her lips primly together and dropped her eyes.

"Ain't there nothing *serious* wrong with you?" Linnea asked incredulously. "Only polygamy? Why it's just like marriage! There ain't nothing to be heartbroke about if all you got to contend with in this life is *polygamy!*"

Linnea said afterwards that the only way she could figure out Mrs. Dancey was just to imagine her as a Catholic girl who was all wrapped up in her religion and who had finally joined a nunnery. Mrs. Dancey had what you might say taken the veil, foregone all earth's earthly pleasures, for the equivalent, to her, of Christ's sisterhood—polygamy.

"Why, she's just deadly in earnest about it," she told Ingeborg. "You'd think that just because she allowed herself to marry Mr. Dancey and be his third wife, she's set herself entirely apart from ordinary people. You'd think she was holy or something. I never seen it strike anybody like that before, have you? And I've seen it strike a good many ways."

Ingeborg thought, and then she shook her head. "It's kind of a peculiar way to strike," she admitted.

Anyway, they never could have been friends even if the water business hadn't come up.

There were three barrels of water for their domestic use out around at the shady side of the house, each carefully covered with a burlap-padded lid to keep the dirt and bugs out. One barrel was ditch water, hard cold mountain water that was turned in the ditches every week by a city employee who lifted the gate and let it run down for some two or three hours. This happened in different localities on different days of the week. Linnea was lucky because the ditch ran in front of her house and she didn't have to pack the water a block or two. Ditch water, not considered pure enough to drink, was used for ablutions and the family wash. A second barrel, never full, at the corner of the house under the rain spout, caught rain water. Drop for drop, this had nearly the value of eau de cologne in all the fashionable scents, for when a woman used it to wash her hair, she had a crown of glory indeed so full of shivers and sparkles of light that it would make the eyes wink to look at it. Also, no other water could be trusted in washing fine baby flannels and other delicate materials. The third barrel held the drinking water which came from a delicious spring. A one-eyed man, driving a one-eyed horse, delivered a barrel a week of the limpidest water in Zion for fifteen cents. He could haul two barrels a trip on his low wagon, which was really only a low platform on wheels with a seat up in front. No other water could touch that spring water for drinking, and it stayed cool and fresh out there at the shady side of the house as long as there was a drop of it in the barrel.

When Mrs. Dancey moved in, Linnea explained to her all about the situation with the water. She showed her the three barrels with their tight lids.

"The ditch water is to take a bath and wash dishes and wash clothes," she said.

"The rain water ain't hardly to be used for nothing. You know what it means to catch rain water in *this* climate. But if you got to use it, it's for washing your hair and the finest flannels."

"The spring water is for drinking and cooking. Nothing else." She made it clear what the spring water was for, at fifteen cents a barrel.

And what did Mrs. Dancey do?

Well, it's hard to imagine any woman performing the way she did. The first week, she used up all the rain water! When Linnea went out around the house and took the lid off and looked into the barrel, she just couldn't believe her eyes! The rain water was all gone!

"Why don't you tell her a thing or two?" Ingeborg said. "The pig!"

"Maybe she didn't understand," Linnea said. "I'd hate to start something. And anyway, that wouldn't bring the water back."

With her in the house, the barrel of spring water could be emptied in two days. "I tell you what I think," she said. "I think she gives Horace a bath in it. She must. Otherwise it couldn't go down that fast."

But there wasn't any shortage of ditch water. Mrs. Dancey never used a drop of it.

That was the business with the water. Linnea had to order two extra barrels a week after Mrs. Dancey and Horace rented the green dining room. That came to a dollar twenty extra a month. Ingeborg said the least Mrs. Dancey could do would be to pay half of it, sixty cents, but Linnea said no, let it go. It showed her, though, how fooled you can be on a person's looks.

After a few weeks, Linnea came to the conclusion that even though Mrs. Dancey was Mr. Dancey's last and latest wife, and the youngest, too, still Mr. Dancey apparently didn't like her very well. At least he didn't come to visit her very often and when he did, he didn't stay very long. He usually picked a Sunday afternoon and would arrive on foot, always empty-handed, with his hat pulled low over his eyes, dressed in sober black. He had a sprightly light-complexioned beard that parted in the middle of his chin and went to each side in upturning tendrils. He had light sparkling eyes.

Linnea wondered how in the world he had come to pick Mrs. Dancey number three, and what she could possibly offer him there in that dire green room on these rare visits. She wouldn't make tea, she wouldn't make coffee. What would she give him? Whatever it was, Mr. Dancey did not have the look of a man who has had good things pressed upon him until they are running out of his ears, when he took leave of Mrs. Dancey. He looked blue and discouraged. But that would change, once he got out of sight of the house and the visit was behind him. One Sunday Linnea happened to be waiting at the corner for the mule-drawn Third Avenue streetcar when he came along just in time to catch it, too. They greeted each other and she saw his gloomy dispirited face. It was quite another that jumped off the car on Main Street and Third South, a face that seemed to have taken a new lease on life. On that occasion he had, by the way, a handkerchief wrapped around his hand and Linnea suspected that maybe Horace had taken a nip out of it. She did not imagine he liked Horace overly well and could not blame him. No, Mr. Dancey did not have the look of a man who has been paying a visit to a cherished woman.

Mrs. Dancey for her part had a shamed and downcast look for days after the tryst, would give a great start if you came upon her unexpectedly and take on a painful blush.

"I just simply don't care for her," Linnea confessed to Ingeborg. "Next time, I won't be so free about renting to a perfect lady. She makes me nervous, and look how mean and underhanded she's been about the water. Next time, I'll look before I leap."

"You might of knowed it wouldn't work," Ingeborg said. "You're as different as night from day. You're big and she's little. You laugh and she bawls. You was born in the church and she's a convert. Why don't you ask her politely to move?"

"I can't do that," Linnea said. "Somebody that behaves theirself and pays their rent, you can't ask them to move. Besides, I can't stand that green wallpaper." She did not want to come any closer to saying that she needed what little money the room was bringing in.

"You could rent to somebody else," Ingeborg said.

"Maybe I could and maybe I couldn't," Linnea said.

She left it at that until the Sunday that disaster struck.

Gunilla, Linnea's only sister, with her three children in the spring wagon beside her, had driven into Salt Lake City from the farm out over Jordan to spend a few days. As always, Linnea was delighted, for Gunilla was her great pet. She hadn't been there an hour when Gunilla knew all about Mrs. Dancey, her manners and appearance. She agreed that Mrs. Dancey ought to be ashamed of herself for getting away with every drop of rain water and squandering the spring water. Also, that she wouldn't touch the ditch water. Gunilla's wrath and indignation over the matter were so comforting that Linnea found she could make allowances for Mrs. Dancey. "She can't help it," she said. "She's one of them miserable skinny sneaky women that's their own worst enemy."

"You mean to tell me she won't even sit down for a sociable cup of coffee?" Gunilla asked incredulously.

"She's a convert," Linnea explained. "You know how fanatic they are. Sit down? Why, you'd have to hogtie her, I guess."

"I wonder what her poor husband seen in her in the first place?"

"I think he wonders, too," Linnea said.

She told Gunilla how hard Mrs. Dancey worked to keep everything that was of the slightest use completely out of sight, using curtains and screens when nothing else would do. "If you happened to knock on the door and her and that little kid Horace *was* happening to be sitting down eating a bite, you know what she'd do? She'd take time to throw a cloth over the table and cover up every dish and every morsel before she'd open the door a crack."

"What for?"

"Be blamed if I know. That's just her way, to hide and cover up everything that has anything to do with living. I've yet to see her go out and empty her chamber pot, so I imagine she does it in the early morning before I'm up or late at night when I'm in bed. Deadly ashamed of it. Deadly ashamed of everything. And sad! You never seen a woman so heartbroken and sad."

"What's she sad over?" Gunilla asked.

"Why, polygamy, of course. And she's got it good, too. She's well supported and don't have to do no outside work. She don't know when she's well off!"

"What did she go into polygamy for then," said Gunilla, "if that's how she feels?"

"She went into it as her bounden duty, so far as I can figure," Linnea said. "Following the Prophet's word right to the letter, that's her way of bringing a *sacrifice*, like a Catholic girl will give up her whole life to being a nun."

"I never heard of such a thing," Gunilla said.

"It would take a convert," Linnea said, "to go at it like that."

"What's her husband like?"

"Not bad a-tall," Linnea said. "Medium sized, light-brown beard, light-brown hair, black suit, blue eyes. More of the kind that's full of the old Nick, if he had half a chance. He pulls his hat down low over his eyes. She's made him sneaky and ashamed-looking too, but I don't think that must of been his natural way. He's took on that miserable sanctimonious look, too, by the time he leaves, like he'd like to sit down and have a good long hard cry, from her, but he drops that after he's gone a few blocks." She told about seeing him on the streetcar. "When he got off, you wouldn't know it was the same man," she said.

"Well, anyway, they got little Horace," Gunilla said.

"That's the part that's beyond me," Linnea said. "She don't even make him a cup of coffee!"

She and her sister were sitting on the front porch on two rocking chairs they had brought out from the house, the children were perched all over the steps, and it was a hot still afternoon, when Mr. Flodden Dancey appeared down the street. "That's him," Linnea had time to mutter, and then to say, "let's go right on talking, let's not act like we're paying a bit of attention." So when he came up the walk and up the steps, the children shifting aside for him so he would have free access, the two women were so absorbed with their conversation that they scarcely seemed to notice him. Linnea did turn vague eyes upon him and happen to say absent-mindedly "How do you do," when he went past her and opened the screen door and went in. The front door was left open during the hot weather. They heard him take the few steps down the narrow hall and knock on Mrs. Dancey's door. He waited and the two women, the children even, outside on the porch, waited, holding their breath. He knocked again. He knocked a third time.

"Oh, she's there all right," Linnea said to Gunilla's raised eyebrows.

Mrs. Dancey was. They heard her open the door now, and Mr. Dancey enter her room.

The man and wife must have spoken in whispers, for never, on any of these visits, was there the slightest sound from Mrs. Dancey's quarters.

"There's never a peep out of them," Linnea said, "not that I listen. But you'd think there'd at least be the rumble of their voices. There never is. Never a sound of a single word. They're always as quiet in there as the grave. What you kids got your ears peeled for?" she asked the children. They were obviously listening, with large eyes.

"Nothing," Bertha said.

"Well, you kids get out in the yard and play. Little kids like you should be playing, not sitting on the porch like you was a bunch of old ladies," she said. "Ain't that right?" she asked Gunilla.

"I'll say it's right," her sister said. "You kids go play."

Reluctantly they did so, casting many a reproachful glance behind them, but soon they were marking out a hopscotch square on the hard baked ground, and taking turns, and had forgotten the grownups. It was not just plain hopscotch but double hopscotch so they had to hop lively.

Something reminded the two young women of their own childhood days when they had lived on Fourth East in the family cottage. They began to chat happily of old times, when they were little girls and Brigham was alive, and used to thunder from the Tabernacle pulpit on Conference Sundays. They reminded each other of this and that, old friends, old fashions, their mother's habits and ways, that mother who, though a staunch Latter-Day Saint, had as good as disowned Linnea when she married Olaf Ecklund in polygamy, and other matters of interest. A time or two, they stopped talking and cocked an ear and listened, out of idle curiosity, but no sound came from the lodger's chamber.

"You'd think we'd at least hear little Horace," Gunilla said softly once.

"He's probably down for a nap," Linnea said. "Besides, he ain't a noisy child. He'll take a finger off you but he ain't much of a one for noise."

"How long does he stay?" Gunilla inquired.

"Who? Mr. Dancey? Not any longer than he has to," Linnea said. "He'll be coming out pretty soon. Maybe we'd ought to go in, so he won't feel embarrassed having to go by us a second time. It's nearly time for a little *påtor* anyway." *Påtor* was the affectionate Swedish name for the "little drop" of coffee they required every so often. She stood up. "Maybe the kids won't notice we're gone," she said, "and we can drink it in peace."

There came a loud thump.

"What was that?" Gunilla asked.

"Maybe Mrs. Dancey has threw her rolling pin at Mr. Dancey," Linnea said jokingly, keeping her voice low.

For an instant, when she saw Mrs. Dancey against the screen door, she couldn't believe her eyes. "Mrs. Dancey?" she said doubtfully, taking a step toward her.

Gunilla, slowly getting out of her chair, turned quickly when she saw the surprised look on Linnea's face and looked to see what she saw in the doorway. "Mrs. Dancey?" she said too.

They observed her extreme and unusual pallor at the same instant and both sisters hastened to her, Linnea opening the screen door and grasping Mrs. Dancey's narrow shoulders in her two hands. "What's the matter?" Linnea said. "Has something happened?"

"My husband," Mrs. Dancey said.

"What about your husband?"

"He's hurt."

Linnea pushed the swaying Mrs. Dancey over to Gunilla, who held her firmly upright, and made a beeline for the dining-room door. She pushed it open, hearing her sister and the frightened half-swooning woman coming after her. She opened the door and saw him at once.

Mr. Dancey was stretched out on the floor like a dead man. "If he was laid out in his casket," Linnea said later, "he couldn't of been laying longer or stiffer. If I'm not mistaken, he even had his hands crossed on his breast." She was not sure on that point, and Gunilla couldn't remember, either, but both remembered that he looked stately and lifeless.

Linnea was instantly at his side and down on her knees beside him. She did not reach for his pulse but instead dropped her head down upon his breast, after unbuttoning his coat and vest. She pressed her ear hard against it and listened, holding her breath. Yes, there it was, his heart beating, bump, bump, bump, bump. "His heart's beating," she raised her head up and announced. Gunilla had meanwhile seated Mrs. Dancey on the meticulously made bed, where she wouldn't stay and from which she at once removed herself, going to sit bolt upright in a straight chair. "So he ain't dead, at least," Linnea said. "Hand me a pillow," she said to her sister and Gunilla took one of the pristine pillows from the bed, bringing it over to her. She took it and put it under his head and began chafing one of his cold hands with her own.

"What happened?" Gunilla asked. "Did he faint or something?"

"Yes," Mrs. Dancey said, "that's what happened. He fainted." She was no longer so pale and was gradually regaining her composure.

"We thought we heard some kind of a bang or a fall or something," Linnea said, rubbing away. "Where do you keep the water? I'd like to have a little to sprinkle on his forehead and maybe touch to his lips."

With such slow secretiveness as to almost seem unwilling Mrs. Dancey got up and lifted up a curtain, reached in to a container which she hid with her skirt, brought out half a dipper of water which she carried over and handed to Linnea, who took it, looked hard at the prostrate man for an instant and then tossed it with a firm swish into his pale face. He gave a gasp and shudder. He blinked his eyes. Then he opened them. His right hand went at once to the right side of his head, his fingers tenderly feeling there. "My God," he said, "feel that."

Linnea leaned over and felt where he indicated. "It's a great big lump," she said, "the size of a hen's egg. Come feel," she said to Gunilla, who came at once. "Come feel if it isn't," she said to Mrs. Dancey, who did not. "What happened?" she asked interestedly. "You keel over in a faint or what?" Horace, she saw now, was taking a nap on his comfortable bed made upon two chairs over in the corner. The commotion had not awakened him. "We heard some kind of a thump or bang or something. We didn't know what it was," she said.

"Mr. Dancey took a fainting spell," Mrs. Dancey said from her straight chair.

Linnea saw that something was missing in this curtained and screened room, some one item. What was it? Something was gone.

Mr. Dancey slowly raised himself up until he was sitting, rather limply and weakly. "I guess I must of," he said. His right hand explored again the knot on the side of his head.

"Well, that was some faint," Linnea said. She had got to her feet and was standing looking down at him. Still rubbing and fingering the protuberance with his right hand, he reached around into his hind pocket, hoisting up his coattail, and brought out his handkerchief with his left, using it to wipe away the few drops of water that still clung to his whiskers and eyebrows. He did not look up or make any move to rise from the floor. Neither did he look at his wife nor she look at him.

Linnea and Gunilla exchanged glances. There was a silence. "Is there —is there anything I can do?" Linnea asked.

"No, thank you," Mrs. Dancey said in her sanctimonious ladylike way.

"No," her husband said shortly.

Little Horace woke up, not going through a stage of drowsy half-awakening but instantly. He had been sound asleep. Now he was wide-awake and on his feet, hanging on the back of one of the chairs that had made his bed and starting to dance from one foot to the other. He saw Gunilla and his tongue darted out. It darted out again, once for Linnea, once for his father. Not the slightest sleepiness remained in his eyes, they were as small and fierce and wide-awake as a shrewmouse.

In her own kitchen, Linnea turned and looked at Gunilla, coming through the door after her. "That kid!" she said. "Did you notice his tongue? He can't look at a person but what out snakes that nasty little tongue. That's one of the meanest kids I ever seen, though I got to give the devil his due and say he ain't noisy."

"Faint," Gunilla said. "He didn't any more faint than I did. Looked to me more like somebody clouted him over the head with a baseball bat. Didn't it look more like that to you?"

"The paperweight!" Linnea exclaimed. "That's what was missing!"

"What kind of a paperweight was it?" Gunilla asked interestedly.

"A great big glass one, green, about as big as a small mushmelon. In there on the taboret in front of the window. The sun used to shine through it. I hefted it once, the day she moved in. For a little thing like that it weighed a ton."

"I bet she hit him in the head with it!"

"I bet anything she did," Linnea said, musingly. "Else why wouldn't it be there on the taboret."

"Hit him in the head!" Gunilla said, sinking into a chair by the kitchen table, the better to think about it all. "I bet anything!"

"He sure got a lump to show for it, didn't he?" Linnea said, starting the fire and pulling the teakettle over to where it would get the hottest the quickest. "Picked up the paperweight. I'd bet my bottom dollar."

"I wonder if his skull was fractured?" Gunilla said, marvelling.

"He wouldn't of come to, if it was, would he?" Linnea asked.

"I don't know. Would he?"

(In later years the rumor got around that Mr. Dancey had indeed at one time or another in his life sustained a fractured skull. At any rate, he did certain things which could not be accounted for in any other way. One of them was, he took to going for milk at the neighbor's, from whom he bought it, with a rubber hot-water bottle. He said this forestalled any possibility of breakage and safeguarded the milk. Secondly, he built a large house on First West and put all of his three wives into it, though no one could say who of them hated whom of them more bitterly. Thirdly, he abandoned them all and refused either to go home or to support them again. And nobody, not even the Bishop, not even the Stake President, could make him do it.)

"What would she do it for?" Linnea asked.

What would she do it for! They happily speculated for hours. A woman like Mrs. Dancey, a good church member like her, a fanatical convert that stuck to the Word of Wisdom like a fly to flypaper, to pick up a paperweight and hit her husband in the head with it! It was not to be believed! It was not even to be thought of! And yet—"A man couldn't fall on his head that hard," Gunilla said, "to make a bump like that!"

"What would she do it for?" Linnea wondered.

Finally they almost doubted that she did.

The next time the rent came due Mrs. Dancey said gently and mournfully that she was not going to pay it because she was going to move out. She said the truth of the matter was, she wasn't so very satisfied with the room.

"I bet it's that green wallpaper," Linnea said. "Well, I don't blame you."

"Oh, no," Mrs. Dancey said, "I like the green wallpaper. I am going to be frank with you, Mrs. Ecklund. "I don't feel like you take your church and—polygamy seriously enough."

"I have four children," Linnea said good-naturedly. "I been married going on nine years. I don't know how much more seriously a person can take it."

"I take it seriously," Mrs. Dancey said with a bereft and grief-stricken face.

"Well, there's all kinds of ways of looking at anything," Linnea said.

"I will also be frank and say I do not think you pray often enough to your God, our Heavenly Father."

"Is that so?" Linnea said.

"Also you and your friends drink entirely too much coffee and laugh entirely too much."

"Oh?"

"And I will also be frank and say I do not think, in fact, I have my serious doubts, that you—well, that you pay your tithing," Mrs. Dancey said.

"I'm afraid that is none of your business," Linnea said with dignity.

"Not ten per cent of your income, like the Prophet said," Mrs. Dancey said.

With still greater dignity, Linnea answered her: "Lots of times," she said, "I don't even *have* ten per cent of my income!"

The day came, and Mrs. Dancey, with all her possessions and her son Horace, who bit the drayman on the finger when he reached for a straw hamper, moved out, never to be seen again.

Linnea had something to remember her by, however. For on the highest shelf of the narrow closet, something sparkled and caught her eye, when she opened the door. She reached up and took it down. It was the green glass paperweight. Linnea hefted it, first in her right hand and then in her left. "Heavy enough to brain somebody," she said. "Now why would she stick it up there? It's kind of a pretty thing. What in the world would she want to stick it up in the closet for, and hide it, so nobody could see it?"

She carried it out and set it on the kitchen table.

When the answer came to her, she threw back her head and laughed. Mrs. Dancey was a regular fanatic on hiding anything that was of any use to her. Anything to wear, or eat, or use, had to be put away in drawers, hidden under the bed, tucked away in a closet or concealed behind screens or curtains. Anything that was of no earthly use to anybody, could be put out in the open, like the jewel case, the china figurines, the glass paperweight.

But if, that Sunday, she had picked up that paperweight and used it to lay her husband out flat, it was no longer a pure ornament, was it? It was a very serviceable item.

Under the circumstances, then, it was of no use to return it to her. She would never display it again.

Laughing, Linnea kept it.

When Ingeborg hefted it, she said if Mrs. Dancey really did hit Mr. Dancey in the head with that, it was a wonder she didn't kill him deader than a doornail. "And if ever you find out why she done it," she said, "you let me know."

"*You* let *me* know," Linnea said. "Why I'd give five dollars any day!"

"I'd give ten," Ingeborg said, "any day!" That meant she would give her right arm, and possibly her right leg and her right eye, to find out. But she never did. Nobody ever did. They had to make up reasons for it as long as they lived.

CHAPTER 4

NOT EVEN Ingeborg Jensen's best friends could say she was pretty. Imagine a blonde young Eskimo squaw, neither fat nor thin, with a large face and high cheekbones, squinting blue eyes and a small knob of ecru hair firmly fastened on top of her head by tremendous bone hairpins. She had a tight red skin with a high gloss to it, the kind that would wrinkle like seersucker by the time she was thirty.

Ingeborg never wore anything very well because of her shape and coloring. She had a torso like a roll of bedding stood on end and thin though large-boned limbs. No delaine, merino, taffeta or calico ever quite became her. There was no such thing as the right piece of goods and the right color. She was outrageous in red, scalded-looking in green, lugubrious in black or brown, overwrought in pink or blue, like a frightened rabbit with a ribbon around its neck. Her feet were determined to pain her and pain her they did, from an early age. She walked as though they were the tenderest feet in the world. She considered them so. So often did she mention her painful, tender feet that one might have wondered whether they were a source of pride. Perhaps they were.

She was seven years older than Linnea and they had been friends ever since Linnea could remember. They were born in houses that stood side by side, to parents that had been friends from childhood. Ingeborg's parents both died and left her an orphan at fifteen, after which she worked at housework to earn her living, thinking of the Skolin home as her home and of Linnea and Gunilla Skolin with as much fondness as if they had been her sisters, visiting there frequently.

Linnea married at nineteen and Gunilla, two years her junior, soon after. By the time Ingeborg was twenty-six, they, and other of her female friends, for Ingeborg was much liked by her own sex, began to worry for fear their dear friend was going to go down in history as an old maid. Even a puce taffeta and a fur tippet had not made a dent anywhere and they began to think uneasily that maybe she was never going to receive an offer. If Gustave Jensen had not come to work as tailor's helper for Linnea's husband Olaf, they wondered what *would* have happened. He was a hunchback with a bushy red beard and bushy red hair, shy and mortified. Linnea put Olaf to work on the matter right away. He told Jensen about a pearl among women that no man had had the wits to want as yet. Jensen, a pious believer who longed to obey the true Gospel and multiply and replenish the earth, was quite shaken and distraught to hear of her, but promised to go to Linnea's to meet her. He took a long time to get ready and comb his hair and his beard, almost as long as Ingeborg took, Linnea feverishly helping her, to get ready.

When he left, Ingeborg said flatly that she would never have anybody like that, with such a funny withered-looking lower portion, short thin legs and enormous dragging feet where the toes turned out like that, and a hunch, even so small you could scarcely see it and didn't know what made him look so crippled and misshapen. Besides, his head looked so big, and he had that awful red hair and beard. She for one wouldn't have him if he were the last man on earth.

Jensen told Olaf sadly that Ingeborg had a "cold eye." He also confessed that he had expected to see some sort of shape and something rather comely in the way of a face. She was a good woman, though, an excellent woman, Olaf told him. Jensen said sorrowfully that that didn't surprise him.

They met again.

"I wouldn't have him," Ingeborg said. "Not if he offered himself to me on a silver platter."

"She has a *very* cold eye," Jensen said dejectedly.

Olaf talked like a Dutch uncle.

Linnea talked like a Dutch uncle. Jensen was a good worker, a dependable man. He would be a good provider. Linnea pointed out to Ingeborg that if she ever hoped to have a home of her own, she would have to have a husband. What had the Prophet said about the matter? (He had said, alas, so much on this, and on every other conceivable subject, that Linnea had more or less lost track of what it was he *had* said, but it was a good policy to mention him from time to time, it gave a solemn tone to the conversation when needed.) Besides, Jensen would never take a notion to go into polygamy!

"He had better not," Ingeborg muttered. "I'd just like to see him dare. I'd like to see him even broach polygamy. Even so much as broach it!"

If Ingeborg took Jensen, she could have a little house, lace curtains and a marble-topped bureau. She could have her own dishes, her own new broom, her own rain barrel, her own copper-lined boiler! Ingeborg said no, he was just like a gnome in the Old Country legends, ugly, and as crooked as a mule's hind leg. She could never think of it!

Jensen almost cried when he spoke of it. She had too cold an eye, too homely a face, too flat a bosom even for him—even for poor him!

They were married the week before Linnea's first child Bertha was born, and they set up housekeeping in a tiny cottage up on Q Street, on the hill, a short block from the cemetery. Here Ingeborg revealed herself to be a frugal and exemplary housekeeper, a fine cook and a bad-tempered scolding wife.

Ten months after their wedding in the endowment house, the happy couple surprised their friends by producing twins, two pretty and healthy girls. They took their hair after him and Jensen was allowed to call them Rose and Lily.

The next year they had a boy, named Bjerstjerne after Ingeborg's father, but popularly known as Chucken because he was so round and fat.

Two years after, they had Helga.

Two years after that, another girl, called Eliza.

Their cottage was as small as ever but Ingeborg accommodated her family to it well, preserving one of her three rooms, as any woman would who wanted to hold her head up in the community, as a parlor, a possession much envied by Linnea until she had one of her own.

Jensen was never known to complain of the married state, but it was supposed he may have looked back on his bachelorhood with nostalgia. Ingeborg was hard to please. It would be nice in the Prophet Joseph's heaven to take his place as the father of five—no, six, for his wife was again pregnant—children, all well-formed, of normal intelligence, but here on earth there must be pleasures to equal and far surpass it. They ate a good deal, of course. One or the other of them, or Ingeborg or himself, was always down sick in winter. There was so much din and commotion that a man could scarcely hear himself think. Sometimes it seemed as though just one thing had any worth or value in a world full of treasures: absolute silence.

Silence, and a well in the backyard, for the poor cripple had to walk two blocks on water day to fill their barrel with ditch water. The buckets were heavy, the trips many, and it was slow painful work.

He also sewed every stitch his wife and their children wore, treading the old Domestic sewing machine long past midnight after ten or twelve hours in the tailor shop at exhausting uninterrupted work so they would have plenty to wear. He even made their quilts, out of sample pieces from the shop, lined with flannelette.

Ingeborg worked hard too, she was loved by her female friends for her many fine qualities, but to her husband she always had that "cold eye" and she used her tongue like a whip. To her children she was an overly indulgent mother. She kept them out of the parlor but otherwise they had the run of the house. She never respected her husband. To her he remained the gnome, the misfit, the only man in a whole world of handsome men who would marry her. She could never forgive him for it.

Her smallest child was nearly three, and Ingeborg was far gone in what was to be her last pregnancy, when Linnea moved into the neighborhood with her four children and became her neighbor. It was nice the two old friends were only three blocks apart, they and the children could see each other almost every day, and besides, Linnea would be near at hand for the confinement. Since she had delivered Ingeborg's five other children, it was taken for granted that she should be on hand when the new baby arrived. She was, and on the twenty-second of January stood by to bring him uneventfully into the world and give him his first spanking. It was also his last for by the end of winter the little red-haired mewling thing died, and lay buried in the cemetery beside a grave almost as new as his own.

The Sunday after Ingeborg was delivered of her last child was the coldest day of the year, a North Pole day full of sharp wind and dark almost before it was light. Linnea went up to the Jensens' a little after one, with Gertrude panting beside her, to see how Ingeborg was getting on.

On this day, the snow was deep and hard-crusted with glittering ice, not to be scattered an inch by the wind. Where one walked as though on glass, it was white and the air looked light, but ahead, the snow was bluish, purple, and twilight fell just beyond one's sight, fell, and stayed, until finally one walked into it and all around found sombrous winter night. Lamps in those houses whose dwellers were not already on their way to the Tabernacle meeting, held from two to four every Sunday, shone blurred and yellow through narrow panes and said it was warm inside, better inside than out.

Down the lighted path to the back door, for a flame burned in the Jensens' kitchen window, Linnea went with Gertrude up on the stoop, knocked and was admitted by a young girl. This was Carrie Page, sixteen years old, a neighbor's daughter who had been hired for a week to feed the children and keep house until Ingeborg was up and around again.

"Hello, Carrie," she said. "Everything all right?"

"Everything's fine, Mrs. Ecklund," Carrie said. "The kids was kind of cross and noisy this morning but now they're playing nice together." They were all in a circle on the big kitchen floor in a scene of great confusion, their blonde or red heads bent over what appeared to be newspaper cut-outs, except Lily, one of the twins, nursing a wooden doll wrapped in somebody's knitted jacket, who perched on a big quilt-covered trunk by the bedroom door. "Mr. Jensen didn't feel very good after dinner and he's gone into the bedroom to take a nap. He said he wished he wouldn't of ate the dumplings, but he didn't only eat one."

"Well, a nap will do him good," said Linnea. "How's Mrs. Jensen?"

"She's all right. I think she's dozed off too."

"And the baby?"

"Him too," Carrie said.

"Well, then, I'll just sit here with you a little while," Linnea said, divesting herself and Gertrude of their outdoor garments and giving Gertrude a little push toward the children. "Go play, Gertrude," she said and her daughter obediently did so, not, however, joining the group on the floor but going instead to her favorite Lily, and climbing up beside her on the trunk to see what might be wrapped in the old jacket in her arms. They fell at once into conversation.

"You kids talk quiet, won't you, right there by the bedroom door where Mr. Jensen is trying to get a little rest," Linnea said to them, and then to Carrie, "I wonder if we shouldn't close the door instead of having it partly open like that?"

Carrie, the dinner just over and the dishes washed, was taking a well-earned breathing spell in a straight chair by the kitchen stove, having given the one rocking chair to Mrs. Ecklund, with the smallest Jensen daughter on her lap. They could see from where they sat the corner of the brass bed in the small dim room. "Oh, he's used to the noise," the girl replied. "All I can say is, he's sure good to this bunch. They could tear the house down and he wouldn't say anything."

"Well, Gertrude, you and Lily be quiet over there, and just talk low, won't you?" Linnea said. "So as not be wake up Jensen?"

They promised they would talk low.

"It worked out nice, putting the bed in the parlor for Ingeborg to have the baby, didn't it?" said Linnea, comfortably rocking and leaning close to the stove. "She wanted to just do like last time, be in the bedroom, and put all the kids here in the kitchen, and not touch the parlor, but I just said to her, now listen, Ingeborg, I said, it ain't going to hurt the parlor a bit to borrow it for a few days. It'll be the best way all around, I said. And it was, too! Don't you think so?" she asked.

"I sure do," Carrie agreed.

The cottage was square and divided through the middle. Half the floor space was kitchen: the other half parceled equally into parlor and bedroom. This was the first time that one fourth of the space was put to actual domestic use, not maintained for company, and Ingeborg was reluctant to do it, or even hear of it. Even she had to admit, however, that it worked out well. However, she would be glad to be up and to have the bed taken out of the parlor, so that once more she could shut the door strictly upon that coldly beautiful retreat.

Rose, the other twin, had the children under the spell of a story she was telling them. The two little girls continued to nurse their dolls on the trunk, Gertrude having taken up Helga's doll in the meanwhile, unperceived by its owner. Ingeborg and her baby went on napping, Jensen went on napping and the fire cheerfully burned. Linnea and Carrie sat in cozy comfort by the stove, quietly chatting.

But with six small children in one room, such peace is an angel's passing through, as fleet as her wings, and before they were aware of their bliss, it was gone. Rose's story palled, Chucken kicked Helga on the shin. Helga, hollering with rage, discovered Gertrude had her doll and hollered louder. Carrie, in her hurry to get to Helga set Eliza down too hard and brought a roar from her.

"Who's getting killed out there this time?" Ingeborg shouted from the bedroom. The baby by her side woke and wailed tinily like a disheartened cat.

"Nobody," Linnea called back in great good humor, taking the doll from Gertrude's arms, quelling her rebellion with a sharp look of just-you-let-me-hear-a-peep-out-of-you-young-lady and giving it back to Helga. "Why?"

"It sounds like somebody's getting killed again, is all. Is that you, Linnea?"

Linnea went into the parlor to greet her friend, look at the baby and ask how she did. Carrie did what she could with the children and succeeded passably well for she herself was a member of a large family. "I'd be surprised if you haven't woke your papa," she reproached them.

"He ain't getting up," Lily offered, sliding down off the trunk and poking her bright red head around the bedroom door. "He's still laying just like he was." She tiptoed a little way in. "Papa," she said.

"Lily, come out here," Carrie ordered. "None of you kids go in there. Come on out here. What do you want to wake him up for?"

He was very still under the woolen patchwork quilt in the brass bed. "Papa," Lily said stubbornly, now she was in the bedroom.

"Come on out here," Carrie insisted.

"Papa," Lily said. She was close enough now to grope through the darkness and touch him, touch his shoulder.

"Lily, I want you," Carrie said sharply.

"Lily, you mind Carrie!" Ingeborg called from the parlor. "Those kids! Do just what they want!"

"Papa, wake up." The child shook him gently. "You said you'd give me a nice sample for a doll dress." All of a sudden she was horribly afraid of Papa in the dark and the cold. She turned and ran back out the door, as if she could never get out fast enough.

"What's the matter with you?" Carrie asked, alarmed, catching her by her apron tie.

"Papa's laying so funny, I'm ascared of him," the child said, white-faced. "He won't move or nothing, and he promised me a nice sample for a doll dress."

"Who promised what?" Linnea asked coming out of the parlor to make coffee for herself and Ingeborg.

"Lily says Mr. Jensen won't move or nothing," Carrie said.

Lily began passionately to cry.

"Won't move?" Linnea went to the bedroom door and peered in for a long moment. Then she turned around with her finger to her lips. "Not one of you kids make a peep," she said, her low sharp voice so full of authority that they stood for a moment like statues. "Not one of you make a peep. Carrie, you go shut the parlor door."

"Why are you shutting the door?" Ingeborg cried. "What's the matter out there?"

"Nothing's the matter," Linnea called in her ordinary voice. "I'll be in in a minute with coffee. You just lay there. We got to shut your door a minute."

"Why? What's wrong?"

"Nothing's wrong. You just lay there and I'll be in in a minute."

They could hear her nervous voice go on and on behind the door.

Linnea took the lamp and went straight into the bedroom. She threw the covers back and looked at Gustave Jensen lying dead in bed.

"What'll we do? What'll we do?" Carrie asked beside her, shaking all over with fright and her teeth chattering.

"You go next door and get Mr. Golightly, and her, too, if you can. I got to send him down to the Tabernacle for my husband. Go fast, Carrie, and get right back here."

There was a high fence alongside the house and Carrie jumped it, cleared it entirely in one leap, a feat she could never do again no matter what as long as she lived, and brought back the Golightlys on the dead run.

"I got to go in there to Ingeborg," Linnea said, "she's carrying on so terrible to know what's the matter. Carrie, you keep the kids quiet." Their fright was such that they couldn't have been quieter if they had been deaf-mutes. "Gertrude, you sit still and don't get in the way. Mr. Golightly, I think the best thing to do's to go down to the Tabernacle and get my husband and have him come up here. Mr. Jensen works for him, you know, or rather worked for him, so maybe he'd ought to be here. I don't know where else to turn." She paused, and bit her lip. "Imagine," she said. "God in heaven. The husband gone, the provider gone, and six kids, one not five days old, and the dead of winter, and hard times. Imagine," she said. "Just imagine." She did not cry, but Carrie was softly crying and Mrs. Golightly had taken her handkerchief out and had it pressed against her eyes. "Mrs. Golightly," Linnea

said, "I guess maybe we'd better go in and get it over with, with Ingeborg. We're coming!" she raised her voice and called to her. "There ain't
a thing in the world to get upset about. Everything going to be all
right. . . ."

In that big domed edifice the Tabernacle they made the announcement from the rostrum, after the choir finished singing "O Ye Mountains
High," that Mr. Olaf Ecklund was wanted outside. Pronouncedly pale,
for this was most unusual, Olaf made his way through one of the big
double doors accompanied by an old friend, Mr. Brunno, who, several
seats away, heard the announcement, saw his pallor, and went out too,
to lend a hand. Mr. Golightly, waiting for them, said in a low voice
that the bad news was that poor Gustave Jensen had been found dead in
bed by Mrs. Linnea Ecklund and she wanted her husband to come
at once.

Olaf's first feeling was one of intense relief that no harm had befallen
either Linnea or any of the children. His next, that Sigrid would be
madder than a wet hen if he didn't go home. It was her Sunday and he
was not supposed to see Linnea on Sigrid's day. He turned to his friend
Mr. Brunno. "If you'd go down home and tell my wife Sigrid that I've
been called up to the—the Jensens," he said, "because of Jensen dying
suddenly, I'd appreciate it as much as anything." Mr. Brunno said he
would be glad to do it, and went at once.

His third thought was of Jensen. Tomorrow the little hunchback
would not be sitting cross-legged on the table, sewing, giving his wince
of pain when he had to straighten up, smelling the iron, making the
coffee . . . patiently smiling . . . saying in Norwegian, "Well, if we
was rich, it would be a different story, eh, Ecklund?" It came to Olaf
that all the time, Jensen's hair and beard had been lighting up the corner
where he sat, like a fire burning, and that there would be no fire burning
there tomorrow. It would be cold without him in the shop. "He was a
hard worker," he said to Mr. Golightly as they hurried up the hill.
"There never was nobody more willing. Too willing for his own good."

"Ain't this a time to leave a widow and six children?" Mr. Golightly
waved his hand to take in the snow and the vast cold twilight. "Ain't this
a time?"

"It's a time all right," Olaf said. "He wouldn't of had nothing like this
happen for the world." He blew out the side of his nostril and wiped
his nose with his handkerchief. A drop of moisture in his eye felt ice
cold. "He didn't have no bed of roses, Jensen didn't. I never seen a man
in less of a bed of roses. But he never said boo."

"Nobody ever had a better neighbor," Mr. Golightly said solemnly.

"He never said boo," Olaf repeated as though he were reading the
carven words upon a tombstone, and he blinked the wetness out of his
eyes.

Linnea had talked the hysterical Ingeborg into sobbing quietness and she lay in her bed in the parlor behind the closed door with gentle Mrs. Golightly on a chair beside her. The baby was fed but threw up. They said that shock had poisoned the breast milk and that they would have to find somebody else to nurse him.

When Olaf and Mr. Golightly arrived at the Jensens', Linnea suggested that they bring the two beds out of the bedroom the first thing, because they would need to lay Jensen out in that room and also keep him there until the funeral. The children could all sleep together in the kitchen. The two men did this. They brought out and assembled the first bed, and while Linnea spread a sheet upon the straw tick, they carried Jensen gently out, so gently it would appear that he was alive and they were trying to spare him from feeling any pain or discomfort, and laid him upon it, while they went in to get the second bed, the one he had died in. This they set up, too, while the children huddled in the corner as far away from the dead man as possible.

Linnea went into the now empty bedroom, quietly dusted and straightened it, in the light from the lamp Olaf held for her. "Everybody should have such clean corners," she pointed out. "Now," she said, "we ought to bring the kitchen table in here in the bedroom, don't you think? To lay him out on? I don't know what else."

They thought so, and did as she asked, putting the kitchen table in the middle of the bedroom. Mr. Golightly said he had an old table on the porch that he and Olaf could bring over for them to eat on while the regular table was in use. It was rickety or he would have suggested it for the corpse, he said. Linnea thanked him kindly.

Linnea first put a quilt on the table, after it had been drawn out as far as it would go and two leaves put in. "I got to pad it a little," she said, "whether he can feel or not. I ain't got the heart to lay him down on hard boards without something under him." Then she carefully spread a sheet over the quilt, and here the two men came again, carrying Jensen that easy careful way, and put him gently down. Mrs. Golightly came in now and they laid him out, doing all they had to do for him as delicately and respectfully as possible, not speaking above a whisper while they worked.

He looked nice when they got through. There he lay, a thick pad soaked in a formaldehyde solution on his face and another over his folded lazy hands. The room was now pitch dark and as cold as ice, for the blind was drawn and the window was open equally from the top and bottom for the freezing air to come in and keep Jensen in a state of preservation until the funeral. The door was shut and rags were stuffed along the bottom. Otherwise they could never have heated the house no matter how much coal they burned in the kitchen and parlor stoves.

The coffinmaker finished the pine coffin shaped like a mummy case, little at the bottom and big at the top, and brought it up in his wagon Tuesday night after supper. Then and only then they dressed Jensen in his temple clothes and put him in it, resting the casket on two solid kitchen chairs. The funeral would be tomorrow. That night, they shut the bedroom window and brought a small lamp in, to burn beside him on a taboret. They also left the door open. Many neighbors and ladies from the Relief Society were there, speaking in low voices, and Olaf and Mr. Golightly stayed throughout the night.

It was bad enough when the door was shut, but the children thought it still worse when it was left open. There was no darkness in the house, but they fretted and whined. Five of them lay in a bed, for Linnea could find no one to care for her children and had to take them with her and put them to sleep with Ingeborg's brood. Carrie also took a narrow edge of one of the beds with the little ones, while Linnea slept on the parlor lounge. That was Sunday and Monday nights. Tuesday night Linnea did not sleep but stayed up to make coffee and feed the watchers who were performing their last duty to Jensen. Mrs. Golightly stayed up that night too.

The bigger children kept thinking the corpse would get up and walk through the open bedroom door right in the kitchen, with horrible big eyes. They scared the littler ones by talking about it. They even scared Carrie though she was almost a grown woman, so that until she was married she felt nervous about going into a dark room and sometimes had awful dreams about Jensen standing by her bed and reaching out for her. They slept, but not for long at a time. One or the other, or two or three, was always starting up and hollering Mamma, and when Linnea or Mrs. Golightly went over and said hush, everything was fine, there was nothing to be afraid of, they were found to be soaked with sweat, and pale as ghosts, with huge pupils to their eyes.

Ingeborg wanted a lamp too, even with so many in the house, and afterwards, when she was alone with just the children, she always let the lamp burn all night, taking off the chimney and turning the wick down low. She slept that way, all the time, though, until she got electric lights, the room was stuffy and smoky with an unsheltered flame like that. She always said she kept the lamp lit all night to scare burglars away.

Everybody was very good, friends, neighbors and church members. They brought bruna bunner and chut buller and big loaves of bread just out of the oven and thin cake and apple and pumpkin pies and gingerbread, and applesauce by the pailful, sweet and spicy.

There was lots to do, cleaning and scrubbing, for the funeral was to be held at home. Ingeborg, in some fever and bedfast for a few more days, was not able to go to the church. The weather was too bad and transportation up and down the hill too uncertain in any case. The washing and ironing of the children's clothes was a real problem, for they were heavy and drying was difficult. Brought in from the line frozen they were as stiff as Jensen himself and could stand alone. With two beds in the kitchen and so many people large and small underfoot, it was hard to clear the table—the one Jensen was laid out on, now returned to its original function—of all the extra food and dishes and prepare a place to iron, or find room on the top of the stove to heat the irons. Every time the children had to go to the outhouse in the deadly cold, which was often, with nine of them, they had to be buttoned, shod, shawled and bundled up as though for a trip to town and Carrie more than earned her small wages just by this never-ending task alone. Mrs. Golightly took down all the curtains and brought them back brittlely starched on Tuesday night at just after eleven so that Ingeborg didn't have to worry about *them* at least. Nobody had a bath except the baby but since all had been scrubbed the previous Saturday night, nobody really needed bathing.

On Wednesday afternoon the funeral took place, with fine fast snow beginning to blow down again outside. All three rooms were used. The parlor where Ingeborg lay ugly and wretched in bed, wearing a long-sleeved high-necked nightgown and a thick wool shawl, the baby beside her, was for the mourners—herself, her children and closest friends. The astonishingly clean and neat kitchen, beds made up, dishes washed, floor swept and newly washed, food covered by snow-white cloths, was for everyone else who came to hear the funeral services. These were held in the bedroom where Jensen in his coffin lay "in state." He was not now a shy unhappy overworked man, but greatly composed like a marble statue which will last for hundreds of years. His hair and beard burned peacefully.

As is the Mormon custom the speakers were five or six of the men who knew him best. They told how hard he worked every day of his life. They said he loved his family and was loved by them, also by his friends. His employer would miss him, they said, for he was a faithful worker. He paid his tithing, too, never once missing. There was many a lesson to be learned from the example of Gustave Jensen. Was he a smoker? No. Was he a drinker? No. Was he a sincere believer in the truth of the Gospel of Jesus Christ of Latter-Day Saints? He was. His every action proved it. God indeed worked in a mysterious way, to cut down such a man in his prime, leaving his grief-stricken widow and five—no, six— innocent children behind, to mourn him and feel his loss. Yet He would provide for them, their Heavenly Father, for not even a sparrow falleth but what He knows and cares. Amen, they said. Amen, Amen.

A fat woman with the usual high sweet voice found in those of her build, sang "Beautiful Isles of Somewhere" all through, unaccompanied.

Bishop Lindfors said the final prayer and the funeral was over. The casket was closed and the pallbearers carried it out slowly, taking it in a cart the one block to the cemetery and the open grave, the women holding the curtains back considerately so Ingeborg could look out through the window and see them make the journey. She watched the shadowy men in the falling snow put Jensen into the ground, saw them standing with their hats in their hands saying the last prayer. She cried, rocking back and forth, while she watched. Linnea was glad when the women left who had held the curtains back, and they once more fell in muffling folds before the window. "They needn't of done that," she said crossly, for she was very tired. "Some people are always sticking their noses into other people's business." She had a hard time to make Ingeborg stop crying. She seemed to feel terrible that on the one occasion in her life that she had *really needed* her parlor (for the funeral of her husband) she had let Linnea talk her into using it as a bedroom! She mentioned it over and over again, sobbing bitterly.

The first thing the women did when the funeral was over was to put the coffeepot on.

Linnea firmly took a cup of the strong coffee in to Ingeborg and made her stop crying and drink it. She obeyed. She even ate a piece of coffeecake, and Linnea, looking down at her while she took this refreshment, thought she had never seen such a poor and wretched face in all her life, the color of a boiled lobster.

She thought, I wonder if Ingeborg ever learned to love Jensen, finally? and answered herself: Of course she did, certainly she did. She must of.

"But did you?" she wanted to say. "Did you, Ingeborg? And him? Did he learn to love you?" but she did not dare. Besides, perhaps it did not matter very much, especially now that Jensen was dead and buried. "Someday," she thought, "when me and Ingeborg is old ladies, I'm going to come right out and ask her—just for fun!"

The Lord did indeed provide for Ingeborg, or so they all said. He took her sickly baby away, for one thing, and she had one less mouth to feed. The little thing wouldn't nurse, or if he did, threw the milk up, and cried steadily, and finally on the whisper of a cry he stiffened and died. This time there was no such elaborate funeral as for the father. With only a few friends and a blessing said at the grave, in a box the women had quilted and fixed, like an oblong sewing basket with a lid, the tiny corpse was buried. Even the mother shed but few tears. He had kept her up so many nights, walking the floor with him. She had never been able to put him down for days and she was worn out.

Jensen was found to owe half the original purchase price of the house, a sum of three hundred dollars. Olaf, Mr. Golightly and several others went around and took up a purse for the widow and her family. From nearly that many contributors they got over four hundred dollars, besides coal, flour and potatoes enough to last out the winter. They suggested she pay off the house so she would never have to worry about a roof over their heads. She took their suggestion and did it. With three months' fuel, staples and a hundred dollars, she would not need to worry about a thing in the world. She could almost be considered well off.

She took up day work, that is, doing housecleaning by the day, and soon she was earning five or six dollars a week, and noon dinner for herself and little Eliza whom she took with her. The other children went to school or stayed at home by themselves. She had, therefore, not a care in the world, which only went to prove that the Lord would, indeed, provide, and that not a sparrow falleth but what He knows what is going on.

Ingeborg was given old clothes in quantity which Linnea helped her refashion for herself and the children. She was never very good with the needle. Her various employers also gave her such articles as would otherwise have been thrown out, out-of-style or cracked vases, wonderfully ornate and not to be used for flowers, a clock, sometimes a very good clock, that could be made to run if somebody worked on it, footlong pincushions with soiled lace and silk covers, so hard a pin would rebound and badly wound the finger before it would stick in, cracked or chipped dishes, a caster set with the vinegar bottle missing, a tiny oval frame enclosing a glass-covered wreath of hair, a saucepan with a hole to be soldered, or half a nutcracker. All of these articles Ingeborg prized. Some she set up in the parlor, some she tried to use, some poked away at the top of the cupboard, or under it, or back in a drawer. She never got anything repaired or passed anything on and Linnea used to say she was just like a pack rat. But Ingeborg said she didn't care, it was lovely stuff and someday it might come in handy.

Eventually she stopped mourning for Jensen, and for her lost baby, but it was a long long time before she quit grieving that her parlor, on the one occasion when she *needed* a parlor, had had a bed in it and was being used as a bedroom. That she blamed Linnea for, and she said it was something she would never get over as long as she lived!

CHAPTER 5

⇉⇇

THAT WINTER, Linnea sewed up a dozen or more bolts of "factory," a coarse white cotton on the order of muslin, into garments. She had not been able to rent the green dining room again, and, as always, she needed a little extra money.

"Garments" were special underclothes all Mormons were required to wear next to the skin, and never divest themselves of, shapeless body clothes split up the middle and made with long legs and sleeves. Later they were factory-knit like any long underwear, and eventually, as times changed, became quite ordinary chemises, as they are now, hardly to be told from other underclothing except that they bear the distinctive marking of the prescribed garments devised by the Prophet to keep the pious wearer from harm—two small V-shaped buttonholed slits about where each nipple would be, a little higher or lower, and an open buttonholed slit a fraction over an inch in length horizontally placed a handspan above the navel. They were not manufactured in those days and had to be individually cut and sewn. Most of them were made at home but some families could afford to hire the sewing done. Sometimes a woman could earn twenty dollars or better at the beginning of winter and again in spring making garments in her own home. She had to work many long hours, of course, to do it, after her regular household tasks were out of the way.

Linnea often sat buttonholing the markings or stitching at the machine until far into the night. Once Gertrude woke to the whir it made. She was sleeping in the kitchen with Stellie. She raised up on her elbow and watched her mother sewing. "Mamma," she said, "you know what I was thinking? I was thinking, the man that wrote that song Home, Sweet Sweet Home—he had some sense!"

"He did have some sense," Linnea said with a smile, looking across at her golden-haired child. "Was you dreaming or what?"

Gertrude stared all around at everything with the large unblinking eyes of the recently sound asleep. Everything looked familiar and dear, as upon a return from afar with a long homesickness behind one, and beautiful, and of great intrinsic value. There was a warm fire, a lighted lamp and a roseate mother sewing under a cloud of lucid Swedish hair. "Mamma, I tell you something," she said, not knowing how else to express her sense of comfort and peace, "I'm glad I ain't dead!"

Linnea laughed and told her to turn over and close her eyes and go back to sleep.

"He *really* had some sense, didn't he, Mamma?" the child said.

"Who?"

"The man that wrote Home, Sweet Sweet Home. Didn't he, Mamma?"

"He certainly did," Linnea said. "Nobody's going to argue with you over that."

The buttonholing of the V-shaped openings and the center-front slit was the most tedious part of the work but Linnea used to say the Prophet could have come out with something worse. He could have come out with open-work daisies or eight-pointed diamonds, and then what? It wasn't so bad when Ingeborg or somebody was there to talk to. The tedious part was when the children were in bed and she had to sit with only the clock to keep her company and the fire in the stove and the teakettle steaming upon it. But then she used to think about things and that passed the time.

For instance, did the children, by any chance, have something? "Something" is a talent which sets one man apart from the others, puts him up higher, as though he were riding around on everybody else's shoulders. People see him and say, What a wonderful mother he must have had!

If anyone had said to Linnea, "Define the word *talent*," she would have said, "To be able to make a statue, to be able to write a book, to be able to paint a picture by hand, to be able to make up a piece of music," only after she had instantly answered, "To sing like Jennie Lind, to act on the stage like Edwin Booth, to play—" and she would have named various musical instruments. The talent she considered the most important of all she would not have mentioned, because she did not know she considered it a talent. That was, the talent to become a millionaire. She would watch for this in her children until they were grown, but idly, and with only half an eye, often forgetting, as she might have determined to find a diamond ring or a purse of greenbacks upon the sidewalk but couldn't keep her mind on it.

Above everything else, Linnea admired the talent for becoming a millionaire, and she loved money and often thought of it, deciding what she would lavish upon every man, woman and child she knew, and some (like orphans and the old and sick) she did not know, and what she and her own family would wear, eat and drink. It was delightful to do this from time to time, especially while tediously sewing, but if she had been arguing the case she would have said that if a person wanted to be perfectly honest, the good things in life probably came in this order:

Health. What good were servants in knee pants if your fingers and toes were dropping off with leprosy?

Good looks. What use were gold doorknobs and being able to fry a chicken in butter if you looked like the devil before day?

Intelligence. What good was taking a trip in a red plush Pullman car and having a sealskin coat, if you didn't know enough to pound sand in a rat hole and everybody had you tagged as a goof the minute they laid eyes on you?

There would not, by the way, be the slightest use for any of these things in Heaven, which thought (on occasions few and far between) sometimes gave Linnea solace. All the talent in the world for money wouldn't be worth a snap of the finger there. Health? Anybody who flew around in the fresh air all the time and maybe sipped honey from the heavenly flowers like some kind of a hummingbird would naturally be as strong as a horse. And suppose you were the best-looking angel that ever stepped foot (or flapped a wing) in Heaven, what good would that do you? About as much good as a sack of salt out on the salt flats. There was no giving or taking in marriage! And what good would smartness do? Suppose you were the smartest angel that ever added up a column of figures in his haloed head? Was God going to step down and let you take over? No, in Heaven the only talent you needed was the talent to get there in the first place, and anything else was just so much excess baggage.

By keeping the mind busy, it was possible to make garment after garment and work marking after marking, sitting still in a chair like a bump on a log, but Linnea didn't favor the job. To get some real satisfaction out of your labor, she always said, what you wanted to do was houseclean, whether in spring or fall.

Conference, held twice a year, when church members and officials gathered from every ward and stake to hold meetings and attend to church business, usually lasted for three or four days and was conducted so as to take in April 6, and October 6. The ladies in Salt Lake City always tried to have their spring and fall housecleaning over by these dates (but just over, so that everything looked at its very best) in order to be prepared for any guests who might show up.

Perhaps on no day does a house look so well as on the first Sunday after the big cleaning, although, if it is the end of March, the parlor is too cold to sit in, with the stove absent (it has been carried out and stored) and the chimney hole covered by the fluted pan. The walls, too, have drawn dampness from somewhere and though the sun may be shining outside and the trees leafing, it is a chilly place. Only a very formal caller, perhaps the Bishop of the Ward, or the Schoolteacher, if they should happen to call, which isn't in the least likely, will be asked to sit in it. Everyone else will be shown its purity and beauty but will be cozily placed before the kitchen fire, and not sorry to be there.

Mrs. Golightly, for one, said that she always felt sorry for the people who were treated like company.

It was quite a novelty for Mrs. Golightly to come to call and when Linnea heard her uncommonly timid knock, she was delighted, as usual.

"Mrs. Golightly!" she said, throwing open the door. "Come in! Well, if you ain't a sight for sore eyes!"

If a small woman in sober dress, with sober hair parted in the middle under a sober round hat can be said to be a sight for sore eyes, Mrs. Golightly was indeed that. Telling her so brought a flash of pink to her cheeks like the unexpected glimpse of an edge of pink chemise. She came in, timidly, saying timidly that she was only going to stay a minute. She was the softest, quietest, mildest, most mannerly little woman who ever lived.

That is why, when Linnea thought back three years to Mrs. Golightly's last confinement, she couldn't really believe she had heard right. She had never mentioned it to a soul, not even Ingeborg. Sometimes she glanced across at Mrs. Golightly in church sitting there like a shy dove, too bashful and mannerly to so much as turn her head, and smiled a little to herself when she recalled what Mrs. Golightly had kept saying during that long night of her ordeal.

She had walked, of course, as all women did, while the pains came and went, stopping to bite her lower lip deeply and grab onto bedpost or bureau, her knuckles white. She really had a long old wait, and a bad time, and the baby was a mile too big (and afterwards she hemorrhaged) but it was surprising how naughty and fierce she was. Coarse, too. That was the especially surprising thing, for a woman like Mrs. Golightly. Every time she saw her husband she said fiercely, "You old fool." Then she said still more fiercely, "You old mule." Most fiercely of all she ended the bitter refrain: "You stink worse than a mule a thousand miles away."

It was not at all ladylike. Linnea bet that if Mrs. Golightly said that once to Mr. Golightly, who stayed there and pitied her and would have done anything he could to help her, she said it a thousand times. It sounded *very* coarse, and also ridiculous. Linnea wanted to burst out laughing, but Mrs. Golightly was so outraged and Mr. Golightly so discomfited that she did not dare.

The minute the baby was born Mrs. Golightly stopped all that and became once again as meek and mild as she had always been, yes, and as delicate and mannerly. Anybody seeing her would never guess that she even knew the word stink let alone knew it well enough to hurl it at her husband, saying he did that very thing worse than a mule a thousand miles away. It was so silly, it made Linnea smile to think of it. She never mentioned it to Mrs. Golightly and Mrs. Golightly never mentioned it to her.

Mrs. Golightly only made about two calls a year, and wisely she picked the very days she knew everything would be looking its very best, including Linnea and the children. That made it a pleasure to have her. Besides, she was free with her praises and seemed to notice everything from the new antimacassar to the left-hand part in Rudie's hair.

She said Linnea had done such a fine job on the housecleaning that the house literally sent out sparkles, like a diamond. "You know," she said, "this housecleaning you've just did, reminds me of when Mamma housecleaned one time."

"Does it?" Linnea said, replenishing the kitchen fire. "When was that?"

"Why, once in—" she looked all around to see if any of the children were in the house, but they weren't, they were playing out in the yard, "in—June," she said. She drew a pattern on the tablecloth with her fingernail.

"In *June?*" Linnea asked incredulously. "What happened? Had she been sick or something?"

"Oh, no. She done her regular spring housecleaning in the latter part of March, just like always. This cleaning in June—that was extra."

"Regular housecleaning?"

"Regular housecleaning, taking up the carpets, washing woodwork, washing windows. Everything. No difference a-tall."

"My goodness," Linnea said in amazement. "What would she want to do that for?"

"Well, I'll tell you," Mrs. Golightly said, again looking around, just to make sure. "That was the summer Pa married Aunt Eunice."

There was a pause while the two women considered this.

"I ain't never told a soul about any of it," Mrs. Golightly said.

Linnea gave her a look that said thank you. She spoke with great politeness. "Your pa didn't only have the two wives, didn't he?" she said. "Just your Mamma and your Aunt Eunice?"

"That's right," Mrs. Golightly said. "Just the two."

"Your pa's been dead going on three years now, ain't he? I couldn't go to the funeral for some reason but I heard it was lovely. I always think it's so lucky to be able to have a funeral in the summer, when there's lots of flowers, and such a shame to have to have it in the winter when there's none a-tall. It makes people feel better, don't you think? Flowers?"

"Them that's left? It certainly does," Mrs. Golightly said. "Mamma, now. Mamma's been dead seventeen years, almost eighteen. There was lots of flowers for her funeral, too."

"That was nice," Linnea said. She set the cups, saucers, spoons and a plateful of coffeecake on the table, brought in the full cream pitcher to stand beside the big sugar bowl, and sat down again with one eye on the blue-enameled pot, waiting for it to boil.

"I was fifteen at the time," Mrs. Golightly said.

"The age a girl needs her mother," Linnea offered sympathetically.

This brought an unexpected tear to Mrs. Golightly's eye, which she brushed away. "Poor Mamma," she said. "She wasn't only a young woman herself when she died. Of course, I thought she was old."

"A real young woman?" Linnea inquired.

"She was thirty-four," Mrs. Golightly said, "but she would of been thirty-five the last day of September so you could really almost say she was thirty-five. My, that seemed old to me. I felt like she was a regular Grandma but of course she didn't really look so old. They skinned their hair back worse than they do now and then some of her teeth was out at the sides but the front ones was good. And here now I've come along till I'm thirty-four myself, just her age. I bet if I died, my kids would think I was an old woman too. I don't feel old, though, not what you'd say old. I feel about like I always did. I guess that's how age is, you never do feel any different than the way you always did, you just feel like you, but here you are getting older every day. People thinking you're older, I mean."

"That's how it is," Linnea said, "exactly. Here I'm twenty-nine myself."

"Yes," said Mrs. Golightly. "So now," she continued, "Aunt Eunice is the only one left. Mamma and Pa is both gone."

"How is your Aunt Eunice?" Linnea asked. "I'd ought to go see her, but it seems to hard to get clear down to Sixth West with the children."

"Oh, she's fine. She's still got the little house she first moved into after she married Pa. I and my two brothers go see her every once in awhile. She never had any children. She's only twelve years older than me."

"Who was your Aunt Eunice anyway? I don't think I ever heard." The coffee was boiling. Linnea got up and set it off to one side, and stood by the stove waiting for the grounds to settle.

"She was Mamma's cousin. Always there when the family had Thanksgiving or Christmas, or going out to Calder's Park or Parley's Canyon for picnics, or down to Liberty Park."

Linnea poured the coffee and sat down again, offered cream, sugar and a piece of coffeecake which her caller with great nicety took.

"Pa was awful good-looking, I guess you don't remember," Mrs. Golightly went on musingly. "Mamma was around eighteen when she married him. You know how some women are, for just thinking the sun rises and sets in somebody. That's how Mamma was."

"There was a girl in Sweden jumped in the lake over some man," Linnea said. "Killed herself. I remember the folks telling about it when I was little. She hadn't even had anything to do with the man, wasn't even going to have a baby or nothing."

"For goodness sake," Mrs. Golightly said.

"Just loved him, that was all there was to it. Wanted this one particular man, and when he didn't love her, that was the end of her." Linnea paused. "But of course she may have been out of her head," she said, "it seems to me some of them said she was out of her head. But most people thought she died of a broken heart, because she loved him and he didn't love her. Imagine jumping in the lake over something like that."

"Imagine," Mrs. Golightly said.

"I guess the poor man hadn't only exchanged a few words with her. *He* was just as surprised as anybody. In fact, one of the most surprised."

"I don't wonder," Mrs. Golightly said. "Well, Mamma wasn't like that. But she just thought the sun rose and set in Pa. Everything had to be just so for him. She used to fuss over his shirts ironing them like he was a king or something. You know he always had to have white shirts working in the Z.C.M.I. and they had pleated fronts. Honestly it seemed like she'd spend a couple of three hours just on one of them white shirts alone. And dumplings with meat inside, half cooked grated potato and half raw grated potato, boiled. He wouldn't let her run the meat through the grinder, she had to chop it in the bowl, chop, chop, chop, and here she'd be working on those dumplings for hours. She used to brush his hair and his beard, started it when they was first married. It was really awful pretty, his hair and his beard," Mrs. Golightly said, smiling uncertainly. "Kind of like Brigham's before he died, thick like that, and wavy, but not a bit gray of course. And he had funny eyes, blue, but with little bits of copper, like. You know how you'll see little flecks of copper in the water off the bottom of the teakettle. Pretty, though. Pa was really a good-looking man if I do say so myself," Mrs. Golightly said. "I take more after Mamma's side. Mamma was little and not one to pay much attention to herself. Her eyes was nice though, real nice. There must have been something to attract Pa to Mamma in the first place . . . whatever it was. . . ."

"I bet she was real good-looking," Linnea said kindly.

"Didn't I never show you through the album?" Mrs. Golightly said. "Next time you come over you remind me to show you through the album. Mamma made every stitch of her wedding dress by hand out of white china silk. Earned the yardage, too, some way, I forget just how."

"I bet it was pretty," Linnea said. "I guess you come right along and wore it at your wedding."

"No, I didn't," Mrs. Golightly said.

"Wasn't you of a size?"

"We was about of a size," Mrs. Golightly said. "It wasn't that. It was—" she stopped and swallowed. "Mamma tore it up and used it for scrub rags when she housecleaned that time in June, the day Pa married Eunice."

Shocked, Linnea looked away. "Oh, my," she said softly.

"I was around six but it's funny how you'll remember some things and forget other things that's lots more important. Some one little thing will stick in your mind and you'll remember it all like it was yesterday, and other things you'll forget."

"It's funny how you will," Linnea said.

"Well, that day, for instance," Mrs. Golightly said. "I don't know. It seemed like Mamma just never thought anything like that could happen. They was good Latter-Day Saints and all, but it just seemed like it never even entered Mamma's head that Pa would—that Pa—" she looked helplessly across the table at her friend, a polygamous wife, whom she did not wish to offend.

"Some people, it never enters their head," Linnea said tactfully. "Some of the best men in the church only got one wife. And here your pa come home and broached it to your mamma, I guess."

"I was only around six but I remember how she keeled over. Just like dead. White as a ghost. I screamed my head off, and then Paul and Harry started in. Poor Pa, for a little while there. I guess he had something on his hands. Mamma come out of it, but she was—like distracted, you know. Not in front of us kids, but her face was all swelled, red in spots and seemed like it had kind of big white blisters, and her lips was swelled," she frowned, remembering, "kind of transparent, and thick, and pale, like with water under them. She acted the same as always around us kids, though, fed us and all. I got scared that night and got up and went out to the kitchen, and here she was," she did not look at Linnea and her face flushed, "down on the floor with her arms around Pa's knees, what you might say crying, and her hair all down, crying and saying how she loved . . ." her voice trailed off miserably.

"Some people take everything so hard," Linnea said. "Whatever happens, they take so hard."

Mrs. Golightly drew a deep breath. "My goodness, how a person will get to remembering something," she said. "Here you housecleaned, and I go see you, and here I get to thinking of all that, that happened so long ago. I never told a living soul before. Anyway, now I got started, I just as well finish. Eunice was Mamma's cousin," she said briskly, "eighteen years old. Pa had knew her from the time she was ten, when he married Mamma, just like he knew all the family. Mamma never any more thought . . . Well, anyway, she grew up to be a big husky girl with big eyes and a big mop of hair, and her cheeks red. You know how some girls will develop early. I mean, here they'll be maybe only twelve or thirteen, and they'll have—they'll be developed—they'll look maybe like women grown, and other girls will be as flat as a pancake and look like maybe they're still kids and here they'll be sixteen or seventeen. You know how some girls will do. Well, Eunice was one of those big husky girls with a big—she was one of those that developed early. She liked Pa, I guess. I mean, I guess he joshed her a lot about her beaus and like that. Aunt Pearl told me once Eunice had lots of beaus. She's only forty-six now, but of course those days are over, she's so fat, she can hardly get out the door, she don't even go to Tabernacle and she's so near by, too. I guess everybody's pretty near forgot how she was real pretty and a lot of the boys was sweet on her. They say she weighs three seventy-five if she weighs an ounce."

"Some people will get fat like that," Linnea said. "And you take other people, they can eat like a horse and stay as skinny as ever. I wonder why that is? I kind of run to fat myself. I guess you got to be careful what you eat, if you run to fat, but I don't know as that would help much, it's probably just natural."

"Anyway," Mrs. Golightly said, "to make a long story short. Here was Mamma's cousin Eunice and Mamma never any more thought of such a thing than fly to the moon. She never even knew how they got so well acquainted, because Pa would just josh her at Thanksgiving and Christmas when the family was all together, about her beaus, or say it looked like she had took to putting rouge on and things like that, like somebody will a relation, or be her partner once in a while playing some game. And then here he come home out of a clear sky and told Mamma he was going to marry Eunice, he asked her, he said, and she said yes, and here he was going to marry her. I don't know, it seemed like if it was just anybody but Eunice, anybody but her. She was eighteen then, already as big as a house but a good shape and an awful pretty face. Of course," she said with sudden overwhelming embarrassment, "it wasn't like *that*. I mean, Pa was a good man and settled here one of the earliest, he really believed the Gospel and always paid his tithing. It was just because he wanted to do like the Prophet said. It wasn't because she was—it wasn't because he—he was awful religious. It wasn't because—"

"No, of course not," Linnea said gently. "I never thought it was."

"Anyway," Mrs. Golightly said, "they got married on June the tenth. Pa had got the house ready for her where she lives now on Sixth West. I don't know how long it was before he come home after the wedding. Maybe three or four days. Maybe just a couple of days. Time don't mean nothing to a little kid, it seemed long to me, but I don't suppose it was over a couple of days. That was as hot a summer as they ever had around here and got hot so early. It seemed like it was about a hundred and ten that day, you could have fried an egg on the washtub turned upside down in the back yard. I knew about Pa marrying Eunice, but Mamma said that was the end of it, not to say any more about it. I don't recall how I knew that was the actual day. Pa was gone like he always went down to the Z.C.M.I. to work. We all got up just like usual, us kids. We got dressed and had breakfast and started playing like kids will do. Paul and Harry had a wagon outside. I kind of stayed around close to Mamma with my doll, kind of close around her. She had that funny swelled-up blistered look and her eyes looked real little and far back in her head, and I'd say something and she'd look at me and then it would seem like a long time before she'd hear me and answer, like she was away down the block or somewhere. She breathed in so funny, like she was trying to pull the air down as deep as she could into her lungs, but she couldn't, it would only go about halfway, and then she'd try again, but it would only go about halfway. I bet you for an hour she just did nothing but walk up and down, walk up and down, breathing like that. You go outside and play with the kids, she said to me, but I just stayed and she didn't seem to notice. I don't know what all was running through her head, but hideous things, just terrible things, I guess, that she'd never say to any living soul. Finally she sat down quick in a chair by the kitchen table and laid her head in her arms, and her back shook all over and it looked like she was crying, but before I got over to her she raised her head and looked right at me. It seemed like that was the very first time that day she looked right at me like she could see me. She wasn't crying. She smiled at me. She said, Come here and let Mamma give you a kiss. She didn't breathe funny like that any more. She said, *What do you say if we houseclean?*"

"I wish I'd of knew her," Linnea said.

"Mamma tore up the wedding dress in scrub rags before I hardly got time to look at it. She said, The material wasn't no good. It's all in pieces. You'll have a lots prettier wedding dress than this. Here I put in all that time making it and here it wasn't no good, she said. She smiled so sweet and it seemed like it was just natural to tear up a white silk wedding dress every stitch put in by hand and use it for scrub rags, she did it so it seemed like it was just natural."

"Anyway," Mrs. Golightly said. "She went ahead and housecleaned. At night after we was all in bed she still was washing woodwork until

I don't know how late. I tell you, she practically took that house apart piece by piece and scrubbed every bit of it. She washed and ironed too. I guess she was so tired when she got to bed, she just fell in. And here it was so hot and her scrubbing the back porch with a piece of the wedding dress and the sweat just dripping off her. But it seemed like it made everything better for her, and for us kids, too, to get in and work like that, she kind of got something out of her system, and never cared no more like she did at first. I remember when she was washing one of the parlor windows she called me to come and look out. The glass was so clear it didn't seem like it was there at all, except it made the air outside sparkle. You know, honey, she said, you wash your windows inside and out and you don't do just that, she said. No, sir, she said. You wash the leaves on the tree, and the hedges, and grass, and sky, and the house across the street, and the church, and the wagons, and make everybody going by look clean and neat, all at the same time. You don't just wash the windows, she said. Don't you ever believe it, she said. You remember that. You remember it about *these* windows especially, she said"— Mrs. Golightly made a V out of her two fingers and laid a tip of them on each of her eyes—"These is the important ones, she said. I think of Mamma saying that even now," Mrs. Golightly said, "when I wash my windows sometimes."

"It all turned out all right then?" Linnea asked.

"Oh, yes," Mrs. Golightly said, "she lived nine more years and then come down with an obstruction of the bowel or something. She suffered awful with it but she was gone in three days, so that wasn't as bad as if she had lingered maybe a month or two."

"And your Aunt Eunice never had any children."

"No, she never had any. Harry was two, and Mamma was still a young woman, you would have thought she would have had another two or three babies herself, but no, she never had any more either."

"Well, that's the way it goes sometimes," Linnea said.

"She still kept on with the shirts, though, ironing those pleated fronts."

"Did she?"

"Yes. But no more dumplings, no more chop, chop, chop."

Washing up the cups and saucers, Linnea thought about Sigrid.

Of course, Mrs. Golightly's mother and Sigrid were two different women entirely. And there wasn't any comparison between herself and Aunt Eunice. If there had been, Mrs. Golightly wouldn't have ever mentioned a word about any of it, she'd have just kept mum.

Linnea could just imagine Sigrid crawling around on the floor with her hair hanging down, for any man living. A man might get down on his knees to Sigrid, but Sigrid would never get down on her knees to him. She thought too much of herself, Sigrid did. Linnea felt relieved to think of Sigrid's pride and haughtiness, her stately carriage, her cold Norwegian beauty.

It's not the same thing at all, she said to herself, Mrs. Golightly's mother and Sigrid, me and Aunt Eunice, yet it seemed to stay like a problem on her mind.

The trouble was, she argued, Mrs. Golightly's mother must of been one of them poor women that couldn't call her soul her own. A woman like that, she didn't have a chance in the world, to start with.

Later on she thought, And Aunt Eunice must of deliberately set her cap for Mrs. Golightly's father! She must of done it *deliberately!*

She almost felt as if she had a bone to pick with the Prophet himself, so heavyhearted and conscience-stricken was she beginning to feel. When Ingeborg came in the late afternoon to send the whole trying matter out of her mind like a puffball blown hard upon, she was just reassuring herself about the following:

Polygamy must be all right, or the Prophet wouldn't have allowed it.

The Prophet must have been all right, or he couldn't have founded a church like the Church of Jesus Christ of Latter-Day Saints.

The Church of Jesus Christ of Latter-Day Saints must be the chosen people of the Lord or they wouldn't have so much influence and property.

Look at Salt Lake City alone.

Look at the Temple. Of course, it wasn't quite finished yet but it eventually would be. And it was going to cost four million dollars.

Were people in the habit of sneezing at four million dollars?

Take the organ in the Tabernacle. It was the biggest organ in the whole world, barring none.

Joseph Smith certainly couldn't have been so *very* wrong, considering all that.

She was glad Ingeborg came so she didn't have to think about it any more.

You could depend on it, Mrs. Golightly's mother was one of those poor little women without a bit of gumption.

As for Aunt Eunice, there wasn't any more comparison between herself and Aunt Eunice than there was between a—a dog and a cat.

CHAPTER 6

WHEN LINNEA RECEIVED the invitation by mail to go to the fashionable
Seely wedding set for the last Sunday in September (the day before
school started), she sat down hard in the rocking chair on the porch and
fanned herself.

Olaf had made Mr. Seely's clothes for the last ten years and become
friends with him as a consequence. Mr. Seely, a strong-willed man, had
no doubt suggested sending the invitation since Linnea did not have the
honor of Mrs. Seely's acquaintance. It rather spoiled things when Linnea
found out that Sigrid had been invited, too, but when she thought it
over she reminded herself that this was to be expected, as Sigrid was
Olaf's first wife. She comforted herself to think that Sigrid would be
madder to hear about her invitation than she was to hear about Sigrid's.

Mr. and Mrs. Seely's only daughter Louise was marrying a man
named Orange Ivins. All Linnea knew about him, which she found out
through Ingeborg who managed to pick up quite a lot of information at
the various houses where she worked, was that he was well off. His
father had left him two thousand dollars and he was the manager of the
whole kitchenware-goods department of the Z.C.M.I., a position of great
importance. "It takes money to get money," Ingeborg said enviously,
"every time."

Mr. Seely was wealthy. He was the owner of the Seely Drug Store,
and had a house which was said to cost over five thousand dollars. Olaf
told Linnea once when they met Mr. Seely and his wife and daughter
taking in the band concert that he bet if Mr. Seely had a cent in the
bank, he had ten thousand dollars.

Linnea was proud of her invitation and wouldn't have missed going to
the wedding for the world. Since it read "Mrs. Linnea Ecklund and
Family," she was also going to take the children and they were looking
forward to it with all their might.

She frequently wondered in the next few days whether Sigrid would go to the wedding, and if so, what she would wear. This bothered her a good deal but she would have died rather than inquire of Olaf whether he knew. She speculated on it. "What do you suppose Sigrid will wear?" she asked Ingeborg one afternoon over their coffee cups.

Ingeborg knitted her brow and thought. "Well," she said finally, "if she don't get something new, I bet she wears her dark-blue foulard with the lace collar and cuffs, and the wine-colored velvet crushed sash. That's her best, ain't it?"

"Her best?" she said frigidly. The mention of this dark-blue foulard brought a kind of ice age down upon Linnea. She had gone through the stages of erupting like a volcano and hotly and smokily desolating the landscape at the time it happened, and now, whenever it was mentioned, or she thought of it herself, she turned to a frozen north of wrath.

Olaf had been given ten yards of navy-blue silk foulard by a goods salesman. While he was trying to decide how to give it to one or the other of his wives (or cut it in half and give Sigrid five yards and Linnea five yards) they both found out about it. They both wanted it. They decided it was the most beautiful piece of material they had ever seen in their whole and entire lives. Sigrid was going to make it up with a bustle and Linnea was going to make it up with a tight basque and a Francine skirt looped up in the middle.

Finally Olaf, in torment, asked Linnea if she would be willing to flip a coin or draw straws with Sigrid for the yardage. Linnea said she would be glad to. He asked Sigrid the same thing and she went on one of her famous crying sprees that lasted three days and three nights. Olaf got so nervous and distraught that he gave the silk to Sigrid and she carried it home from the shop and hardly got in the house before she cut it out. That was two years ago, but Linnea still could not hear the mention of dark-blue foulard without feeling like a female Guy Fawkes.

"Well, whatever it is," Ingeborg said, gently sidestepping the dangerous issue, "I bet it will be tight-fitting. She's one woman that sets an awful lot of store by her shape."

All Linnea had to do when she wanted to be hardhearted was to think of Sigrid's ways and of her vanity and the dark-blue silk, so that was what she thought of while she climbed the stairs to the second floor where Olaf had his tailor shop up above Carter's Gun Store. She told Olaf she had to have some extra money so she could take the children and go to the Seely wedding without wanting to sink through the floor; she had to buy a present of some sort and not only that, she needed quite a few little things in order to be presentable. Olaf didn't have the money, and Linnea felt sorry for him and wanted to desist, but the thought of Sigrid's perfidy and beauty goaded her on. She began by wheedling in a half-flirtatious way and ended by quietly sobbing into her handkerchief. It worked, and Olaf gave her eleven dollars he could spare about like the Prophet could spare one of the golden plates from the Hill Cumorah.

When Linnea took it, she cried afresh, thinking that Olaf looked pale and work-worn. She gave it right back to him, the tears streaming down her cheeks. "I don't need it," she said. "I didn't want to go to the darn old wedding anyhow."

Then Olaf had to take her on his lap, though she was a real lapful, weighing a hundred and sixty-five pounds—at least ten pounds more than Olaf—and soothe her, and comfort her, and kiss her tenderly, and tell her that he didn't need the eleven dollars. His goodness and kindness undid her again and started a fresh fountain, while she clung to him and told him she wouldn't any more deprive him of the money than fly to the moon. He had quite a struggle to make her take it but he finally succeeded. This often happened when she coaxed Olaf into giving her extra money—she felt so sorry when she got it that she returned it, and he had to coax her into taking it back. If Sigrid had known about this, she would have sworn that this was one of the reasons that Olaf was such a fool over Linnea and she would not have been far wrong.

The wedding was set for four o'clock Sunday afternoon and by a little past two of that bright day Linnea was all ready, and so were the children. They all had a bath the night before, and clean underwear, and she put up the girls' hair in rag curls. It was no easy job to comb it and there were many low moans and outright shrill cries, much wincing and screwing up of faces, for the golden tendrils were like tight springs; the minute they were released from the hand they hopped right up close to the head and there they stayed quivering, but they had a fashionable look and that was all that mattered.

"Now just go sit on the porch, and don't get mussed up," she said.

Earnestly aware of their duty and the solemnity of the occasion, Bertha, Gertrude and Stellie, their new hats firmly on, the elastic sawing at the plumpness under their round small chins, carefully hoisted their blue challis skirts up at the back so that only their muslin drawers should be exposed to the hot top step.

Mamma came out too, having nothing to do inside the house, and sat down in the rocking chair, taking Rudie who had toddled out with her into her arms so he wouldn't get into mischief. Her daughters shifted around to see her better, for it was very nice to sit leisurely on the porch like this with Mamma and have a real wedding to look forward to. Mamma made signs that she was going to put Rudie to sleep and make him take a nap until it was time to go. She did not dare to say this in so many words and risk his fiery dissent, but the girls caught her meaning and when she started "Good Night, Ladies," they quietly hummed along with her. The softness of Mamma's lap and bosom, the hot and quiet sunlight, the rippling shade of the vines, the creaking of the chair, the humming of their clear tender voices, all combined to make Rudie lose his hold on reality in a very short time and soon he was soundly sleeping.

"Now, how you kids going to act at the wedding?" Linnea began conversationally, rocking back and forth.

"Nice, Mamma." "Quiet." "Like little ladies." "One helping of ice cream, if they have ice cream." "Like you said." They had been well drilled.

"No wanting to run outside and play with any of the kids."

"Oh, no, Mamma."

"No getting off from me where I can't keep my eye on you."

"Oh, no, Mamma."

"No acting-up during the refreshments."

"Oh, no, Mamma."

"No wild Indian shenanigans."

"Is there really going to be ice cream and cake?" Gertrude asked, uneasily wriggling.

"Sure," said Mamma.

"What else?"

"What do you mean what else?"

"About the bride's veil and white satin and all the pretty things like that."

"I told you all that before."

"Tell it again, Mamma," they chorused. "But first I got to go tinkle," Gertrude announced, "wait till I get back, before you tell, Mamma."

"No, you don't got to go tinkle," Mamma said. "The least little thing, you get all excited and right away have to tinkle. You sit quiet there for a minute."

"I *really* got to go, Mamma."

"Why can't you just sit there where you are for a minute? I seen you go around the house out to the back not twenty minutes ago."

"You don't care if I go, do you, Mamma?" Bertha said, getting up.

"Of course I don't care. Since when did I care?" Mamma asked impatiently.

"Can I go, too, Mamma?" Now Stellie was dancing beside Bertha.

"Of course you can go. What kind of notion is this all of a sudden? Run on out and then come back and behave yourselves." They tore down the steps and around the house hand in hand. "Don't run! I meant walk." She looked down at her remaining daughter, shifted Rudie's weight against her arm and went on rocking.

Gertrude looked back reproachfully, with tragic eyes. "I was the one had to tinkle," she said. "I guess I'm supposed to go my whole life and never tinkle. I guess that's what you want."

"No smartness, if you please, young lady," Linnea said. "There's no occasion for smartness. You can go tinkle when the girls come back." They could hear the slam of the privy door, called by all of them the Swedish word meaning little house, and the sound of running feet on the sidewalk. They were already on their way back. "All I said was, you always have to go tinkle whenever you get a little stirred up about something. All I wanted you to do, was every time you got to go all of a sudden like that, to wait a few minutes. I thought I told you kids not to run," she said as Bertha and Stellie, out of breath, again took their places on the top step. "In your new dresses."

"Why?" Gertrude asked.

"Why what?"

"Wait a few minutes?"

"Well, to learn a little control. When you get to be a young lady you'd ought to have a little control, wouldn't you think? You want to be nice and polite, don't you?"

On this point, Gertrude was easily influenced. More than anything else, as soon as possible or a little sooner, Gertrude wanted to be an irreproachable and inestimable young lady with rats in her hair, bone hairpins, jet earrings, a tight corset and a Carlotta train. She stood up. "Is that long enough to wait?" the willing little pupil asked hopefully.

"That's fine," Linnea said. "That's the way to do. Once in awhile, wait a little bit like that."

"Can I go now?"

"Sure you can go. You don't have to ask me when you got to go tinkle. Walk," she called after the bobbing ruffles and flying streamers that whisked around the house, "not run." She waved a fly away from Rudie's pink nose. "You kids," she said. "The notions."

Gertrude did not come back as soon as expected. Linnea, Bertha and Stellie chatted amiably together about weddings, veils, orange blossoms, presents and ice cream. The children were as proud as their mother of the beautiful gift which had been chosen, wrapped, and now reposed on the kitchen table to be carried to the wedding. It was a combination sugar bowl and spoon holder, a red glass bowl with a rim of silver loops to hold twelve teaspoons. It could be used for oyster crackers instead of sugar, the man said.

But where was Gertrude? It must be all of fifteen minutes since she ran away to tinkle.

"She must of fell in," Bertha said wittily.

"Gertrude!" Linnea called. "Gertrude!" louder. No answer. "Gertrude, you answer me right this minute!" Rudie opened his eyes drowsily, his pupils still huge and black with slumber. "Now I've gone and woke up Rudie."

"You answer Mamma!" Bertha shouted.

"You shut up," Mamma said, trying to joggle and rock Rudie back to sleep again at the same time.

"What, Mamma?" Gertrude's voice came weakly.

"You come on back out here. You been in there long enough! There, there, Rudie, go to sleepy-bye," she said to her small son, beginning to sing again to him and stopping to ask, "What's she saying, Bertha? She's hollering something."

"She says she can't."

"Can't what?"

"Come out."

"Why not? Is she caught on a nail or something?"

"Her hat, she says."

"Oh, for heaven's sake go get her and see what's the matter. Tell her to quit hollering. That's a fine way to do on Sunday. What will the neighbors think?" The situation sounded to Rudie as if it had interesting possibilities. His pupils narrowed to pinpoint size. He flatly refused to go back to sleep again. In fact, he refused to continue at all on that island of Circe, his mother's lap, and became a man of action. He stuck out his legs. His face got red. Linnea knew he would scream if not set at once on his feet, so she stood him down. "Go to Bertha. Go play with Bertha," she said. "You watch he doesn't get dirty while I go see what Gertrude's up to."

"What you up to now, young lady?" she asked, flinging open the unlatched backhouse door. Gertrude had her head down the big hole. Hearing Mamma behind her she pulled it out with a jerk and in doing so the back of her skull got a sharp blow. Her hand went instantly to the place under her jumbled curls and she rubbed it hard. "What you doing down in the hole? Where's your hat? Your hair's all mussed up. Did you hurt yourself?" Mamma's voice grew high and higher. "What's got into you?"

"Nothing, Mamma." This was not the moment to cry about the bump.

"Where's your hat?" She very well knew with a sinking heart where Gertrude's hat was. "What you done with it?"

"Nothing. It's down there."

"Down the hole." Mamma stated this with tragic finality, her hands on her hips. "Your new hat. For the big Seely wedding, that you ought to got down on your knees and thanked heaven that you got an invite to go in the first place!"

"I couldn't help it, Mamma."

"If you'd of had it on your head where it belongs, it wouldn't of fell down any hole. Come on out of there. What did you take it off for?"

Gertrude came out of the toilet humbly, greatly crestfallen, still rubbing her head. "It fell down the big hole. I just took it off a minute, it hurt under here," she stuck her chin up to show the mark from the tight elastic, "I just laid it down not even near the big hole, and it started sliding and I grabbed, and here it went and fell down the hole." She looked up at the high dudgeon in Mamma's face. "I never meant to."

Mamma reached over and gave her a shake. This was insult upon injury and brought a roar from Gertrude. Her tears bounced down in a stream.

"Quit that bawling," Mamma ordered. She was inside the privy now, bent over, peering down into the deep dirt-walled trough through the smooth-edged big hole. "Quit it right this minute or you don't go a step." She straightened up and looked over her shoulder at the sobbing Gertrude. "Go next door and ask old Mr. Castleton if we can borrow his rake. Quit that bawling."

"My—new—hat," Gertrude chanted miserably.

"Go on and get Mr. Castleton's rake. Go on and hurry up. We haven't got all day." Gertrude went. "You kids go on back to the front porch," she said, as Bertha and Stellie with Rudie between them appeared with interested faces around the house. "There's nothing for you to do here. Take Rudie on back around to the front."

"Can't we stand back and watch?" Bertha asked.

"There's nothing to watch. This ain't a runaway, or a fire, you know. Gertrude's hat's down the hole, is all, and I got to get it out. You go on away. I don't want you getting all mussed up."

"We won't get all mussed up. We'll just stand where we won't get in the road, Mamma," Bertha said. "Yes," Stellie agreed anxiously.

"Well, all right, but don't ruin your outfits and don't bother."

"We won't, Mamma." The three children, even Rudie was interested, stood back and surveyed the scene: the toilet door wide open and Mamma's black silk back and handsome bustled behind with the black silk cord and tassels.

"Here you are, Mrs. Ecklund," a man's deep voice said.

Linnea craned around. "My goodness, Mr. Castleton," she said, seeing her white-bearded neighbor. "You didn't need to bring it *yourself*. Gertrude, I just wanted you to borrow the rake, not bother Mr. Castleton." Her cheeks were red with embarrassment.

"Gertrude here tells me she's lost a hat down the hole," the old man said. "Bran new, she tells me."

"My goodness, I can get it out," Linnea said hastily. "I wouldn't of bothered you on a Sunday like this. Thanks just the same."

"Won't take a minute," her neighbor said. He rolled his sleeves up, pushed his hat back on his head and stepped into the toilet with her. She moved aside by the little hole and he took a stance before the large one, putting his rake expertly down it. Her uneasiness concerning the lack of refinement in such a place as a privy and the unladylikeness of being there at all, for any business whatsoever, vanished as she watched Mr. Castleton fish for the hat. "You kids be still out there," she called out, without taking her eyes off the maneuvering rake, "stop that silliness out there." They were giggling and carrying on like a bunch of monkeys. "Kids," she explained to Mr. Castleton. "What they won't think of next."

What they had thought of was that Mamma was unprecedently in the toilet with a man.

"Mamma's in the backhouse with Mr. Castleton!"

Hearing from the laugh-smothered excitement in his sisters' voices— even Gertrude was caught up in it—that this was a situation out of the ordinary, the delighted Rudie broke from Bertha's restraining hand and made a dash for the lightly swinging privy door. "You come right back here, Rudie!" Bertha called. He caught at it, gave a pull and a slam, and Mamma was not only in the toilet with Mr. Castleton, she was in there *with the door shut.* They sagged with laughter. Mamma pushed the door open almost before it got shut, in time to see Rudie running off from the scene of his roguery. "If you kids don't stop it, you're every one of you going to be left home from the wedding and then some. I've had about all I'm going to stand today. Don't let Rudie get around to the front!" she said sharply. Bertha made a swoop and caught him by the tail of his jacket. "That's right! Tear his coat off his back. We'll be a pretty-looking sight at the wedding, I must say! Stellie, quit looking so silly. Gertrude, you're going to be punished good for this, I can promise you that."

"I ain't looking silly."

"I never did nothing, Mamma. *Not on purpose.*"

"No back talk, either. Not a peep out of any of you."

"I ain't talking," Bertha said smugly.

"You're a buttinsky. I got a mind to leave every last one of you home."

Mr. Castleton stuck the rake out the privy door. On it dangled Gertrude's new hat. The children gave a shout of laughter. "He got it! Mr. Castleton got Gertrude's hat out of the toilet!"

Linnea took the hat off the rake herself and anxiously examined the extent of the damage. It was considerable. "I can't tell you how much I thank you for all the trouble you've gone and been to, Mr. Castleton," she said. "If you leave the rake, I'll clean it up and send one of the girls over with it in a little while. I sure thank you."

"Oh, the rake's all right," Mr. Castleton said. "How's the hat look?"

"It'll take some cleaning," Linnea said. "I don't know if it will dry or not. It might pucker, too. I don't know if Gertrude can wear it. She might have to get out her old one."

"Oh, *Mamma!*" Gertrude fairly leaped upwards in her anguish.

"Well, you should of thought. You'd always ought to think beforehand. She'd always ought to think beforehand, shouldn't she, Mr. Castleton?"

"My old hat!" Gertrude wailed. "I can't wear my old hat to the *wedding!*"

"Everybody ought to think beforehand," the old man said. "Only that ain't much comfort right about now, is it, Gertrude? But your ma'll clean up your hat all right—"

"Say thanks to Mr. Castleton for getting it out, Gertrude."

"Thanks, Mr. Castleton."

"Say it nice."

"THANKS, Mr. Castleton."

"—and it'll be just like new to wear to the wedding, you see if it ain't," the old man finished. "You dry them tears, Gertrude. Your ma'll fix it up."

Linnea tried hard. She got soap and water and a stiff brush and went to work on it in the kitchen, but there was a large stain on the under side of the brim that wouldn't come out, Mr. Castleton's rake had clawed the crown, the water spotted the streamers, and the straw being very cheap and ill-woven, it buckled. It was simply ruined, that was about the size of it. "I guess you're just not going to be able to wear it, Gertrude," Linnea said sympathetically, "and I want you to stop that crying now, like a good girl. You been sitting here crying for a quarter hour at least, and you're going to make yourself sick. It was a accident, and you said you couldn't help it, and we won't say no more about it. Go pour out some water and wash off your face and dry it and then we got to get ready to go. It's pretty near time."

"Oh, Mamma, won't it dry off? Can't I wear it? My old hat's *ugly*."

"Look at it," Mamma said gently. It was a droll and dismal sight. She twirled it around on her finger. Gertrude stared at it with tear-swollen eyes. "Your old hat will do fine. Nobody's going to notice a little girl anyway."

"No," Bertha said.

"Then let me wear yours, missy!" Gertrude glared volcanically at her sister.

"No smartness, if you please," Mamma said. "I don't want to hear another word of smartness out of any of you today. You go do what I said and we'll all get ready and go now. Bertha, is Rudie ready? Stellie, pull your sash down. It's hiked up over your stomach." Mamma meant what she said. Disconsolately Gertrude dragged off to the wash basin, poured out water, splashed her sorry eyes. "Here. I got to comb your hair again," Mamma said and did it briskly. This was a painful business, as has been said, but the sight of Stellie bringing Gertrude's old brown hat in from off the hook on the back of the bedroom door was what really brought on the hurricane, the flood. Mamma stopped these by her own brand of miracle and set the hat firmly on her Gertrude's head. "You go out and sit on the front porch," she said. "We'll be out in a minute. I got to get things straightened around a little. This had ought to be a lesson to you, young lady," she said, "one you'll never forget. But go on out there and cool off a little. Nobody's going to hold anything against you. We'll be out in a minute. And I don't want any more bawling, if you please."

Gertrude heard him calling her before she got through the screen door. "What you want, Mr. Castleton?" she asked, going out on the porch, her breast still heaving and her cheeks wet.

"Hey, Gertrude!"

"Where are you, Mr. Castleton?"

"Over here!" So gnarled an old man in snuff-color was hard to see in the branches of gnarled lilac, black currant and gooseberry bushes that divided their properties.

She found him by his discolored white beard and two pieces of blue glass eyes hopping up and down like bright twin birds on a bent little twig. "What you want?" She ran down the steps to him.

"Ma couldn't make nothing out of the hat, huh?" He took in her woebegone face and dejected carriage. "Had to wear the old one, huh?"

Gertrude's lip trembled.

"Old lady wants to see you." He jerked a thumb over his shoulder at the window where Mrs. Castleton held the curtain aside and beckoned.

"I better ask Mamma," Gertrude said.

"Oh, come on. It ain't going to take but a minute." He turned and she followed him. "Old lady wants to give you a word of advice about losing hats down toilets."

The Castletons were an old couple who lived mostly to themselves. They went out rarely, had few visitors, and were in bed at dusk and up at dawn. She was said to be "poorly" though she could do her own work, and her husband never left her for very long at a time. They were amiable to the neighbor children but discouraged "running back and forth" with such firmness that they were almost never bothered. Thus, for all Gertrude knew of Mrs. Castleton's character, it was perfectly possible that she was going to give her a word of advice about losing hats down toilets. It was no very happy prospect. "I got to go right back in a minute," Gertrude said.

The novelty of going around and into the Castleton's kitchen, with the table not cleared from their late Sunday dinner—they had had chicken, for there was the carcass on a platter, and ruby jelly in a glass dish shaped like a swan—dried the tears on Gertrude's face and made her forget momentarily her embarrassment and loss. Unfamiliar rooms are always too dark or too light, Gertrude noticed, and at first they have a peculiar smell, nice or dreadful, but peculiar. This smelled shut up. This was too dark. Strange rooms are always too bare or too full. If the latter, the furniture is very large and sticks out everywhere. The picture frames are large and hang high on the wall. It is quite a while before these frames enclose pictures; a black horse and a white horse wild under a lowering sky, their manes and tails churned to foam over their swiftness; or a man and a lady in a swing, barefooted, swinging; or a woman holding her baby up to look out the window at a bluebird; or a dead pheasant and grapes and apples, one nearly peeled and the knife there, the peeling curled down over the polished table, or two well-dressed children about to go over a cliff for a butterfly eluding the boy's yellow hat but an angel is there behind them with hands stretched out and high humped guardian wings. The ceiling in this aberrant room is either so high as not to be discovered at all, or so low it is like crawling into a cave to go under it, the floor a mystery of ingrain carpet or perplexing bare boards. Unknown, composed of glare or darkness, the triggest room under these circumstances may look untidy, sluttish.

Gertrude's bewildered eyes took in the bones on two flowered plates, the red jelly in the swan-shaped dish, the old cat in the window, but little else.

"Old lady here wants to talk to you," Mr. Castleton said.

Mrs. Castleton stood in the doorway to another mysterious room, her hands behind her back. She was a toothless old woman with red eyes and skimpy ashen hair. "Pa tells me you lost your bran-new hat down the toilet."

"Yes, ma'am, I did, but he got it out for me with the rake only I can't wear it, it's spoiled," Gertrude said breathlessly.

"Got special for the wedding, I suppose?"

"Yes, ma'am."

"That was a fine way to do, wasn't it?"

Gertrude hung her head, noticing on the floor an ironwork footstool with a soiled red plush top.

"How did you happen to let loose of it?" the old woman asked.

"Well, I—" Gertrude swallowed hard, and blinked back her tears.

"Pa tells me you got to wear your old one. That right?"

"Yes, ma'am."

"That it? On your head?"

"Yes, ma'am." Her face was red, and she was blinking faster, determined not to cry.

"There ain't nothing wrong with that. Hadn't ought to be ashamed to wear *that* hat! Liked the other one better, though, h'm? H'm?"

"Yes, ma'am," Gertrude said. "Lots better, because it was prettier, that's why."

"Liked it better than an old ugly hat like this, of course?" She brought

a hat out from behind her, a little hat for a little girl, and held it up for
Gertrude to stare at in a kind of swoon. It was a gypsy bonnet of Tuscan
braid, the brim faced with heliotrope *satin de Lyon,* shirred, the crown
encircled by a *rouleau* of the same silk, with strings of ribbon to match,
held in place by gilt ornaments and the trimming completed by a cluster
of pale blue ostrich tips on the front of the crown. What the intricacies
were, how its elegance was arrived at, Gertrude had no idea—she only
knew it was a hat for a little girl, from the looks of things her own
unworthy self, and that it was the prettiest hat in the world.

"Gertrude!" That was Mamma calling over on the front porch. The
family was ready to depart.

She did not answer, could not come out of her spell to move or speak.

"You go holler Gertrude will be right out, Pa. Tell Mrs. Ecklund
she'll be right out," the old woman said. She shuffled over and took
Gertrude's old brown hat off. Her bony palm ran over the soft hair of
silvery, pinkish, viridescent blonde and smoothed it. "Half the kids in
Salt Lake is towheads," she said, "ninety per cent. Be kind of a relief to
see a little nigger once in awhile." Delicately she placed the marvelous
hat on the quaking head, delicately adjusted it, tied the satin strings.

"You—see a little Indian kid once in awhile," Gertrude offered, in a
strangled voice. "They got black hair."

"Yep," said Mrs. Castleton, "they're a relief."

"I seen a eyetalian once."

"Did, h'm?"

"A Indian lady come to our house and Mamma give her a jelly glass
full of sugar and two onions and some potatoes. She had a little baby on
her back in a—in a thing. The baby had black hair."

"Black hair, h'm? Get kind of sick of ninety per cent towheads around
here," Mrs. Castleton said. She stood back and surveyed the hat. "Climb
up on that chair there and look in the glass," she said.

Gertrude, clumsy and dazed, climbed up on it. It was hard to see in
the dim mirror hung a little too high on the dark wall.

"How's it look to you?"

She could only guess at what a blinding sight her beauty must be.
"Mrs. Castleton," Gertrude said, "oh, Mrs. Castleton oh, my."

"Well, it's yours, Gertrude. You don't never need to bring it back.
Jump down off that chair now and go on over to your mamma. I guess
Pa's gone outside to tell her where you been."

"Oh, my, Mrs. Castleton," she said again at the door, turning back,
wanting to give her a kiss and not daring.

"It looks fine. Wasn't only wore a time or two. It belonged—I bought
it for—" Mrs. Castleton stopped. "If you keep something long enough,"
she said, "it'll come back in style as sure as you're a foot high. That's
what they always say. You keep a little girl's hat and thirty years after

some other little girl will come along and—" she stopped again. "No throwing this one down toilets, understand?"

"Oh, no, Mrs. Castleton!"

"On the head, understand?"

"Oh, yes, Mrs. Castleton!"

"Well, go on, your mamma wants you. She'll be wanting to give you a licking. I must say," the old woman said, "I must say—you're a sight for sore eyes."

Gertrude went, but first she mustered up her courage and came back and with great speed threw her arms around Mrs. Castleton and drew her head down and gave her a frightened kiss. In her soft withering face the old woman had a few sharp bristles like the thorns around the rose, and Gertrude was pricked by them but she did not notice at all.

CHAPTER 7

THE WEDDING was performed that morning in the Endowment House, in the presence of a few close relatives, so there was no chance to see the ceremony, but it meant little anyway in comparison with the reception held that afternoon.

Linnea and her children approached the Seely residence much as they would have approached the turreted castle of a Grand Duke. "Little did I think," Linnea said in even a softer voice than her usual one, "that me and my family would be walking up the front walk and going to knock at the Seely front door, but that just goes to show that a person never knows, don't it?" They turned in where the big cement hitching block said SEELY at the curb, and went through ugly brick gateposts. The house, of chocolate brick and yellow frame, stupendously ornate, with double porches, a latticed one up, a pillared one down, a balcony on one side, tall windows half of stained glass in red, blue, purple, yellow, green, and half of clear glass, a steep green roof and high multiple chimneys, was so large and grand a sight that Linnea had to cough once or twice with nervousness as she went up the narrow cement walk through the wide front yard.

Even Gertrude forgot her new hat, Bertha her jealousy of it, and Stellie the mosquito bite with the top scratched off and warmly bleeding, (but the blood wouldn't show on her black stocking) which had kept her occupied in a simian side-crouch for the last two blocks. There were flower beds of many shapes like at Liberty Park in the big green yard, and snowball and rose bushes. Box elders, mulberry and poplar trees were aristocratic there like members themselves of a snobbish moneyed family, taller, bigger and more shade-giving than other trees. You can judge trees by the company they keep.

In Mormon circles tobacco-using is as taboo as more unmentionable vices, the Prophet having for all time proclaimed it so with his Word of Wisdom, and even though a few frail sinners cherished a pipe or smoked a cigar, they usually did it in secret as they would have done what the Gentiles might consider worse things, behind closed doors. These men, then, on the Seely porch, that hot autumnal afternoon, were not smoking, but had only come outside to stand together as some men immemorially do, fleeing from the party inside. They wore their Sunday best, tight pantaloons, high shoes, velvet waistcoats and starched fronts, gleaming cuff buttons, stickpins and watch guards. Among them, there was enough hair of one shade or another in their mustaches, beards and the flowing locks that hung a little below their earlobes to stuff a good-sized mattress. They all, or nearly all, had their hands in their pockets and were standing or lounging in the usual way. There were perhaps eight of them but to Linnea, coming up the broad stone steps with a fast-beating heart, her brood pushed in close around her so that movement was somewhat hampered and she had to give Gertrude and Bertha a shove or two to keep them out from underfoot, there seemed a good twenty, and so shy and blank her eyes suddenly became, she would not have recognized Ólaf himself if he had been there with them.

They talked together as men talk, and hearing *Congress* and *tariff* she went by without a look, up to the open front door, twice as big as an ordinary front door, and stood there. She could dimly see inside down the dark hall with the double doors on either side. There must be hundreds of people moving about. She could hear a clamorous buzz. Whether to knock or not, she did not know for an uncertain moment. It might not be polite to walk right in, and on the other hand, if she knocked and no one heard her she'd have to stand and keep on knocking like a fool. She clutched the beautiful wedding present in her arms, feeling like a know-nothing, and then the man nearest her spoke. "Walk right on in," he said behind her. She did, quickly, pushing one after another of the children in before her, without looking back, her head high and her cheeks red as though he had offered her an insult.

A stairway high and dark, with a landing halfway up and a stained-glass window to sort the sunlight in separate colored strands and let it all down in taut streamers like a decoration, had polished banisters flung wide at the bottom like arms outstretched at the end of the hall. The children nudged each other to look at this, at this, at this—at the marble lady on the pedestal without an arm in the world, at the marble man all ready to throw a marble cake pan at somebody, at the naked marble baby nursing a marble bottle. And this—oversized flowering plants in jardinières as big as a washtub. And this, oh, this—portières in the doorways, tasseled, made of BEADS, pure beads, with long bead tinkling shimmering fringe. Linnea herself was taken aback by the splendor she saw as they waited just inside the entrance door. People down at the end of the hall passed back and forth in front of the stairway and went through one portière or another into the teeming rooms, but she could not seem to recognize anybody. Most of them were Tenth Ward people. She wished Ingeborg had been invited and could have come with her.

"What are we supposed to do now, Mamma?" Bertha inquired softly.

"When do we give the present?" Gertrude asked.

Linnea put a stop to their insubordination with an icy look. "Who's the mother?" she asked. "You?"

Bertha shook her head.

"You?"

Gertrude looked ashamed.

"Well, then. See that you behave yourselves."

"I—think—I—seen—the—bride," Stellie whispered, "right—in—there."

"Where, Stellie?"

"Now I don't want to hear a peep out of any of you," Linnea said, taking her skirt firmly in her left hand, holding the present tight against her right breast and advancing magnificently, "not a peep. Come on."

Money wasn't everything. Not by a long shot, it wasn't. There were a lot more important things than money in this old world. At the por-tière-hung doorway that led to the vast parlor she was still trying to think of one of these important things, which seemed to elude her for the moment, when Mr. Seely came through the musical bead fringe. Other people passed back and forth. She said how do you do to him, but seeing that he did not recognize her, she went up to him and told him who she was.

"Good!" he said, beaming. "Good!" He had insisted on inviting his tailor, Olaf Ecklund, and Olaf's two wives, also another polygamist, a business acquaintance and his wives, only to point out again to his own spouse (as he did on any occasion which offered the slightest excuse), a thin and sour-faced woman who now came up and took him by the arm, the bliss of plural marriage. They numbered no such families among their close friends, Mrs. Seely, though a devout Latter-Day Saint, being unresponsive to this celestial edict from the Prophet. Mr. Seely was a man of perhaps fifty-five, and he badly wished to take a second and possibly a third, wife, a young and handsome woman or two with what he called some "go" or "git up and go" to them. His wife flatly refused to consent to this nonsense, as she called it. Oddly enough, though Mr. Seely was a strong-willed man who did almost exactly as he pleased in every other respect, he did not dare go against her wishes in this matter. However, he never quite gave up trying to change her and bring her around to his way of thinking. "My dear," he said, looking first at Linnea and her children and then down to his thin-lipped wife, "this is Mrs. Ecklund. Her husband is my tailor. He and I have been friends for ten years. This is one of the ladies I mentioned to you," he said significantly. "Remember?"

Linnea bowed and smiled and said pleased to meet you, and her three

small daughters did the same. Rudie, in her arms, though he was a big
boy of three, merely stared around him.

Mrs. Seely said how do you do.

"Look at this lovely *family*," Mr. Seely went on, still more significantly, "*three* lovely girls and one lovely *boy*. Now isn't that something
fine? Isn't that something to be proud of? A man with a couple of
families like that isn't going to have to worry much about the salvation
to come, is he now?"

Linnea kept on smiling but she thought Mr. Seely was rather a silly
man even if he did have a drugstore and a bank account.

Mrs. Seely merely smiled in rather a sour way and said, reaching out
a bony hand and pushing back the bead portière, "It was very nice you
could come, Mrs. Ecklund. Will you just walk into the parlor and make
yourself at home?" Linnea thought she said to her husband, "Why don't
you hire an artist to make an easel picture for you so you could show it
to people and they would understand what you mean?" but perhaps she
said something else.

"I seen her looking at my hat," Gertrude murmured as they moved on.
"Didn't you see her?" Bertha sniffed, disdaining to answer.

There was no broad daylight in the room Linnea and her family entered, though it was richly afternoon outside. The blinds were all pulled
down in the large room and a Milky Way of candlelight and lamplight
illuminated the dozens upon dozens of women's white or heat-wave-red
faces, and hirsute men's, pallid or like a lobster. It made jewels of their
eyes, turned frocks, tailcoats, fans, necklaces, even cravats, into magic
raiment. It took some seconds for the multitude to become scarcely a
hundred, in quite ordinary party best, but to the children they were never
less than a thousand in the indescribable garb of Kings and Queens.

The bride they saw as through a glass darkly, and never got up to for
presentation, she was so encircled, was even beyond this: from quite
another sphere. She was an angel in melting white that wrapped her
like a cloud. She gleamed underneath the cloud like moonlight. She had
a face and hands of lily, hair of orange blossoms, no feet, for whoever
heard of a bride having feet? She hovered made of tulle and tissue above
the carpet imponderably. She was blown down from the cottonwoods,
pure mist, you could walk through her like fog or a rainbow. She was
Beauty itself you could grab and have nothing for your pains.

When the children escaped outside to the grass-grown backyard and
carriage shed, under the trees, other of their contemporaries with whom
they struck up a shy acquaintance having drawn them out to where
earlier arrivals already played, and joined these in the quiet game of
Tippy Tippy Thatchwood someone had begun, they kept thinking of
the splendor inside, as one might recall having run one's hands through
a chest of unset jewels, letting them fall in a cascade, and for a long

time the bride was all there was for them of loveliness not of this earth.

Linnea, anchored to reality by the pull of Rudie's fat hand, soon became acclimated and more at ease in the scene of glory. When Olaf came up behind her and took her by the arm, she gave a little jump of surprise, so absorbed was she in taking it all in.

"Hello, my dearie," Olaf said, using his favorite term of endearment.

"Hello, yourself," Linnea said smiling delightedly and looking him up and down. "My, you look nice in that black broadcloth," she said. "Like you got money!"

"I would have," he teased, "if you didn't lobby it away from me all the time."

"No, but you do," she said. "More like a businessman. That's what I like so well."

"I am a businessman," he said. "But say! I ain't the one that deserves the compliments. It's you!"

"Me?" she said, looking downwards at the tight fawn-colored gloves that busied themselves with the carefully wrapped present, her old black purse swinging on her arm. They were new. So was her lace collar. So was the pike-shaped hat trimmed with black velvet bows that rode high on the lemon-pie-colored mass of her bound-down hair. That was all she had bought for herself. She was wearing her black silk dress, of which she had grown very tired after five years, but it had been such excellent material to start with that it looked as if it were going to last another five. Her beloved mosaic brooch was pinned on under her plump chin. "Me?" she repeated happily. "Oh, I don't look like much, but the girls look nice. I guess they're out playing in the back yard. They come and asked me if they could go. I made them new challis dresses, and Rudie here his new blouse."

Olaf reached down and picked up Rudie, giving him a squeeze and a kiss on the cheek. "You met the bride yet?" he said.

"No," Linnea said shyly. "I ain't but just got here."

"Well, let's go over and meet her. I've knew Louise since she was a little girl ten years old. She used to come in the shop sometimes with her pa. I don't care much for her," he turned his head and said softly. "Kind of a snippy type." This last was whispered and Linnea had a hard time to make it out.

She saw what he meant when they went over and met the bride. She was standing on a sort of platform about a foot high and her proud husband stood beside her. He had a large pimple on the end of his nose which gave him such a helpless and girlish look that Linnea lost all respect for him at once even though he was the manager of the kitchenware department in the Z.C.M.I.

Olaf greeted them and then introduced Linnea. "This is my wife," he said.

"Pleased to meet you," Linnea said with great good manners. "I wish to congratulate you both. I hope you will have a long and happy married life."

"Thank you," the bride simpered, slipping her hand through her groom's arm and drawing close to him. "Didn't I *already* meet a Mrs. Ecklund?" she said, knowing very well that she had, and only to see if the faces before her might reveal some secret.

"Yes," Olaf said uncomfortably.

"You met my husband's other wife," Linnea said. "Zion ain't the place to get excited about something like that. Where you want to go if you want to get excited over something like that, is to Boston or someplace where they don't have polygamy. Around here there's quite a lot of it because this here's a Latter-Day Saint city and the Latter-Day Saints believe in polygamy, so it ain't nothing to get all excited over." She held her head high.

The bride squeezed her husband's arm and looked up at him, batting her eyes rapidly. She had baby-size teeth with a gap between each one. "Well, I tell you something, Orange," she said, "if you try anything like that, I know somebody in Zion that's going to get all excited and it's going to be me."

Her husband, Orange, looked shocked. "Oh, I couldn't afford it," he said in a high and girlish voice.

"You want to keep that good and quiet," Linnea said, "if you don't want to cause a epidemic of broken hearts around amongst the girls. I can imagine how they'll take a piece of news like that."

"Well, congratulations," Olaf put in hastily, and when some newcomers crowded up he got Linnea out of the way. "You see what I told you," he whispered as they walked over and stood by the big bay window, "about her being the snippy type."

A spot of color blazed in Linnea's cheeks. Her lips wanted to tremble and she was having a hard time controlling them. "What did they ask us for?" she said. "It ain't as if they didn't belong to the Church. What do they think we are? Freaks or something? What did they ask us to come to their old reception for?"

"Don't you mind, my dearie," Olaf said. "Both Louise and her mother is just scared to death they're going to lose their men to another wife. That's all that's the matter with *them!*"

"So that's it," Linnea said. "Well, what did they ask us for?"

"I got no idea," Olaf said. "But what do you care?"

"I care, because I ain't in the habit of being made fun of. I got a blame-good notion to go home. Get the kids together and go home," she said.

"Don't do that, my dearie," he said. "Why, look. They've started to pass out the refreshments. There goes the ice cream. I wouldn't blame you a bit, I'd take you and go myself, only—only old Seely is such a good customer, and I guess this blatherskite of a husband of Louise's is going to come to me, too."

He looked so sorry and sad that Linnea's heart went out to him. "Well, it ain't your fault," she said. "*You* can't help it if people ain't got any manners."

Ladies were coming through the bead fringe with large china dinner plates on each of which reposed a silver spoon, a Fujiyama of strawberry ice cream and a wedge of angelfood cake with paper-thin lemon frosting. Willing hands stretched out for these, and the fortunate ladies whose honorary task it was to serve went back to the source of supply for more. It was rumored there was also fruit punch somewhere and small-handled glass cups of a lavender liquid began to appear here and there.

"I tell you what," Olaf said. "You find a couple of chairs and I'll go get us some ice cream and some punch."

"I'm so riled up," Linnea said, "I almost don't want none." She leaned over and patted his hand. "But since old Seely's a good customer and everything, and since it ain't *your* fault, and since I'm here anyway, why, all right, you can go and get some."

"Some what?" said a voice behind her.

She whirled quickly, knowing the voice as well as she knew her own, blushing, because she had been patting Olaf's hand. She would rather have had Sigrid see her stealing from the tithing box or setting fire to a house than being tender with Olaf.

"Some ice cream," she said. "Hello, Sigrid. Have you had your refreshments yet?"

"No, I haven't," Sigrid said. She was wearing the dark-blue foulard with the lace collar and cuffs. The wine-colored velvet sash fit snugly around her slender corseted waist. She was not wearing a new hat but her old one with the burnt umber ostrich tips was extremely becoming. There was a frosty bloom to her face. Sigrid was a pretty Norwegian woman and that meant she was just about as pretty a woman as she could be, cool as a mermaid, slender, swift, pale. Linnea always felt a little vulgar beside her and large as a continent, with a high temperature like a bird's, overcolored, with too big a stack of too yellow hair.

Olaf took his handkerchief out of his pocket and patted it around his mouth and chin and dabbed at his forehead with it, as unobtrusively as possible. He shifted Rudie from one side to the other.

The two women looked at each other.

Linnea was not going to speak first, and give a compliment, as though to placate and desire to please Sigrid, but she did. She always did. Sigrid managed to keep silent just enough extra seconds to make Linnea blurt out something. She used to vow that sometime when they met she was going to keep silent even if it took an hour, until Sigrid had to speak first, but so far she had never done it. "You sure look nice today, Sigrid," she said.

Sigrid smoothed one of her lace cuffs. "I can't see why," she said. "I haven't got one new thing. But I just said to Olaf, nobody's going to pay any attention to *me* at the wedding."

"Well, anyway, you sure look nice," Linnea repeated, a kind of slow poison working in her veins.

"I can't see why. I haven't got one new thing." She looked at Linnea's new hat but did not mention it.

What the Prophet hadn't seemed to understand somehow, came into Linnea's mind, was human nature. Women's human nature, that is. The only way polygamy would really work like he meant was for one ugly repulsive old man with about a million dollars or five million dollars to marry a bunch of women that didn't care anything about a man anyway and were tickled to death that he didn't get ideas in his head and want to sleep with them every night, a bunch of women that merely wanted to be supported and not have to work. Of course, even then they'd be mean and jealous, that was how women were. They would always want more clothes and more of everything than the others had, also they would want this repulsive old man to like them best, even if they couldn't stand him, just to show the other wives a thing or two.

The Prophet Joseph—in fact, all men chosen by the Lord to sit down and think out religious matters—didn't take into consideration human nature.

It would have been bad enough if Linnea and Sigrid had been married to an ugly repulsive old man with a million dollars, but Olaf was a young man, with just his earnings. He had a neck like a pillar, a smooth chin, a soft thick mustache, a fine nose. He had breadth to his shoulders, a big chest, a deep voice. He could sing like a bronze bell booming, he could dance a polka with the friskiness of a colt and had a strong warm arm to slide around a lady's waist. In his handsome tailored suit he looked like a businessman with money.

Sometimes Linnea thought that if Olaf had made enough for two wives and six children to live off the fat of the land, instead of barely enough for them to survive, they would have got along like lambs. But then she looked hard at Sigrid and Sigrid glanced haughtily back at her and it didn't seem to be so much of a question of money after all.

There was almost no safe topic. "It's sure a warm day for September, ain't it?" Linnea said.

"It sure is," Sigrid answered. "Have you been to pay your respects to the bride and groom?"

"Yes."

"She's sure a beautiful young girl, ain't she?" Sigrid said, quite loudly. "And just as good as she is beautiful."

Olaf thought as he looked at his two wives looking at each other like dolls with china faces, that it was a good thing they almost never met. At the beginning he had had a kind of Bible illustration in his mind, of two women strolling with their arms around each other's waist, speaking in soft voices, perhaps even singing duets together. He wondered how he could have been rumdum enough to even imagine such a thing. It was a blessing that they lived in different wards and so attended different meeting houses, and that their friends were different.

They were both blonde, for in spite of being light-complexioned himself, Olaf was partial to blondes, but there the similarity ended.

Sigrid was saving. She could do with a handful of coal in the stove and the dampers shut tight, all day, and one lamp was light enough at night.

Linnea shoveled the coal in by the bucketful; the comforting flames flew up, warmth was in all the corners, under the flesh the very bones were warmed, moved slickly at the joints, could hop and jig. Instead of letting it die down beforehand, the fire would still be going strong when she went to bed, coloring the darkness like a dark red rose. Linnea turned up the lamp high, would just as soon light two as one, light three as one, if she had them. The good light, she used to say in Swedish, the good warmth, the way other women say, the diamonds, the rubies. . . . Linnea never counted noses, she always cooked more than she needed, providing she had it, in case four or five people should happen to drop in. Potato dumplings for supper meant a washtub full of potato dumplings, yellow, soft, unutterably delectable. There never were enough drinkers for all her rich coffee, fragrant and scalding. She did too much work for nothing, any kind of work somebody helpless or sick had to have done, scrubbing or washing, without pay, but just let someone offer her even twenty cents an hour for general housecleaning and watch her swell all up and act like a mean empress: I'd catch ME scrubbing the floors for that Mrs. Keith, she'd say. There's not money enough in the world to pay ME to get down on MY knees and be a slave to anybody. I'd catch ME doing a washing for that Mrs. Catling, she'd say. ME, she'd say. For some reason Olaf could not grasp, performing the services of a midwife and occasional home sewing were not beneath her: she would willingly take these jobs and accept remuneration for them. Any other work was taboo. The trouble with Linnea, she had too much pride, the deep-down kind.

Sigrid was different. The pride she had was for what showed. She knew how to cut corners and save. In winter the fire was out before bedtime, her room was never red with extravagant firelight. She counted noses. She didn't make a full pot of coffee for two people. She wanted the best of furniture for her parlor but she could go without cow's cream. Who knew whether you used cow's cream or skim milk? The house could be cold all day, the range in the kitchen lukewarm to the touch with a bed of gray-headed red coals in the bottom that wouldn't fill a pie tin, but she had to look nice when she went out. What showed. What people could see. This was what was important to Sigrid, not comfort. Of course she was vain, and why wouldn't she be? She was still beautiful to look at even now at thirty-seven. Nobody here could hold a candle to her, if you were talking about *looks*.

Linnea was something else again, not beautiful. All she was, was full of light like a sun or a moon. You waited for her to come up so you could look at her, reach to her, bask underneath her soft rays. All she was, was big and bright, pearly, deaurate, irised, of lobelia, apricot and pearl, transparently shining. All she was, was what you'd rather cut your right hand off than do without, not beautiful. All she was, was full of light.

The three stood in discomfited silence, Rudie still listening to the tick of his father's watch. There was a buzz all around them of guests finding or refusing seats, standing and chatting and feeding on strawberry ice cream with tinkling spoons. The bride had gone off to change her dress and get ready to go on her honeymoon. The groom, too, was nowhere to be seen. Olaf did not know what to do. They would all three have to partake of the refreshments. Each of his wives would want to eat with him, or at any rate apart from the other where she could begin to breathe and talk like a natural woman again. He tried over various sentences in his mind. Well, how about some ice cream? (*Gaily*) Well, what about some ice cream for you girls? (*Jocularly*) How would you girls feel about a little ice cream? (*Sportively*) You girls want to fill up on some ice cream? (*Waggishly*) He discarded them all. (*Sadly*)

It was Rudie who extricated him from this predicament, who sent him from the frying pan into the fire. "Present," he said, pushing the watch away from his ear and pointing to the package in the crook of his mother's arm. "Pretty. Awful pretty present."

"Oh, is that your wedding present?" Sigrid asked.

"Yes," said Linnea. "I got to go lay it down now."

"In the dining room across the hall, on the big table, is where you're supposed to put it."

"Yes," said Linnea, who didn't, "I know. Well, good-bye, Sigrid, it was nice to see you."

"Wait a minute," Sigrid said. "I'll walk along with you. I got to go through the dining room anyway and look out around the back for George. We got to start to get ready to go home pretty soon. Hattie we left home with a sore throat."

"Oh, I'm sorry to hear that," Linnea said, and was, for she thought

Sigrid's sixteen-year-old daughter a gentle and nice-dispositioned girl. They made their way through the maze of little rented gilt chairs, murmuring guests and florist's wicker baskets and vases of flowers. "Can I do anything?" she asked as she would ask a perfect stranger, but at the same time meaning it, for Hattie's sake. The sight of the dark-blue foulard bustle slightly in front jabbed her suddenly and she felt the sharp sting of her old jealousy.

"Oh, no, thanks," Sigrid said. "It's just quinsy. I know what to do. She's nearly over it."

Olaf, saved for the moment from choosing one and enraging the other, followed along behind them with Rudie in his arms.

The dining-room table was pulled out to its full length, a huge oblong with a dozen or more leaves, covered with a white linen cloth that touched the floor all around and flowed in points on the carpet a yard long at the corners. The blinds were drawn in this room, too, but here a brilliant prismed lamp as big around as a buggy wheel was lighted in the ceiling as well as numerous candles, so it was as bright as day. There were several ladies and gentlemen admiring the beautiful gifts of glass, silver, china, crystal and silver handsomely strewn on the damask surface. Mrs. Seely was there at the end, admiring too, no doubt, but looking a little pale and fatigued in her wine-red dress.

She looked curiously at the two women and at Olaf just behind them. "I bet you're wondering if the children got anything to eat, aren't you?" she said effusively. "Well, they're all out on the back steps. We've sent their plates out there and they're having a fine time, all eating together."

Linnea said, "Now, that was awfully nice of you. But I really wanted to look at all the pretty things and to bring this." Shyly she handed over the present she had brought. "I guess I should have put it in here right away, but I got so kind of interested in everything in there, I just sort of hung on to it. Everything looks so nice. I guess I really should have gave this to the bride."

Mrs. Seely took the package. "Why, thank you," she said. "You didn't necessarily have to bring a present."

"Oh, my goodness, I certainly wanted to bring a *present*," Linnea said.

The lady began to unwrap it. Everybody stopped looking at everything else to see what was to be added to the collection. Sigrid's curiosity, too, got the better of her and she let George fend for himself a little longer with ice cream on the back porch while she stopped, too, and watched.

"I've been undoing most of the presents for Louise," Mrs. Seely said in an artificial tone. "Poor child, she hasn't been able to call her soul her own these last few days." She untied the ribbon bows and shook off the wrapping of thin paper. "Well!" she said. "If this isn't pretty!" She held up the piece for all to admire.

Linnea blushed happily. "It's a sugar bowl," she said, "and the little gaps around the edge are for spoons."

"Well, what an idea," Mrs. Seely said. "If that isn't an idea."

Sigrid cleared her throat. "It's just like mine," she said pointing down the table at an identical sugar bowl and spoon holder, red glass and silver.

"Well, for goodness sake," Mrs. Seely said with rather a frightened look in her eyes, "I declare I didn't notice that. But you know what the old saying is? If one's good, two's better."

Everybody smiled politely. After all, it was nothing out of the ordinary to see a duplication of presents at a wedding. It always happened.

Sigrid's face was white, her voice, when she spoke again full of fury, though she did not shout. She turned to Olaf. "Olaf," she said. "Why didn't you tell me Linnea was going to get the same present I got? At Jensen's Jewelry," she said.

"I didn't know it," Olaf said. "I didn't even know that was what she was going to get. She never told me. Did you, Linnea?"

"I ain't seen you," Linnea said, "for quite awhile." Her face was white, too.

The guests began to gaze upon the scene with more interest. "What's she so mad about?" somebody said softly. "Lots of people buy the same present." "They're both married to the same man," somebody else whispered. Others came wandering in, stopped to see and hear whatever it was that was going on. "What's the matter?" "Two ladies brought the same present." "They're both married to the same man." "For heaven's sake." There was a little flurry of suppressed laughter.

"You knew it," Sigrid said to Linnea. "You knew what I was going to get. You did it on purpose to embarrass me, to make a fool out of me."

"How could I know it?" Linnea asked. The color was coming back into her face. "How could I possibly know? And why in the world would I want to embarrass you any more than I would want to embarrass myself? It was just an accident," she said.

"Why? I guess you know well enough why! I guess you'd ought to know why!"

"Now, Sigrid," Olaf said. He put Rudie down and the little boy ran at once with scared eyes to his mother who picked him up. Olaf patted Sigrid's arm. "It was just an accident," he said. "You'd ought to take it like a joke."

("What's wrong?")

("It's two women having a fight. They both brought the same present.")

("It's two ladies both married to the same man.")

("It's the tailor and his two wives.")

("Isn't that the funniest thing?")

"Accident!" Sigrid said venomously. "I'd ought to take *her* like a joke, I suppose, or *you* like a joke. Well, don't think I don't! You keep your hands off me." She was still speaking in her ordinary voice.

"Her awful mad," Rudie said.

"No, she ain't," Linnea said comfortingly to the child.

"Well, my," Mrs. Seely said. She glanced over to the doorway where her husband stood, staring open-mouthed at the scene. "Here's your fine polygamy for you," her bitter little eyes said.

"Go get George," Sigrid said. "Go get George and tell him to come on. We're going home." She hurried to the door, but Olaf did not follow. "Olaf," she said turning.

"I'm not coming with you," he said.

"Olaf."

"Go on with her," Linnea said, pushing Rudie's hair back from his forehead, stroking him as one strokes a cat.

"All right," he said.

They went out, and Linnea stood there reassuring her nervous child. It was very quiet. Linnea bit her lips and then, not finding anything else quite as easy to do, laughed a little. "Well, my," she said. "That's two women for you." She laughed more, joined by all the others. "My, oh, my," she said, laughing, her eyes bright.

"Say, I think I see two fruit bowls just alike!" a woman in green taffeta said. "That one and that one!" She pointed gleefully.

"And how about these two—no, three—cut-glass water pitchers?"

"They're not just exactly alike."

"I wonder who got their hair pulled out over *them?*"

"Wait till you see the other fellow!"

Everything anybody said was hilariously funny now and they all roared with laughter. The eyes on Linnea were warm, friendly. Mrs. Seely went out with her head high and Mr. Seely went after her, apologizing, as though he had been guilty of a crime. The woman in green taffeta came up and put a hand on her arm. "Have you had your refreshments?" she asked.

Linnea turned and smiled at her. "Well, no, I ain't," she said, "but I feel so foolish over all the damage I done to this nice reception that I don't think I could swallow a bite."

"Sure you could," the woman said. "You didn't do no damage. Everybody's smiling, ain't they?" Everybody was. Wherever Linnea looked she saw a friendly smiling face. She began to feel as light as a feather.

The woman in green put her in a comfortable chair by two Tenth Ward ladies who at once included her in their pleasant conversation about inflammatory rheumatism, tapeworms, carbuncles and cramps in the stomach, which interested Linnea very much, and soon came back with two of the china plates, one for her and one for Rudie, generously loaded with pink ice cream and angelfood cake. "Now, don't spill," Linnea told him. "Hold the plate on your knees and bend down to it so your spoon don't have so far to go."

"I've just been out and peeked at all the children on the back steps. They're having a fine time," the woman said, "eating and laughing. Have you got any out there?"

"I got to get mine rounded up and get ready to go home now pretty soon," Linnea said.

"Oh, you got plenty of time. You just sit there and eat your ice cream and enjoy yourself."

The woman in green leaned over Linnea and spoke in her ear. "I hope everything will be fine," she said, "with—her, and your husband. You know."

Linnea looked up with beaming gratitude. "Oh, everything will be fine, I'm sure."

"I've got the same thing myself to contend with," she leaned down and whispered. "Here we were married thirteen years and here John came along with this minx and married her. So my sympathy's all with you. . . ." She gave her a quick pat and was gone, before Linnea could open her mouth.

Linnea nibbled at a spoonful of ice cream, a frown between her brows. She was sitting here under false pretences. She wasn't the first wife. She was the second! But then, the woman in green didn't stop to listen. She dreaded to run into her again and was wondering how she could collect the children and slip out and go home without anybody at all seeing her, when a gentle hand was laid on her shoulder. She started guiltily.

It was Olaf, smiling down.

The Tenth Ward ladies were talking about galloping consumption now. One minute you could be just as well as I am now, and three hours later you could be dead.

"Listen, my dearie," he said.

With the hotly blushing face of a girl, Linnea quickly finished her ice cream and asked the ladies, who did so graciously, to excuse her. She put Rudie's plate and her own on a taboret already stacked with soiled plates and took him up in her arms and went off with Olaf.

"Listen, my dearie," he said. "Sigrid's gone. Her and George had a chance to ride with some folks going down that way."

"Why didn't you go with her?" Linnea asked, not looking at him.

"Because I want to help you get the kids home."

"You ain't been home in a long time," she said.

"You know why not," he said softly. "Because the town's swarming with U.S. Marshals, that's why. A man can't come and go as he pleases.

But this state of affairs ain't going to last forever. There'll be something done."

"Then you better not take a chance and come home with us," Linnea said. She was busily looking at the faces that passed for the face of the woman in green taffeta, so she could avoid her, feeling guilty and ashamed.

"If there was a whole army after me, it wouldn't make any difference," Olaf said. "And like I say, the time's going to come when I can go and come as I want." He meant when the polygamy issue was settled and the government agents withdrawn from the city, if that time ever came.

"If Sigrid would drop dead, you could come and go," she said. She was looking for another door to the back, so she wouldn't have to go through the dining room where the woman in green taffeta might be, who thought she was the first, or sinned-against wife instead of the second, or sinning, wife. "I don't mean that, exactly. She's got more cause to hate me any day than I got cause to hate her. I'm just onry, I guess. I don't mean I want her to drop down dead." She started to the end of the hall beneath the stairway and thought she would try the door there, to see if it led outside to where the children were playing.

"You ain't mad, are you, Linnea?" Olaf said at her side.

"Not at you, I ain't. But if you want to know the real truth—no, I ain't going to say it," she said. She opened the door and it led to the large and busy kitchen, a dim and hazy place where what seemed like dozens of women scurried back and forth. She hurried through it to the back door, not looking at any of them. She opened it and was on the vast back porch. A great many boys and girls of all ages, with plates upon their laps, sat along the railing and up and down the stairs. She found her own and signaled to them that it was time to go home. Reluctantly they finished their ice cream, brought their plates and spoons with them, which Linnea had them put down in a mannerly way on the edge of a running board in the kitchen.

She looked for Mr. and Mrs. Seely, but they were nowhere to be seen, so she could not say farewell to them. She did not look very hard or long, afraid she would meet the woman in green taffeta who might in the meantime have been told that Linnea was wife number two. But she did not have to, for here the woman was, coming down the stairs from the second floor. Linnea gave her a shy smile. The woman looked through her, and around her, and past her. She came down and went into the parlor.

"She found out," Linnea said softly to Olaf.

"Who found out? Found out what?"

She sighed, looking after her, but at the same time she felt better, as though she had a weight taken off her chest.

CHAPTER 8

HALF THE BIG SKY was red with sunset when they went up the hill home. The round moon on top of the eastern mountain looked like it was made of tissue paper. Three or four diamond stars the size of muskmelons glittered high overhead.

It was a long time since Olaf openly walked with his family up the street, Rudie in his arms, his wife beside him and his three little daughters parading behind, when they didn't get around to the front and run backwards up ahead, facing their parents, miraculously running backwards and not falling, so as to tell them some wonderful thing. Olaf heard all about the hat in the toilet, all about Mrs. Castleton giving Gertrude the new hat she was wearing, all about everything. He had to say it was the prettiest hat he ever saw in his life at least ten times until Linnea made Gertrude stop asking and drop back behind them where she belonged. Then Bertha had her turn, and Stellie, dancing up ahead, said when she got married she was going to have a veil as long as from here—hop, hop, hop, hop, hop, hop, hop, hop, hop—to here. And she was going to eat a whole gallon of strawberry ice cream all by herself.

Linnea didn't really cook much supper except that she rustled up a fire in the stove to boil up a pot of coffee. They ate the fresh bread, sliced thick, yellow butter, delicious common "mouse" cheese, garlic sausage, apricot preserves translucent and perfumed, and leftover sweet soup, with appetite, the three girls on the bench along one side of the table, Rudie in his high-chair (to be discarded soon for his three-year-old behinder was no longer of a size for it) and Linnea opposite them, Olaf at the head of the table, where the Papa should be.

They mildly protested but while it was still shadowy twilight and they could see each other's shapes plainly in the bedroom without a lamp, the children had to go to bed, for it was the first day of school tomorrow. There were no curl papers for Linnea to put in as she considered braids quite good enough for everyday and would make two tight wet pigtails apiece in the morning, but there were "chores" such as prayers and other duties. Bertha must double up with her sisters tonight. Was Papa going to sleep here? the children wondered. Maybe he was and maybe he wasn't, Mamma said. Bertha could crawl in with the girls. They were all in Mamma's bed anyway tonight, because that was in the bedroom, and Mamma would sleep in the narrower bed in the kitchen, usually slept in by Gertrude and Stellie, whether Papa stayed or not. What more did they want? A drink of water? Well, all right, but that was the absolute end. If Mamma heard another peep out of them, they knew very well what they'd get. Now, were they all settled? Yes, they were. Well, here was one more brief kiss on each little mouth. (There were no germs in those days.) Would they go right to sleep? Yes, Mamma. Good night then, darling. Darling. Darling. School tomorrow. Sleep tight.

Linnea came out and shut the door carefully behind her. Olaf was sitting in the rocking chair rocking back and forth. She went ahead and cleared the table, put the food away in the pantry, and with half a teakettle of hot water washed up the few dishes, dried and put them in the cupboard, carrying on an animated conversation about trivialities. If there was something on their minds, something troubling their hearts, they did not speak of it then. They talked about the wedding, and Linnea told all about the woman in green taffeta who thought she was the first wife and thought Sigrid was the second wife. She must have found out though, because she certainly gave her the cold shoulder later. Did Olaf notice?

Linnea hung up the dish towel, took the lamp from the drainboard and set it in the center of the empty table now covered by a clean plaid cloth. "How would you feel about another cup of coffee?" she said. "Now the kids are in bed?"

"Fine," Olaf said. "Maybe a little weaker maybe, not quite so strong."

She made another pot of coffee and poured it out. They sipped it the way the Scandinavians do, like brandy fanciers sipping fine old brandy. With darkness had come a chill on the air that meant it would be colder from now on, that today might have been the last hot day, that tomorrow in the early morning the breath would start to show on the air. The fire in the cookstove began to feel good, began to be something one needed to pull one's chair up closer to. Linnea got up and shut the kitchen window where the white curtains billowed. "It's turned off cool," she said. "That wind's cold."

"Linnea," Olaf said. "I been doing a lot of thinking about things. You been awful mad a lot of times about the way things was, haven't you?"

"Yes," she said. "I sure have. But I ain't only been *mad*, remember."

"You knowed how it all would be when you married me," he reminded her.

"Nobody knows how anything's going to be beforehand, for sure," she said slowly, "even if they think they do. If they say they do, they're lying. They just think they know. They got to find out for sure, when they do something, how it's all going to be. They can't imagine it, beforehand. So how could I know? How could I imagine? Actually imagine, I mean?"

"Well, people ought to be able to. They can pretty near imagine."

"Did you?"

"Did I what?"

"Did you imagine how it would be to have two wives?"

"Why, yes. It ought to be just like having one wife, only—"

"It ought to be, you say. Only it ain't, is it? It's like having two wives, ain't it? Two separate people. Like having me and Sigrid? Like me bawling up at the shop and wanting a little extra money for the wedding you didn't really have to give me, ain't it? Like Sigrid being so mean and mad when I got the stove new, and whatever I get, she's got to have just as good, and whatever she gets, I got to have just as good, ain't that right? Like her not coming near when I had a one of the kids, like me not going near when she was down with her miscarriage? Like me not being able to stand the sight of her and her not being able to stand the sight of me? Like today, with the wedding presents?"

Olaf cleared his throat.

"It was kind of funny, though," she said. "A funny thing to happen. Me buying the exact same thing she bought and bringing it to the wedding as big as life. Both of us being married to the same man. No wonder they laughed around there." She laughed herself now reminiscently. "But honestly, she's a numskull," she said, "if she'd of just kept her mouth shut, nobody would of known a thing about it, Mrs. Seely would of set my piece on the table, and if somebody had happened to of spotted there was another one there already like it, nobody would've said a word and that would of been the end of it. But no, she's got to start hollering and make us both look silly. She's just a numskull, is all she is. I'd of kept my mouth shut."

"You shouldn't talk like that, Linnea." It made him uneasy. She might start finding fault with the Gospel next, and what would that lead to? A mess for sure. Either there was some sense to it all, or there wasn't. This was a pretty time of day to start arguing about the Gospel after all these years. "You, of all, Linnea," he reminded her, "that before you was born your folks joined the Church and come across the plains by handcart, walked every step across the plains to get out to Zion, brought you up a good Latter-Day Saint, done everything they could—"

"I know," Linnea said. "I guess I maybe ought to be ashamed of myself."

"You wouldn't want to go back on everything and everybody now, would you? Where would you go? You wouldn't pick up the kids and maybe go to Iowa or somewhere, and not know a living soul, would you?"

"Well, no, I wouldn't want to do nothing like that exactly."

"You wouldn't want to never sing the old songs again, Come, Come Ye Saints and O Ye Mountains High and Do What is Right again, would you? And never take the sacrament again or see none of the ladies in the Relief Society no more or have the elders in to lay on hands when one of the kids is sick?"

"They're pretty husky kids." She rapped a couple of times softly on the wooden arm of her chair. "Knock wood," she said.

"Yes, but suppose they wasn't?"

"Well, my goodness, I didn't say I was going to Iowa. Why would I want to go to Iowa in the first place? I didn't say I was going to apostatize. The way you talk, you'd think I was going to apostatize all of a sudden after here I am going on thirty and born and baptized and married in the Church and four children. I didn't say nothing like that. All I said was, Sigrid is a numskull."

"That's what I mean."

"Well, she *is* a numskull."

Olaf rubbed his eyes tiredly and then clasped his hands around his knees, leaning far back in the rocker. He looked at Linnea. Absent-mindedly she had taken the bone hairpins out of her hair and they lay in her lap. The hair was fallen down over her shoulders and in curving tail-ends across her breast and down her back to her waist. She washed it last night and the least breath could have lifted it up and blown it around, it looked so light in weight and as slick as a blade of barley. The clock stubbed its toe on the quarter-hour with a little ding! and it was eight-fifteen.

"I guess you'll be wanting to go home now pretty soon," Linnea said.

"This is my home as much as that is."

"Yes, but—"

"As soon as the polygamy problem gets straightened out with the Government, I'll be able to come home whenever I want to, I can come home every other night."

"And stay with Sigrid every other night."

"Linnea, listen. You wouldn't want me to leave her, would you? Look how much older Sigrid is than you are!"

"Eight years. That ain't so much. She's prettier'n me. And the kids is nearly grown. Hattie's going on seventeen and George is going on fourteen."

"She didn't put anything in my way when I wanted to marry you, remember," he said. "I owe her a lot for that."

"Pooh," Linnea said. "What could she of done?"

"Maybe a lot of things. Anyway, she didn't do nothing to try to prevent me. You and I been married ten years. She and I been married seventeen years. You wouldn't want me to go ahead and leave her high and dry now, would you, with no support or nothing? She don't make friends easy like you do. She ain't got the way with her you got. She's lots more set in her ways."

"She's awful blame pretty, I know that. And a pretty woman ain't never as helpless as a homely one."

"That don't mean nothing. You wouldn't want me to have the heart to leave her? We'd have to stop believing what we believe in. We'd have to leave the Church. What would we amount to, leaving the Church? We got to believe something. What would we believe?"

"I didn't say that." Linnea sat thinking. "She sure thinks it means something, being pretty, don't you fool yourself. It does, too. I wouldn't mind it myself, I can tell you. If I was as pretty as her, I'd give you a run for your money."

"You're beautiful," he said.

"Me?" she said. "I'm too big and fat."

"No, you ain't."

"Yes, I am." She smiled across at him.

"You give me a run for my money."

"Olaf," she said, and drew a deep breath, and paused. Then she started over again. "You know what, Olaf?" she said. "I ain't going to be mean no more. I'm going to turn over a new leaf. I ain't going to say another mean jealous word about Sigrid."

"Come and sit on my lap," Olaf said.

She did as he asked her. "I really ain't," she said. Her hair was a thicket to lose the way in, off the main road, with the light of her face shining down between its branches. He wandered off in it.

"Ain't you?" he whispered, holding her tighter.

"Olaf, tell me," she said, "who do you love best?"

"Now what kind of a question is that to go and ask?" he said tenderly. "What kind of a question is that?"

"But who do you, Olaf?"

"You know who I love best."

"Who?"

"You know well enough."

"Me?"

He took her face between his hands and pulled it over close to his own. He kissed her. Then he looked into her eyes and looked away. "I'd hate to even live if you wasn't alive somewhere," he said, not at once but taking quite awhile to find the words.

The knock at the door came sharp and loud. Linnea was off his lap instantly. He sat very still in the rocking chair so it wouldn't squeak, gripping the arms. "It's too late for anybody," she said softly. "It's past eight-thirty."

The knock came again, louder. "It might be—" She moved to the door, turned the knob. "But maybe it's just somebody's sick or something." She opened the door. "Who is it?" she said.

"You gone to bed, Mrs. Ecklund?"

"Why, no," she said, relieved. "My goodness! Mrs. Castleton! I never expected to see *you* at this time of the night!" She opened the door wider. "Come on in and make yourself at home," she said. "It's my next-door neighbor, Mrs. Castleton," she said over her shoulder to Olaf.

The tottering old lady tugged on a large shawl-covered bundle and dragged it in over the doorstep. "I won't stay," she said, out of breath, "I see you got company."

"It's just my husband," Linnea said. "My goodness, sit down. We was just sitting here talking. Don't you want a cup of coffee? It's still hot. We just had some." She found her hairpins and began hastily twisting up her hair, her cheeks stained red high along the cheekbones.

"Well, I can't stay but a minute," old Mrs. Castleton said, but accepted the rocking chair Olaf got up and offered her. "I don't want to take your chair," she said. "Pleased to meet you."

"Go ahead," Olaf said. "Pleased to meet *you*."

"Feels nice and warm," she said. "Don't give me no coffee, Mrs. Ecklund. I wouldn't sleep a wink. Well, maybe just half a cup," she said.

Linnea poured it out and brought it to the gnarled twigs of her hand. "I sure want to thank you for that beautiful hat you give Gertrude," she said. "Honestly, I just about fell over when here we was ready to start and she come running from your place with that beautiful hat on," she said.

"You'd never believe what we paid out for that hat," the old lady said.

"Yes, I would, too," Linnea said. "It's sure a beauty. Gertrude nearly went out of her head, she was so glad." She was very surprised to see old Mrs. Castleton at this time of night, in fact, to see her at all, for she had never called on Linnea in all the months she had been here except once, to borrow a starting of yeast, and had never extended a real invitation to call.

"So this is your husband," Mrs. Castleton said, looking hard at him.

"Yes, ma'am, it is," Linnea said.

Olaf got out his handkerchief and blew his nose.

"Nice-looking fellow," Mrs. Castleton said.

"Thank you," Linnea said, "I think so too."

Olaf was going to blow his nose again but Mrs. Castleton changed the subject, so instead he took a straight chair and settled himself uncomfortably upon it. Linnea took another, opposite him. "How was the wedding?" the old lady asked.

"Just lovely," Linnea said. "She had a white satin dress and a long veil that was sort of wrapped around her feet when she stood there and people went up to her, and she was wearing orange blossoms. She looked just simply lovely."

"Wax, probably," Mrs. Castleton said.

"Wax?"

"The orange blossoms."

"Oh, the orange blossoms. Well, I don't know. They may of been, for all I know. I didn't look close. Was they real, Olaf?" she asked him.

"I don't see how they could of been," he said. "We ain't got no orange blossoms around here."

"I guess they wasn't," Linnea said. "I didn't smell nothing, come to think of it, only the regular flowers in the vases."

"I don't know her, but we got some friends that know him. Big booby."

"Oh?" Linnea said. "The bridegroom?"

"Regular big booby. I bet you wonder what's in this big bundle?" the old lady asked abruptly.

"Why, to tell you the truth, I didn't—didn't pay much attention to it," Linnea said, not knowing which would sound the more mannerly, to say she wondered or to say she didn't.

"Don't pay many calls," Mrs. Castleton said, "waste of time. All right when you're young. Waste of time when you get old. Pretty near everything's a waste of time when you get old. How old would you take me for, say?"

"Oh," Linnea said, "that'd be pretty hard to guess."

"How old would you take me for, Mr. Ecklund, say?"

"Well, I'm not so good at guessing ladies' ages," he said uncomfortably.

She smiled in triumph. "I'm eighty years old. Was eighty in February. Pa's eighty-two. We're no chickens any more, Pa and me."

"For goodness sake," Linnea said, who assumed she was a good deal older, perhaps in the nineties, "I never would of thought it."

"Me either," Olaf said obligingly.

"But to get back to this here bundle," she said, nudging it with her toe. "You're a proud woman, Mrs. Ecklund, I know you, you don't want no old clothes give to you. I see you, how proud you are. Not smarty or uppity acting or nothing like that, but proud inside, like a proud woman. But after your little girl Gertrude was there this afternoon and I remembered that hat and give it to her, Pa and me went through a old trunk we packed thirty years ago. You'd be doing me a big favor if you'd take it off my hands. I set too much store by it all. I wasn't never going to part with a bit of it, not even her little mittens or nothing."

She bent over and untied the bundle. Linnea saw various small articles of girl's wearing apparel, so old-fashioned as to seem at first glance like costumes for a play, but of astonishingly new-looking and excellent material, challis, wool, velveteen, silkaleen and one little dress of pure velvet. "I want to give you these here," she said. "They been well kept, no moths has got to them or nothing. You're handy, you can fix your kids up something out of them, to wear. They got nice trimming, braid and all, and pretty buttons. Villa was a great one for pretty buttons."

"Well, my, I don't hardly know what to say," Linnea said. "You don't want to go and give me all these things."

"Yes, I do. Ought to of gave them away years ago. At first, they was just a torture to keep around. But it seemed like I had to keep them, although I cried till I was weak in the head. The older you get, though," she said, her eyes wet, "the more your tears dry up on you. Nothing don't seem worth crying over, no more. I ain't shed a tear now in a long time over Villa. In fact, these here things of hers that was such a torture at first to have around, has got so they been kind of a comfort to me, knowing they was stacked up in the little trunk in the front bedroom. But today," she said, "it sort of come to me I'd ought to be able to give the clothes away, where they'd maybe do some good. Pa come home and told me about Gertrude losing her hat down the toilet and how bad she felt, going to that big wedding and all, and I went and dug out that hat of Villa's. And then I got thinking, well, why not give all the stuff away, where it'd do some good, so Pa and me got it all together this afternoon."

"The hat was just beautiful," Linnea said, "and not a bit old-fashioned looking. Just beautiful. Really, it was too nice for you to go and give away." She saw that this was an extraordinary hour in the old woman's life, had been an extraordinary afternoon and evening. She'll probably be sick tomorrow, she thought, I'll have to run over and see how she is tomorrow, she's so stirred up over something, and then staying up so late like she's not used to and drinking that coffee and all.

"Well, sir," Mrs. Castleton said, "so I got the hat out, and I seen how Gertrude just looked like her eyes would pop right out of her head. And I put it on her. Villa had that same light hair like that, but my boys is dark-complected, I guess she would of turned darker if she would of— growed up. So anyway, Gertrude had the hat on and I seen that face of hers and them eyes. So when she run out and Pa come back in, we got to talking and I said, well, we had a lot of things little girls could wear, and we went and got in the trunk and brought all the things out, and I said to Pa I was going to bring them over to you and give them to you to fix for the kids." Her toothless old mouth trembled.

"I just don't know what to say," Linnea said.

"I can easy part with them now," the old lady said, fingering her eyes. "I can part with them as easy as pie." She leaned over and smoothed the pure velvet hem of the neat little dark red dress. "This here's the last dress we got her. She was going to speak a piece at the Friday Night. 'When the starry vapors gather over all the starry spheres, And the melancholy darkness gently weeps in rainy tears.' You ought to of seen how she could learn something off by heart. Great long verses, and she could learn them off by heart. I bet if she'd of lived, she'd of knew all kinds of long verses, probly thousands, all by heart."

"Villa, you say her name was?" Linnea asked softly.

"I'll tell you how it was," Mrs. Castleton said.

Olaf looked again at the clock, slyly, out of the corner of his eye. Let one of these old ladies get started like that, and they just went on and on. He sighed, glancing at the narrow bed in the deeply shadowed corner, neatly and cleanly made up, where he would sleep with Linnea at least until daybreak or a little later. He had to go home to change his clothes before he went to the shop. After all, he was wearing his only good suit, and his only really handsome linen shirt, and his best thick cravat. He'd have to go home and change them before he went to work. It was no very pleasant prospect, but it was hours of darkness off. He drew a deep sigh. So stern a rebuke for it did he see in Linnea's eyes when they met his that he abandoned all thoughts of any overt disclosure of his boredom and, to please her, merely cleared his throat, crossed his legs and took on an appearance of polite listening. She gave herself up wholly to her garrulous old guest, paying her words the closest mind, as though the woman spoke something of great interest.

"Me and Pa was married sixty-three years ago. Well, sir," she said, "I was seventeen and he was nineteen. He was a good catch, Pa was. Had this big farm. Back east, where we was raised," she said. "His folks died off, and here he had this big farm. I ain't never told you this before, have I?" she asked.

"No," said Linnea.

"Well, sir, we started right in and had our family, Eddie, Pete, Ernest and Avery, every last one of them two years apart, and then we didn't have no more kids. Years went along and no more kids. Well, sir, I got along in my thirties or so and I got to wanting a girl. I got to thinking how nice it would be to have a girl around the house, to do for, and the first thing you know I couldn't think about nothing but that. Dead set on it, you might say. I got to kind of dreaming about her, how she'd look, how she'd be, I'd always be thinking how I'd dress her, how her and me would go to town Saturday, what we'd do, how I'd talk to her when we was sitting peeling apples or something. I was alone so much and I had it all figured out. You know when we joined the Church?" she said.

"No, when did you?" Linnea asked.

"The year after the war was over. Villa'd been dead six years. The missionaries come through and we was every one of us converted. Then we come out here to Utah. The boys took up farms. Me and Pa bought the little place next door here. I didn't feel good enough to go on a farm. It seemed like after Villa died, I never did feel good no more. But I was going to tell you," she said, "about wanting my girl. I had a long wait on my hands. My youngest boy was eighteen and fixing to get married, Eddie was twenty-four, Pete was twenty-two, Ernest was twenty—and here I come along and was going to have this baby. Well, sir, all I could think of was now I was going to have my wish come true. Pa used to tell me I shouldn't get my head so set on it, I'd be disappointed sure. That was the way it always happened. I'd have a boy for certain, he said. But I knowed better. I knowed what I'd have. I'd have my girl, that's what I'd have.

"And sure enough I did," she said, "on my own birthday, and here I was forty-one years old. I just couldn't get over her being born on my own birthday. Even now it seems like that was wonderful. I mean, it was fine enough as it was just to have her at all, without her needing to put herself out to be born on my birthday. That made it all the better, of course, like it kind of maybe meant something some way. But to make a long story short," she said. "Mr. Ecklund here won't want to hear all this old stuff, so long drawn out."

"Sure, he does," Linnea said passionately. "Don't you, Olaf?"

"Sure, I do," Olaf said, thinking how it would be daybreak before a person could say Jack Robinson. It was twenty minutes to ten right now.

"Anyway," Mrs. Castleton said, "I named her Villa. I thought Villa was such a pretty name."

"It is," said Linnea, "it's an awful pretty name."

"I just was dead set on that girl," the old lady said. "Here she come along and looked just like I imagined. Like a little girl on a Christmas postcard, with all this light hair of hers and her little face and her little arms and legs. The boys was all gone then, married and gone. It seemed like I didn't have no other family but her, never had had. But then, I'll come right out and say that I never took the pleasure in them, that I took in her.

"I'd dress her up in something, maybe this merino or something," she picked up an edge of a blue skirt, "and put her little hat on, after she got older, and she'd take her muff in her hands and she'd walk right along with me, just like a lady out for a walk. It seemed like she never got mean. My heart used to hurt sometimes, to see her doing her little lessons at the table, with her head bent down and her face so serious, studying away there. I'd wish she'd be mean sometimes, not always so good the way she was. She was nine years old," she said, "when she—" she said, and stopped. "The way it was," she said taking a fresh start, "I'll tell you just exactly how it was."

She held herself sternly together now. "Some of the boys come over and was helping Pa around the place. It was October, just as sunshiny and bright as could be. Big blue sky. Looked warmer than summer but there was a cold wind that'd tear right through you. Well, sir, me and Villa was around in the kitchen. It was Saturday. I had my cleaning done and was doing my baking. I let Villa have some bread dough and she went to work and shaped up two little loaves of bread and put them in a tin, and I put them in the oven for her, to bake. The boys was raking up the yard and the first thing you know they got a big fire going out back of the house. Well, it was burning good and Villa seen it through the window and you know how kids get so excited over a bonfire and got to make a beeline for it. Well, out she went, out the back door in a flash, and right for the fire. She didn't only have her little thin dress on, silkaleen, like this one," she pointed at a sleeve protruding from the pile, of thin sprigged silk, "only it was yellow instead of lavender—I got her the two dresses at the same time. I knowed it was cold outside, and first I just hollered at her and then I grabbed up her cape and went down the back steps after her." She stopped talking and just sat there. Neither of her listeners spoke and sat there too, the clock ticking. "Well," she said. "She got out there so fast, and right up to the blaze and the wind come up strong, and here the flames just jumped out and her skirt caught fire and her long hair hanging down her back. She yelled bloody murder. We all ran, all of us. If she'd of just stood there. But no—she took out across the stubble field, so fast, so fast, honestly, like a streak, away she went out across the field, screaming, the wind just blowing wild. It was me that caught her," she said. "The boys was faster than me any day, but it was me that caught her and—and—she didn't die for two days."

Linnea could not look at the old lady. "God in heaven," she said.

"Her little loaves of bread," Mrs. Castleton said. "I remembered and took them out of the oven when they was done. Funny how I'd remember and take them out for her. She was nine years old. She would of been thirty-nine now. This here is good material," she said. "You think you could maybe fix it over into something? You're not offended, are you, to have stuff offered you? I don't mean it—like you give somebody old clothes."

"I know," said Linnea. "Sure, I can make it over. I ain't offended a bit."

"I ought to of give it away years ago where it would do somebody some good. I was downright selfish when it come to Villa, more'n I ought to of been."

Linnea considered before she spoke, in order not to wound. "Mrs.

Castleton," she said. "You mentioned that at first it was just torture
for you to have the things around."

"It was," said the old lady, "I'd get to looking at the stuff. Of course,
it seemed like everything was torture them first years—"

"But then, you said it seemed like it was kind of a comfort for you to
have that little trunk around, full of—Villa's clothes, in the front bedroom," Linnea said.

"Well, you know what I meant. It seemed like it had got so it *was*
a sort of a comfort. But like I said to Pa today after Gertrude made us
kind of start thinking this afternoon, I said we'd ought to give them
things away where they can do some good. When we're gone, they'll
just be something done with anyway, I said."

"But you're going to live to be a old old lady," Linnea said gently.
"When you're gone will be a long time off."

"Oh, I don't know," the old lady said. "I don't know about that."

"You asked me if I'd be offended," Linnea said, "and now I got to ask
you if you'd be offended. Because you see, Mrs. Castleton," she said,
"we're going to get these nice and beautiful little clothes together that
was bought and made for I bet one of the nicest and most beautiful
little girls that ever lived, and I'll take them for you over to your place,
and then you go on in and put them back where they belong, and you
just keep them as long as ever you live. They was a torture and then
they was a comfort to you, and they'll be a comfort to you till the day
you—till Villa her little beautiful laughing self comes dancing up and
takes you by the hand and all your sorrows are done with and over,
forever and ever, and yourself younger than the day she was born. . . .
Some things," she said, "it seems like we just got to keep, like we was a
church and the things was the sacrament cups or something. Sometimes
they're real, like these, Mrs. Castleton, and sometimes they ain't real at
all, like dreams, but certain things we got to keep."

The tight old lips loosened and shook. "I can give them up, as easy
as pie," she said uncertainly.

"Sure, you can," Linnea said. "You proved it. All a person needs to
do to prove something, is to go right ahead and prove it. That's what
you done. Nobody wants to see more than that." She knelt down and
began delicately folding the little garments as though they were made
of dew-strung cobwebs, delicately folded the four corners of the sheet
over them, delicately retied the cotton cord. She stood up and then she
bent over and took up the bundle. "My," she said, "it's quite a load. I
wonder how you carried it over here."

"It didn't seem so heavy," the old lady said. She got to her feet. "Well,
I've stayed, for sure. Wore out my welcome, I'll bet. Stayed till the last
dog was hung. You're sure you ain't offended?"

"Of course I ain't," Linnea said smiling. "You're sure *you* ain't?"

"Oh, no, I ain't," Mrs. Castleton said. "Good night, Mr. Ecklund. I hope I ain't talked a ear off you."

"Good night," he said. "No, you ain't. I still got them both."

"I guess Pa will think I've run off and left him for another man. I wouldn't never let Pa have nobody but me," she added. "Not that he ever so much as ever hinted he ever wanted anybody else. But he'd of been a pretty sight, wouldn't he, fifty-eight years old at the time and maybe taking a notion he wanted to start another family or maybe two or three other families? He'd of been a pretty sight, I must say. That's the only thing I ain't quite reconciled to, the polygamy. Don't see no sense in it. Present company excepted. No offense meant," she said, "I hope you won't take it as such. You got a sweet woman here, Mr. Ecklund. Awful sweet woman. Awful good neighbor. Not one of them buttinskys. Good night," she said, "Pa will think I've run off for sure."

When Linnea came back Olaf had his coat hanging neatly on the back of the chair, his cravat loosened and was sitting on the edge of the bed unbuttoning his shoes.

"It's real chilly," she said, closing and locking the back door, "after such a hot day."

"You got the old lady home, did you?"

"Yes," she said. "I set the bundle down on the kitchen floor. She give me a kiss on my," she put a hand up to her cheek, "on my face here."

"That was nice serviceable stuff," Olaf said conversationally. "You could of made all three girls some good warm clothes out of it. Not that you have to have things give to you. But why wouldn't you take it? I kind of got to wondering."

"Why, I couldn't," Linnea said in surprise. "It didn't have anything to do with pride."

"Why couldn't you?"

"Well, don't you see?" she demanded. "The time had come when she just naturally had to give it away, *so she could have it back.* Don't you see?" she said.

"Yes, but suppose you'd of kept it? She couldn't of had it back then. If she'd of give it to Ingeborg or somebody she couldn't of had it back. A person that had a nice bundle of clothes give to them like that, they'd keep it. They wouldn't go giving it back to the old lady," Olaf said.

"Oh, you numskull, Olaf," Linnea said, unlacing her stays. "You don't understand. You don't see what I mean. Maybe pretty near everybody has to give up what they love best, sometime or other in their lives, so they can *have it back.* I mean, a time comes, when if they don't give something they got, away, they can't keep it no more, even if they got it under lock and key—and if they give it up, why, even if the one they give it up to, keeps it or not, that's immaterial, why, they really get to keep it then, forever. Don't you see? Just because we got something we love, that don't mean that's all there is to it. Every once and awhile, we got to earn it all over again some way or other. We got to. One way to do it's to give it away.

"Besides," she said, "we live right next door, she sees the kids all day long, how do you think that poor old soul would feel to see them colored pieces of silkaleen or flannel or merino run by the window, that she knows every thread of, like some people know their gospel? How would that be? It'd be like turnin' a knife in her heart, no matter what she says. It looks like you'd ought to know that." Linnea pulled her big cambric nightgown over her garment-clad body, wonderfully soft and full without the tight corset and thick camisole that now lay rolled up on the sewing machine. She began to make a rough braid of her hair. "You don't understand," she said, "all you do is think things out with your head. There's times when you got to think out things somewheres else besides your head." She laid her fist, doubled around the braid, its silky palomino horsetail end sticking out, on her breast. "Here, is where you got to think sometimes."

"Even when you lose by it?"

"Who said I lost anything?"

"Well, you lost all that nice material."

"She was awful keyed up, poor old lady. It seemed like today was some kind of a turning point with her or something. She never stays up late like this. She never even comes here. She ain't never been here but once before. I got to go over tomorrow and see how she is. Poor old soul, it was kind of a turning point in her life or something. She was so glad to get home with her things, you could just see it written all over her face, and so tired and wore out, but so kind of happy and peaceful, some way, when we said good night. I felt happy and peaceful, too, like we'd worked out something together to the best interests of both of us, her and me. I don't know how to explain it but that's how I felt."

"Didn't you?"

"Didn't I what?"

"Lose all that stuff? Not that I wanted you to take it. Just for the sake of argument." He eyed her tenderly.

"What do you want to argue all the time for?"

"I don't want to argue," he said. He came over to where she was bending to blow out the lamp, gave her a little spat. "You go on to bed. I'll blow out the light. I don't want to do no arguing," he said.

CHAPTER 9

DECEMBER THAT YEAR was as frozen solid as the summer iceman's chunk of ice and maybe because it was so cold, things happened that were difficult and sad. But that's what people said in hot weather when difficult and sad things happened. "Maybe because it's so hot," they said. "Maybe because it's so cold," they said, now. One thing they promised without fail. Whatever the weather was, hot or cold, "when it changes," they said, "things will be all right." When it rains. When it stops raining. When it warms up. When we get a cooling spell. When we have a good fall of snow. When the winter breaks. . . . It will be better then. That's what people always said, knowing so well that what was, was never as good as what would be.

Ingeborg scolded and fretted, for she had to go out cleaning several times a week and her hands, in soapy water most of the day, were so chapped from the blustery winds that they were raw and had open wounds that ran a yellow and bloody ooze and would not heal though she put good lard all over them and wore cotton gloves at home. She never had time to dry them properly, being sent from one dripping task to another, often outside, as when washing windows, and she complained of this. She would have complained worse if she had had no cleaning jobs to go to, disagreeable as they were, but it did seem very sad, she said to Linnea, who could see her point, that here some women like Mrs. Kimball and Mrs. de Brewell and Mrs. Salisbury, not mentioning any names, just had everything handed to them on a silver platter and never so much as had to poke their nose out the door but even had meat and staples brought right to the house in a delivery wagon. They didn't even so much as have to cook it, for what should they have but a *cook*, mind you, and all in the world they had to do was shovel the food down, and sit around. They had hired men building up their fires all over the house for them and keeping them up, so that every room was warm, not just the kitchen, and not a one of them would so much as lift her hand. And here other people, poor widow women with maybe five kids to support, had it so hard that it was just terrible, with raw sore hands and everything, and going up and down the hill in the blizzardy cold, and that was just the way it was, wasn't it? No matter what anybody said, it didn't look fair, and even the Prophet himself couldn't make it look fair unless he did some pretty slick talking.

Of course, as Linnea reminded her, and she herself well knew, Ingeborg had a good many things to be thankful for. She had a strong back and a good stomach. She had work. She could get a good night's sleep at night, peculiarly as she went about it. Besides, her children were all straight and normal, not one of them with a hunched back like their father's. There was coffee in the world. There were loving friends to drink it with. And though times were hard and her wages so small she would have been ashamed to tell to the penny how much she got for her hard work, still she kept her family clothed and fed. Not like princes, of course, but adequately, and she sent them to school. She could be, as Linnea told her many a time, proud of herself. She could hold her head up with anybody.

Ingeborg had even been able to save money for a strange purpose. Various of her well-wishers tried to dissuade her from it, at least until the weather was better, saying that in the winter months, when the ground was frozen, it might be double the cost. But she said as soon as she had the money saved in the handsome humidor Mrs. de Brewell had given her because the monkey faces carved all around made her nervous, and besides, Mr. de Brewell didn't smoke and the humidor had belonged to an uncle who lived to be ninety-six and drank and carried on until a person was ashamed to mention him—Uncle Orrion, it was—as soon as Ingeborg had the money saved in the humidor, she was going to have something done that just had to be done, no matter what anybody said. She was going to have Jensen's grave moved!

After all, she was Jensen's widow, wasn't she?

She'd ought to know what she could stand and what she couldn't, shouldn't she?

If she wanted to have Jensen's grave moved from where she could see it every minute of the day, to a new plot down in the hollow, where she couldn't, why, that was her business, wasn't it?

She was sick in bed when they put Jensen there in the first place, as Linnea would well remember. For all Ingeborg knew, she said, she was at death's very door at the time. She had had no say in where they were going to bury Jensen. Mr. Golightly and Bishop Lindfors and Olaf himself had appointed themselves a committee of three to pick out a nice lot for the Jensen family. It had not been expensive and they purchased a plot big enough as years should pass for the whole Jensen brood to lie, one after one, until all of them were accommodated. Mr.

Golightly was the one who had been so pleased to pick that very plot, thinking that the widow might derive comfort from looking out of her window at the marker on her husband's grave and see the little mound it made against the sky. He mentioned it at the time.

But Ingeborg did not like it at all. For several months she was very quiet about it but then one day she burst out to Linnea that it made her nervous, that she didn't want to have to catch a glimpse of it any more. It had got so she didn't even want to look out of the window. And it was the first thing she saw when she came up the hill home at night.

Ingeborg was not quite herself these winter days, but her sore hands bothered her and she had had a quinsy attack just before Christmas that left her easily fatigued and ready to weep when the least thing went wrong. Linnea was of the opinion that if she went normally to bed, and slept, in a dark room full of fresh air, she would soon be much improved. But she pooh-poohed this. Whether she kept a lamp burning all night to scare away burglars—was she not an unprotected widow woman with a brood of five to watch over? (all the more reason why nobody would bother to steal from her, Linnea said)—and if she paid for the coal oil didn't she have the right to use it anytime she wanted to?—why, the lamp didn't keep her from resting. As a matter of fact, once she got to sleep, she slept as well as anybody. No, she would soon have enough money saved to have Jensen's grave moved down in the hollow, and the baby's moved, too, and then she would feel much better. Ever since Jensen died, Ingeborg had a very peculiar way to go to bed, a very peculiar way to put the kids to bed.

Along about bedtime first one child and then another would go and lie down like a ripe apple dropping off a tree, as though for a nap, not getting regularly undressed. They might take off their shoes and a few of their heavier garments. Ingeborg would find them sprawled and sleeping and would then straighten them out and cover them up, very thoroughly, with heavy woolen quilts. Too thoroughly, in fact, for if you ever happened to feel of them they were sopping wet with perspiration. Ingeborg herself would do much the same thing. "I think I'll lay down and take a little nap," she'd say and would do so. Like the children she would take her shoes off, and perhaps her outer skirt and the waist she was wearing, if it were heavy. Everything else she left on. Her nap would last until morning as she took the precaution to have sufficient covering near, or over her, so that in case she got cold she would not have to get up but could reach out and get the extra quilt and go right back to sleep. It seemed as though she never wanted to give in at night and say: Now I am going to bed. She just wanted to pretend to take a nap. The lamp was left burning every night, all night. She took the chimney off, flipped the little metal wick slot back and turned the wick down low. In this guttering fashion it smoked awfully and anybody coming in from outside could hardly breathe for a minute, the room was so stuffy and smoky, but Ingeborg was used to it and it seemed to give her great comfort.

It was, as her friends had predicted, and as she found when she made inquiries of the sexton and others, substantially more expensive to have a new grave dug for Jensen in the dead of winter when the ground was frozen solid, and Jensen exhumed from his offending resting place and reinterred in it, with the baby's little coffin put in on top of him, than if Ingeborg could have waited until late spring or summer. She thought it was wise to bury the baby this time in on top of his father. Not only would there be no additional cost for digging a new, though tiny, grave, but it seemed like maybe both of them would like it, if they knew. Not that they did, of course, being both in heaven, but it just seemed like it was better for them to be right together, like maybe the father was holding his child in his arms, than all soul alone. If Ingeborg had not been flat on her back, she told Linnea, she would have seen that things had been done a lot different. Imagine! Burying a husband right where every time you came up the hill, or looked out of the window, all you could see was the mound of his grave and his marker. Ingeborg dabbed at her eyes and wiped her red nose hard. Now that was a fine thing, wasn't it?

Linnea said that well, they had all done the best they could, none of them could possibly suppose Ingeborg would feel like that about it. Of course, maybe when spring came and Ingeborg's hands got better she wouldn't feel like that about it, exactly.

But she would, Ingeborg said. She would bet anything she owned it was that busybody Bishop Lindfors who did it. Linnea reminded her that Olaf and Mr. Golightly were also on the burial committee.

"Whoever was on it," Ingeborg said, "that's just men for you. That's the way men'll go and do every time. Give them half a chance and that's the way they'll go and do!"

Linnea did not argue or point out to Ingeborg that after all, at the sudden death of her husband she had been left almost penniless and that these same unfeeling men had canvassed the town for contributions of money to pay off her house, purchase a grave plot and casket, and give her something to go on, and had given at the same time all that they themselves could spare. For Ingeborg was in no mood to be reasoned with.

Linnea was worried about her old friend. The flesh was going off her large bones. She looked awful. Ingeborg had never had the disposition of the born angel but now she was so cross and fretful, she cried and complained so steadily, that Linnea felt genuinely concerned about her. Her hands really were very bad, and she got so she didn't even seem to enjoy a good cup of coffee any more. She might have a growth of some kind, she might have galloping consumption, Linnea thought, worrying about her. If she died, who would take care of the kids? Linnea was her closest friend. But how could she take more than one or two of them to raise? And what would happen to the others? They'd have to be separated from each other, parceled off to maybe complete strangers. But how could Linnea take them all? She had four of her own and another baby coming in the summer and they were about all she could seem to do for, with times so hard.

Olaf came home very seldom now for the government men were after the polygamists strong, and with two families to provide for, even though not in a manner to suit either of his wives, he could not risk another prison sentence.

Linnea would be glad when the polygamy question was settled and peace between the Mormons and everybody else established, although sometimes she feared that if it were, she might find herself with no name, five children and no husband.

She worried more right after she knew she was pregnant again. It seemed like a woman wasn't all of a piece to deal with things when she was pregnant. It seemed like things maybe scared her more, future things, that hadn't even happened. Because she felt weaker and softer and not able so well to take things as they came—and her tears, too, which was unusual with her, flowed easier, not only for all human suffering, or breaking the handle off a cup, or running out of coffee, or scorching a dresser scarf, but for pity of her own self.

She wished Olaf would come home once in awhile. With the weather so bad she couldn't get downtown much and almost never dropped in on him for a chat in the tailor shop. The last time he was here he told her he was trying to get a place for her out in Bountiful. She said she never lived on a farm and didn't think she would like it but he said it would be good for the kids to have some fields to run their heads off in. It was very healthy out in Bountiful. The place he knew about was ten acres, and it had a good two-room adobe house on it. She asked him what he thought she could do with ten acres and he said, nothing. He said a neighboring farmer would work the place and he would give her a share of what he raised, potatoes, hay for the cow, and stuff like that. She would have a cow and she could learn to milk. Think what it would mean for the children! He made it sound very nice and Linnea decided she would try it, at least, and see how things went. Besides, as Olaf said, out in the country like that there wouldn't be spies all over. He could come and be with her and the kids much more often. He probably could come out every Saturday night and stay all day Sunday! It would be wonderful.

"If Sigrid lets you," Linnea said bitterly. And then, still more bitterly, for with a new baby coming she felt sorely tried, and put upon, and it was hard to be reasonable and good, "I suppose if the Government decides no polygamy, I suppose me and mine will be out. I know whose welfare *you'd* look out for and no mistake." She wanted to hurt him. "Well, I wouldn't care," she said, "I'll have you know. As far as me and mine is concerned, we'd get along fine. We don't need no help from anybody. We don't want you to love us or do nothing for us. We'd get along fine!" She said this proudly, with a high chin, and tried not to wink or blink, and Olaf could see how desperately she wanted to mean it, how she wanted to be as proud as the Queen of Sweden, or prouder, and was, perhaps, at that, just for wanting to be. His heart melted at the sight of anything so foolish and so womanly, and he reached out and took her hand. "I ain't a bit sorry about the baby," he said. "You always have such nice kids. I ain't a bit sorry."

"Who said anything about being sorry?" she asked fiercely.

"Nobody. I just said I ain't sorry, is all. I hope it'll be a boy, so Rudie'll have a brother and not just grow up with nothing but sisters." He patted her hand and lovingly looked at her.

She softened and smiled, winking and blinking, and that made her tears fall down like a rainy branch shook. "I hope so, too," she said, wiping them away with a corner of her apron. "Maybe we could name him Cyril, Olaf. I just think Cyril's the prettiest name, don't you? So many of the ladies are naming their kids Cyril. It's awful popular now."

"Well, we'll have lots of time to talk about that," he said.

After she had had a long talk with Olaf, she always felt reassured and safe.

It didn't seem as if anything could go wrong again, and Linnea made plans for her baby that was coming in June, and made plans to move out to Bountiful as soon as school was out, the first week in May, if Olaf got the ten-acre farm, and though she was more easily upset over any little thing than she had been, and cried and laughed over little or nothing, still she faced the remainder of the long winter with equanimity.

But she did worry about Ingeborg, and was tender and sympathetic with her in her querulous melancholy, though she thought it nonsense that she was so set on having Jensen moved from one grave to another, as though that would solve all her problems.

It was an afternoon in late December and Ingeborg, off work early, had come in for coffee. Linnea thought this might be a good time to try and reason with her. It had been a long time since she or any of Ingeborg's female friends (she had no others) had said a word about the matter, for Ingeborg grew so emotional if anybody said boo. Indeed, so unlike herself had she grown these past few months, that she was actually secretive about the matter, though anyone knowing her tenacity of purpose was aware that she had no more abandoned it than her own hope of heaven and was stubbornly piling up the hard-earned pennies until her goal was reached. No one broached the subject any more, but Linnea thought she would today, as Ingeborg looked so ugly, sick, bony and plagued by demons.

"Ingeborg," Linnea said, handing over her cup of coffee and passing the lump sugar. "Are you still saving?"

"Now that's a fine question to ask anybody," Ingeborg said crossly.

"The reason I asked," Linnea said, ignoring this, "is because if you are, you'd better use your money and go and see a doctor, that's what you'd better do. I know you got a notion you don't want your girls to grow up vain and so you keep your looking glass hung over with a towel so they can't stand and make faces before it. Naturally under them circumstances you can't look in the glass yourself, so you do up your hair and pin on your brooch without it—"

"Nobody can say I don't look neat!" Ingeborg said.

"Sure you look neat. Nobody ever said you didn't. But that ain't what I'm talking about. What I'm talking about is that you *ought* to take a look in the glass for a change! You've lost flesh and your eyes is sunk in and you just naturally don't look like yourself no more. What I think is, you've got something the matter with you that had ought to be tended to by a good doctor! That's my honest opinion," Linnea said.

"No, I ain't!"

"How do you know you ain't? If you'd take that money you been saving up ever since last fall to have Jensen's grave moved, and go and spend it getting examined and maybe getting medicine you need, you'd be a lot better off. Somebody's got to talk to you, Ingeborg. You're just plumb silly on this notion you got to get Jensen moved. That's not going to make you feel any better. My opinion is, you got something the matter with your stomach or bowels or chest or something. You got to go see a doctor. That's what you'd ought to spend your money on, to get yourself well so you can take care of your family. They ain't got a soul, remember, but you. So for them if not for your own sake you've got to go see a doctor and not spend your money on foolishness."

"I never thought I'd live to see the day you'd talk to me like that, Linnea," Ingeborg said. Her face grew very red and her forehead looked shiny and scalded. Once, if she had considered herself insulted, as she did now, she would have got up and stalked out, but today she only proved that Linnea must be right by pushing her cup away, putting her bony arms on the table and dropping her head on them, weeping terribly. A lump came in Linnea's throat when she looked across the tablecloth at her poor friend. She had such a hard lot. Something about the sight of her skimpy colorless hair skinned back and the scalp gleaming through, her pathetic topknot no bigger than a baby's fist furiously twisted on top, her fierce bone hairpins, her scrawny red neck, her wretched shoulder blades jutting out under the ugly brown calico, hurt, and Linnea bit her lips hard to keep from blubbering.

"Ingeborg," she said, "Ingeborg, listen. I ain't butting into your business because I want to be mean. I just think you're sick with something you got to go and see a doctor about."

Ingeborg raised a worn wet face. "I'll go," she said, "just as soon as I get enough saved up so I can get Jensen moved."

Linnea sighed deeply. She got up and went and stood by the window looking out at the snow. "I never knowed you to be so stubborn," she said. "I sure never thought I'd see the day when dear good Ingeborg would be so bullheaded and stubborn. Why, you can't any more afford to go and spend your money for something like that, sick as you are and with times so hard, then I could affort to—to" she groped desperately for a simile—"to go down to the Z.C.M.I. and buy a solid gold chamber pot!"

Behind her, Ingeborg sniffed mournfully.

Linnea turned around and walked back over to the table. She dropped down in her chair again. "For goodness sakes," she said, "how much do you still got to save to go ahead and get Jensen moved?"

Ingeborg blew her nose and wiped it hard and figured. "Seven dollars and forty-one cents," she announced.

"How long do you figure it will take you?"

Again Ingeborg calculated, wrinkling her brow. "About fifteen weeks," she said.

Now Linnea figured. "But that'll be the middle of April! The way you're going you might be passed clear on by then! Anyway, are you figuring the higher price, the way the sexton told you it would be in the winter like it is now, or the lower price it would be in the spring when the ground's soft and the men would only have to work half as long?"

"The high winter price," Ingeborg said.

"What you doing that for?" Linnea asked impatiently.

"Well, because Christmas came along, and I give the girls each a doll and Chucken a nice picture book, and put a orange each in their stockings, and bought five of them little candy canes—you know, they brought the dolls and Chucken brought his picture book when we come over here and eat Christmas dinner—you know, you seen 'em, Linnea," Ingeborg said, "and it stands to reason that would make *some* difference."

Ingeborg's logic was so confusing that Linnea gave it up with a sigh. "Ingeborg," she said, "what if somebody let you borrow seven dollars and forty-one cents right this minute? You mean that above everything else you'd actually have Jensen moved?"

"Yes," said Ingeborg toughly. "Right away. Tomorrow or next day."

"You wouldn't be a bit better off than you are right now. In fact, you'd be worse off."

Ingeborg was stubbornly silent.

Linnea stared at her. There was only one thing to do. She would have to get the money from Olaf even if it meant making a scene that would make all other scenes look sick. She hated to do it, but she would have to. "Listen," she said, "I think tomorrow I can get the money for you. I think I can let you have the seven dollars and forty-six cents."

"Forty-one cents," Ingeborg corrected her.

"—forty-one cents. But not till tomorrow evening."

Ingeborg's face lit up like a sunrise. "I could make arrangements—I could have him moved day after tomorrow!" she said, her voice uneven with gladness as though she were saying, "I got me a magic lamp now— all I got to do is rub and whatever I want'll come true!"

Linnea looked at her and hoped she wasn't doing the wrong thing for her friend, wasn't being lax when she should be strong, indulgent when for her welfare and survival she should be severe. She wore an anxious, puzzled look.

"Oh, say," Ingeborg said, the sun sinking in her face, "you can't afford to let me borrow no such amount as that. I don't know what I'm thinking of, even to so much as consider it."

"I got plenty," Linnea lied. "I been doing fine with the sewing, and— and one thing and another. That ain't it. It's just—"

"By the middle of April it will every cent be paid back, just like I'd put fifty cents in the humidor every week!"

"I ain't worried about that," Linnea said uneasily.

Ingeborg laughed with relief. "Say," she said, "what's gone wrong with the coffeepot? Don't it work no more?" She got up from the table and went to the stove, taking the pot expertly off it with a dish towel wrapped around its scorching wood handle and brought it back and filled up the cups, more like herself than in a long time. Dubiously, Linnea looked at her.

She wondered if God Himself knew all the gulches in the human heart, and decided that He'd be a pretty smart Fellow if He did.

So poor Jensen was moved to a new grave down in the hollow, where his widow couldn't see it from her window and in fact had a hard time seeing it when she went to find it sometime later, to place some of the first roses upon it, for it was in such a thicket of bushes and willows, the modest and weather-despoiled marker staked out on such a small patch of thorny wilderness that it was nearly indiscoverable then, and in a very few years was quite lost to human knowledge.

To Linnea's amazement Ingeborg at once improved. The very day they set to work rousting Jensen out of his resting place and shunting him to another, and the baby with him, she took on her old brisk look.

Linnea took her brood up for supper that night and Ingeborg's eyes were so bright, her color so good, her appetite so reckless and her laugh so ready, that Linnea could not believe this was the same woman she had considered seriously ill. She made allowances for the excitement of the day, however, and looked for a relapse. But none came, and Ingeborg was quite herself again. She even put on so much weight that she had to let out the seams of most of her dresses, and Linnea looked on, marveling.

By extraordinary good fortune, too, soon after Jensen was moved, Ingeborg found a cure for her sore hands. She always thought the new grave had something to do with it, because, her goal reached and her desire accomplished, she was nice instead of cross to the Indian squaw who came to her back door and asked for something to carry away with her. If she had still felt "mean," as she told Linnea, she might have turned the woman away with the merest token (for she was too superstitious, and too poor, to send away a beggar empty-handed). Since she felt "good," released and disburdened, she was kind to the squaw and gave her, besides sugar and tea, an apronful of sliced dried apples and a jar of bread-and-butter pickles.

She told Linnea the Indian woman looked closely at her hands. Ingeborg said she said, "You got um sore hands." Ingeborg said yes, they were chapped and sore and oozed like that with discharge and wouldn't heal. The squaw said, "Me fix um, make um all better," and the next day she knocked on the door and presented her benefactor with a small bundle tied up in a dirty rag. This proved to be a lump of something that looked like mud and partially chewed-up leaves. Without much faith Ingeborg followed the squaw's directions and plastered it on her hands. In three days they were healed and gave her no more trouble.

For quite a while afterwards whenever Linnea saw an illness that had no name she always thought of Ingeborg, and thought: Now if only somebody would discover what that poor soul *wants* more than anything else, and give it to him, he would probably get better. It taught her a lesson she could never do much with, though she was uneasily glad of knowing it all the same, as though she had suddenly been shown how to make rain, about the mind, and the notions the mind has, and how with its notions it can do as much damage to the helpless body as typhoid fever, dropsy, gangrene or worse. She believed that the Indian's mudpack may have helped but she also thought that Ingeborg's hands would have recovered, as the rest of her disconsolate self recovered, the minute she got what she wanted: her husband's grave moved from where she could see it to where she couldn't. Linnea never looked at her hale and hearty, doing the work of two women, or three, without thinking: Ah, my girl, if I knowed deep inside of YOU I'd know a thing or two about everybody, myself included. . . .

CHAPTER 10

INGEBORG gave Jensen's new grave site credit for everything when none
of her children came down with the diphtheria that struck that winter.
For years it got credit for every piece of good fortune that befell her or
hers. "Now if I hadn't just gone to work and INSISTED on having
Jensen's grave moved—" she used to start out and say, such and such
wouldn't have happened, so and so would have taken place. Gradually
she forgot it, however, as she gradually forgot where Jensen was actually
buried, except vaguely "down around in there someplace, in among
those willows," and after that it got but little credit for doing anything,
except being lost. But now it was still fresh in her mind and Ingeborg
was sure that if she hadn't put forth every effort and had Jensen trans-
planted, every last one of her kids would have succumbed to the
epidemic. Linnea never knew why the Lord spared hers, and always
thought secretly that maybe He knew how much she cherished them
and just didn't have the Heart to take them away. Of course, this
wouldn't bear investigating. She had trust in God's special watchfulness
for her, and faith in the asafoetida, but she took other precautions too.
Every day, while they hid in their house from the raging diphtheria,
the snow lolling against it so heavily with high elbows and knees they
could hardly open a door against it, she lined the children up two or
three times and in good white light from the kitchen window blew
sulphur down their protesting throats. She kept their bowels open with
quarts of lukewarm cassia tea they gagged on and pleaded not to have
to drink, though her floundering trips to the outhouse with the slopping
chamber pot were three times as many as a consequence. Not only
that, their chests were rubbed with grease every day and chest protectors
made of soft old woolen were kept securely pinned on. Also, she kept
the kitchen, at least, where they all stayed, as warm as toast, not skimp-
ing on the coal in this trying time no matter what she would have to do
later. All these measures combined, no one alone she could afterward

point to, though the senna tea, being the most horrible, was likely the real exorciser, and kettles of good soup, and the Lord's love, kept them safe. The last alone, maybe, though at the time (she felt conscience-stricken to think of it later) she would not have sat back and depended on His love alone, any more than fly to the moon.

The days in durance, the contagion lurking everywhere invisible and deadly, went by with a kind of idyllic swift happiness they all wondered at later, that it was there and then. Linnea took even more pains with her housework than usual, and the house they were confined to never seemed to gleam and shine more. Out of the main stream of life, with nowhere to go, no one to see, in a lost pocket of the white world, in the Lord's vest pocket, Linnea with her four children had ease and joy. Of course the children fought sometimes, and once Rudie stopped his mother's heart by vomiting but he got better right away. Towards the last they ran out of nearly everything but flour, and yet it was a time to look back on and say, We was snowed in, lots of kids died with diphtheria, they died like flies, we couldn't stick our nose out the door, and the funny thing is, *we was happy* as a bunch of larks. . . .

Sometimes they just sat around the stove and scuffed their heels, or curled up like puppies on the lounge, or moved out of the swath of Mamma's cleaning as bushes lean back from the wind, or stood with their noses pressed against the freezing window. They balanced, wrestled, lay and sat. But they had work to do, too, and did it, the three girls, for Mamma well knew about the devil and idle hands. This was when Bertha, Gertrude and Stellie learned to crochet, cross-stitch, make a lazy daisy, a buttonhole, sew a fine seam and do other things—knead bread, roll a coffeecake and iron a ruffle. But Linnea did not weary them with too much to do. They played all the games they knew, said all their pieces, sang all their songs, cut paper dolls and dresses out of brown paper, played house, gave programs, held Sunday-school services (never on Sunday) and ate delicious starches until they were all as fat as cabbage roses.

The time the supper dishes were done until they went warmly to bed, in sweet clean clothes, was the best part of the day. Linnea was not so foolish as to risk bathing them, and maybe by this one rash act un-doing all her careful work, so they were not of the cleanest except for hands and faces which fairly shone. The lamp lit, Mamma's sewing in her lap, the stove replenished and the grate red, this was the time for sprawling and talking, singing, and telling of long ago.

Whatever Mamma told, it sounded interesting, for she would go fast, or pause, or whisper, or talk loud, just when she should, and she made little gestures with her hands that were like a picture drawn on paper, so plainly was what she told to be seen by the motions she made in the air. And she could be old or very little by her lips and voice and beautiful eyes, so comic her listeners died laughing, so lugubrious they sniffled and bawled.

Every child had her favorite story.

Bertha, being ten going on eleven, liked best to hear about the emigrant girl who came and worked for the O'Laughlins. O'Laughlin was a rich mining man who was just a common miner until he was past thirty and then what should he do but strike it rich by discovering the Four O'Clock Mine. O'Laughlin made so much money he didn't know what to do with it. His wife and kids got everything they took a notion to want. Well, sir, the emigrant girl was Brita Stollstedt and though she herself had never seen her, Linnea knew people who knew her well, and so she could speak with authority. She was sixteen, so bashful she didn't want to go no place, and she worked for the O'Laughlins as upstairs maid.

One night she did something just terrible but she didn't mean any harm by it. The O'Laughlins being out and the servants nowhere around, she crept into Mrs. O'Laughlin's bedroom, only nobody in that house called it a bedroom, they called it a fancy French word meaning a bedroom such as you never saw in your life, as big as a church, all pink satin and lace curtains four yards long and a bed with a pillar at each end to hold up a roof of chiffon like a big cloud—and she got into Mrs. O'Laughlin's clothespress and what should she do but put on a rose-red velvet ball dress with a train as long as from here to the corner and metallic embroidery, and got into Mrs. O'Laughlin's satin shoes with diamond buckles though they were too small for her, and wrapped a tulle stole dyed to match the dress around her bare shoulders, never thinking, of course, but what she could get into the clothes and out of them, and put everything back where it belonged, without being discovered. She was all dressed up, but she had her hair hanging loose down her back, because it wasn't fixed fashionably enough and she wanted to try something that would suit the dress—when they came home! The O'Laughlins! Brita didn't hear them, she was looking so hard in the one big mirror and the two mirrors on either side of it that could swing back and forth so you could see yourself a dozen times at once, and anyway, the carpets were so soft all over the house, you couldn't hear a living soul until they were practically on top of you. Mrs. O'Laughlin turned the silver knob and walked into the bedroom with the French name, and her screams brought Mr. O'Laughlin who came a-running.

Brita was too scared to do anything except stand like a statue in the velvet dress with her hand reaching for her hair, and turn red and white and red and white and finally keel right over in a dead faint.

Mrs. O'Laughlin was so mad she didn't know what to do. They brought Brita to, finally. Her mistress was all for firing her, at the very least, but Mr. O'Laughlin felt sorry for the girl and after a lot of talk about it, they let her stay. She was as good as gold after that, you can bet! Nobody could have asked for a better little servant. Mrs. O'Laughlin always acted cold and like she bore a grudge when she gave her orders, and no matter how hard Brita worked she never got a word of praise, but Mr. O'Laughlin used to treat her kindly and sometimes he used to smile at her in a kind of a teasing way that made her remember what she had done that night and blush all over.

And then, about a year after, what should Mrs. O'Laughlin do but come down with a terrible bronchitis and die, although they had a doctor come out all the way from New York City to look at her. Their children were in fancy schools, or married, and at first there was talk that Mr. O'Laughlin would sell the house, but instead of that, he traveled all around in the East until he kind of got over his sorrow. And then he came back home down there on South Temple, for he had kept the servants on all the time and they had it just as spick-and-span as could be, and settled down. And then! What should Mr. O'Laughlin do but call Brita to him and ask her to marry him! She keeled over in a faint then too, they said. But she said yes, and they were married, and she made him a good wife, though even more of a spendthrift than the first Mrs. O'Laughlin, once she got onto the trick of spending money, and where the first wife had three party dresses, Brita had six, but that was natural considering that she was quite young and hadn't had any particularly easy time in her life up to then. Mr. O'Laughlin didn't fall in love with her that night his wife caught her dressing up in her clothes, because of course he was married and when you are married you can't fall in love with anybody else, but he kind of got his eyes opened to her, and so, when his wife died and he was thinking over who all he could marry, he thought of Brita in that red velvet dress and married her!

This story was Bertha's favorite, although it had no moral except that the thing to be was a blonde young lady seventeen or eighteen in a red velvet dress where a millionaire could get his eye on you and, when his wife died, marry you, and they never walked down South Temple without she'd run ahead and hang onto the wrought-iron gates and look through to the big O'Laughlin mansion with its glittering windows and handsome lawn and hope to see somebody, maybe the heroine herself! But she never did, there was never a thing stirring, the O'Laughlins were traveling in Europe or somewhere, so all she could do was stand and stare and think, *This was the very house,* until whoever she was with got nearly to the corner and then had to turn back and shout for her to come on and hurry up.

Stellie liked best to hear about the eagle carrying the baby off and never bringing it back, and Rudie could listen a thousand times to the story of the boy just his size that was stolen by the Indians—they gave him bows and arrows, a horse and feathered headdress, were kind to him, and when he grew up they made a Chief out of him, and you couldn't tell him from a real Indian, except that he had blue eyes, like Rudie's.

To Gertrude, however, the best of all possible stories was the absolutely true story of the littlest man who ever lived. It took a while to get fairly into it, for there was quite a long prologue, but Gertrude never minded that. In fact, it made the story all the better and was like eating the cake first and saving the frosting till last.

Mamma picked up the coal scuttle and poured some coal into the range—not much, for it was nearly bedtime, but enough to keep them cozy—and then came back and sat down in the rocking chair, giving it a hitch nearer the stove though the light didn't shine over her shoulder right afterwards and she had to give up her sewing, her hands idle on top of it in her lap. "Let's see, now, where was I?" she said.

"*My* story," Gertrude said eagerly. "You was starting in on my story."

"Oh, yes," Mamma said. "Well, it's not what you might call a real *story*. It's just about a little midget named Tom Thumb. He had another name, a real name like anybody would have, but they went to work and called him Tom Thumb, because he was in a show, in the American Museum in New York City."

"It is too a real story, Mamma," Gertrude protested jealously.

"All right," Mamma said. "I mean, not a fairy story. Well, the way I happened to hear about all this was—you know before I married your father I told you I worked for this lady named Mrs. Muller. Mrs. Muller had this dressmaking place down on State Street and Third South. She was hard to work for because she was so particular, but she was a very fancy seamstress that came from New York City, and she could make the most beautiful dresses you ever laid your eyes on. I just done plain sewing for her and I wasn't there only one winter. What she come out here for, I guess she heard there was lots of rich people, like some of the rich men in the Church and mining men and like that, and she thought their ladies would want fancy clothes and she could make lots of money. Maybe she could of, too, in time, but she couldn't stand it out here and went back to New York City. She said Salt Lake was just nothing but a howling wilderness." Mamma always had to begin with the dressmaking establishment and the howling wilderness, but they wouldn't have had her start any other way for the world.

"Was the littlest man in the world still there when she got back?" Gertrude asked.

"I don't know. I guess so," said Mamma. "Anyway, this Mrs. Muller was awful particular about everything, it was hard to suit her, and when she got mad she'd just start in to scream and holler something terrible, and once Evelyn Fogergren that sewed for her too, at the same time I did, put a Spanish flounce on a skirt wrong and she grabbed it and tore it all to pieces. It was such good silk she couldn't hardly tear it either. But when she wasn't mad she was just as nice as could be and we had coffee in the afternoon just like as if we was home, we'd cook up a cup of coffee on the back of the stove, and when everything was going along to suit her and we'd maybe all three be sitting around doing handwork (so much of sewing was handwork then—I'd overcast seams till I couldn't see straight), why, Mrs. Muller would start in and tell us all about New York and the houses there, and carriages, and stores, and how it was lit so bright at night you could stand right on the street and read a newspaper, and how the ladies dressed to go to the theayter with diamonds even in their hair—instead of just one theayter, like we got the Salt Lake Theayter, there was five or ten there, every last one of them as big as the Tabernacle—and she'd tell about the big restaurants where the waiters wore knee pants and white wigs—"

"What for?" Stellie inquired.

"I don't know," said Mamma. "All Mrs. Muller said, she said the waiters wore knee pants and white wigs."

"Don't be a buttinsky," Gertrude said severely. It was hard to wait for the most important part.

"I ain't a buttinsky," Stellie said.

"You hush, both of you hush," Mamma said. "Anyway, Mrs. Muller told us about all them things, store windows with real live people in them—one man that could stand for hours without even blinking his eyes, and you could watch him and watch him and he looked just like a wax dummy, you couldn't any more tell he was alive than fly to the moon—and she told us about the American Museum. It cost a quarter to go in but Mrs. Muller used to go every week or two—"

"To see Tom Thumb! To see his little wife!" Gertrude breathed reverently. The time was nearly here and her heart beat fast in anticipation.

"Not only to see him—"

"And her," Gertrude said.

"—but to see lots of things. Why, do you know," Mamma said, "this American Museum was run by a man named Barnum, and this Mr. Barnum would get things from all over for people to see. I guess there never was such a place as the American Museum, to hear Mrs. Muller tell it, there was four floors of just nothing but the most wonderful things you could imagine, and they had what they called a Lecture Hall in the building where there was shows and performances."

"Tell about the fattest lady in the world," Bertha said.

Gertrude gnawed her knuckles with impatience but this was interesting too, so she nodded. "Yes, tell about her," she said.

"Well, there ain't much to tell," Mamma said. "All this lady was, according to Mrs. Muller, was so fat that she could hardly move. They had to have a special chair built for her of all ironwork underneath and I guess a special bed too that wouldn't fall down. Her arms and legs was as big around as that table." All the children looked wonderingly at the round marble-topped table in the corner and back at Mamma. "And her face was as fat as this." She made a circle with her two arms. "And if a person would ever feel of her hands, they'd be just as cold as ice no matter how hot it was outside, her blood didn't circulate right or something, she was so fat. They said she never ate much neither. They said she ate just like a little bird. But anyway she wasn't only twenty-six or so when she died. She was just too fat to live, and they had to build a coffin four times as wide as a ordinary coffin and dig a grave four times as big and they had to hoist her out through the window, mind you, with a block and tackle, like she was a pianoforte or something, they couldn't take her out the regular way. She was the fattest lady that ever lived, and she weighed eight hundred pounds."

They all sighed in wonderment.

"There was everything in the world you could imagine in that American Museum," Mamma said. "Waxworks that was just the spitting image of famous people and most of the time with their very clothes on —like that Queen that got her head cut off in France, I think Mrs. Muller said it was, that they say after her head rolled in the basket, her eyes blinked and her lips moved like she was trying to talk—with her very dress on, of yellow satin embroidered all over with silver roses. And her hair was fixed the funniest way, done up about three feet high and powdered white with a little ship on top, a perfect little sailing ship that Rudie would of just loved"—Rudie made a chirping noise to show his pleasure upon hearing this—"with sails and everything, and not so little, either. About this big." Mamma showed them the size with her two hands about eighteen inches apart.

"Was that after she got her head chopped off?" Stellie asked, thrilled.

"No silliness," said Mamma, "there'll be no more about the American Museum if we're to have silliness."

Stellie huddled down meekly.

"Of course it wasn't after she had her head chopped off. It was before," Mamma said. "And there she stood, all made of wax, and painted and fixed just like she was in real life. There was lots of wax Kings and Queens and President Lincoln sitting in a rocking chair right like he was that night twenty-five years ago watching that show on the stage when that young fellow come in at the back and shot him in the head. The fellow hollered something in some foreign language that meant *it serves you right,* or something like that—"

"What did he holler that for?" Gertrude could not resist asking.

"Because he was mad at President Lincoln."

"What was he mad for?"

"He was just mad, is all. How should I know? Shall I tell this or shall you? Because when we get smart-alecky and interrupt people all the time, why, then the first thing we know we can go ahead and tell the story ourself if we think we can tell it better. Now, do we listen or do we get smart-alecky?"

"We listen," said Gertrude.

"All right, then," said Mamma. She did not look cross. She just looked sober, as she ought, but then she smiled a little like handing over a flower just picked. "This young fellow that killed President Lincoln was there made of wax too. Mrs. Muller said he was a actor and was just as handsome as could possibly be, with black hair that hung clear to his shoulders in curls like a girl's and a beautiful black mustache. Imagine a nice young man like that being so mean. I don't think he could talk English. President Lincoln being the President, he didn't sit down in the audience with the rest of the people when he went to the theayter. He sat in what's called a box, you know, them balconies like stick out on either side of the stage—they've got them at the Salt Lake Theayter, you must of noticed them when you went to see the matinee that time."

"The Christmas Fairy," Gertrude said.

"Like porches with railings around them," Bertha offered.

"That's right. Well, anyway, President Lincoln was at the theayter to see a show the night he was killed and he was sitting in a box. At the American Museum they had it all just exactly like it was—the box, and President Lincoln, and Mrs. President Lincoln—she wasn't a very pretty woman, Mrs. Muller said, more kind of dumpy, not what you'd call pretty at all—and this young fellow was standing there pointing the gun at his head. Just imagine," Mamma said. "That must of been some sight to see." She paused, while they all imagined it. "There was wax-works upon waxworks, down a whole long corridor. It would take pretty near a day just to look at the waxworks, I guess, without going near any of the rest of the stuff. Like a white whale," she said, "not dead, or mounted, mind you, but swimming around in water in a glass case that must of been twice as big as this house." She reached down and took Rudie up into her lap, holding him snugly as if he were very little instead of nearly four, and beginning to rock back and forth. "And a man that was tattooed over every inch of his whole body," she said. "And two boys that was joined together, where one went the other had to go, Mrs. Muller said. They each had a head, and each had two arms and two legs but they didn't only have but the one stomach between them, and that way, they had to eat twice as often as ordinary people, or they couldn't only eat half as much as ordinary people, I've forgot which. And there was a lady with horns just like a cow, and a colored man as white as snow—"

"I don't mean to interrupt, Mamma," Bertha said with a politeness befitting an oldest daughter, "but how could they tell he was a colored man in the first place if he was as white as snow?"

"They could just tell, is all," Mamma answered with equal politeness, that befitted the mother of a polite oldest daughter. "Mrs. Muller said they had this colored man there as white as snow."

"Oh," said Bertha, perfectly satisfied.

"And they had a mermaid, half woman, the upper half, and half some kind of a fish, a salmon or something, the lower half, but if I'm not mistaken she was already dead by that time. It seems to me Mrs. Muller said she was dead, and stuffed, and in a glass case. And they had a man so double-jointed he could tie himself up in knots he couldn't hardly undo, they was so complicated. He pretty near had to have help to get untied. And there was a man there that was a real giant, as tall as a lamppost or taller, as high as the ceiling, and—"

"And Tom Thumb," Gertrude said, "oh, please, Mamma, Tom Thumb."

Mamma rocked Rudie and looked down at her big pleading eyes. She smiled. "And Tom Thumb," she said, relenting. "The littlest man in the world."

Gertrude let her breath out in a great windy sigh. It was now, it was here, it was time. "How little?" she whispered. "How little?"

"Well, I tell you," Mamma said. "You imagine a real little man that would just about come up to Rudie's shoulder, or someone about as high as a stick of kindling wood, or the leg of that chair,—not even that big, not the height of the lamp there, not as big as Aunt Gunilla's baby when you stand her up, not as big as that doll we seen in the Z.C.M.I. window, not any higher than *this*," Mamma spread out her hand about a foot from the floor, "and that would be Tom Thumb," she said.

Gertrude stared at the empty space she measured off as though he were standing there and Mamma's hand were lightly resting on the top of his head. "A really little man," she said in a kind of trance, "a really truly little man. Not a baby or a little boy or anything like that but a *grown-up man* with whiskers, a little little MAN, the littlest in the whole world. Oh, Mamma, but I'd like to have *him*, I tell you."

"He had little suits made just like anybody, little Prince Albert coats and striped pants and velvet waistcoats and everything," Mamma said. "Rudie here couldn't begin to get into them." She patted his plump knee. "And little tiny boots Rudie couldn't even get his big toe in." Rudie thrust out his legs proudly. "Little tiny gloves that wouldn't go over Rudie's hands, little high silk hats that would just sit right up on top of Rudie's head—" The honor done him by this description was almost too much for the small boy and he stretched out so extremely in all directions that he would have slid off Mamma's lap had she not taken a firmer hold on him. "Either you sit still or you go to bed this instant," she said. "I know you're big but you behave yourself." When the pride passed from her son and he curled up again and was quiet she smoothed his soft hair and went on, "He had his own carriage, no bigger than a baby buggy, but perfect, like a real carriage, like Mrs. Kimball's or better. It was pulled by the four littlest horses that ever was known, and when he'd ride down the street in it, policemen had to clear a path for him, so many people crowded around and gawked."

"I'd gawk," Gertrude said, still in her trance. "Nobody could make me move. I'd just stand there and gawk and never move a inch."

"A policeman could make you move," Bertha said. "A policeman's got a club, and anybody that won't move, they hit them on top of the head."

"They wouldn't hit me on top of the head. Nobody could make me move," Gertrude said stubbornly. "I'd just stand there and watch Tom Thumb, and see the little horses and the little carriage."

"Oh, no, you wouldn't, missy. Would she, Mamma?"

"You hush up, Bertha. Now don't start bawling, Gertrude. You could anyway see him till he went past, if he went past and you was in New York City. Of course he wouldn't only go past once in a while," Mamma said.

"I'd fix it so I could see him *all day long*," Gertrude said fiercely.

"We won't get all on edge over something like that," Mamma said. "We'll cool down and act like little ladies, if you please. Or we get sent to bed. There was quite a few little midgets in the American Museum, Mrs. Muller said, because this Mr. Barnum was always looking around for midgets, there was maybe seven or eight, but none of them was so small or so wonderful as this Tom Thumb," she said. "He was just a sight to behold, according to Mrs. Muller. Nobody might of ever been good enough for him to marry and he might of just gone on and been a old bachelor," she paused and they all burst out with laughter, for by doing something with her face and making some motions with her hands, they could see before them an old gray-headed and bewhiskered bachelor about a foot high with doll's spectacles on his nose, a minute vest with microscopic gravy stains upon it, and gaiters, "if it hadn't been," she said, "that somewhere or other along the line this Mr. Barnum stumbled on a—"

"A little lady," Gertrude helped her, hanging on every precious word.

"—a little lady, just as perfect a little lady as TomThumb was a perfect little man. She was eighteen years old, and not a quarter-inch higher than he was. And can you imagine! She was just as smart as a whip, had her little education, could read little books and do little sums, like a schoolmistress!"

"Could she read big books and do long division?" Stellie asked.

"I don't see why not," Mamma said.

Gertrude had a horrible vision of the perfect little woman being crushed under the teacher's big Geography and winced. "Oh, no," she said, all out of breath, "They'd be too heavy for her! She couldn't! That little thing!"

"Well, she could open a big book up on the floor and crawl on the pages and read the words if she wanted to, I should think," Bertha said.

"Sure," Stellie agreed. "Like a fly."

"But she didn't *want* to! She never did that, did she, Mamma?" Gertrude begged, for they were trying to ruin the beautiful story of utmost and incomparable smallness. "Did she, Mamma? She just read little *tiny* books about as big as pillbox she could hold with her little hands on her little lap in her little chair, and did little *tiny* problems, didn't she?"

"I guess so. You kids shut up now," Mamma said. "Anyway, this Tom Thumb was going on for twenty-two or twenty-three—"

"But he never grew *a bit*," Gertrude put in passionately.

"Of course he never grew a bit or he wouldn't of been a midget, silly, the littlest man in the world. He was going on for twenty-two or twenty-three," she continued, "and he never had so much as even looked at a young lady or sparked nobody the least bit or even so much as asked to call, because there was nobody little enough, and smart enough, and pretty enough, to suit him, and it likely began to look to him as though there never *would* be nobody. Maybe he'd have to live all alone his whole life. All soul alone!"

"Poor little Tom Thumb," Gertrude whispered.

"He had them little horses, though," Stellie put in. "He had that little carriage. He had lots of things!"

"But no little lady to marry," Mamma said, "until this Mr. Barnum happened to stumble onto her. She was living with her mother and father and sisters and brothers, in a house just like anybody else. Everybody else in the family was just regular size except her. The people that has a little midget is just regular size. Tom Thumb's folks was just like anybody else. Any father and mother can have a midget, when they least expect it, depending on the will of the Lord."

"I wish He'd give *us* one," Gertrude said. "Oh, my. Oh, my." She clapped her hands.

"God forbid," Mamma said. "Don't *never* say nothing like that." She looked superstitiously around. "That would be something."

"And what happened then?" Bertha asked.

"Well, they brought this little woman, Lavinia Warren, her name was, to New York City and put her in the American Museum. And Tom Thumb got acquainted with her there."

"And they got married, didn't they?" Bertha said.

"You shut up, Bertha. You're trying to get the story done too quick!" Gertrude said furiously.

"It wasn't so easy as that," Mamma said, "because this little lady didn't say yes so quick. Tom Thumb saw her, and the minute he laid his eyes on her he was just plumb out of his mind, he was so in love with her. You can imagine how little she was, and how perfect, like a little ornamental statue, and had her hair fixed in buns and curls like a society lady. And here she had her little ears pierced and diamonds dangling from them, and little stays on like a grown woman, with a waist about as big around as my wrist, and all these little flounced dresses made and these little high-heeled shoes. She was a sight for sore eyes, I can tell you."

Gertrude laughed aloud with pleasure, never taking her eyes off Mamma's face. "That little woman!" she said in ecstasy. "That little *thing!*"

"Well, sir, Tom Thumb fell in love with Lavinia, but he wasn't the only one. Somebody else fell in love with Lavinia, too, another midget, but not nearly so little as Tom Thumb, in fact one of the bigger midgets—as big as Rudie, not little at all"—Rudie was too close to slumber in the hot room to be excited by this mention of his own great size and all he did was cuddle closer—"a little man they called Commodore Nutt. *He* fell in love with Lavinia, too," Mamma said, "and it looked for a while as if maybe Lavinia was going to marry *him.*"

"But he wasn't the littlest man in the world! He wasn't nearly the littlest!" Gertrude said wildly.

"No, but he was very nice. Lavinia was supposed to have liked him very much at one time. In fact, for awhile it looked like Tom Thumb never *was* going to get her. He bought her beautiful presents and she wouldn't even take them. He had a little watch made special with a heart outlined in diamonds on the back, and her name engraved in it, and his own picture in the locket side, and she wouldn't take it. Oh, he bought so many things for her! But Commodore Nutt was sparking her, too, and finally poor Tom Thumb, who was so in love with her, when he saw he wasn't making any headway, just about dwindled right away. He lost flesh and he got pale, and he never took no pleasure in his food or nothing, walked the floor at night, and that little minx just kept him dangling. It got so serious, it looked like he would maybe dwindle right away and die if something wasn't done pretty quick."

Gertrude, her eyes very wide and fixed on Mamma's lips, was biting her thumbnail in desperation.

"Mr. Barnum, that owned the Museum, was all for Tom, because he was the first midget he ever had and anyway because he liked him better. He studied what to do and finally he hit on the scheme that he would send Commodore Nutt away to be in another show, in Boston or somewhere, so Tom Thumb could get his licks in and have Lavinia all to himself. But Commodore Nutt wouldn't go. He said, No, siree. He said he'd rather quit his job any day than go. And then! What do you think happened then?"

"What?" "What?" "What?" said the three little girls, who well knew.

"Why, the next day Tom Thumb was leaving the stage when here this Commodore Nutt come up to him and called him some awful things. Commodore Nutt said Tom Thumb was dirty and underhanded and snuck around and got Mr. Barnum to try to send him away so Tom Thumb could get in his licks with Lavinia like the sneaking underhanded no-account he was. He said Lavinia couldn't stand the sight of him. In fact, since Commodore Nutt had told her what a sneaking underhanded thing Tom Thumb had tried to do, Lavinia probably wouldn't even so much as *speak* to him, let alone anything else.

"Well, sir, poor little Tom Thumb stood there just absolutely flabbergasted. He didn't even know what Commodore Nutt was talking about because he had never said a single solitary word to Mr. Barnum. So he just stood there with his little mouth hanging open. 'I don't have no idea what you're talking about,' he says. 'Oh, you don't, don't you?' says this mean and fresh little Commodore Nutt. 'No, I don't,' says Tom. 'Well, maybe this here'll teach you,' says this big bully about the size of Rudie here, and what should he do but give Tom Thumb a punch in the nose, and knock him down, and sit on him, and begin punching him *when he was down,* when that's the lowest thing anybody can do, to jump on somebody and punch him *when he's down.* Especially a midget as you may imagine. And! Who should come along right that minute but Miss Lavinia herself and when she seen what was going on she lit right into Commodore Nutt like a whiz and pulled his hair and shook him and scratched him with her little tiny hands until he didn't hardly know for a minute what had happened. And she give him a push and pushed him clear off Tom and then she knelt down beside him and wiped his nosebleed with her little handkerchief and helped Tom sit up, and then stand up, and brush himself off. His lovely little suit was ruined. And then she turned on Commodore Nutt and she called him everything she could lay her tongue to. She said anybody that would pick on a man half his size ought to be horsewhipped, and not only pick on him, but when he had him down, to keep on punching him, she said, why, she never saw anything to equal it in her life. She said she was ashamed she was even so much as *acquainted* with him, let alone anything else. Well, sir, Barnum came in to see what was the matter, there was such a crowd around in back of the stage, and of course he said Commodore Nutt never told the truth about the matter at all, because Tom Thumb didn't even know that Barnum wanted to send Commodore Nutt to Boston, let alone suggesting it. Lavinia put her little arm around Tom and had him lean against her going off to the dressing rooms and from then on they was sweethearts. And Commodore Nutt went to Boston and was glad to go."

"And then they got married and lived together forever in a tiny little house," Gertrude said happily.

"Say, Mamma. Was Tom Thumb a coward?" Stellie inquired. "Why didn't he hit back?"

"It wouldn't look like Lavinia wouldn't want no husband that wouldn't so much as hit back," Bertha said interestedly. "I don't see as he did so much. All he did was let Commodore Nutt beat up on him. I don't see how that's so wonderful."

"HE WAS THE LITTLEST MAN IN THE WHOLE WORLD," Gertrude said. "Haven't you got no sense at all? Here this great big Commodore Nutt goes and hits him before he can do a thing and goes and sits down on him and keeps on hitting him!" Her cheeks were red, her eyes flashing. "Why, Commodore Nutt was as big as Rudie!"

"That ain't so big," Bertha teased her. "Rudie ain't so big."

"Yes, but look how *little* Tom Thumb was!" She spluttered in her vexation. "You kids make me so mad I wish—I wish—"

"Now don't say something you'll have to beg pardon for." Mamma got up, put the sleeping Rudie on the bed in the corner and began to undress him. "It's past nine," she said—nobody could remember hearing the clock strike—"and it's time you kids got your shoes and stockings off and done your chores and got ready for bed."

"While we're doing it, couldn't you just tell about the wedding? Just this one time?" Gertrude began hastily to unbutton her shoes to show her good intentions.

"Well, maybe," said Mamma. "Maybe this once." She lifted Rudie in his outing-flannel nightgown and stuck him between the sheets, pulling the bedclothes up around his ears. She sat down on the edge of the bed and began to unbutton her own shoes. "They finally fixed on the day, Tom Thumb and this little woman," she said. "And was going to have their wedding in a church like ordinary-sized people. And did, too. The little bride wore a white satin dress that was made every stitch by hand in Europe, the most beautiful little wedding dress that was ever made, Mrs. Muller seen it later, so heavy embroidered with them little tiny seed pearls that it would pretty near stand alone—and here it had a great long train to it that went out fan-shape behind. She was a sight to behold with her long lace veil and her tiny little kid gloves and her little shoes, and here she was carrying her bunch of flowers just as big as you please, a nice bouquet of perfect little roses each one no bigger than your finger-nail, and got out of her carriage and went walking up the church steps. And Tom Thumb wasn't no slouch that day either! He looked like he just stepped out of a bandbox, so handsome and spruce, and he was shaking like a leaf."

"Oh, goodness," Gertrude said, delighted, pulling her nightgown over her head. "I wish they was *here*. I'd just never do nothing but look at that little bride and groom!" She ran and jumped in the rocking chair, still warm from Mamma's cushioned behind, her bare feet in under her, and rocked hard.

"Well, sir, the most important people in the whole United States was invited to that wedding, and they all come, too, even the very President I think Mrs. Muller said though I'm not sure. There wasn't no tickets sold, don't you ever think. It was run just like a real wedding, which it was, and nobody could get in that church for love nor money without they had an invite. Why, at six o'clock in the morning the police had to rope off the street, such a crowd gathered, and they rode on horses and had to keep making people get back. That must of been some sight. Mrs. Muller said she never seen anything so cute in her life as that little bride and groom coming through the great big enormous church doors after they was married, and coming down the steps. She claimed she seen them. There never was anything to equal it, she said."

"And they went and got in their little carriage, with the four little horses pulling it," said Gertrude dreamily, rocking back and forth, her hands clasped around her knees.

"Yes," said Mamma.

"And went home to their little house where they had little furniture and dishes and knives and forks and spoons, and little pillows and little quilts, and went in their little front door. They opened it with their little key and went in, and shut it behind them, and was happy *forever after*, wasn't they?"

"I don't know. I should imagine so," said Mamma. "Anyway, that's the end of the story. Come on now, and get to bed, you kids, so I can blow out the lamp." She drew back the curtain, letting in the moonlight. "Maybe it'll be so people can get around tomorrow," she said. "I wouldn't be surprised but what we won't be snowed in much longer."

Gertrude gave a deep sigh of pleasure. "That little Tom Thumb," she said. "That little Lavinia all dressed up. I guess that's just about the best story in the whole world!"

The next afternoon, fuzzy and blue-gray with no ray of sunshine the whole day and the last of the snow beginning to fall in flakes as big as a four-bit piece, was when they saw Mr. Whitehead come up the hill behind the old horse in his rickety wagon on his way to the cemetery. He sat hunched on the high narrow seat, with the reins held loosely between his mittened hands, and looked neither to right nor to left. His bearded chin rested nearly on his chest, and his shoulders sagged so wearily under the fluttering snow that it seemed as if he would never be able to straighten them up again. There was someone, more than one, in the wagon bed behind him, in boxes, with an old quilt spread over the top of them that was covered now with drifting white flakes.

Bertha saw him coming and told Mamma and Mamma left the board where she was kneading bread and came to the window with her hands all floury and little pieces of dough stuck to them which she picked off while she watched out the window and carefully rolled into a ball, rolled it and rolled it, watching, and when her tears fell fast she wiped them away with her bent wrist but got flour in her eyebrows anyway. When Stellie and Gertrude saw Mamma and Bertha at the window, they had to come and crowd around and look out, too, and then Rudie had to come, and Bertha lifted him up and sat him on the window sill, pressing against him to hold him on the narrow space. They talked softly about what they were seeing, that the man in the wagon was Mr. Whitehead— whose wagon was the first to come up the hill here in many a day—and that he was going to the graveyard to bury one of his children, or two, or three, or more. Oh, who could the Whiteheads possibly spare of the seven, all so agreeable, such playmates, such a help to their mother? Not Deseret, the color of nut brown, going on eleven, with the constant smile and the motherly ways. Why, one hot Sunday afternoon she packed that big baby all the way down to the Tabernacle, and the sweat was just running off her, her hair curled all around her face like she'd been in swimming. Not Frank in cut-down pants, with a pink face like a girl's, that never would snitch on anybody and was so good at numbers but so poor in spelling. Not Russell, in only the First Grade, that tried so hard to make his letters right, his face would get as red as a beet and he'd chew on his tongue, and the slate pencil would screech until your blood would run cold; that wore the heavy shoes three sizes too big so his feet would have leeway to grow (but if it was Russell that was dead the shoes would be three sizes too big forever). Not Cynthia. Why, Cynthia was the youngest! Not that big fat baby on a blanket in the sun in the yard, with her round bare feet and legs kicking and her round bare arms and hands waving—hollering and crowing with two teeth up and two teeth down, and a puff of thin bright hair like a white down dandelion you could wish on and blow away—like she was last summer. Not these. Not Letha, or Ted, or Emma, the other children in the Whitehead family. Not *anybody*. They couldn't spare a one! Who were these in the home-made wooden coffins under the snowflake-covered quilt in the back of the wagon? When nobody could be spared?

Mamma cried, so Bertha cried in imitation, and then they all cried, Rudie too, because Mr. Whitehead was going up to the graveyard all alone in the snow, behind his old horse, to bury some of his children. Everybody was afraid of the diphtheria, most folks were snow-bound, so no one had come to be with the Whiteheads in their trouble, nobody at all, the snow or the fright kept them away. The meeting houses were shut, people were forbidden to congregate, and no funeral service could be spoken. Mr. Whitehead would maybe read a few words of the gospel up there in the graveyard over his children, by himself, with the snow coming down. The wind was up now, whistling, cold enough to freeze his tears. He would hurry and put one little coffin after another into the frozen ground, frozen solid, and would pile the dirt on them fast, as a mother will hurry to get her cold children into bed and covered up and warm again, and safe and snug—he would pile the dirt on, to keep them from the weather, hurry to make them snug and warm. Linnea bit her lip hard and rubbed the tears out of her eyes with her floury wrist but they came faster and faster.

"Mamma, why did any of the Whitehead kids have to die?" Stellie asked, not wiping her tears, letting them splash and sprinkle.

(Four of them, they found out later.)

Mamma wiped her nose on the corner of her apron and prepared not to cry any more. "Because they had the diphtheria," she said. "That's why. Now you kids quit crying—there's no sense in it—you can't bring nobody back to life by crying. Stellie, you and Gertrude get back to your embroidery, see if you can't get all the lazy daisy done. Rudie, you show me how nice you can cut out paper dolls like I showed you out of that piece of paper I give you, and Bertha, you come on and I'll let you help me." She turned away from the window briskly.

"No, but what I mean is, Mamma, why did God *let* the Whitehead kids die?"

Mamma walked over and stuck her hands in the dough again, kneading it. She knitted her brows, thinking, while her children stood around the table waiting for her to make the much needed explanation. "Well, I'll tell you," she said. "God never *personally* was on earth, was he? By that I mean he never was a man and had a house and a wife and a family of kids, did he? Or worked for a living or slept in a bed or knowed what it was to set down to a good square meal when he was hungry? Jesus, now, did, but that's a different proposition altogether. What I'm talking about is God, like you asked me. Since God never lived right on the earth like a man, *he* don't know why we're all so attached to it. It's a mystery to *him*. On the other hand, he knows how nice Heaven is in the Hereafter, because he lives there. He's all for it, like we're all for Salt Lake or Mrs. Muller was all for New York, because it's so wonderful that it's really got every other place that was ever thought of, beat a mile. Naturally, God can't get it through his head why people hate so to die or hate so to have their folks die, when they get to go *there*. He knows—he ain't blind, see—he knows that life on earth ain't no bed of roses. It never was and it never will be. Well, sir, if you take Heaven now, Heaven is just literally what you might say a bed of roses. So naturally God thinks who wouldn't like to change *this* for *that*? Is anybody so rumdum they wouldn't like Heaven? he thinks. Like I think, is anybody so rumdum they wouldn't like Salt Lake? Like Mrs. Muller used to think, is anybody so rumdum they wouldn't like New York?"

"How about Hell?" Bertha asked practically. "How about if a person goes to Hell?"

"That's a entirely different story. We ain't talking about Hell. We're talking about Heaven," Mamma said. "As I was saying, life ain't no bed of roses. Take for instance now—the nasty cold winter and the diphtheria. Take thousands of things, one worry right after another. The reason we happen to like it so well is because we're used to it, like the Eskimos like the snow and ice. Everybody likes what they're used to, and they don't like what they're not used to. That's what you call human nature. Take sour-sweet beans. We always had sour-sweet beans so we like sour-sweet beans. But remember Esther Golightly? I give her some on her plate that day and she took a mouthful and turned right green in the face. I told her to go ahead and spit it in the stove. I said she didn't have to eat it if she didn't want to. So that's how it is. We love what we know and we hate what we don't know, even when it's good, like sour-sweet beans or Heaven. We know earth, so we like it. We know life, so we like it. We don't know death, so we hate it. That's all there is to it. Once we're woke up to the fact that most of what we *don't* know is as good, or a hundred times better, than what we *do* know, why, then we're going to be a little nearer over on the right track."

"But you cried, Mamma. Why did you cry?" Bertha asked.

"Well, look," Mamma said, shaping a chunk of springy dough into a loaf, flipping it top down in the soft white grease in the bottom of the pan and then turning it right side up, ready to bake, and reaching for another loaf-size lump. "I was crying because it's *natural* to cry," she said. "Not because I got any doubts that *God* ain't done the best thing. Not because *God* ain't fixed it so it's the luckiest thing that ever happened to the kids themselves, and maybe to their folks too. No hard times for them kids, you can bet. From now on, them kids is sitting pretty."

"Wasn't you crying 'cause it's *such a shame* people got to die at all instead of living forever?" Bertha asked anxiously. "If they like to live? The way you said? If they want to live? The way you said? Forever? Wasn't you crying about that?"

"Bless my soul, no," said Mamma. "Ain't you paid a bit of attention to what I been telling you?" She repeated some of it again, even more persuasively, with several bright smiles, adding that once Heaven was got used to, people simply couldn't be pried loose from it, even if they had once been Lillian Russell or John Jacob Astor and lived off the fat of the land.

There was a pause, while they all considered the matter.

"I sure like to be alive," Gertrude said thoughtfully.

"Sure, you do," said Mamma. "Me, too. That's because we're used to it. That's the way it's supposed to be."

"Well, but if Heaven's so much better," Bertha argued, "why don't people just take poison and get there as quick as they can?"

Mamma sighed with exasperation. "I'm ashamed of you, Bertha," she said. "Heaven's what you might call a *reward*. You don't get to go there for nothing. You got to do something for it, and what you got to do is, you got to live until God gives the high sign you can quit. Now, God give the Whitehead kids the high sign they could quit even though they was just children and you wouldn't think *they* had earned it. But that's just like sometimes a young fellow will get rich when he's only about twenty-two or twenty-three and other people maybe got to work hard till maybe they're seventy or so before they got anything laid by, if then. You see?"

"At least," Bertha said, "why don't we wish we'd die as quick as we can?"

"That *would* be smart," Mamma said with fine irony. "That would be like me not doing no more washing or cooking or taking care of you kids, just because I was sitting around wishing I owned the O'Laughlin house and had a carriage and a million dollars in the bank. You'd come to me and say 'Mamma, can I have a piece of bread and preserves?' and I'd be sitting there on my backside twiddling my thumbs and I'd say, 'I never made no bread, I never made no preserves, I'm just sitting right here wishing I had the O'Laughlin house.' Or you'd say, 'Mamma, I got no clean underwear to put on.' 'What's that make any difference?' I'd say. 'I got no time to do no washing. I'm sitting here wishing I had a million dollars in the bank.' Now, wouldn't that be smart? Wouldn't you kids think you had the smartest and the best mother in the world if I sat around all day wishing for something I haven't got?"

They all laughed at the absurd picture of Mamma sitting around wishing. But Bertha, the oldest, was a little less than satisfied. "It ain't the same thing," she said slowly, having a hard time to find the words. "We're *bound and determined* to die and go to Heaven sometime, whether we particular want to or not. But even if we wanted it and sat back like you say and just wanted and wanted it, we ain't *bound and determined* to get the O'Laughlin house or a million dollars. Heaven, we're *bound and determined* to get. A million dollars, we ain't. That makes a big difference."

Mamma brushed her hands off, slid the puffily filled pans close together and picked up the clean quilt she covered them with for the second rising. She refolded it and spread it across them. The talking was a great comfort. The feeling of a too-small steel cage locked too tight was gone from around her chest, the terrible lump in her throat had vanished. She smiled down cheerfully.

"The main thing is," she said, "not to think about all them things and rack your brains. Let thinkers that got nothing better to do than worry themselves to death thinking, think about all them things. All you got to do is to live every day, doing the best you can, and tomorrow will take care of itself. It will. You don't got to worry your head about nothing. All the worrying's been done already by Something or Somebody a thousand times smarter than you are. Your two cents worth put in ain't going to do much good. You know how smart Mrs. Haight is, that's a teacher with a education and a framed diploma? You can't ask Mrs. Haight nothing she don't know, I bet. Well, the Lord—or Whoever's running all this—" She opened her arms wide, taking in all the earth, the oceans, and every last sun and star in a great embrace. "The Lord," she said, "well, the Lord's so much smarter than Mrs. Haight he'd make her look like she didn't have sense enough to add two and two. He's so much smarter, and bigger, and kinder, and stronger, than anybody else, that there's just no comparison. Mind you, and that's who's running things! Him! And he never takes five minutes off but just sticks to the job every minute night and day. So what's the idea of *us* worrying? I tell you something," she said, "once you get thinking like that, and leave everything to the Lord, you'll be so happy, why, you'll be so happy, you'll just—"

"—just *never* want to die," Gertrude said solemnly.

"Pshaw," said Mamma, "talking about dying! Why, you'll live to be a hundred and five! All of us will! What do you say we get in and make some taffy?"

This was so wonderful and unusual a proposition, Mamma thinking sugar was bad for their teeth, that they all let out howls of joy. She shushed them and went over and pulled open the sugar bin. "Just remember what I said now. Do your best. Don't cross your bridges till you come to them, and when you come to them and cross, don't never look back. Be happy. Be busy. Don't never ask why of nothing or nobody. You're alive. Take life for granted. You'll die. Take death for granted. *That ain't the end of you.* Take Heaven for granted. Then you won't be all ate up with worry and dissatisfaction. You'll be fine. You'll be sitting on top of the world." She scooped out two cups of sugar into the old granite-iron saucepan.

"Sufficient unto the day is the evil thereof," Bertha recited. "That's what I had to learn in Sunday school."

"What's that mean?" Gertrude asked suspiciously.

"Tell her, Bertha," Mamma ordered.

"Why, it means *sufficient unto the day is the evil thereof,*" Bertha explained.

"Oh," said Gertrude. "I just wondered."

CHAPTER 11

THERE ARE steadfast friends, the same today and the same tomorrow, enduring, unchangeable. And there are the other kind—as good, maybe, in the long run, but hard to put up with. Mean and uppity, a chip on their shoulder, one day, and so good and friendly that butter wouldn't melt in their mouth, the next. Good friends, proved so, but difficult. The world and the weather belong to these.

For instance, here was snow piled as high as houses, here was cold-hearted wind, an uppity moon, a sulky sun, for days, and weeks. Here was sickness smelling horribly, death, grief, despair, for what seemed too long to stand. And what happened? You know what happened as well as I do. All of a sudden the sky softened deliciously into baby blue and baby pink. The birds blew in tuneful and loud and settled down to stay, letting bygones be bygones. Branches of green reached down to pat the hatless head, shake the hand, grasses reared up with the flattery of a cat around the knee. The moon turned into a cooing pigeon, the sun to somebody that would give you his last *sou*, his bottom dollar, without a scratch of the pen and no security.

Was the ditch hard enough to walk on? Not a peep out of it? Try walking on it now, but take your shoes and stockings off first. Listen to it, noisier than birds, but soft to bare ankles, dabbling fingers, like a current of air. Did you think you could not bear the white face of snow another minute? How's this one suit you, of lilac, bluebell, cowslip, the pink and perfect may? There are no turtles to speak of, so their voices cannot be heard in the land, but the winter is past. The sickness is over and gone. Spring is here. Butter wouldn't melt in its mouth. It would give you its shirt. And what shall you do but forgive and forget?

Bountiful was a fine place in spring.

The first Sunday that Olaf came out from Salt Lake, after Linnea moved to the farm in Bountiful, she said she wanted to have a heart-to-heart talk with him.

"What I want to get straight," she said, "is that I ain't a farmer. And if you think I'm going to start in and farm this ten acres, you got another think coming. I'd catch Sigrid doing it."

"Nobody wants you to farm," he said. "You and the kids can just live here, like as if you was renting in town. There ain't any healthier air in the world."

"Air!" she said. "And another thing I want to get straight is this. The cow's a nice little Jersey, and she gives good milk, and if I got to milk her, I got to milk her, but it ain't something I'd *choose*."

"Of course it ain't something you'd choose," he said soothingly. "You did wonderful, to learn so quick."

She tried not to beam at this compliment. "The neighbor boy showed me how. It wasn't so hard to learn. But milking ain't something I'd *choose,* I want you to know. Although Bonny's a very nice little Jersey cow."

"I do know it," Olaf said. "The main thing is, out here in the country I can come and see you, while in town I couldn't. There ain't never been more government agents or U.S. Marshals than there is in Salt Lake now. They're hid around watching everybody like hawks. So that's the main thing." He looked admiringly around the clean room where they sat. "It's a mystery to me," he said. "Here you ain't been here a week and you got the place looking like a doll house, a regular bandbox."

She smiled. This compliment rather took the wind out of her sails. She was going to tell him what a disappointment the two-room adobe house with no pantry had been at first sight, also what she had resolved when the chimney fell down and she had to have the neighbors come and help her put it up again. But now she decided not to. The house did, as Olaf said, look very cozy and attractive. She could put up with it for a while if she had to. There were plenty of people who would give their eye teeth for as nice a place as this. "I just wanted to get it straight that I'm no farmer," she said gently. "Otherwise, I got no complaints."

To the children, the farm that summer was an unending revel. Ten acres of their own, an area as big as all Salt Lake, all Utah put together, to tear over, of cold-footed warm-haired grass, gnomish peach trees, strawberry and tomato plants, irrigation ditches, watercress, catapulting water bugs, flowing wells of tasteless and colorless ice-cold water, in hot sunshine and no shade (or small shade like a cool bath in a darkened room) in the midst of rich fields where rabbits ran, snakes ran, and birds dashed by singing a carol and screech—this was for Bertha, Gertrude, Stellie and Rudie the delight of the world. They never left off prancing from morning till night.

Mamma would not let them go barefoot, and skirts and sleeves were long, petticoats many, the face grew scarlet and dewy down the starched cylinder of the sunbonnet with the tight-tied strings and the flap behind, but Mamma said just because they lived in the country was no reason for them to imagine for a minute they could run around like burnt wild Indians. She wanted them to be little ladies with white complexions and soft feet and secret cool hair, or know the reason why. It all depends on what a person is used to, whether they can stand something or not. The children didn't mind the myriad garments of cambric, muslin, gingham and foulard, all the mirrory starch, the buttons and snaps. They leaped lightly in spite of them.

When Ingeborg came out with her brood to spend a few days, Linnea said she was ashamed to confess she had got into the habit of going to bed with the chickens and getting up with the chickens, but honestly it was broad daylight at five or earlier and the birds and everything carried on so. Naturally, if a person got up at that time of day, a person was pretty limp by the time twilight fell, and was glad to go to bed, and slept the sleep of the just. The large-bodied, thin-winged mosquitoes that danced over the dark evening grass might try to get in, buzzing and whirring, but the mosquito netting tacked over every window, and the snug screen door, kept them out. There was no trouble from *them,* or from the exaggerated moon or exaggerated stars or summer moonlight white as snow in every corner of the room, from the fresh and eddying wind or sounds of running water in the night. A person *slept* in the country, for some reason or other, that Linnea had to admit.

And got up early. And that was how it was Gertrude that met the morning-glories face to face. It was quite by accident. They were almost all open and ready for business, when Gertrude ran out to get the butter off the cooler over the well, but a laggard caught her eye, unopened, not ready for business, stirring, though, doing something on its stem. She stopped to look . . . and saw . . . how a morning-glory opens . . . of its own accord, by its own vanity, like a parasol, the pupil of an eye, something unnamed and wonderful opening its mouth for air. Of pink, purple, white and blue, of taffeta material never touched by anyone, they looked out, looked upwards in green on green, were morning-glories, the glory, the miracle of the morning. She almost fell over backwards. After that, Gertrude was the earliest one up, to see them asleep, first, and see them awake, after, with never diminishing astonishment and admiration. What ways they had. How they did. The early mornings were bright-colored but cold, with a cold ground underfoot. It warmed up soon, though, and ripened and softened, even birds' songs, and everything and everybody was as ripe and soft as a plum by the time night fell, the falling sun ripest and softest of all, like a nearly rotten peach. And Gertrude watched the morning-glories close up shop and go to sleep, like people, all summer long, in the evening.

There were three sets of neighbors who lived fairly close. The

Barneses, the Myers and the Taylors. Linnea liked them, as she usually liked people. Mrs. Taylor came to call. Mrs. Myers came to call. Mrs. Barnes came to call.

Mrs. Barnes said afterwards if she'd have been a day later—and she nearly was, she had strawberries to put up—it might have been just too bad. But she just decided to drop everything and run down the road a piece to introduce herself to the new neighbor, the new neighbor being Linnea. That was on a Saturday. In the polite conversation that took place between the two ladies (Linnea was glad she blacked the stove and had a clean apron on and buns to offer with the coffee) Mrs. Barnes was overjoyed to hear the news that the new neighbor was an experienced midwife. Mrs. Barnes said it was wonderful news because there was no midwife right close around. Later she said if she hadn't found that out the very day she did Grace might have died and *both* the twins instead of just one, if they had had to wait to get somebody clear out from Salt Lake.

"My Grace," Mrs. Barnes said, "is in the family way, and while she ain't expecting for another month, it's nice to know there's somebody can do for her within hailing distance."

"If I'm not down myself," Linnea said, "I'll be glad to attend to your daughter. But I'm expecting about then, myself."

"I just never paid no attention to *your* condition. I did and I didn't," Mrs. Barnes apologized. "I seen you was, but then it slipped my mind when I got talking. Grace ain't so well," she said. "She don't look so well. She's skinny as a rail but on the other hand she's as big as a house. I'm afraid her baby's going to be a regular moose. She kind of worries me."

"Oh, she'll come through fine," Linnea said comfortingly. "You see if she don't."

"I don't go nothing on her man," her neighbor said. "He ain't much on the work, if you know what I mean. No trade. But one of these big handsome know-it-alls. Dances. Sings. Mustache. Always giving the ends a curl. Grace just thinks the sun rises and set in him."

"That's always the way," Linnea said.

"She's home with us now. He's off hunting a job. He's one of these fellas don't like working around the farm. Me or the girls'll catch her bawling every little while. She ain't but eighteen."

"Poor little kid," Linnea said.

"Poor little kid is right," Mrs. Barnes said. "Last year this time you should of seen her—primping and dolling up, laughing and carrying on, prettier'n a picture, thinking she was sitting right on top of the world." Meditatively she twisted a ring on her fat finger. "Life sure clamps down on a person, don't it?"

"Yes, but it lets loose, too, once in awhile. That's the main thing."

"Who's going to do for you, Mrs. Ecklund, when *your* time comes?"

Mrs. Barnes asked. "Me or my girls could help out with other things, but them or me ain't so much on the nursing end."

"My sister Gunilla's coming out to stay. I'll be in good hands."

"Fine," Mrs. Barnes said. "The neighbors are good as gold around here. They'll do what they can."

"It may be I can help out with your Grace. If I ain't down myself, I'll sure be glad to lend a hand when the time comes."

Mrs. Barnes said afterwards it was just like it had been ordained. The next day was a Sunday and what should Grace do but slip and fall off the back steps that she had run up and down every day of her life, and what should start but the pains, and what should flow but blood to scare the wits out of all of them.

It didn't matter a bit that Olaf was there and had to go back by evening, Linnea grabbed her black bag and went with Venie Barnes, a fourteen-year-old with a face as white as paper.

"You give the kids their dinner at one o'clock," Linnea said to Olaf, "and if I ain't back when it comes time for you to go, why, bring them on over to the Barnes'. The Barnes' is the ones with the big brick house over in among them cottonwoods."

"You put me in mind of a volunteer fireman. There's certain people gets excited over a fire, certain people gets excited over a baby on the way. You ain't in no shape to go," he said crossly. He had been looking forward to a good dinner and a long day of cheering companionship with her.

"I don't care what I put you in mind of," she said. "Someday I'll tell you what you put me in mind of, and that's somebody who acts like a big ninny if everything don't go just to suit him."

But she kissed him good-bye and gave him a little hug and turned back and waved to him when she and Venie got out to the road.

Mrs. Barnes always swore it was Linnea Ecklund that saved Grace's life but Linnea said pshaw, she wouldn't of died, though she was one of the sickest girls you'd ever want to lay your eyes on.

When Olaf brought the children over at five o'clock, Linnea was so busy she scarcely had time to bid him good-bye and tell the children to play nicely and quietly in the yard and not be a botheration to anybody until she called them. Gertrude whispered that they might get hungry, and Linnea said fiercely, just let her catch them hinting around for something to eat like somebody that hadn't been taught manners and she'd make them wish they hadn't. But if somebody offered them something, well, that was a different story. They could say thank you politely and be sure to eat like little ladies.

"How's things coming?" Olaf asked, when the children ran off at Venie's bidding to play.

"She's an awful sick girl," Linnea said, "an awful sick girl. The baby looks to me like he's here today and gone tomorrow, if you ask me. It's twins."

"Twins, huh?" Olaf said with the pleased astonished look people always get on their faces when they hear this news.

"Or soon will be. But nothing to bank on, from the looks of this one, blue and sick." Linnea drew a deep sigh. "It was these here steps she fell off of." They were standing on the back porch talking in whispers. "Her man ain't nowhere around, they've sent for him but they can't locate him. Well, I got to go in," she said, kissing him. "It ought to all be over pretty shortly."

"You want me out next week, Linnea?"

"What a question," his wife said. "What a question! Of course I want you out next week, like I want the sun to come up tomorrow."

"You won't have no accident, Linnea?" He started down the steps reluctantly. Holding onto the post, she leaned toward him and he came back up a step or two to kiss her again. "Fall down or nothing?" His face was uneasy.

She smiled at him, her eyes gentle. "Me?" she said. "You couldn't kill me with a axe."

The Barnes family consisted of the Mrs. Barnes who had come to call on Linnea, another almost identical Mrs. Barnes, her sister, two married daughters with husbands (one absent), five other daughters between the ages of three and seventeen, six boys from two to twenty-two, and four or five grandchildren.

No Mr. Barnes was ever seen. Another neighbor, Mrs. Myers, told Linnea privately that when Mr. Barnes married his third wife, his first wife Mrs. Barnes and his second wife, the first Mrs. Barnes's own sister, banded together and ran him off, Church or no Church. They had one of the biggest and nicest farms in the whole country, and one of the biggest and nicest red-brick houses, and one of the biggest and nicest barns and ten cows, and all the children were good and industrious.

Mrs. Myers told it this way: Mr. Barnes said it was his farm and his two wives had no business running him off just because he married a thirty-year-old widow, one of these little snips with frizzy bangs, always trying to show off how she wore such a small-size shoe, and fluttering around and screeching with her corset laced up so tight she was blue in the face. The two Mrs. Barneses said maybe it *was* his farm and maybe they *hadn't* no business running him off, but just let him try to step his foot on the place and see what would happen, they said. There was ways of dealing with a old goat like him, that two nice-looking healthy women wasn't enough for, with thirteen children between them, that he had to get ideas in his head and sneak around behind their backs and take up with this little snip and buy her a watch and a muff and no telling what all. There was ways, they said. He'd wish he'd of never been born. Mr. Barnes said he never would of believed they could act so mean. But he'd show them what was what, he said. They'd see where to head in at. He'd have the sheriff out, have them arrested, and sue. Try it, they said, go ahead and try it. All they wanted him to do was step his foot on the place! That was all of a year ago, Mrs. Myers said. He hadn't come near yet. He was living with this little snip on *her* place that *she'd* been left with, and no very easy pickings either from what a person heard tell. The two Mrs. Barneses hardly noticed he was gone, the children knew their duties and everything went like clockwork around the farm.

Linnea heard the clatter downstairs that meant some thirty men, women and children were sitting down to supper in the huge dining room around a table with two dozen leaves put in and three tablecloths to cover it. She heard the chairs being dragged to the table, the clamoring voices, laughter, the scrape of feet. Then the hush that meant the blessing was being asked, but not the voice that asked it . . . then the clash and tinkle of china, glass, table silver, the voices and laughter again.

This was a house where they had to put plenty of food on, she thought. A wash boiler full of potatoes, gallons of milk, bushels of shelled peas, pounds of butter, mountains of bread, bowls of plum jam. She had been served such a dinner minutes before on a tray, quietly beside the sleeping Grace, so she knew what all they had. It was a good thing they raised it all, she thought, and didn't have to try to buy it. Maybe if she and Sigrid could have clubbed together, in the same house —she grew feverish with horror thinking of it—it would have been different, they could have got ahead more, made things easier for Olaf. But she knew she thought it like thinking any other utterly impossible thing, like imagining that if they had all been Chinese they could have made a go of it better. The two Mrs. Barneses were sisters, fond sisters, exactly alike and nearly of an age. That made a big difference. This was as happy and prosperous a home as anybody would want to see, and it showed that polygamy really *would* work if people set their minds to it, the way the Prophet said. Of course, the two women had run their husband off, sent him packing (it served him right too, the old coot) but it was still a polygamous household in spite of that and worked like a charm. Mothers and children lived and worked together in peace and harmony. But she and Sigrid under the same roof would have had each other's eyes scratched out in a week. Linnea sighed, knowing how they would act.

She had nothing to do now for a breathing spell but sit by the wooden bed with a headboard that missed the ten-foot ceiling only by inches and watch the torn white rag of a girl, her worn linen face, against the best pillowcases. Lamplight made a person look sicker than otherwise, but she was sick enough. Her eyelids with their ragged fringe never fluttered. You had to bend over her to see that she breathed. Linnea sat and looked at her. The mother of twins, and here she was only eight years older than Bertha, with a pelvis hardly wide enough for a baby rabbit to squeeze through, let alone a girl of six pounds and a boy of six and three-quarters. Bigger and stronger in every way, he was dead, the boy, and laid out in the small bedroom at the end of the hall. He died at five-thirty in the late afternoon just when Linnea swung the other one up by the heels and spatted her hard to make her give a gasp and start punily to cry. She lay now in the cradle and didn't act right, big as she was, but had an ugly old-woman frown on her face and the cold tint of death.

Linnea wandered over and stood looking down at her, reaching down and took one of the little claws meditatively in her hand. Tears came, or the hint of tears, with a need to swallow a lump the size of a plum that stuck in her throat, and it struck her as curious, suddenly, that she should cry over the little thing's having to die. It was the best thing in the world that she was exempt, right at the beginning like this, from failure, from torment, from the thousand and one ills and woes of life. She was getting off easy. The only catch was, if the baby could have her choice she would take a chance on life, would say, I'll take a chance on it, Lord. I'd just as soon if it's all the same to you, I'll have a whirl at it, if you please. . . . A grown-up woman like Linnea herself would say it, even now, who certainly ought to know better. Ask this little newborn, and if she could speak, she'd say sure, why not, a while, forever, as long as anybody else. There must be some sense to it, quite a good deal of sense to it, if people felt like that about living, if people hung on like they did with teeth and toenails. . . . Linnea opened her fingers and looked at the little unsubstantial premature hand lying on her palm. It made a clutching motion . . . the first grip on the ladder. Under the soft blankets the little no-account feet would be pawing, ready for the long, long climb after the reaching hands, up the ladder, rung after rung. "Let her go ahead then," Linnea said harshly to Someone, blinking, "if she wants to so bad! What would it hurt to let her have a try at it like anybody else?"

But when Mrs. Barnes came up after supper and the two women looked at the baby again, she appeared still worse, and Linnea whispered that it didn't look to her like it would be long before this one would be gone too.

The young mother barely spoke and they went over to her. "The baby died, didn't he?" she whispered. "Dexter? I was going to name him after Dexter."

"Dexter's her husband," Mrs. Barnes said.

"Yes," Linnea said. "But he was an awful sick little baby. It was lots the best for him."

"You got a girl, though, too, you want to remember," Mrs. Barnes said brightly.

"She ain't dead?"

"Of course she ain't dead! What are you talking about?" her mother said.

The girl's lips worked and her eyelids closed tight. "I heard what you said," she murmured. "She ain't going to hold out either. Where's Dexter?"

"We sent Anna's man after him but they ain't back yet." Mrs. Barnes bent down close to her daughter.

"Not him. The baby. The dead baby."

Linnea swallowed. "He's laid out nice," she said. "Now you better not talk no more. You better just drift off to sleep and get you a lovely long nap."

"In the back bedroom," Mrs. Barnes said.

"Don't—you dare—bury him," she said.

The two women looked at each other.

"Until—the other one goes. They got to lay together, being as they're twins, him and her, in the same coffin."

It was not a whim. She absolutely insisted on it.

Down in the kitchen at midnight, having coffee around the big table, they talked it over, the two Mrs. Barnes, Linnea, a married daughter, and the two oldest single girls, soon to be married themselves, who were much chastened by the day's happenings.

"If you ask my honest opinion," Linnea said, "I don't think the baby's going to hold out long. I don't think it'll live more than a day at the most. It wouldn't hurt to keep the other one like she wants and bury them both together."

"But that's so silly," the married daughter protested. "It had ought to be buried tomorrow morning, and suppose the other one don't die for maybe three or four days?"

"For that matter, suppose it don't die at all?" Linnea said. "My honest opinion is, it will. But suppose it don't?"

"It's so hot, too," the first Mrs. Barnes said worriedly. "Only the end of May and hot as fury. How can we keep it?"

"Well, for that matter, you can get ice, and keep it packed in ice," Linnea said.

"Why, the boys'd have to go clear to Salt Lake for ice," the married daughter demurred. "Ten miles there and ten miles back, the busy season, and everybody's got their work cut out."

"We could spare somebody," the second Mrs. Barnes said.

"Why not just bury it and not say nothing to Grace about it? And then when the other baby dies, bury it, and she'll never know the difference," one of the single daughters offered, a buxom girl with a tiny ruby engagement ring who tonight was a little less anxious to marry in June than she had been before.

"No, siree," the first Mrs. Barnes said. "I as good as promised Grace and when I as good as promise I stick by what I as good as promise. The boys'll go after ice and we'll keep that baby until the other one's ready to lay alongside of it in the coffin. When I as good as promise, I keep my word!"

"That's right," the second Mrs. Barnes agreed, "it's little enough if it makes her happy."

"We'll start a couple of boys for ice in the morning," the first Mrs. Barnes said. "That Dexter of hers! Wasn't to be found, huh?"

"Joe said he looked all over for him. Couldn't find hide nor hair of him," the married daughter said. "I knew when we took him on last year to help with the planting he wasn't nobody to trust."

"Like fun you did," her mother said.

"Well, it wasn't supposed to be for another month. He would of been here then, probably," the young girl with the ruby ring said. She too had been impressed with his good looks, his easy careless ways. "You got to give the devil his due," she said. "After all, Grace wasn't expecting for another month. Who could imagine she'd go to work and fall off the back porch?"

"Her husband's off hunting a job," the second Mrs. Barnes said in an aside to Linnea. "He could of had all he could do around the place here, and got plenty for it, room and board for the two of them and a share in the profits, but no, that wasn't to his liking, farm work's too low for him, he's got to go off and find something that'll keep his hands like a woman's and won't take the curl out of his mustache."

Linnea stayed five days with the Barnes family, her children with her, and pulled Grace through. She said she had little to do with it, man proposes and God disposes, but both the Mrs. Barnes and the married daughter said that without her care, and all the fussing she did, Grace's chances wouldn't have been worth a dime.

Every morning one of the boys or maybe two of the boys, usually a big one and a small one, drove into Salt Lake with the wagon and brought home hundreds of pounds of ice shoveled over with sawdust and concealed from the blazing sun under old quilts and a canvas cover, to keep the dead baby sweet and frozen solid like a salmon while he waited for his sick little sister to die and join him. A coffin was built to accommodate both of them, lined with china silk. Still the little twin remained, but not seemingly with any real intention to stay and make a go of it. She procrastinated and mewed all day and all night long, and wouldn't hold a bit of milk on her stomach and grew smaller by the minute. "She can't last much longer," Linnea would say. The grip on the finger was weaker. She didn't mean to climb so far, so high. Maybe she didn't mean to climb at all.

Secure in the knowledge that her foolish wish was being carried out, with no matter how much trouble, and that the one baby would not be buried without the other but that they would lie together in the tiny coffin as they had lain together in her womb, Grace, the mother, rested easier and was recovering. She looked as if a breath of wind would blow her away and had cheeks and eyes like a starving Armenian and hands and feet like a skeleton in the graveyard, but she was going to get well.

They brought Linnea's cow over to the farm too and put her in with the rest of the cows. Bonny's acquaintance with the magnificent bull was more than a casual one and when she had a calf in due time the Ecklund children nearly went out of their minds with joy. Flossie told Gertrude at school that now they two were related "by blood." To Bertha, Gertrude, Stellie and Rudie these days with the Barnes family were days of incomparable happiness. There were playmates by the dozens, food to founder on, a million pleasant and interesting things to do. Not by the shed, though, the little shed out back of the kitchen with the door locked with a padlock. The grownups tiptoed past it. The children made a wide detour around it. It exuded coldness on the hottest day. The voice dropped down to a whisper there.

In this shed the dead baby lay, waiting, on a big canning table with ice placed all around him. It was better here than in the second-floor bedroom. The ice could melt and drip and the grooved floor could carry off the water. It would have been terribly hard work to keep him upstairs, running with pails and tubs of water every minute down such a long flight of steep stairs, to empty them. Here, all they had to do was carry in the ice and arrange it around him and let it melt as it would. Grace didn't mind about him being in the shed, she knew about the hard work. It was clean and snug. Nothing could get in to him. Gunny sacks on the roof were wet down twice a day. The great project, and everyone lent a hand, was for him to be preserved most fresh and babylike until his sister died, for him not to change to something hideous.

Linnea stayed five days and then she took the children and went home. She could go every day and see how Grace was doing until she was on her feet, and for the rest, her mother, aunt and sisters could do what had to be done. All that was possible Linnea had done for the living baby, everything she knew how to do. It was as bad off as at the beginning. The family could do what she did, she said. They could keep the little thing warm, try to make it swallow from a medicine dropper the slightly sweetened water, or cow's milk, or plain water, jiggle the cradle, walk up and down with it in their arms, see what good it did them.

The time of ice had been fun at the Barnes'. When the boys drove in the yard with it, and while they were carrying it into where it had to go, all the children could dance around and chip off little pieces, wash them off at the pump if they had sawdust on them, and suck the ice. Even when Linnea took her family home, they waited out by the main road for the wagon to go by and the boys still gave them pieces of ice. It got so it seemed as if it all would last forever, the boys' journey, the ice from Salt Lake, the almost forgotten reason for their trouble, the frozen doll in the padlocked shed.

The following Sunday Linnea left Olaf for a little while and ran over to the Barnes' to see how they did. Grace was sitting up in bed with a tray across her knees. She would do, Linnea decided once and for all. She was over the worst. There wasn't anything could happen to her now.

Since Mr. Barnes was gone—and good riddance, his wives said, though they once had loved him fondly and would cherish him still if he hadn't made such an everlasting fool out of himself—the two Mrs. Barneses shared the big front bedroom. They had the sickly baby's cradle in there with them, where they could watch it better. Linnea leaned over and looked at the little one. "She looks about the same," she said, "not much different."

"We can't go on forever with that ice," the first Mrs. Barnes said. "The thing is, I'm not sure the dead baby's going to keep much longer, ice or no ice. It looks to me like it's starting to—" She paused, unwilling for delicacy's sake, to go on.

"Well, Grace is so much improved she probably won't hold you to your promise much longer. She wasn't just in her right senses when she took such a notion," Linnea said. "Even before I left and went back home I started telling her she'd ought to let you bury the dead baby because this one was going to live, or might be going to live. I thought maybe you could kind of get around it that way."

"That's what I say, too," the first Mrs. Barnes said, "but no, sir, she won't have it. This baby's going to die, she says, and that's all there is to it. I know she heard us talking that first day, and of course the little thing *is* going to die, but why do you suppose she's so stubborn about it? Sometimes I think maybe she don't *want* the baby or something."

"That ain't it," Linnea said. "I've put it in her arms a time or two. I've saw how she held it and looked down at it like it was made out of rubies and diamonds. It's something else." I think I know how her mind's working, Linnea thought, but it was hard to put into words. She's going at it by a roundabout way. If she says it'll die, it'll live and fool us all. She's fighting a hard old battle with death and all she's got to fight with is that one dead baby and that ice and her fierce words about the living child: it'll die, it'll die, it'll die. "I think I kind of see her idea," Linnea said, "but it's hard to put into words." She eyed the wizened baby again, screwing up its face, and took up the little hand again, weighing it speculatively as you weigh a coin.

"Anyway," the first Mrs. Barnes said, "me and Lucy decided *definitely* if the baby ain't dead by Tuesday morning we got to go ahead and bury the other one anyway, even if Grace goes through the ceiling. We can't keep on with that ice business. It's all just as silly as can be. That baby's got to be buried and buried it's going to be, promise or no promise. Tuesday."

"For sure," the second Mrs. Barnes added.

But Wednesday morning came and Linnea saw the wagon heading for town, saw it coming back. The children ran up from the main road sucking ice. She smiled a little, thinking of the lenient grandmother, the bullheaded young mother doing the best she could, the bullheaded baby that wouldn't do one thing or another. It wasn't worth a nickel, not a nickel, but it was living, it wouldn't, wouldn't die. She heard the children shouting down by the irrigation ditch and not stopping to think at all she dropped down on her knees beside the bed. It was no snap to do it. She was as big as a house and the whopping baby inside her gave her a kick or two to remind her what was what. But she folded her hands respectfully and shut her eyes respectfully and spoke respectfully so only One could hear. "As long as she ain't give up," she said, "sick as she is and such a poor color and won't nothing agree with her, as long as she's hung on like she has, like a cat glomming on to a bird, couldn't you just go ahead and give her a boost? Give her a little lift? Give her a chance? Honestly to goodness, I bet she'd grow up to be one of the nicest girls you'd ever want to see, smart in school and everything. I bet she'd learn like a whiz. I bet she'd have a Sunday-school class and maybe sing in the choir. She'd be well worth your trouble. I bet you it'd just amaze you. Everybody's so interested if she's going to hold out, Lord, all the neighbors along the way that been interested in what they're hauling all that ice for and have been told. They're rooting for her, just like I am, like anybody roots for somebody that *don't give in*. So you catch ahold of her, Lord, and give her a good big pull, will you? It'll tickle us all nearly to death to have you do so. In later years, you'll pat yourself on the back and be glad you done it—you see if you won't. Thine is the kingdom, and the power, and the glory forever. Amen."

She got to her feet heavily. "Well, at least it won't do no hurt," she said.

Thursday morning the wagon went by for ice. Friday morning it went by. Saturday morning it went by, but that was the last time there was Salt Lake ice to suck.

Sunday afternoon at two o'clock they held funeral services for Grace's boy-twin Dexter who was not pretty enough to look at in the short wide

casket, now, and so the lid was shut down tight upon him all through
the ceremony. Nobody looked down on his face or bid him good-bye,
nobody knowing him even to nod to. Grace's husband was there with
his fine mustache and gentleman's hands and Grace was not so sorrowful as she was proud and happy. She held the girl-twin Dolores in her
arms, mewing still, but louder, angrier. The dead baby was buried all
soul alone.

The Bishop said the Lord's Will would be done, and not a person
there doubted it. Linnea thought again modestly that her supplication
had done no hurt, thought again shamelessly that not only had it done
no hurt, it had very possibly turned the trick. But she put the notion
away as big-headed, at the same time feeling a warmth of gratitude at
her heart as soft and light as an omelette. No more than she would have
told Olaf when he did her bidding that it was her idea, would she have
told the Lord about this. All she said to Him was, as she would have said
to Olaf: You had a fine idea. You did the right thing.

CHAPTER 12

"MAMMA," Gertrude said one morning, "you know what Mr. Taylor asks me every time I see him working down by the fence or any place? 'How's your ma,' he says."

Linnea smiled. "That's nice of him," she said.

"He *always* wants to know how's my ma."

"Do you say 'She's fine, thank you'?"

"I say she's fine, thank you, but what's he want to know for?" the child asked.

"It's just his way to be polite," Linnea said. "The Taylors are good neighbors." She had informed none of her children that a new baby was expected within the week, and they had no suspicions of it. It would come as a great surprise but at the same time an anticlimax for the arrival of the children's favorite aunt, Linnea's sister Gunilla, and her family of their favorite cousins, on Wednesday, would dim the luster of anything subsequent . . . even the birth of a brand-new brother.

It was a pleasure to get ready for Gunilla, bake beans, bread and coffeecake, scrub and clean till the little house sparkled like a gem. The day her sister was expected Linnea hurried and got the children brushed and combed, the breakfast things done up, put on a stiffly starched Mother Hubbard and waited, first peeping out the window and then out the door, for her to come.

It was another scorching day but the stove in the kitchen blazed away merrily, the blue enamel kettle of rich chicken soup on its slick top rollicking with steam. She made herself a cup of coffee to bide the time, though she had already drunk her usual midmorning cup. She sat at the table, sipping it, and noted with pleasure how white her tablecloth was. Her curtains were white, too, and with the heavy green blinds pulled far down, they made the room look cool, and deliciously lighted, as with snow. If any stove was blacker and shinier than hers she would like to see it, she thought. Gunilla would say, "How nice your house looks!

There's nobody can beat you for making a cozy home whether it's big or small! I tell you, it's just as pretty as a picture!" Nobody ever made you feel so good and clever as Gunilla did. Linnea, smiling, carried her empty cup and saucer over to the dishpan, brought the teakettle over and poured boiling water over it. Usually she left a cup and saucer, or even several, and plates, too, until she had enough dirty dishes from the next meal to make it worth the trouble to wash them, but today she couldn't have even a soiled spoon around, with Gunilla coming. She dried the dishes, took the dishpan outside and threw the small amount of water over the climbing rosebush, wiped it with the dishrag and hung it on the nail over the water bucket. Then she put the china in the cupboard where it belonged—the cup swinging on a hook, the saucer on top of a pile of saucers. She was proud of the way her cupboard looked. She stood back, her hands comfortably clasped on her bulging stomach, her head cocked on one side, and looked at it. Her dishes were pretty, all the plates standing on end in a row across the backs of the shelves so every leaf and rose and swirl of gilt upon them could show. She reached over and shut the clear glass doors.

It was too bad not to have a pantry, she thought for the hundredth time. A woman needed a pantry. But Olaf said they didn't have the money to put a pantry on at the end of the kitchen and she would have to get along with this cupboard, for foodstuffs, and pots and pans (these were in the compartment underneath) as well as dishes, until they could have a proper pantry built. Of course, they were lucky to have been able to buy such a high, capacious, glass-doored cupboard as this, second hand, so reasonably, although it cost three dollars to haul it out from Salt Lake. It was nine feet tall, six feet wide, about a foot deep, built of heavy walnut. A pair of glass doors covered the upper shelves, walnut doors concealed the bottom ones. It looked fine, solid and substantial. It did not stand, however, as steady as Linnea could wish, but had a tendency to teeter forward and she thought the next time she housecleaned it and had it emptied out, she would drive a few long nails in the back panel to hold it firm against the wall. But there was time enough for that. On the third shelf above she could glimpse the loaf cake she baked last night after the children were in bed. She frosted it last night, too, with white frosting and sprinkled over it coconut. They would have it for supper tonight.

She wandered out on to the front step and looked again down the road, but Gunilla's wagon was still not in sight. Linnea was awfully anxious to see her sister. Bertha's, Gertrude's and Stellie's sunbonnets, of identical blue check, bobbed among the pussy willows down by the irrigation ditch and she heard their shrill voices. A sudden banging around at the side of the house meant that Rudie was also near by. She strolled out to find him. He was busily hammering a nail into a board with an unhandy stick of kindling, his fat face red with his exertions, his bottom, against his heels, not an inch from the dusty ground.

"You're going to get yourself all dirty," she said, standing and looking down at him, "your clean blouse and your stockings and everything, and I wanted you to look like you just stepped out of a bandbox for Aunt Gunilla. What you making anyway, Rudie?"

The little boy banged another time or two, manfully, and then said, "A wagon."

"My, that's wonderful," Linnea said, "but don't you think maybe you'd better come around and sit on the steps with me for a little while and cool off and you and me will watch for Aunt Gunilla?" Her son came willingly and she took him first to the kitchen to wet and brush his hair for the third time. He stood still while she performed this ceremony, his wide eyes circling the room idly. Looking upwards at the cupboard he saw the rough white corner of the coconut cake and, electrified, gave a shout of pleasure.

"Oh, no, you don't," Linnea said. "That cake's for tonight's supper."

"I want CAKE, Mamma!"

"Tonight," she said, "for supper, after you eat all what's good for you." She stepped back from him. "There," she said, "you look just lovely."

Everything looked lovely—every inch of the house, her children, herself, waiting for Gunilla. The clock said twenty-five to eleven and Gunilla had written that she was certain to be here before noon dinner on Wednesday, with her family, prepared to stay through Linnea's any-day-expected confinement. Taking Rudie by the hand she led him out onto the back porch. There she could sit with him on the vine-shaded steps and watch down the road for Gunilla's wagon. For a minute or two, at least. A three-year-old boy could be expected to sit quietly beside one on a shimmering summer day about as long as a hummingbird would sit quietly, and have a conversation.

"Do you like to live around here, Rudie?" she asked companionably. He nodded, kicking his heels.

"It's a nice farm, ain't it?" she said.

It was so quiet they could hear the clock ticking in the kitchen through the nettinged back door, hear what the high sweet voices said down by the willows, hear the drone of bees, a dog barking over at the Barnes place, the breath of wind in among the morning-glories. It was hot wind. The day was going to be a scorcher. The heat was not something invisible—you could see it dancing over the flat fields planted to timothy and clover, the ditch-banked willow-edged road, the far-off rail-road tracks, the few poplars, the stunted fruit trees, clear over to the hazy foothills. It rolled and fluttered like a veil. Linnea sighed with contentment. Really, the whole Bountiful countryside was beautiful, and a fine place for the children, just as Olaf had said. The satisfying thought of her spotless house, her many preparations for the beloved guests who would arrive any minute, made her smile. There wasn't a pin out of place. She could put the dinner on the table in twenty minutes. What children—except her own, of course—were so agreeable, so little trouble, as Gunilla's? What face was dearer to her across the table, what gentle eyes over the rim of a cup, what laughter to the ear or hand on the arm, than Gunilla's own?

A scream from the willows shattered her complacency. She scrambled up from the step clumsily, reassured by the glimpse she had of the three sunbonnets. At least, none of them was drowning in the shallow water.

"You stay here and don't get dirty," she admonished Rudie who had stood inactivity as long as he could and was now ready to make up for lost time. "I got to go see what they're up to. That sounded like Gertrude's voice." The scream came again, louder, shriller, like the whistle on a steam engine. "I got to go straighten them out." Linnea made her way as fast as she could down through the clover field to the irrigation ditch.

"Yelling like that!" she said angrily, "so they can hear you clear over to the Barnes' place. I never heard anything to beat it. Three little sisters, that their favorite aunt is coming, and instead of playing nice together, acting like a bunch of hoodlums. Now what's got into you?" she demanded.

They stood perfectly still, with willow wands in their hands, waiting for her, Gertrude full of passion yet. Linnea made her eyes as stern as possible, but had a hard time to keep them so, for never, she thought, looking down at them in counterfeit wrath, were there three prettier little faces, or brighter, bigger eyes, or finer mouths or clearer cheeks or hair escaping from checkered sunbonnets more like actual gold, never in striped chambray and black-buttoned high-top shoes were three forms more dainty.

"Now who started all the rumpus?" she asked.

"Bertha did!" Gertrude said, breathing hard.

"I did not!"

"What started all this?" Linnea inquired of Stellie.

"Bertha said she was *all Swedish*," her youngest daughter said obligingly. "And she said I was half Swedish and half Norwegian."

Gertrude made a spluttering sound like a firecracker about to go off. "Now you hush up and wait till you're spoken to," Linnea warned her, "Stellie's talking."

"But she said Gertrude was half Swedish and half Norwegian and half Danish," Stellie went on.

"Half *Danish*," Gertrude panted.

"Well, you ain't," Linnea said, trying hard not to smile, "you're every last one of you half Swedish and half Norwegian."

"Bertha, too," Stellie said, sliding over closer to her furiously angry sister. "She ain't any better than we are. See, Gertrude? Mamma says so."

"Bertha, too, of course. You all got the same mother and father. You're all just as like as peas in a pod. What do you want to go and make up something like that and cause a lot of trouble for?" Linnea asked her eldest child. "A great big girl nearly ten years old that ought to know better?"

Bertha had the grace to blush. "I thought I was all Swedish," she said, "because I'm the oldest."

"Half *Danish*," Gertrude muttered between her clunched teeth. "She said I was half—"

"Now hush up," Linnea said, and burst out laughing. "If you was, it wouldn't be any terrible hardship. Such notions! Here I was thinking I had such nice little girls and now I'm beginning to believe I got a bunch of rumdums on my hands!"

Stellie laughed, too, and Bertha joined in, embarrassedly, but it was harder for Gertrude to unbend in her stiff indignation like a suit of armor. Finally she did, though, at the sight of Mamma's merry face, and it cracked and fell away and she laughed, too, but she gave Bertha at least one more dirty look that was meant to flatten her out dead on the ground before she did.

"Now then," their mother said, "let's all go up to the house and sit down on the steps and wait for Aunt Gunilla, shall we?"

"Oh, look at the dust!" Stellie suddenly shouted. "I bet they're coming now!" There was a cloud of dust, and a wagon full of bobbing heads like a load of pumpkins and the old fat brown horse that stepped along like a girl in her teens, and it was Aunt Gunilla, right on schedule, coming down the road. The three little girls began to bound with joy.

"Come on, come on," Linnea said happily, "let's go down to the road and meet them where they turn in!" Grabbing Stellie by the hand she set off swiftly through the willows along the ditch, Bertha and Gertrude, whose heart had softened so amazingly in the last moments that she actually rubbed shoulders with her sister, following behind. Linnea turned once to glance back up at the house, but Rudie was of course all right, he would be banging away at his board again.

It was seven weeks since Linnea and her sister had met, too long, too long. She felt the tears of gladness rush to her eyes. She hurried and they all hurried, with little peals of laughter and excited talk, the children not walking, but hopping and skipping like so many jumping jacks.

And here were the big dusty wheels of the wagon rolling to a stop and here was the dear old brown horse with his dusty hide patterned by cowlicks and shining with sweat, with that area as big as a barn around him full of his captivating smell, snorting and slobbering and stomping his feet like he could have gone twice as far, twice as fast, and was willing to prove it anytime in the best of good humor. And here was the buggy whip stuck in its holder that Aunt Gunilla never used, and here were the loved the rosy the laughing loving family faces—Aunt Gunilla's, Hilma's, Thurval's, Oscar's, Bernice's, whose baby's face had changed in seven weeks from a baby's to a very little girl's, Alfred's, that Gertrude sought of them all as Joseph sought the Golden Plates and found and smiled at (but did not kiss). . . .

And some of the children on the wagon rolled off and started hopping and skipping on the ground, and Gertrude clambered on, and Stellie clambered on, and the two mothers, the sisters, shouted and threw kisses at each other and wiped away tears, and Gertrude grabbed the baby and kissed her and for a minute the baby was startled, did not know her cousin, considered puckering up her lip and crying, but then she remembered and smacked Gertrude back with a resounding kiss and Gertrude nearly died laughing. . . .

Somehow or other they got turned in at the gate and the horse went up the short roadway to the house as fresh as a daisy and all their laughing and talking made them sound like a bunch of raggle-taggle gypsies O, and here they were in the back yard. Then, such kissing and hugging! And hopping and skipping! And going around in circles!

Aunt Gunilla started handing things out of the wagon—hampers, boxes, buckets, baskets, with canned fruit, and eggs, and jam, and a five-gallon can of honey, and a dishpanful of *skorpa* and pies in their tins tied up in snow-white dish towels . . . and Mamma said, "You must be clear out of your head bringing all this stuff!" kissing her sister, and crying and laughing, "you'd think I couldn't feed a flea!"

Aunt Gunilla said, "I had the stuff on hand. It would just of gone to waste!"

Mamma had the baby in her arms, squeezing her.

"But how are you, Linnea? How are you? I ain't thought to ask. Are you fine?" Gunilla said.

"You ask me if I'm fine! I never was better in my life!" Linnea said.

"You're sure big enough—big as a house," her sister said admiringly. "I never saw anything to beat it."

Everybody picked up something and carried it though both the mothers had to shout for Hilma and Bertha who were disappearing hand in hand around the house. "Where do you think *you're* going?" they said.

"I got everything fixed," Linnea announced at the back door. "I can have dinner on the table in twenty minutes."

They were all there, all crowded around her. They all saw it happen. There wasn't one but watched it through the white mosquito netting of the locked screen door and stared in horror and couldn't move a muscle, until Linnea could, the instant after it was too late—the way mothers think lightning-like and can—and bolted through the thin material of the door when the crash came like Babel falling, like Nauvoo falling, like the house falling down. It was not she who screamed, it was Gunilla and all the others, amid the fiendish noises of the horrifying demolition. Gunilla caught sight of him first and made the frenzied sound that turned them all to stone, that half-instant before Linnea got through the door. . . . Rudie, up in the cupboard after the cake (Linnea knew what he was after), hanging like a monkey to the edge of the third shelf, his feet on the edge of the first one, the glass doors flung wide, the chair he had climbed from directly beneath him, all the cups on all the hooks dangling shrilly like a flock of little birds under the hawk or over the hunter, all the upright plates weaving, wavering, like sinners on the last big day of retribution, all the bowls and lids and pitchers quivering and hopping in the agony of waiting, and the too narrow, too tall, heavy cupboard coming forward in an awful avalanche so slow you would have time to grow old and die and rot in your grave before it pitched over. Linnea bolted through, she would have caught it and held it off her boy if it had weighed ten thousand pounds, but it had crashed, was fallen, was come down in ruins—every cup, every plate, every dish, the pots and pans underneath rolling out, in inexpressible din . . . shatter, bang, crash, crash, splinter, bang. And the ear-splitting screech from the buried child shooting up like a rocket, exploding in mid-air, Mamma, MAMMA. . . .

"Keep them all out," Linnea said fiercely. "Gunilla. My God, my God."

They stayed out, the children, twittering with fright, Hilma holding baby Bernice so tight she yelled in rage. "Rudie pulled the cupboard down on top of him." "Rudie's smashed under the cupboard." "The cupboard fell on Rudie." "Is Rudie dead?" And Gertrude beat on the door with both her fists and didn't seem to have sense enough to walk through the rent netting and driveled no, no, no, no. But Gunilla was right behind Linnea saying God help us, God save us. There was no room for anyone else in the room, in the ruins. No boy, no finger, no shirttail, no capped toe, no yellow curl showed under the done-in cupboard.

"Wait, wait," Gunilla said, but she had a basket of eggs and did not know where to set them down. "Wait, it's too heavy—you'll kill yourself." And set them down in the corner and hastened with crunching steps through the splintered china to help her ashen sister lift the weighty piece off the child. When exposed to view he lay like a marble boy of wry shape that Linnea tenderly felt of and lifted, crying, and held, murmuring, and carried across the wreckage and laid upon the bed in the other room. . . .

The children all crowded into the kitchen with their frightened twitter and panic eyes and Gunilla drove them out again and they clustered like bees outside around the doorway buzzing. She ran into the room where Rudie lay upon the bed, in frigid insensibility, with an awful trickle of jewel-red blood dribbling out the corner of his ivory mouth, with Linnea still feeling of him, and saw he was breathing. . . . "Thank God, he's breathing," Gunilla said. And Linnea motioned her away like an empress bigger than life-size. She went back in the kitchen and went to the door and said, "Now you kids set whatever you was carrying on the back porch here or on the steps, and Hilma, you hang onto Bernice, and all you kids go on out and—unhitch the horse and water her and give her some hay. I'll call you just as soon as we know what's what."

Gertrude said, "Oh, Rudie ain't *dead*, is he, Aunt Gunilla?" clasping her hands. "He's the—the baby of the family," as though this would absolve him from any thing, even Death. She was crying and sweating and had bubbles of saliva on her lips.

"Of course he ain't dead," Gunilla said matter-of-factly. "He's just shook up a little, is all. Now you go play. All you kids go play. And I'll call you." She wiped the beads of perspiration off her face with the pretty handkerchief pinned to her blouse. It was hotter than fury, her clothes had a wet plastered feeling, especially her close corset, and she thought, Rudie certainly picked a day for it. She went back through the devastated kitchen with soft steps through the broken china and back to the bedroom.

Linnea was sitting beside her child now, holding his head. "I've felt every inch of him," she said. "I don't think there's no bones broken. I could move his legs and arms and everything." She had got a dish towel and wet it and was passing an end of it over his face. "His color's coming back now. He just got knocked out."

Gunilla looked at him fearfully. "But the blood coming out the corner of his mouth. I thought maybe . . ." she could not go on.

"He just bit himself or got cut on a piece of china. See, here's the place." With a look very like pride Linnea pulled his lower lip down and showed Gunilla the little gash inside.

"Of all the things," Gunilla said, and sat down weakly on the foot of the bed.

Linnea's face was still very pale, but she laughed, patting Rudie's temples with the corner of the towel. "Imagine," she said, "pulling that big cupboard down on top of him. Such a naughty boy. Such a naughty, naughty boy. Up there after that coconut cake. Why, he's never done such a thing before in his life."

The child opened his eyes hazily, his pupils overly large. "Mamma," he whimpered.

"There, there," she said. "Mamma's right here. You just lay still and everything's going to be all right. . . ."

Back in the kitchen Gunilla, with the broom, inspected the damage. It was staggering. She and Linnea with the mighty heave that freed the tumbled boy had brought the cupboard upright and set it once more against the wall. Both the panes of glass in the doors were broken and one frame hung crookedly on a single hinge. The kitchen chair Rudie had climbed upon was splintered but it still had its four legs and it was this, rolled on its side, that kept the heavy cabinet from "smashing him," as Gunilla said wonderingly, "flatter than a pancake." Only three cups of all the china cups Linnea had held so dear, two plates of all the plates, one platter and a cream pitcher were left intact. The cake was a sight to behold and Gunilla swept its mauled frosting, far-flung coconut and crumbled insides up with the rest of the damage.

Linnea came and stood in the doorway and watched her, with one eye—the other never left her now-reviving son on the bed—while she cleaned up.

"Your poor china," Gunilla said pityingly. "All your pretty china you always been so careful of."

"That don't matter a bit," Linnea said in a cheerful tone. "I can always buy *china*."

"Of course you can," Gunilla said, who somewhat doubted it, packing out a second big kettleful to dump back of the barn. "And you couldn't buy another *boy*." But her heart felt heavy when she poured the shards out on the cinder pile . . . the sugar bowl, the fluted red jam dish with the gold edges, that came from Sweden, were Grandma's, were maybe a hundred years old . . . these hurt to look at, like personalities of importance gone all to pieces. Linnea took such pride in her dishes though she wasn't stingy about using them. Nobody had ever been asked to eat or drink in Linnea's house without having the best ware she owned set before him, even if it was nobody but an old fishmonger, and the way she always set them up so pretty and swung the cups on hooks, and packed them overconscientiously, so that never a thing had been even so much as cracked when she was going to move, anybody could see she was just dead set on them. The oval bowl, in twenty parts on the refuse heap, that had been Mamma's, painted with pea vines in blossom all around the edge, one of the presents from Mamma's own wedding . . . the loss of this alone was something disproportionately hard to bear. Linnea would feel it for a long time. The more Gunilla swept up and carried out, in tinkling oddments, the sadder she became, until the tears actually ran down her face and she had to wipe them away and blow her nose hard before she could go back in the house. Behind her, when she went up the stairs, she could hear the wondering ohs and ahs of the children, gathering at the pile and fingering with little clinking noises the bits of broken glass. "Don't a one of you kids cut yourself," she called back crossly in a way very unlike her usual tender self, "or you're going to get a blame good licking. The first one that cuts theirself."

Rudie, except for a noticeable pallor, was none the worse for the havoc he had wrought, but shamefaced, and sat on his mother's lap (what her pregnancy had left of it) with the shyest of downcast looks.

"Now I know just as well as I know I'm sitting here," Linnea said to Gunilla, who was wiping up the sticky floor where the frosting had lain with a wet scrubrag, "that Rudie never any more intended to gouge out a piece of that cake, and steal it, any more than he meant to fly to the moon. All he meant to do was climb up there and pick off a little corner of frosting and some of the coconut and sample it. He *never* meant to tear the house down and do all that damage. Did you, Rudie?"

He cried softly and buried his face in the folds of her dress. She put her arms tighter around him and held him closer. "You'll never do nothing like that no more, will you, Rudie?" He shook his head wretchedly. She kissed the back of his ear.

"This here's all that I guess is going to be worth saving," Gunilla said, with a sigh, pointing to the little stack of china on the table. "Everything else was busted."

Linnea did not even wince. "And cheap at the price," she said. "I had more'n what I knowed what to do with anyway. . . ."

That is how it happened it was nearer two than twelve that the sisters and their children sat down to eat. But Rudie was all right, and except for the vanished coconut cake, all the other good things Linnea had prepared were there to be eaten. In a memorable way, too, for there were not enough dishes to go round or begin to go round and so the children had to eat like what Gunilla called "starving heathens," each armed with a spoon, all out of one bowl, or out of two bowls, or out of a tin piepan or some other strange dish. But it was like a holiday or a picnic, for Rudie was not dead, and everybody loved everybody else with all their might, and each person would rather be there than with the King of Sweden.

Linnea said ruefully that maybe it had served her right. She had maybe been a little too cocky over the way she had her house all dolled up for Gunilla and everything all fixed to run as smooth as clockwork, and she just needed to be took down a notch. And Gunilla said she better hush talking like that. Why, the house looked just beautiful—anybody could see without half looking how hard Linnea had worked, and if there was anybody in this God's world that *didn't* need to be took down a notch it was her.

The children drifted outside into the blazing afternoon but without much noise and lazily, for they were as full as ticks, and Rudie, grown sleepy, was put to bed for a nap beside Bernice who already slept there in dewy innocence, and then was the time for Linnea to heat up the coffee again and share with her sister a second cozy cup with elbows on the littered table and hands cupped under the chin. They were much alike, these two women, with identical eyes and teeth of the same shape, but Gunilla was somewhat smaller and three years younger. They had never had a disagreement.

"I tell you something," Gunilla said, "when that cupboard fell down on Rudie I thought I was going to have heart failure."

"Me, too," Linnea said.

"But you was as cool as a cucumber."

"I didn't feel cool."

"It's the biggest wonder in the world you didn't keel over in a dead faint, in your condition and all. It's the biggest wonder in the world it didn't start your pains. That's all *I* can say."

"Why, I—" Linnea said, and her face looked suddenly startled, "I never been the—the fainting—" and with that her face looked still more startled for what seemed a very long time and her head dropped down between her arms on the table, her heavy body sagged and rolled sideways. Gunilla got to her instantly but too late to save one of the three remaining cups and saucers that her spasmodic movement sent crashing to the floor. "If that ain't *hell,*" Gunilla said with a profanity unusual for her and rushed for the water bucket. "We won't have a dish left to bless ourselves with."

It proved not difficult to restore Linnea and the first thing she did when she opened her eyes and shook back her dripping hair (Gunilla had given her a good sousing) was to laugh and say well, if that didn't beat the Dutch. If she hadn't gone and fainted just as sure as God made little apples. And the first time, too. Out like a light, she said. Imagine. Gunilla ran for the broom and swept up the broken cup and saucer—"I'm thinking strong of going into the business," Gunilla said, and they laughed like a couple of loons. Linnea described in the most minute details how it felt to swoon, and they marveled over the extraordinary sensations.

They got up to do the dishes and that very instant Linnea's pains started and she gasped, "Well, I guess this is what I been waiting for," and lay down a little while on the lounge by the stove. But then she got up and started the first mile of the miles she would pace before the next dawning came and she had her eleven-pound boy.

Gunilla, all alone, was busier that hot July day, the hottest day of the year, than a cranberry merchant, but she came through with flying colors. She had nine children from the ages of eleven to one to watch over, feed when suppertime came, inspect the feet of when bedtime arrived—for no child was ever allowed to go to bed with dirty feet and the boys, at least, who had gone barefooted, had to scrub their feet in the little green foot tub before they could retire. Not only that, she had to make a paste of soda and water to daub this upon the innumerable bumpy mosquito bites with the tops scratched off, and blow whoo, whoo, whoo, when the bitten hollered about the smarting. She had prayers to listen to, admonishments to speak, about noise and disturbances, threats to deliver, kisses to bestow. . . . Later, when they were asleep, she had the supper things to clean up—before that, the dinner things—and kindling to cut, and coal to bring in, for Alfred and Thurval had not brought enough, and water to heat and keep boiling, coffee to make and drink with Linnea, and comfort to give and tenderness. . . . All through the long hours she kept up a steady easy soothing chatter composed of gossip, reminiscence both humorous and sad, sanguine forecasts of things to come, and whatever was just too good for words . . . it made the time go faster.

"You done the same thing for me, over and over," Gunilla said when Linnea was sorry it was such a job, *such a job,* "and more, too, and I'd be a fine sister if I didn't at least try to take a hold around here and do a little something."

Rudie and Bernice slept in the bedroom where Linnea was soon to be brought down to the second bed in the last gale of her pains like a bough brought down under goose-egg hail, but the other seven children, on the lounge and a cot, slept with amazing peacefulness in the lamplit kitchen. It was not an ugly place, but big, clean and comfortably dim, with a cool night wind blowing off the green fields through the mended screen door and out the open window—so cool a wind in spite of the day's heat that the crackling fire in the stove felt good and Linnea wore a shawl around her shoulders over her nightgown when she walked softly up and down. They talked . . . and the little sleepers never stirred under their quiet voices, but only slept better, and safer, and deeper, and sounder, except when they roused by one and one to use the pot but then they scarcely wakened. They did what they had to do with shut eyes and fell back to bed like logs and did not even ask what Mamma and Aunt Gunilla, Mamma and Aunt Linnea were doing up so late at night. . . .

The women went over more times than one the fall of the cupboard and Rudie's miraculous escape, but Linnea never looked at the battered piece sadly or had a grieving word to say about the loss of the well-beloved dishes. "It just goes to show," she said, "what matters and what don't matter. Yesterday, if I had of broke a one of them cups and saucers, I would of sat right down and bawled my eyes out—to say nothing of the red glass bowl—but today, with Rudie all in one piece, that might of been laying dead—he *could* of been laying dead—I kind of got my eyes open as to what means something and what don't."

"Me, I was kind of heartsick for a while there," Gunilla said meditatively, "I might as well tell you."

"Me, I wasn't," Linnea said with a staunch smile. "Never for a minute. What's a old cup and saucer anyway?" (Full of tradition? History? Hanging on a hook? Thin enough to see through? Only a thing of beauty. Only a joy forever.) "What's a cup?" she repeated. "What's a old cup?" Regret she would not name or recognize, but in her heart it turned and twisted like a thin blade. . . .

CHAPTER 13

⟫⟫ ⟪⟪

AUNT GUNILLA said the new baby they were half delirious about was brought in the night by the stork. Not a child in the house but believed it without a shadow of a doubt. Bertha and Hilma said at first, while they were eating their breakfast in a kind of Christmas-morning flutter, that they wished they had seen him, the stork, that's what *they* wished. They would have picked out a girl, because girl babies were cuter than boy babies. Gertrude disagreed shrilly. No baby could be cuter than this one, she said. He was an armful certainly—Gunilla estimated his weight at over ten pounds though she had no scales—with a tranquil face, indolent eyelashes and a round head fuzzed like a peach with a nap of satiny white hair. Linnea said his name was Parley. She had given up all thought of Cyril. For some reason, that day, she was sick in bed in the bedroom with the blinds pulled part way down, and Aunt Gunilla carried the new baby in to her and laid him, to keep her company, on her arm. This was where the children saw him, tiptoeing in, one after one, with almost scared eyes, to see the miracle.

"Well, what do you think of him?" Linnea asked each one, smiling an inward-turned smile.

They all answered in various ways, as children will, sometimes with a question. "What makes him so red?" "Why don't he open his eyes?" "When can he run around?"

"He don't know *me*," Stellie stated wonderingly.

"No, but he will," Linnea promised.

"Why are babies always so little?" Gertrude inquired with great interest.

"He ain't little. You'd ought to see a *little* baby sometime!"

"He looks little, though, Mamma, honestly he does. Why are they so little?"

"Because they're babies, of course. What a silly question. If they was big, they wouldn't be babies."

"Do we get to keep him?"

"Sure, we do."

"We're lucky, that's all, huh, Mamma?"

Linnea smiled. "I'll say we're lucky," she said. "Anybody that says we ain't, don't know what they're talking about."

Even Papa arrived at noon, by a great coincidence. He didn't know about Rudie pulling the cupboard down on top of him, or the new baby, or anything. He had to be enlightened by every member of the family. He was terribly surprised. He was just in time for dinner.

It was a day like a holiday, full of activity, fun, food and surprises, and memorable to Gertrude for another reason also: it was the first day in her life she knew how it would feel to hate Papa. That morning, with the morning-glories to watch in the company of Alfred, *skorpa* to dip for breakfast, jobs to perform for Aunt Gunilla, such as buttoning and unbuttoning the smallest children and lugging in water from the well, playing, talking about the new baby, was full to overflowing. It was not until Papa had arrived and had his dinner and was sitting in the rocking chair by Mamma in his shirtsleeves, that Gertrude was smote as by lightning with the grand idea. She must go to the Barnes', to the Taylors', to the Myers', across the fields and down the road to the Crossroads, even, to the three cottages there, to spread the glad tidings. At each door she would knock and say WE GOT A NEW BABY AT OUR HOUSE. Alfred could go along. Out of breath with excitement at the very thought—why she hadn't done it before breakfast she couldn't imagine—she rushed past protesting Aunt Gunilla who said, "Don't go in the bedroom, Gertrude. Your Mamma and Papa wants to have a little visit together without you kids running in and out," and straight up to Mamma's bed. "Mamma," she said. "Mamma, can me and Alfred go and tell everybody about the baby?"

"What do you mean everybody?" Mamma asked.

"Oh, you know," she said impatiently. "Flossie's mamma, and that new girl name Beulah's mamma, and Mr. Taylor, and down at the Crossroads, and all over. Everybody!" She danced from one foot to the other.

"Did you help Aunt Gunilla all you could?"

"Oh, yes, Mamma!"

"Well, I don't see why not then," Mamma said.

"What's she want to do?" Papa asked, who had been thinking of something else and mopping the sweat off his forehead, for today was another scorcher.

"Tell people!" Gertrude said.

"Go around and tell people about the new baby," Mamma explained.

"You just go on outside and play," Papa said, "play around in the yard here. You got no business traipsing around the neighborhood bothering people with something that ain't no affair of theirs."

Gertrude turned horrified eyes upon Mamma, eyes filled full of instant tears, and was speechless, with lips that puckered at the corners. And for the first time she knew how it felt to hate Papa. It felt sickening, like being butted in the stomach by a goat, it weighed heavy, it was hot as a fire in the stove, then it got cold, ice-cold, under her ribs.

"Play around the yard here," Papa repeated. "That's the place for kids. You don't need to go running around the neighborhood."

There was a dead silence, so that they could hear the clock tick. Mamma got a funny look on her face. "And what, may I ask, do you mean by talk like that?" she said.

Papa would not look in her eyes but a little to the side of them. "Well, you know," he said. "All this trouble—they're checking up all the time —the government agents—I got to do enough sneaking as it is—they arrested Monteith—they're always arresting somebody—there ain't no sense in *advertising* a new baby. You know that, yourself."

"Gertrude, you run on outside and play," Mamma ordered. "I'll call you back pretty soon. You run on outside like a good girl." Gertrude went, with a glittering look at Papa that was meant to stretch him out dead on the floor.

Linnea raised up on one elbow and settled herself, pulling the baby in close to her breast. "What am I?" she said softly. "Your no-good woman or your wife? Whether I was out of my head enough to bury myself out here in the country and leave Sigrid a clear field and free sailing or not. What am I?"

"What do you mean, what are you?" Olaf said, uneasily. "My wife, of course."

"Do I come out to a community and hide and shut myself away like a no-good woman that some man's keeping, or do I make friends with my neighbors and hold my head up amongst them and act like a honest woman with a husband to back her up or don't I?"

"You act like a honest woman," Olaf said. "You *are* a honest woman. I didn't mean no—I just meant—"

"My baby comes along," Linnea went on icily. "I've made friends with my neighbors. I been here two months. What kind a woman would I be not to make friends with my neighbors in two months? Am I Miss Friddle with forty-seven cats? We call on each other, we like each other, the way the Lord meant. Are they blind, that they don't know I got a baby coming? Is there one amongst them that would tell the authorities and get you took up again for polygamy? So how do I act? Do I hush up my mouth like the baby was a nameless nothing or do I show my new baby off proud like any mother shows off her baby proud, saying this here's Parley, my baby, he weighs over ten pounds and looks like his father?"

"Oh, Linnea," Olaf said, "I didn't mean nothing like—"

"Gertrude comes," Linnea went on, "half out of her mind she's so glad about her new little brother, and wants to tell the neighbors, her eyes shining, so tickled she can't hardly stand it. Can I go tell everybody, she says. What else would she say? And what does her papa sit there and do? You mind your own business, he says. You shut up about this baby. Never tell a soul, he says. This baby's a nameless nothing and your mother's a no-good woman that lives with a man that ain't married to her. I ain't got but one family, he says, and that's Sigrid's family, and I ain't got but one wife, he says, and that's Sigrid, living in a nice house in town and lording it over everybody—" her voice broke and she began to cry.

Olaf was down on his knees beside the bed, trying to put his arms around her, trying to kiss her, trying to wipe away her tears. "Sweetheart, sweetheart," he begged, "I just said—I never meant nothing like that—"

"Oh, no," she said, "I guess not, I just guess you didn't. . . ."

It was perhaps half an hour later that Aunt Gunilla called Gertrude and told her her mother wanted her in the bedroom. She went in and Mamma, smiling, with pink cheeks and eyes as blue as azurite, half sitting up, sipping coffee from a cup, said, "You and Alfred can go now, if you want, and tell the neighbors about the baby."

Gertrude pointedly ignored Papa. "Can we go down to the Crossroads, too?" she asked.

"Well, it's pretty hot today," Mamma said, "and that's pretty far, but if you want to, you can."

Her daughter kissed her good-bye, and was kissed in return. Then she started for the door.

"Don't Papa get no kiss?" Mamma asked.

Gertrude glanced at her father who was smiling and looking tender and sorry. "No," she said.

"Why not?" Papa said.

"Because I—because you—because—" She fumbled with the doorknob. The hatred, that had had time to freeze solid, was breaking up now, breaking off in chunks under his sorry look, floating, melting away. . . . This was the day of that, the first she had ever felt for him. It was a memorable day, the birthday of Parley's life, the day she thought: I hate Papa, I wish he was dead. It was also the day for something else, wonderful, but that came later.

She did not hate Papa now, with that tender sorry face. She ran to his open arms and he gathered her in and gave her a big kiss and she gave him a big kiss back, thinking how his mustache scratched like a bramble, thinking how his lips under it were slick and cool as patent leather.

"You go on," he said, squeezing her shoulders. "Spread the good news.

Tell the neighbors we got a new baby here at our house that'll knock their eyes out."

She did, Alfred with her, on winged feet.

That early evening, after supper, the wonderful thing happened. The two Mrs. Barneses had been to call in the afternoon—they came right away after Gertrude was there to make her announcement—under a black cotton umbrella, with clean aprons on, bringing a milk bucket full of soup and two pies. It was all they had on hand, they said. Tomorrow they would do better. They said they never saw a prettier new-born baby. They had seen plenty, they said, but they never saw a new-born baby to equal Parley. Mr. Taylor brought a dishpanful of fresh-picked strawberries. He said the baby looked like a baby that was going to grow up and make them all sit up and take notice. He said his wife would come to call tomorrow and stood ready and willing to do anything she could, to lend a hand, if a hand was wanted.

Linnea never said anything but she kept glancing at Olaf while they were there with a beaming look, and he smiled at her whenever he noticed. Nobody could have shook hands nicer, or talked nicer, or acted nicer, than Olaf, she said later to Gunilla. He just needed to be sat down on, that's all. Every man needed to be sat down on once in awhile.

From the Crossroads, the widow woman Mrs. Olander and her daughter sent by one of the section hands who had to pass that way, a freshly laundered crocheted bonnet and sweater, used but with a lot of wear in them still, a loaf of bread just out of the oven and congratulations. She said she would try to visit the mother and baby tomorrow, if her dizziness passed over. The stonecutter sent congratulations, too.

But in the evening! Who should come driving into the yard in his spring wagon behind his trim mare but Mr. Myers, and what should he unload but a barrel and two boxes, and what should be in them— when Olaf, his face red with embarrassment, had helped to carry them into the kitchen—but just the thing they needed worse than anything else in God's green earth—and that was DISHES.

Yesterday, after the children were there, Mr. Myers said, and Gertrude told his girls and their mother about the cupboard falling down on top of the boy and all the dishes being broken like that, smashed all to pieces, and they only had three cups left—they were going to get a set tomorrow, Linnea put in hastily, it was just for these couple of days that it was hard to get along—why, they all got to poking around in the cupboards and pantry and up in the attic and here and there, and they resurrected this little bunch of dishes, he said, and if Mrs. Ecklund could use them, why, here they were, and she'd be doing them a favor—they just took up room and should of been carted out long ago.

Gunilla took them out one by one from their careful paper wrappings, and exclaimed so much—the children, or Olaf, had to run back and forth

to the bedroom to show Linnea who looked feverish with excitement in
the last red rays of the sun—that she grew quite hoarse. It was no
wonder! Part of the dishes matched each other and belonged to the same
set, but most of them were one of a kind or two of a kind—of nice china,
some, of pottery, some, but all beautiful, as dishes used to be, cups,
saucers, plates both big and small, platters, glasses, a water pitcher, even
a yellow mixing bowl.

After Mr. Myers went home loaded down with thanks, the giddy
children, their aunt and mother no less light-headed, had to try them
out, and this one had pie, that soup, the other some leftover hash on the
novel crockery, exactly like a party. Then, while Aunt Gunilla washed
them all up, and Bertha and Hilma dried them, Papa nailed the cupboard tight to the wall with long nails so it could never fall forward
again, and took the broken doors off. Aunt Gunilla, knowing so well
her sister's ways and having them herself, arranged the open shelves in
the old way . . . plates standing upright in the back, all the cups on
hooks . . . and the whole family admired it and said it looked almost as
good as it used to.

Her husband could have a breathing spell, Linnea told him, before
he needed to get a new set of dishes. Not that she was going to get along
forever with these. She'd catch Sigrid not having a set of dishes to her
name. But maybe for a month or two he could have a breathing spell.

He was glad of it. He was more than glad. But he said bravely that if
she wanted her set of dishes, she could have them tomorrow.

The summer lasted a long long time in Bountiful, like an epopoeia,
full of the morning-glories, Kelly-green grass, the pale poplars and paler
willows, skies too blue, too pink, like a blue-eyed Norwegian woman in
a pink dress.

Visitors came for a day or a week at a time to the Ecklunds, among
them Ingeborg with her children, all of them the picture of health. Jensen's new grave was beginning to be really lost now, not just hard to
locate. It grew harder and harder to find down in the cemetery's hollow,
and Ingeborg's skin troubles were all cleared up. She and her brood
flourished. Linnea thought her boy Chucken too wide across the behind
for a boy, with a face too much like what she called in Swedish a "doll's
backside," but otherwise they were a fine family and she loved Ingeborg
as of old.

Parley doubled in bulk like a batch of bread, a handsome baby with
the disposition of an angel. Rudie, after the cupboard fell on him, developed a little limp that stayed. He didn't set his left foot down as he
used to, but he said it didn't hurt him. Linnea felt of his foot over and
over and couldn't feel anything, only he didn't run very fast. He never
ran very fast again, but perhaps he wouldn't have anyway.

Olaf came often, almost every Saturday, staying over Sunday. Linnea, constantly improving her small house by work and imagination (she never had had less money), caring for her family or taking part in what social life, small as it was, the community had to offer, was quite contented with life in the country. But she was homesick for Salt Lake, too, for she hadn't managed to get in even for a day's shopping. She thought of it often, its cement sidewalks, big bustling stores, street lights with the moths pelting round them, the park, the mansions, the stylish ladies, the linden trees on Brigham Street, Temple Square, the streetcars . . . She told Ingeborg she never could get used to the frogs croaking at night. If anything gave a person a God-forsaken feeling it was frogs croaking, and the echoes. The children would stand in the yard at twilight and holler hello or come play with me and this echo would come eerily from miles away, like voices from the departed. And when the moon wasn't shining it was as black as pitch outside. You could stand in the doorway and look out and there wouldn't be a light for miles, just solid blackness.

The summer lasted a long long time, like verse after verse of a ballad, but when it ended, it ended like a man falling dead in the street of heart trouble. One night, all in one night, severe winter came, a white horse of snow rolling over Bountiful, snorting and rolling in its meadows, its fields. The proud trees were brought to their knees with ice and it came to the onlooker how yielding, what easy marks they had been all the time, if anybody had known. The roads got sluggish. Winter came, and stayed.

Visitors, then, from town, were few and far between. Even Olaf seemed neglectful, arriving on the little train only once maybe in two weeks, but he caught a bad chest cold, Sigrid was sick for awhile, and occasionally the roads were impassable. Also, Hattie, Olaf's and Sigrid's daughter, had such a bad gathered ear that they thought for awhile she was going to die, and what with one thing and another he could not come as often, nor nearly as often, as before. Linnea understood this and it was herself who begged him not to make the trip out if the weather was too bad or if he didn't feel just right or something was wrong with his other family. But she always felt hurt, and lonely, and abandoned, when he didn't, even though it was at her urging, as a woman will.

At first, when he brought Mrs. Sterling and her two small children Estelle and Johnny, out to stay with her, she was mad enough to shoot him, but she didn't say so in front of the woman and only in a restrained voice to him alone in the bedroom. However, in no time she took a great liking to her, and more than once during the blue moon of bleak season that followed, she blessed Olaf for bringing to her such pleasant company, able household help and satisfying companionship.

Mrs. Sterling came from Ogden. Her husband, serving a mission to spread the Gospel of Jesus Christ of Latter-Day Saints in Norway, had been gone three quarters of the two years required of him by the Mormon church. At first, Mrs. Sterling was contented to stay at home in the small house they owned and look after her boy and girl, but as time went on and money grew scarce, she became bored and uneasy. An expert tailoress before her marriage, she decided to go back to work, rented out her house and took her children to Salt Lake City. Olaf gave her a job and she and her family took two rooms in a private dwelling. All would have been well had she not, innocently, become involved in a very vexing situation that was for a while a dangerous one as well.

Sigrid, who hated her for what she termed her bald-faced gall (Mrs. Sterling had a way of throwing back her head and showing all her teeth when she laughed, breaking out with little trills of song and doing audacious things such as putting her foot up on a chair and tieing her shoelace, right in the shop), could never believe there was any innocence about it. No, sir, Sigrid said. Mrs. Sterling *meant* to get poor Brother Bell in that mess and herself threatened so that she had to leave town. A *lady* wouldn't be caught acting like that. It was the biggest wonder in the world she hadn't got her glommers on Olaf, and the truth was, Sigrid said, she probably had, or he wouldn't have hired her in the first place.

Linnea, when she heard about it, said it could have happened to anybody. Everybody knew how woman-wild that old Brother Bell was, as silly as silly could be, even if he *was* a banker and had more property than he knew what to do with, and was a pillar of the church. It wasn't for not coveting them that he didn't have more wives than Brigham Young and Heber C. Kimball put together, to say nothing of lady friends. It was his stinginess that prevented him, and that mean wife of his, and those mean children. Brother Bell's two boys looked just like girls, the girl looked like a boy, and not a one of them was married yet though the youngest was going on for thirty. Neither busybody Mrs. Bell nor the busybody family had never been known to do a tap of honest work, except to spend almost all their waking hours seeing that the Church did not collapse because of any misdoings in Choir practice, Conference, Relief Society or Mutual, and that everything was done according to the strict word of the Prophet.

Who didn't know how Brother Bell pawed this woman and that woman, and sashayed around in those skin-tight pants and wore a wig and waxed his mustache although he was way past sixty, until it was a perfect scandal? The thing was, Olaf should have told Mrs. Sterling what an old woman-chaser Brother Bell was, and then, when he came up to the shop about his suits and tried them on and was fitted, Mrs.

Sterling could have sat in her corner doing her work perfectly quiet and he maybe wouldn't have got his eye on her. The smiles and singing and laughing, the cocking the head on one side, the gay friendliness, the miniature hourglass shape, had fatally attracted Brother Bell, there was no doubt of it. But then! maybe all she had to do was sit there and be a member of the opposite sex, nothing else, though as still as a mouse and with her eyes riveted on her work, to set him going, Brother Bell being what he was.

Linnea did not dislike Mrs. Sterling when she was introduced to her in Olaf's shop. She thought her likable and recognized in the woman another of her own kind, easygoing, well-intentioned, warmhearted. Her prettiness was not of a sort to cause unrest, for she was small, and dark, with gleaming black eyes, one veering a little to one side, a light olive skin and black hair. To Linnea, as there was only one Church, there was only one kind of female beauty: the silver, jonquil or topaz blonde, tinted with pastels on a white ground, eyed with viridescence or azure, a little over life-size. Any other comeliness was not quite authentic, certainly nothing to get nervous over. She would have thought so, she felt, even if she herself had not belonged to this category and had been dainty and dark as a gypsy, but of course there was no way of proving this. Sigrid, in blonde perfection, was as big a threat as she ever hoped to encounter, and Mrs. Sterling, as different from Sigrid and Linnea's self as night from day, could be accepted, therefore, without prejudice.

After the first shock, Linnea was pleased that Olaf brought the lady out to Bountiful to stay. Mrs. Sterling could not get back in her Ogden house until early spring when her husband returned from his mission, for it was leased until then. She could not, or thought she could not, after what developed, remain in Salt Lake and continue her job with Olaf. To go out to Bountiful and stay with Linnea seemed the logical thing to do, and proved so. Mrs. Sterling stayed there four months, sharing the expenses, which helped a good deal as times were hard. The women became fast friends, and neither she nor Linnea ever regretted the arrangement.

Olaf said it never entered his head that Brother Bell would take such a fancy as that to Mrs. Sterling. It should have, Linnea said, everybody knew what a chaser he was. Why, it was a perfect disgrace the way he acted. Well, it didn't, Olaf said. Anyway, Mrs. Sterling was sitting there sewing and Brother Bell came in. She looked up and smiled and got to talking to him—not that she lagged any, she didn't neglect her work to sing or talk or laugh, no siree, she kept right on and could sew rings around anybody else he ever had working for him, except poor Jensen—and Brother Bell got to talking to her. And the first thing anybody knew, he was dropping into the shop every day and casting sheep's eyes at the lady and acting like a loon, like a moonstruck calf that didn't know whether he was a-foot or a-horseback. It may be, it *may be*, Olaf said, that Mrs. Sterling could of let up then with her friendliness and joshing, but it just wasn't her way and she didn't any more than a bird will all of a sudden stop acting like a bird and start in acting like a pollywog. Brother Bell got wilder and wilder over Mrs. Sterling. He got so he'd even bring her things—a tightwad like him, imagine—a sack of gumdrops or horehound candy and once he even brought two bits' worth of chocolates, and all kinds of calendars. She said she never thought for an instant, him being old enough to be her father and her happily married, with a husband on a mission—but it ought to have, perhaps— that he would get such a notion as he got, and declare himself desperately in love with her. She said she didn't see how it could hurt anything for him to walk home with her a couple of times and carry her umbrella and lunch basket. She had him in to see Estelle and Johnny. It was as much her fault as his, maybe, but she maintained to Linnea that it wasn't. She said she hadn't meant to lead him on *at all*.

Brother Bell really kicked over the traces for Mrs. Sterling. She never took him seriously, and she used to joke about her conquest, looking up from her pressing at the clock and saying, "Well, it's about time for my handsome young sport to show up," or, biting off a thread, "I wonder where the lady-killer is today," or, "I'm about due for a free calendar and a dime's worth of licorice." Mrs. Sterling was an honest woman then and Brother Bell had been smitten before. He had actually stammered out a proposal, but Mrs. Sterling only laughed and it would probably have all blown over. Somehow or other, however, it got to his wife's ears and to his children's ears, and became no joking matter.

They waited upon Mrs. Sterling in her rooms, the gray-faced wife all in black like a widow at a funeral, the frightening influential family. The two sons looked like a couple of women dressed up in men's clothes, Mrs. Sterling said, with women's faces and awful, soft, white hands, and the daughter looked like one of the Council of Twelve masquerading as a woman with his beard shaved off. It sent shivers down a person's back, Mrs. Sterling said. The daughter was the spokesman. She said they very well knew what was going on right under their very noses, they knew who was making laughingstocks of them all, who was flaunting them. Mrs. Sterling tried to say something but they would not let her. They sort of surrounded her, she said, encircled her, pressed in upon her in a way that made her want to scream for help but she kept mum so as not to frighten the children, and out of shame that such a scene as this could happen to the wife of a man on a mission, who should never have got herself into such a predicament.

Her mother Mrs. Bell had been driven nearly distracted by the situation, the terrifying Bell daughter said. She walked up and down and moaned all night. She could not sleep. She could not hold anything but the lightest food on her stomach such as omelettes or gruel and even then was blown up with gas until it was just pitiful, all from the anguish Mrs. Sterling was putting her through. For they did not blame their father, no, indeed. His whole life long he had been a God-fearing man, never swerving by a hair's breadth from the path of righteousness. He was a man of substance, a pillar in the church, a man to be reckoned with in the community. The breath of scandal had never blown upon his name.

It was the old story. Mrs. Sterling had bewitched him. There was not a doubt in the world. She wanted Brother Bell to marry her, make her his polygamous wife, rule his life, relegate to inferior status his faithful spouse who had stood by him through thick and thin, twist him around her little finger, squander his money in life and inherit all he had when he died. But! they had a program arranged to forestall her wicked scheming, they said. They would write to her husband in Norway, exposing all. They would go to the church authorities. Mrs. Sterling would be excommunicated. They would blacken her name until her children would sneak through life with their heads hanging, for shame of her, and despise her for what she had done.

None of that frightened Mrs. Sterling so much as the look in the eyes of the pale-faced beardless men when they said, pressing in closer, in their high precise voices, that there were yet *other ways* to deal with such as she, and when the awful Bell daughter said too there were other ways of which she would not speak. Mrs. Sterling might find herself with a face people would run from instead of chasing, for instance, an ugly face for a change, a disfigured face. She might lose a child by a sad accident, under a runaway horse's feet. Mrs. Sterling might wake up some morning and find herself dead and buried, the daughter said, and very little torture she could do to an innocent wife and very little money of a great fortune she could squander or inherit *then*.

After they left, the lady in black and her brood, Mrs. Sterling got cold all over: they were odd and misbuilt, somehow, their minds too. They might have meant what they said, and didn't just say it to sound like a bunch of tragediennes on the stage. She went to Olaf and told him what had happened. She must leave, Mrs. Sterling decided hurriedly. She could not reoccupy her house in Ogden for several months. Olaf suggested that she go out and stay with Linnea in Bountiful until spring. After all, it was ten miles from Salt Lake. There wasn't much danger that Brother Bell would come out there and bother her, especially if his family had put the fear of God into him the way they had put it into her.

She decided not to write to her husband about the matter. He would be home in four months, five, at the most, in March or April, and she could tell him the whole silly story then.

Linnea and her children liked Mrs. Sterling and her children, and were glad they had come. The more, the merrier. Estelle was seven, a thin darting girl with black bangs. Johnny, five, was rounder, and had a tic, a way of constantly batting his eyes that was fascinating to watch and still more fascinating to imitate until Mamma put a stop to it. He was never without his white lace collar and the pair of shiny black rubber boots that Rudie (and for that matter Gertrude and Stellie) would have given his soul's salvation for. Mrs. Sterling bought them for him the day before they came to Bountiful and it was all she could do to persuade him to allow her to pull them off at night before he climbed into bed.

Gertrude liked the look of Mrs. Sterling, her hair frizzled up, her yellow chintz waist and dark-green skirt, her tight belt buckled with tortoiseshell, her tiny buttoned shoes. It was pleasant to look at her and pleasant to hear her. She knew as many songs and stories as Mamma and was at least as patient. No matter what she was doing, she would lend an ear if a child had something to communicate. They were especially glad that Mrs. Sterling, Estelle and Johnny were there when the snow came.

Somehow, that winter, Linnea and Mrs. Sterling and their seven children, in two rooms, lived the life of Riley. The women were busy much of the day, cleaning and cooking, but they had time to prot over coffee, and the children always found something to do or be or make, that kept them contented and happy. The lamplit evening by the stove, as always, after the supper dishes were washed up, was the best part of the day.

Then was when Linnea, with sewing in her lap and Parley nursing or Parley asleep, would start a song and Mrs. Sterling, with sewing in her lap, too, would join her, and then they all joined in one by one. Or Linnea would sing by herself a Swedish song they didn't know, or Mrs. Sterling would sing a song, usually very melodious and full of pathos, and quite new. "This is all the style now," she would say. They learned these songs in no time. Gertrude picked her favorites by the words, not the tunes. For a long time she loved best a song that went

> Last night I dreamed
> A pretty lit-tel sta-arling
> Came tapping softly on my window pane,
> And in its bill
> A message from my da-arling:
> I know that you will call me back again. . . .

until she sang it so much she got sick of it and everybody else did too.
Mrs. Sterling knew a wonderful riddle.

> *I have a little sister*
> *That goes peep, peep, peep.*
> *She wades in the water*
> *Deep, deep, deep.*
> *She climbs the mountains*
> *High, high, high.*
> *But my poor little sister*
> *Has only one eye.*

"What is it?" Mrs. Sterling would say. A STAR, of course. But like a
paper plate, or a cigarette, a riddle is only good *once,* so it is more or less
impractical.

Estelle was the one who knew the beautiful song about Santy and was
flattered to be asked to stand and sing it, twisting her thin hands behind
her back, too shy to look directly in anybody's eyes.

> *A-WAY in the NORTHland where CHRISTmas trees GROW.*
> *Where the POlar bear FROlics knee-DEEP in the SNOW.*
> *There IN a big PALace all GLITtering BRIGHT*
> *Lives DEAR jolly SANta, the CHILdren's deLIGHT.*
>
> *He has a big WORKshop and IN it he MAKES*
> *All SORTS of stick CANdy and SWEET frosted CAKES,*
> *Drums, TRUMpets and DOLLies and TOYS without END,*
> *This dear jolly SANta, the CHILdren's best FRIEND.*
>
> *The NIGHT before CHRISTmas he FILLS up his SLEIGH*
> *And WITH his eight REINdeer he GALlops a-WAY,*
> *And DOWN through the CHIMneys while LITtle folks SLEEP*
> *This DEAR jolly SANta with PREsents will CREEP.*

Mamma started them off on a fad of saying "There never was yet a
boy or a man who better could mend a kettle or pan, a bucket, a dipper,
a skipper, a pan, than happy old Roger the tinmaker man!" as fast as
they could, as many times over, without drawing a breath. Bertha was
the champion of that exercise but she paid dear for it: she was very
nearly purple when she had to give in and breathe and her eyes looked
as if they were going to pop right out of her head. Mamma said she was
the champion and now she wasn't to do it any more, it made everybody
nervous to watch her, a person could bust a blood vessel that way. But
it was exhilarating to say it as fast as you could say it, as many times,
without drawing a breath, and the children loved to do it.

Mrs. Sterling used to recite a little verse looking straight at Parley, as
if it were recited especially for him, and he got so he thought so too,

for baby as he was, he used to catch Mrs. Sterling's eye and rear back against his mother's shoulder and crow so loud they all had to burst out laughing to see him perform. It became his exclusive property. Mrs. Sterling would say it solemnly and dramatically.

> Eight fingers and ten toes,
> Two eyes—but one nose!
> Baby said when she smelled the rose,
> "O what a pity! Only one nose!"
>
> Twelve teeth all even and white,
> Lots of dimples—but one nose!
> Baby said when she smelled the snuff,
> "DEAR ME! ONE NOSE IS ENOUGH!"

and Parley would nearly jump out of Mamma's arms, it tickled him so.

The women almost never left home except once before Christmas when they got Venie Barnes to stay with the children and went into Salt Lake City on the D. & R. G. for costume material for the church costume ball at the Crossroads, yards and yards of thin glazed cotton, red for Linnea, yellow for Mrs. Sterling. They spread the stuff out gloriously for the children to see and everybody exclaimed over its beauty. Red! Yellow! Fifteen yards apiece! How the little ones would have liked to go, but this was only for grownups.

Linnea and Mrs. Sterling made a great fuss over getting their costumes ready. Nothing was talked but the ball. They cut and sewed their flimsy dresses as carefully as though they were of damask at five dollars a yard, with gores and tucks and linings worthy of the finest material. Mrs. Sterling was to go as a lady all in ruffled yellow, with a low neck and short sleeves and her hair hanging down around her shoulders. Nobody knew definitely whom, or what period in history, she represented, including the lady herself, but once she told Gertrude the yellow dress was to be assumed as being made of pure cloth-of-gold. Gertrude assumed it with little effort and great enthusiasm and under her eyes Mrs. Sterling became the Princess of Sweden.

Linnea had a joke up her sleeve: she was going as the Belle of the Ball. Her red dress had a wide ruffle around the bottom, and even a train, and a crushed girdle, and embroidered on the back, with narrow green braid, were the written words BELLE OF THE BALL. Once the children had it explained to them just exactly what belle was, how it meant the prettiest and most popular girl there, with all the young men falling over each other to dance with her, and be her partner for refreshments, they enjoyed the fun enormously. Mamma also would carry a cowbell in her hand, you see, which she would ring from time to time. They considered this very witty and daring. Belle of the Ball, you see. Cowbell, you understand. Mamma *not* the prettiest and most popular girl there, at all, but just Mamma, an old married lady of thirty with five children at home! It was really irresistibly funny.

The great day of the Ball arrived, and the costumes were nearly done, except that Mamma still had the snaps to sew on hers. Noontime dinner was a sketchy picnic-like affair—five-o'clock supper would be still sketchier and more picnic-like—and everybody had big bright pupils that day and laughed at nothing. It was a day full of freedom and excitement.

After Brother Bell came and went, it almost got out of hand, there was so much effervescence and uproariousness, and Mamma said she didn't know what had got into them all, even Parley in the highchair, whose hair stood on end and whose cheeks burned red as a rose, it was like they'd all taken a snort of something. But it was the orange and red costumes all over the kitchen like wildfire let in, it was their having been shut up so long by snow, it was the Ball that night, it was the season, for Christmas was near.

Mrs. Sterling had her costume on for a last look in the glass and a last parade before the children that afternoon, "dress rehearsal," she said, and Mamma was sewing her snaps on and drinking a cup of coffee at the same time, when Brother Bell actually came and knocked on the door. Gertrude, her face pressed against the cold pane she had been occupied with blowing and then drawing faces upon—she could do this and admire Mrs. Sterling at the same time—saw him coming down the road. "A man's coming down the road," she said.

Mamma said, measuring out her thread, "Just somebody going by. Mr. Taylor or somebody."

But he turned in and came towards the house. "Oh, no, he's coming here," Gertrude said.

Mamma flew to the window then to take a quick look, Mrs. Sterling at her shoulder to take a quick look, too, through the clear circle Mamma rubbed in Gertrude's lacy breath. "You don't suppose it's another one of them *sneaks*," she said, meaning the government agents who would track down the polygamists for another year until the problem of multiple marriage was settled once and for all.

Mrs. Sterling made a funny noise like coughing and swallowing at the same time. "It looks to me like *him*," she said, squeezing Mamma's shoulder convulsively.

"Brother Bell! Oh, Lordy me!" Mamma said, laughing. "That old chaser! Out here in Bountiful to pay you a call! Imagine the nerve. You go in the bedroom and take Estelle and Johnny. I'll tell him you've left for parts unknown. Imagine."

Mrs. Sterling started for the bedroom, but something stopped her in her tracks and only many years later did Gertrude realize what it was.

That it was that shortcoming, that imperfection, that human failing Vanity, that stopped her. Herself in the yellow costume with her black hair hanging down around her shoulders, as pretty as she would ever be in her life again, stopped herself by her vainglory, like somebody colliding with a wall.

"Maybe I'd ought to explain to the poor man why he mustn't come out here anymore. It would be too bad to hurt his feelings," Mrs. Sterling said.

It would be too bad to hurt the feelings of any admirer, anybody who admired . . . it really would. And Mrs. Sterling looked so fetching, so delectable, right this minute, trying on her costume for the last time before the ball. She knew she did, it was too bad to waste her prettiness, her downpour of hair, her heyday eyes, one that veered a little to the side, her bare front, her bare slender arms . . . wouldn't it? Oh, it really would! Her eyes beseeched Linnea. To run and hide in the bedroom? Abate? Diminish? Snuff out the gold dress? Quench her shining there?

Linnea saw the vanity she lay helpless in, like an arm in a sling, like a fly in honey, and smiled. He knocked, then, Brother Bell, at the door. "You better go let him in," she suggested gently, "it might honestly be better, if you explain to him yourself. We better make him a cup of coffee before he goes back—it must of been a cold old trip out here from Salt Lake."

But Brother Bell said piously that he did not drink coffee. He sat by the fire looking old and cold, with his mustache limp, trying to give the ends an upward curl every little while, in tighter pants than ever, his nose dripping as it thawed, so that he had to wipe it frequently with his fine linen handkerchief, in a dainty surreptitious female way, never once giving it a good hard blow, and said, no, thank you, he did not drink coffee. It was to the quiet staring children he addressed most of his remarks on the subject. "No, I tell you," he said, "you keep to the Word of Wisdom and you'll never regret it. Don't drink coffee, tea and strong liquors. Don't take up with filthy tobacco, you boys. Eat but very little meat. Keep the fast day when it comes along." He gave a little curl to his mustache. "Honor thy father and thy mother," he added, as an afterthought.

"But it's so cold outside," Linnea said hospitably. "I thought maybe you'd like something to warm you up a little."

Mrs. Sterling's heady beauty in the yellow costume was doing that. She perched in rosy confusion on the edge of a straight chair, wetting her lips nervously from time to time, her hands clasped around her knees. "Brother Bell really doesn't drink coffee," she said. "He really does keep to the Word of Wisdom."

"I try to do so," Brother Bell said again to the children who didn't seem to be taking their large eyes off his face. "As a matter of fact I may go so far as to say that I have succeeded in doing so: I have kept the Word of Wisdom. And my Maker, I may say, I really may say so, has seen fit to heap blessings upon me for so doing."

Linnea thought of his ugly wife all in black, his frighteningly peculiar children, but then she remembered all his property and the Bank on Main Street. "It's fine if you can do it," she said. "Me, now. I'd die off on the vine without a cup of coffee. Winter mornings—I don't know how you do it, Brother Bell."

"A big glass of sparkling cold water," Brother Bell said, "pure and clear."

"A person had really ought to," Mrs. Sterling said ambiguously, "if a person had any gumption to them." She fawned only because Brother Bell admired her so. Nobody could blame her for it.

Linnea gave her a sly wink. "It's not so easy for the Swedes for some reason or other," she said politely. "It might be different for the English. They just had that nasty tea to start with anyway. It wouldn't be much of a chore to give THAT up."

"Oh, I don't know," Brother Bell said.

There was a silence, then, so deep that the clock could be heard ticking, the glowing coals heard dropping down in the grate. Even the steam jetting out from the teakettle spout seemed unusually loud and Linnea, laying her costume down, went to the stove and set the kettle back over the reservoir.

Brother Bell cleared his throat, wiped his nose again, put his handkerchief away in his hip pocket and gave another twist to his mustache. "You have a nice-looking little family, Mrs. Ecklund," he said, "I know your husband well."

"Thank you," Linnea said. She picked up her costume again but only folded it this time as she meant to retire soon to the next room on some pretext and take the children with her, so that Mrs. Sterling could talk to the man in privacy and tell him what she had to say.

"Little girl," he said to Stellie, who instantly got back of Bertha so that she could not be seen. "Do you go to Sunday school?"

"Oh, yes," Mrs. Sterling said, "I should say they do. When the weather's not too bad. They all go. Mine, too."

"They're pretty regular," Linnea said.

"We *like* Sunday school," Bertha announced piously.

"Who was Emer?" Brother Bell catechized. Nobody had the faintest idea. "Don't you read the Book of Mormon?" he asked the children in pained surprise.

"They're pretty little to know it all through," Linnea said. "They got plenty of time."

Oratorically Brother Bell began to recite, his eyes fixed on the place up above where the stovepipe went into the chimney, the children staring at him in bewilderment. "From the Book of Ether, Chapter nine," he announced. "Verse sixteen. 'And the Lord began again to take the curse from off the land, and the house of Emer did prosper exceedingly under the reign of Emer; and in the space of sixty and two years, they had become exceeding strong, insomuch that they became exceeding rich, having—verse seventeen—having all manner of fruit, and of grain, and of silks, and of fine linen, and of gold, and of silver, and of precious things, and—verse eighteen—and also all manner of cattle, of oxen, and cows, and of sheep, and of swine, and of goats, and also many other kind of animals which were useful for the food of man; and they also— verse nineteen—also had horses, and asses, and there were elephants and cureloms, and cumoms; all of which were useful unto man, and more especially the elephants, and cureloms, and cumoms.' You must be familiar with the wonderful Book of Ether," he said.

Alas, they were not. The words echoed in Gertrude's ears—elephants, cureloms and cumoms—with horns, with tails, with wings, with hoofs, with scales of gold, green, pink and crimson, with eyes like firecrackers lit ready to go off, bigger than houses, twisting and turning, flying up over the tabernacle, leaping over the Wasatch Mountains—like band music they resounded, and Mrs. Sterling in yellow suddenly looked like the picture of a circus lady bareback on a horse . . . she caught her breath, listening and thinking . . . elephants, cureloms, cumoms.

"It doesn't hurt a person to know the Gospel," Brother Bell said. "It never hurt a person yet to know his Book of Mormon."

In the bedroom, for soon Mamma corralled them all in there, while Mamma was changing Parley's full diapers on the bed, making as if to hold her nose and saying pyew, pyew, pyew, in mock distress, with her eyes beaming at him, so that he roared with laughter, Gertrude said, "What's a curelom, Mamma?" the circus visions with her.

Mamma snapped a big safety pin shut. "Some kind of a animal," she said. She pulled the other corner of the diaper up tight and shoved in another pin expertly, while Parley kicked in wild merriment.

"A cumom, too?" Gertrude asked.

"You can search me. Some kind of a animal, though, I guess," Mamma said. "They're all dead now, probably. Must be. You don't see none of them running around nowhere."

"They must sure been a sight for sore eyes, huh, Mamma?"

"They must of been," Mamma said, and thought a minute. Then she swung her dry baby up off the bed to her shoulder. She began to laugh. "But they wasn't the only things that's a sight for sore eyes," she said. "I wouldn't be surprised but there's things walking around on two legs right this minute that'd tickle the life out of you."

"I didn't mean *tickle*, Mamma—" Gertrude began.

"Well, I do," Mamma said. "There's things so blame ridiculous right in the world today, that a curelom or cumom would curl up and wither away and die of shame!"

Puzzled, Gertrude heard the last of the band music fade into nothing, the last wing winnowed by, the last scale coruscated, the last flashing tail whipped through the last echoing canyon, all the circus riders in yellow dresses went away. . . . "I just meant—" she said, in a sort of melancholy.

But Mamma cut her short. "I tell you what I'll do," she said. "If you kids will all sit down in a circle and be real quiet, I'll tell you a story." She herself sat down on the edge of the bed, Parley on her arm, and flipped her breast out of her dress. She pressed his mouth against the nipple and then covered up both breast and the scarlet top of his head with his little blue shawl. They could hear the murmuring voices of Brother Bell and Mrs. Sterling in the kitchen behind the closed door. For all they knew, Brother Bell might still be reciting the Book of Mormon.

Mamma told them the story of the Bad Housekeeper and the Lily.

"Once upon a time," she said, "there was a lady that lived all alone in a nice little four-roomed house. You would of thought she'd of took some pride in it," she said, "a nice little house like that. But no, siree, not her. She was so filthy dirty that you wouldn't believe it even if I told you *how* dirty she was. All I can say is, she never housecleaned from one year's end to the other, never scrubbed, never washed windows, never did nothing. Laid around and read novels, likely. Well, sir, one day a old lady come to her back door. She had a lily in her hand. 'Here,' this old woman said, 'I want to give you this here lily.' The lady took it, saying thank you, not knowing what else to do. 'Put it in a vase,' the old woman said, 'put it in water.' Well, sir, the lady went back in her dirty house and looked at it. This lily was the most beautiful-looking thing you ever saw, big and snow-white, as fresh as a starched bib and smelling so sweet it the next thing to overpowered a person. Well, the lady looked around for a vase and found one, but it was so dirty she felt ashamed to put the beautiful lily in it, so what did she do but wash it with soap and water till it fairly shone. She carried it into her filthy parlor to set it on the marble-topped table," Mamma said, "but *that* was so dirty that she had to clean it and dust it. Then, of course, the beautiful lily in the clean vase on the polished table in the corner stood out like a sore thumb. So she had to clean the corner! And then the corner stood out like a sore thumb so she had to clean the room! And the room stood out like a sore thumb, so she had to clean the next room, and the next room, until the whole house, and the back stoop, and the front stoop, and yard, and walk, was so clean you could eat off it! And everybody nearly fell over dead because this here dirty housekeeper had gone and cleaned her house until it just sparkled like a diamond! And when the neighbors asked her what in the world had happened, she said it was *all on account of the lily.*"

"What about when the lily died?" Bertha asked, who knew the story well.

"It was a magic lily," Mamma explained, "and the old lady was like what you might call a fairy godmother, so the lily didn't die for a long, long time, and when it did, it didn't make any difference because the lady had got into such good habits that she couldn't stop doing her housework no more, but kept right on till the day she died! And lived happy ever after. And that's the end of the story," Mamma said.

"I'd sure of liked to seen that lily," Gertrude said. "It sure must of been a beautyful lily."

"It was," Mamma said, "but no more beautiful than any other white lily. Any other white lily'd be just the same way and work the same stunt. It all depends on *who,* though, I guess," she said. "It seemed like the lady was just ripe for it. . . . Well, anyway," she finished briskly, "that's the end of the Bad Housekeeper and the Lily."

When they came out of the bedroom, leaving Parley napping there, Brother Bell was gone to catch the three o'clock train, and Mrs. Sterling flew to put the coffeepot on. "Don't it beat all?" she said. She tossed her hair over her shoulders, and laughed, showing all her teeth.

"It sure does," Linnea said, settling down with the red costume and preparing to put on the last snap. "It'd be too bad if he went to work and set them Lammanites onto your heels, though, just when you've got moved so nice and everything."

"Oh, no danger of that!" Mrs. Sterling said.

"For your own sake, I wouldn't like to see it," Linnea went on gently. "Old Sanctimonious making tracks out here. Preaching the Gospel." She laughed, too, stopped, though, laughed harder. "Don't it beat the dutch? Book of Ether! Verse sixteen, if you please. Old Tight Pants! Cold water for breakfast! You'd think a man'd have some shame to him once in awhile."

"Oh, he won't," Mrs. Sterling said. "A man won't." She wandered to the mirror waiting for the coffee to boil and looked in. "I bet I looked a sight," she said, "in this costume. I told him we was fixing to go to the party." She smiled across the room at Linnea and Linnea smiled back, shaking her head.

The lie she told lifted lightly, like dandelion fuzz, and blew away.

Mamma won the grand prize at the ball, if you please! The children hopped with joy when they heard of it the next day. Mrs. Sterling was pleased, too—who had been very popular indeed, by the way, and Linnea joshed her for weeks about it—she said there wasn't a one there had a costume to hold a candle to it! "Your ma would sashay around ringing this cowbell, see," she'd say to the girls who had to be told the story several times, while they always laughed as though they were hearing it for the first time, "in and out among the dancers. And here you'd see on her back them words embroidered *Belle of the Ball*. People just roared. But your ma wasn't no wallflower, I can tell you that! Not her! She danced pretty near every dance, except when she wanted to sashay around ringing her bell."

"I wasn't no Belle of the Ball," Linnea would say modestly.

"I'd like to know who was, then," Mrs. Sterling would maintain. "You got the grand prize, didn't you?"

She had, there was no arguing that. The grand prize was a shiny new lantern of which the whole household was extremely proud.

"I danced the Sally Wally, too, didn't I? and sat down flat on my rear end," Mamma would say. For she had! Somehow or other, dancing the Sally Wally with Mr. Goff, the stationmaster, she had got her train wrapped around her feet and down she went right smack on her behind! It was the biggest wonder in the world she hadn't pulled Mr. Goff over on top of her. Somebody said even if Mr. Goff was the stationmaster, he couldn't get to first base with Mrs. Ecklund's *train*. Oh, it was too funny for words!

Everybody was there—the two Mrs. Barneses and their grown children (Grace, the young mother, came without her husband for he was gone again), the Taylors—Mr. Taylor did most of the fiddling for the dancing —the stationmaster and his two sons and the daughter who taught school. Mrs. Goff, his wife, was expecting and didn't feel up to the dance which was no great wonder as she was forty-four and hadn't had a baby in sixteen years so she didn't show up, but everybody else did, even perfect strangers.

It was a great success! Linnea and Mrs. Sterling talked about it for weeks, and never once did the children take the shiny new lantern out to the barn or out to the toilet but what they thought of it, so that the party became enlarged as a Grand Duke's Grand Ball and shimmered in their memories lit bright as if a thousand candles burned upon the scene of it.

Christmas itself, sad to relate, was rather an anticlimax. There was an orange in every stocking, and some hard candy, but Santa Claus didn't break his back bringing them presents. The house was too much buried under snow, the snow on the roads too deep, the moonlight too scanty or the chimney too small, something, anyhow, was amiss, for old St. Nick gave them a lick and a promise and not much else: a new pair of stockings apiece, yes; a new suit of underwear apiece, yes; a roast of pork for dinner, yes; but presents, no, except a new penny for each in an empty pillbox. He had long got shed of the dolls, trumpets and toys without end of which Estelle sang so sweetly. A game of checkers for the whole family, tiddledywinks for the boys, and a gingham cat for Parley, were all he managed to hang onto and bring. Because the old fellow didn't give two cents for them, as Gertrude bitterly said, Christmas was always a good deal less of an occasion every year than it promised faithfully to be, but along about Thanksgiving of next year they would be carried away by the same old delusion again.

The heavy dinner was a triumph, though, and for most of the afternoon they were as stuffed as a bunch of owls just home from the taxidermist's, fat and stupefied. Mamma and Mrs. Sterling took a nap in the afternoon with Parley between them, and slept so soundly that even a halfhearted but shrill fight between Bertha and Gertrude did not disturb them and the girls had to settle it themselves. Papa would come out later in the week with a big sack of candy and a small gift for each of the children, and a pair of earrings for Mamma's pierced ears, but today something kept him away.

Mrs. Sterling said when she got up from her nap yawning and stretching that she would have told them the Christmas story she heard once, if she could, only she couldn't remember it. She said it was just wonderful: there was a mean old man with some outlandish name, and some ghosts dragging chains behind them, but it was a Christmas story for all that—she forgot how it went—and it all ended happily with a big dinner, and a little crippled boy climbed up on the table and hollered "God bless us every one!" It was really too bad she didn't know it to tell, the children would have liked it, she said.

By bedtime, for some reason or other, the day began to seem an enjoyable one, not tedious and disappointing at all, and they retired almost convinced that it had been a very merry Christmas.

CHAPTER 14

IT WAS quite a coincidence that the day Mrs. Sterling got the letter from her husband saying he would soon be released from his mission and on his way home, she should receive a letter from Brother Bell. She let Linnea read both of them. She decided not to show her husband the letter when he came home, for Brother Bell had said perhaps more than he meant to.

Brother Bell had visited Mrs. Sterling twice more during the winter, but though the two women were uneasy about the matter, no repercussions had as yet been felt from the direction of his family. Linnea said this seemed odd. Of course, they didn't know about it, Brother Bell had covered his tracks well, but being the type the Bell family was, you'd think they'd keep a close watch on the old man. It was funny they'd be in the dark about him coming out here. It was funny they didn't try something, after showing off that way and threatening to do all those dramatic things like disfiguring Mrs. Sterling's face and running down her children and tattling to her husband and even murdering her! For naturally they must have meant murdering her when they spoke about her waking up some morning and finding herself dead, what else? But there wasn't a peep out of any of them. Mrs. Sterling had inquired, and Brother Bell said his wife Mrs. Bell was sleeping all right now and could eat and didn't have so much gas on her stomach. It would amaze you, the gas she had been known to have on her stomach, he said. He also said his children were busy with their church work, doing the work of the Lord.

Brother Bell hinted broadly in the letter that he would like to be on very cozy terms indeed with a "lovely woman" like Mrs. Sterling. He had taken certain steps, he wrote, so that this paradise on earth would be possible. He was no longer referring to a plural marriage with her, which he had once suggested and she had refused to consider, being already happily married, but to a connection he called "higher in the eyes of God."

Linnea and Mrs. Sterling laughed their heads off. "I'd like to know what the 'certain steps' are," Mrs. Sterling said. "It ain't come out in the Deseret News that the roof has fell in on his family, and they ain't been found full of ground glass on the floor in the parlor. What in the world could the man of done, to be able to write so bold all of a sudden? As if I'd leave John," John being her husband, "for a tottering old knee-sprung woman-chaser like him!"

"Maybe he's turned over all he's got to his wife and kids," Linnea suggested, "and they got nothing more to be nervous about. So you'd have pretty slim pickings, no matter how high you and him stood in the eyes of the Lord, and it wouldn't be no skin off their nose. That's what it looks to me like. Once they've glommed everything, they don't care what he does, any more than you'd care what happened to the old sock your money was salted down in, once you've took it out and put it somewheres else."

"I wouldn't be surprised but what you're right, Linnea," Mrs. Sterling said. "The nerve of the man!"

That was exactly what had happened but they were only making guesses then.

"You know what John looks like?" Mrs. Sterling asked, thinking of her husband.

"Just by that picture you showed me," Linnea said. "He's a nice-looking man."

"He's handsome, downright handsome, Linnea," Mrs. Sterling said solemnly. She folded up both the letters and stuck them in her pocket.

"I know. That's what you said. You was telling me."

"No, but what I mean is, he's one of these big tall men. With blue eyes, see. These great big blue eyes. Neither one of the kids inherited them. And this blonde mustache and this blonde hair parted on the side and he's about this broad across the shoulders, see"—she measured off nearly a yard between her hands—"and he's so particular with himself. His tie's got to be tied just so and everything. I tell you the girls in the Ward could of scratched my eyes out when we got married. He's been a good provider, too, paid for the house, and it cost five hundred dollars! He's kind of inclined to take these mean spells, though, and maybe won't speak a word for two or three days till I feel like I want to pick up the teakettle and throw it at him or something, but that's just his way. When you see him, Linnea, you'll have to admit yourself that he's downright handsome."

Linnea was sure of it. "Imagine that old Brother Bell thinking he could even get to first base with you," she said.

"Yes, imagine," Mrs. Sterling said.

She left the first part of March and went back to Ogden with Estelle and Johnny. Linnea cried when she went, and Mrs. Sterling cried, too. "It's going to be a lonely old place here without you," Linnea said, and when she washed up the last coffee cup that Mrs. Sterling had used, and found one of her dark bone hairpins down beside the dresser and ran across some ravelings of yellow thread, she cried again.

It was a lonely old place, and the weather helped more than anything else to make it so. Never was there a colder, wetter, snowier, muddier spring in all history than that one out in Bountiful. The sun almost never shone. Nobody came near the place except an occasional passing neighbor. Ingeborg could never seem to get out even for a day's visit and it had been months since Linnea saw her sister Gunilla.

Olaf, who might have triumphed over the inclemency, was tied hand and foot by a new watchfulness on the part of those "snoops," the government men. He wrote Linnea that he simply did not dare to visit her. With two families depending on him, he could not risk another term of imprisonment. She believed him and did not believe him. Sometimes she thought he had ceased to love her and sometimes that it was all Sigrid's fault. It was sure, however, that the federal agents were watching the polygamists closer than ever owing to pressure from Washington.

The first Mrs. Barnes came over for a little visit one afternoon and the two women got their heads together and talked about a lot of things. For instance, polygamy.

"What would you think about it if they abolished it?" she asked Linnea. "I wonder how it would be for a change? One husband, one wife?"

Linnea rubbed her forehead, studying. "It wouldn't be so bad at that," she said, "for the women. For the men, too. For the children, too, for that matter. I've thought more times than one that, Prophet or no Prophet, Joseph Smith had little to do to start such a hubbub as all this polygamy has been ever since it began. It ain't worked a pin's worth no matter how people has tried and it looks like Joseph would of knowed it wouldn't, if he knew straight up. People is people, you know. They're enviers, even the best of them, and nine times out of ten they're looking out for Number One. If he'd of been dealing with a bunch of angels it might of been a different story, but he wasn't, he was dealing with common ordinary people. Sometimes I got my doubts about Joseph," she said, "not that he was the Prophet of the Lord, you understand, but whether he was quite all there, all the time."

The first Mrs. Barnes said that was merely a man for you every time. However, that didn't have anything to do with the *Gospel*. Herself, now: she and her sister had run their husband off for sashaying around so smarty and getting him another wife—as if two wives wasn't enough for any man! But they still believed the GOSPEL, even if they wouldn't let neither him nor that woman, especially that woman, come onto the place and start telling them all where to head in at! Why, to see her acting so silly around Mr. Barnes (that old fool) and uppity to them, would of been more than flesh and blood could stand. But as far as the truth of the *Gospel* was concerned, why, it was as true as ever! The faith of the first Mrs. Barnes, of both the Mrs. Barneses, stood as unshaken as ever in THAT.

"Me, too," Linnea agreed. "It ain't the Gospel. The *Gospel's* all right." She thought it over. "It's just the buttinsky men. I notice they never let the women have a word to say on nothing. Is there a woman in the Council of Twelve? No, there ain't. You bet your boots there ain't. Is there a woman in the Quorum of Seventy? No, there ain't. There never was and there's never likely to be."

"I couldn't really say I'd like to get mixed up with no church business," Mrs. Barnes protested modestly.

"I would," Linnea said. "I'd like to tell that bunch of high-and-mighties where to get off at for a change."

"The kids is who has to suffer in this polygamy mix-up," Mrs. Barnes said, "it seems to me like. I wonder if they'll ever get it settled?"

"What settled?" Linnea asked, thinking of something else.

"The trouble with the Government over plural wives. Or whether they'll just drag on and on with it."

"That's the doggone men for you," Linnea said. "Women would of had it settled and forgot about by now."

"What if the men can't live with their polygamous wives no more when they come to some agreement with the law? If the Government says they can't?"

"Well, I feel sorry for some of them then," Linnea said. "There's wives that'll hang on like grim death to a nigger's heel. There's husbands that'll be tore apart limb from limb by their darnfool crazy women. This one'll want him and that one'll want him. Me, now. I'd say good riddance to bad rubbish, if it was me." She walked to the gray window and looked out. Olaf had not come to Bountiful for a long time. "Sometimes I feel like saying it anyway. Between you and me and the gatepost."

"But you're into it now," Mrs. Barnes pointed out gently. "You got your kids. And your husband's an awful nice man. A *nice* man. You got to stop and think of that."

"Oh, I'm not going to do nothing rash," Linnea said.

But a few weeks later, her patience at an end, she did do something rash, and Olaf was the most surprised man in Zion. Yet he might have expected it.

CHAPTER 15

LINNEA MISSED Mrs. Sterling very much, but she was busy, the children were active and entertaining. If the spell of bad weather had not continued so long, if Ingeborg could have come visiting, or Gunilla, she might have borne with her place of isolation. The dreary days were broken sometimes by some little happening that "livened things up," but not often enough.

One advent was the trouble Mrs. Goff had when her baby was born. The stationmaster at the Crossroads sent for Linnea and she went to do what she could, taking Parley with her. Her coming was almost, or looked so for awhile, of no avail: the baby was stuck and wouldn't budge an inch. He stayed that way for hours while Linnea did everything she could think of, until finally things got to a pass where it was either one thing or another. Then she just took the bull by the horns and caught hold and pulled and worked until the baby "came loose," as she said. Mrs. Goff's subsequent hemorrhages nearly scared the living daylights out of her but she stayed right on the job and forced sweetened liquids down her by the gallon and before too many hours went by she could tell the worried husband that his wife and baby were going to hang on. He cried as if his heart would break and said if there was anything Linnea ever wanted, she just had to speak the word. She patted him on the back and said pshaw, it wasn't her, it was just luck, and she didn't want anything else than just to know they were going to make it now. For awhile she had had her serious doubts, she could tell him. . . .

But she did ask a favor of Mr. Goff, and Mr. Goff moved heaven and earth to oblige her, and not so long afterwards either . . . a favor she wouldn't have thought of then.

The loneliness seemed to kind of prey upon her out there in Bountiful that everlasting wintry spring, she told Ingeborg later, with Olaf never coming near, although he wrote often and repeated over and over the reasons why he couldn't come. She had none too many supplies,

little money with which to buy more, and the days dragged by like a
crippled army, so alike and so depressing that sometimes she wanted to
scream right out loud. She got to wondering what had ever possessed
her to go out there in the first place, leaving everything she knew and
loved, leaving Sigrid to wallow in all the advantages, to bundle up the
kids and shut herself off like that in the country. She decided she must
have been out of her mind. Sigrid liked the arrangement very well indeed, she should imagine. In fact, Sigrid was probably behind the whole
thing. Afterwards, when she could be more reasonable, she had to admit
that it was her own fault and Sigrid didn't have anything to do with it.
As Ingeborg pointed out, who was quicker to make a move than Linnea?
She *liked* moving, Ingeborg said. She was as anxious to try out life on a
farm as anybody, and she liked it all right in the summer. It was just
when things weren't going to suit her that she got restless and had to put
an end to it and start something new.

But Linnea let day after tiresome day go by without making a move.
She did everything she had to do. Sometimes, for a moment, with the
children good and quiet about her in the lamplight, sewing, singing
songs or telling stories, snug and warm and out of the weather, she was
even happy, but not as she had been happy. Linnea out of town, out of
the world's way, out of the light, was Linnea with a heart of lead, all her
bravery motionless like a shot pheasant, all her assurance hanging limp
as a flag in no wind. But Parley was still very small, money scarce, the
cold extreme. She let one more day go by, and another day . . . until
the sun shone again, perhaps.

The straw that breaks the camel's back is really just that: a straw.
Linnea did not recognize it until the back of her endurance was broken.
When Bonnie had to be brought in from the field and Linnea started
after her with a black umbrella pressing upwards against the downpour,
when she untied her and came dragging her through the mud, she
never thought that this was the straw dropped gently down from fate's
careless fingers . . . for one never knows.

It was somehow one of the most infuriating incidents that had ever
happened to Linnea. The umbrella kept veering off sideways, the sleety
rain came from all directions so that she was soaked to her very skin in
a moment, the slick mud was like glue and she clopped and slopped
through it, her feet leaving holes the cow stepped into, with a sucking
sound. It was only by the greatest miracle her sodden shoes stayed on
her wet chilled feet at all. And Bonnie, though generally the best-na-
tured beast in the world, wouldn't come ahead as she ought but pulled
back and pulled back until Linnea was almost bent double trying to
drag her along. And carry her umbrella as well! "I've got a notion to
give you a blamed good licking," she muttered, but she didn't mean a
word of it. Bonnie was a great favorite of hers, both for her sweet nature

and good looks, and besides, she gave quantities of rich milk. Now especially that she had her cunning calf Beauty, Bonnie was in little danger
of punishment.

In her mind's eye, like a picture in a frame on the wall, Linnea saw
herself at this moment in the rain and mud dragging her cow along.
Where was her vanity now, that had made of her self a spotless spruced-
up citified woman that any man would be proud of? Her hair blew
around her face in sodden strings. She was without her corset, and had
left her dignity in the drawer with it. Her Mother Hubbard was ugly
and shapeless, her shoes a caution. Another year of this and what would
she be like? She! who went to the wedding at the Seely's, who could go
to the Tabernacle and sit there as handsome as anybody, who could
window-shop down Main Street, who could drink coffee with friend
after friend—what would she be like? A cow, that's what! As dumb and
heartless and soulless and clompy and manure-heeled as a cow! And not
in a class with Bonnie either.

She stopped tugging and pulling suddenly and let the rope go. "No,
sir," she said out loud, "I'll be damned and double-damned if I'll do it!
No, sir, by God Almighty," she said, glaring upward through the rain
and closing down her umbrella as though she had got safe at home
under a snug roof. "I might not set the world on fire and I might be just
as poor a sight and just as no-account in one place as another, but I'll be
damned and double-damned if I stay buried in this HOLE, pulling a
COW around without a CORSET on and nobody to care whether I
live or die! I'll be TRIPLE-damned if I will!" she said. "Was I born to
be planted out on ten acres like a tree and left there? No, I was not!"
she said. "Was I born to have some double-damned man plant me where
he wanted me and leave me there? No, I was not," she said. "Was I
born with sense enough to get in out of the rain? No, I was not," she
said, "but I'll LEARN some sense or I'll fall over dead trying. A house
don't have to fall on me!"

And there it was. That was the last straw, that broke the camel's back.
A little thing, for size it up and it's always some little thing. Not the
cupboard falling on Rudie, not the mosquitoes or flies, not the loneliness
and isolation, not the frozen potatoes, not running out of fuel and keeping the children in bed two days, boiling her coffee over the flame of the
lamp, until Olaf sent out the load of coal he promised, not running out
of flour and being two days without *that*, not getting scared to death in
this God-forsaken place that every cough was pneumonia and every
stomachache an obstruction of the bowels. No. It was dragging a cow
through the mud in the rain with her shoes making that nasty, sucking,
clopping, slopping, mucky sound every time she lifted her feet and the
cow pulling back and her wet hair blowing in her eyes like a witch's.

She put Bonnie in the barn, wiping her off gently with a dry rag and patting her, saying with half-embarrassed laugh that she hoped she hadn't offended her ladylike ears there when she turned the air blue with her swearing. "I'll take you with me, never fear," she said, "and little old Beauty too. I'll take you both *someway*. You won't be left here to rot, I can promise you that!" Bonnie turned puzzled Juno eyes upon her and when she went out the door, lowed a time or two in deep mystification.

"I got to go down to the Crossroads," she told the children, "and I want you all to be as good as gold until I get back. Bertha's the oldest, so she's the boss, and you kids do what she says. But don't go at the bossing too hot and heavy, Bertha," she said, changing her clothes as though for a trip to town, combing her hair and otherwise making herself as presentable as possible. "Use an easy rein. Just see that nobody gets in no mischief but otherwise let them do pretty much what they want."

It was still pouring when she left the house but bravely she set out in it, her umbrella held jauntily over her head, her corseted figure as straight as a string. It was biting cold but she was alight with newly awakened pride and an anger so bright it threw out sparks, so she did not feel it.

• While Mrs. Goff, still rather pale and looking older than her forty-four years, her month-old baby over her shoulder, bustled about pulling the diapers down that were warming by the stove and pushing a chair up close to the grate, Mr. Goff said what was it? Whatever they had was hers.

"Whatever we have is yours, Mrs. Ecklund," his wife said. "I wouldn't be here now if it wasn't for you. The baby wouldn't be here now." She patted him softly on the back.

"Oh, yes, you would," Linnea said with an embarrassed face. "My goodness, I didn't do anything much. I tell you what I want, Mr. Goff."

"What?" he said smilingly.

"A boxcar," she said.

"Well," he said. "That's a pretty big order."

"You're the stationmaster," Linnea explained in some haste. "That's why I ask you. You can do anything you want with the trains. I've got it all figured out," she said. "I want to leave here. I want to go to Ogden. I haven't got the money for a big lot of transportation. I've got the five kids, the furniture and dishes, and Bonnie the cow and her calf. I thought maybe you could fasten a boxcar onto the passenger train that goes up to Ogden, and I'd have my stuff all loaded on, and then me and the kids could climb in, too, and we could all ride up there. Whatever the expense was . . . I could . . ."

"Don't talk to me about expense," Mr. Goff said.

"No, don't talk to us about expense," his wife echoed, jiggling the baby up and down. "But what are you going to do in Ogden, Mrs. Ecklund, if you don't mind my asking?"

Linnea bit her lip and looked down at the toe of her shoe. "My friend Mrs. Sterling that stayed with us, lives there," she said. "I can spend a while with her. I can get some kind of work to do there, sewing or something. It's far enough from Salt Lake so I never need to—" she paused and swallowed. "When my husband comes out, if he comes out, if he ever comes, looking for us, I don't want him told where we've went."

Mr. Goff took his pipe out of his pocket and found a match, lit it and began to puff. "It's a kind of a hard lot, ain't it?" he said.

"I bet. I can imagine," his wife said. "I never would stand for it myself."

Linnea looked up. "If I'd of been the *first*, I never would of stood for it either, I guess. But I'm the second and there you are. Sigrid's maybe bigger than I ever could of been under the circumstances." She paused. "Or else she was off her base to start with. Or had something in mind. I don't know. The whole thing's a mystery to me." She put a hand to her forehead, let it drop down into her lap. "Sigrid's his first wife," she added.

"The Church'll settle it," Mrs. Goff said soothingly. "The Government'll settle it all some way."

"They'll have to be a bunch of Solomons then," Linnea said.

"Don't you think—" Mr. Goff began.

"I never would of asked you for a big favor like a boxcar if I didn't think that was the best possible thing I could do," Linnea said. "I thought maybe you having influence could do it, if anybody could. Fasten a boxcar at the end of a train going up to Ogden. Of course, if it'd be more trouble than you'd want to go to . . ." She stood up and took her umbrella from out of the corner.

"Lots of times a person'll feel one way one day and another way the next. Maybe you'll change your mind," Mr. Goff said. "You been a good neighbor the little while you been here. We'll be sorry to lose you."

Linnea reached over and pulled the blanket gently back from the baby's head. "He's a husky," she said, while the pale mother crooked her neck and smiled sideways at him. "He looks like five months already, don't he?" Gently she put the covering back. "He'll have the girls doing some stepping some day, I'll bet." At the door she said, "It might look kind of peculiar to you settled folks, but it's all I can seem to do. Sometimes all you can seem to do looks peculiar, you know. Or else you're planted out on ten acres like a tree."

Once Mamma set her mind to anything she didn't let any grass grow under her feet but went ahead and did it. "We're going to move," she said. "We're going to Ogden."

"Are we, Mamma, are we?" all the children said, clapping their hands. Because Mamma decided it, it was the best thing in the world to do, like going on a picnic in Emigration Canyon.

In no time, Mamma did the thousand and one things that had to be done, packed all the dishes and canned fruit, crated the furniture, bundled up clothes and bedding. Mr. Goff came through with the boxcar, and more than the boxcar, and the day after but one, Mamma and her brood, Bonnie and the calf Beauty, were on their way to Ogden and Mrs. Sterling's small house. They would not stay there long, Mamma said, just long enough to breathe easy again, and then Mamma would find work and they would move to their own house.

With that perversity often seen in nature, the early morning they locked the empty house and rode away in the Barnes' wagon (two of the Barnes boys had loaded all their goods on the boxcar in two trips, one last night and one this early morning with Bonnie and Beauty hitched on behind)—leaving not a scratch of the pen to say where they had gone and strictest injunctions, along with affectionate good-byes, to their neighbors not to tell if anybody asked—that morning, like a wayward woman, proved the softest and fairest ever seen, of shell-pink and dusted gold, with a bluing rinse for the white clouds. There wasn't enough rain left for a tiara, or wind enough to flutter a bonnet string. By some wonder-working, a green down appeared, as a beard grows on a boy in the night. The buds took a notion to pop out. From somewhere the birds came back. It was spring, perhaps the first and last day of spring, for from the looks of things tomorrow was going to fall right smack dab in the middle of summer. If it had been sweet like that before!

It wasn't such a bad little stone house, either, Linnea thought. It heated well. The two rooms were big. It had looked pretty when it was cleaned up. Linnea took quite a long time to lock the door, while everybody waited in the wagon. What made it kind of hard to leave even a place you hated was that things happened there that had cost so and so many days of your life. She thought of some of them: Parley being born, friends' visits (who could never come there again, any more than they could go back to a certain year). Things happening and things being, no water better and colder than that spilled out from the flowing well, no moons bigger, no nights blacker or whiter . . . and echoes, and frogs, and tomatoes and peaches, that got a hold on a person like a pet in the house you didn't care for to start with, but later cared, and knew it to your sorrow when it was lost or sick. She cared now, like that . . . had that nagging pain of caring, of feeling sorry. Olaf was the one to blame! Never coming near, mind you, and five kids, one a baby in arms. Linnea could see Sigrid ten miles out of town, on a farm, Olaf never coming near. She could just see her! The sorriness went away. In her mind's eye she dragged Bonnie through the mud again.

"No, sir," she said, "it's a free country! I won't be PLANTED." She locked the door and threw the key away. "By God Almighty, no."

The boxcar was there on the siding and Mr. Goff was standing by the rolled-back doors. The Barnes boys drove Bonnie and her calf up and inside, where all their possessions were piled. "I sure don't know how I'm ever going to be able to thank you," she said. "This nice boxcar and everything. I don't know how else I would of got everything took, the kids, and the cow and all."

"That calf's a little beauty," Mr. Goff said, when the heifer stuck her head out blinking and ran her tongue up her nose hole.

"Her *name's* Beauty!" Gertrude said proudly.

Mamma wrapped the brown shawl closer around wide-awake Parley whose heavy weight had already brought the sweat to her upper lip. "All right, you kids," she said, "in you go. I don't know how to thank you," she repeated to the stationmaster.

"Wait a minute," he said. "You're going to go in style."

"I know it," Mamma said. "You kids get on in, and don't keep jumping around like that. I'd just as soon try to raise a bunch of hy-yeenies." She smiled her going-away-good-bye-all-good-things-must-end-the-best-of-friends-must-part smile and put out her hand.

"You're really going to go in style," the man said kindly. "I fixed it up with the conductor. The boxcar goes on behind. You and the kids ride up in the parlor car."

Mamma looked shaken then, behind her smile, like a lady caught in her corset cover, and paled a little. "Oh, my, no," she protested. "That's just too much of a good thing!" Her face got red and the tears that never came while she was locking the door came now, or threatened to. They arose glistening.

Mr. Goff cleared his throat and turned away. "Nobody that done for my wife and baby like you done is going to ride in a boxcar. Her and her kids ain't, if I got anything to say about it," he said.

"It was just *luck,*" Mamma said, with a break in her voice, but he was starting to walk away. "Bertha," she said, "you go on up in the boxcar and untie Beauty and bring her down."

"What for, Mamma?" Bertha said, but she went up the incline and did it.

"Now you go after Mr. Goff," Mamma said, "and give it to him. Say she's a nice little Jersey calf. Say I shouldn't of tried to raise her anyway but should of had her butchered like Mr. Taylor said. Say she was so cute and Bonnie was so stuck on her we just couldn't get rid of her, but say he'll be doing us a favor if he either raises her or—listen," she said, "tell him we don't know how to thank him, we don't know what to say. . . ." The tears were running freely now. "Come on, kids." She caught them one by one by the shoulder and marched them ahead.

"We're going to ride in the parlor car," she said. "We're going to ride in style."

Mr. Goff didn't want to, he said she was a valuable animal, but he kept Beauty and was holding on to her rope on the station platform when they all pressed their faces against the moving windows and waved good-bye. Mamma dried her eyes right away in the beautiful very quiet green plush car and sat up straight. She got the kids settled and told them not to put their feet up on the seats like a bunch of country jakes, and to look out at the scenery—didn't it beat everything, how the weather had been, and now, just when they were leaving (like a rebuke), spring had broke out all over the place like measles?—and then she put Parley to her breast and looked at the scenery herself, crestfallen, a little crestfallen, but a little and more and more happy—because Ogden was something else again and she wasn't going to be planted like a tree.

Nobody in the world could have shown more delight—Mamma said so afterwards, she said she would never forget it—than Mrs. Sterling, and Estelle, and Johnny, when at Mamma's bidding Bertha knocked on the door and they all stood still on the little front stoop and waited for it to open.

It was a nice house, just as Mrs. Sterling had said, of a size for a doll to keep house in, with a window, a door and a window across the front, and gingerbread trimming. The curtains, clean panes and green plants on the sills, the swept walk and scrubbed steps showed that a good housekeeper lived there. Mamma told Mrs. Sterling that right away. "You can tell from the outside that a good housekeeper lives here," she said. Inside, it had the clean-in-the-corners look that Mamma's rooms always had, that look of attention bestowed and pleasure taken in the bestowal, that made her rooms so comfortable to be in.

Almost as if Mrs. Sterling had had a feeling in her bones, she had cooked up a potful of brown beans and was just taking the bread out of the oven. She kissed every one of them and said something nice, and took Parley out of Mamma's arms and hugged him and said if he wasn't the sweetest little old baby that ever drew the breath of life, why, she'd like to know who *was,* that's all. In no time they were divested of wraps and made at home, in no time fed. "It'd take something," Mamma said afterwards, "for me to forget that woman. If she'd of been my own sister she couldn't of put herself out more, and in that lovely way, so that it didn't seem like she was putting herself out at all."

There were beds a-plenty! Of course there were! Bonnie? Bonnie could stand in the coal shed! No trouble at all. And the children could run outside and play, it was so warm and bright. "You know," Mamma said, "speaking of bright. If it had been nice like this a day or so ago it might of been a different story all around. I tell you I got to thinking that cold and mud and onryness was never going to end." Now that they were here, had all walked up from the station, their coming seemed ever so slightly rash, and she felt a little embarrassed to speak of it. The drayman, hired on the way, was bringing their things up this afternoon. "I hope that drayman gets here," she said. "I'll just have him unload in the shed or somewheres, because we'll be going in a day or so."

Mrs. Sterling poured what coffee was left in Linnea's cup in the sink and filled it up again from the boiling pot. "It wasn't supposed to be," she said comfortingly, dropping back down in her chair and propping her elbows on the table. "The winter weather wasn't supposed to break until you was just so sick and tired of it you couldn't stand it a minute longer and had to pack up and get out."

"I was dragging Bonnie through the mud—" Linnea started to explain.

"The Lord just naturally meant you was *supposed* to come up here to Ogden. Or you wouldn't be here! If it hadn't of been the weather, it would of been something else. Because what I say," Mrs. Sterling said, "is, what is to be, will be. Don't you think so, Linnea?" It was a favorite saying and sounded good to the ears right now, like an ouzel over a waterfall.

"I'd of been stuck out there for life," Linnea said, wanting to hear the song again.

"Of course you would!"

"The kids could of got sick and died. Olaf never come out but a time or two since you left. The polygamy trouble piling up and him being scared of the government men—I tell you I got so I just wanted to scream. But of course he did give us what he could. He always has give us what he could." She saw his kind eyes, his kind face before her suddenly and looked another way.

"You did exactly right!"

"And what I thought was," Linnea went on, "government or no government, church or no church, settlement or no settlement, I'd wind this thing up once and for all—"

"But you ain't off the *Church*, are you, Linnea?" Mrs. Sterling asked.

"Oh, no." She looked surprised. "I ain't off the Church. I was born in it, just like you. Anything you was born in, you can't be off of, any more than you can be off of your own folks. You can have a tiff with your sister, but you always make it up. It's the same thing." She took a sip of coffee. "Oh, no. I ain't off the Church," she said. "The Church may be off me, though. No, I'm just off polygamy, is all. I've had enough to last me awhile."

"Well, what is to be, will be," Mrs. Sterling reiterated her sweet song. "Only I'd hate to see you and the Church—"

"I'm just off Olaf."

"He can't help it because them spies is after him, or that the weather was so bad and he couldn't get out. You can't imagine how hard he works in the shop. I was right there with him. I seen him. Working till his hands shook and he couldn't thread the needle. He tries as hard as I ever saw a man try, Linnea!" At the sight of her friend's face going blank, then soft, then anguished, she added quickly, "Only don't think about that now. You've set your head one way and you might as well stick to it as any other. It's all for the best, I'm sure of it. Everything's going to turn out *all right*."

It was as good as being at home, to be at Mrs. Sterling's, as good as being at Aunt Gunilla's. It smelt and tasted and felt like home. Mamma said she was going to take hold in a day or so and get work and find some rooms for her family. Mrs. Sterling said she could stay right here. Her husband Mr. Sterling was expected within days but that didn't make a bit of difference. Mamma said she wouldn't even think of such a thing as that, but she'd stay a little while, with gratitude.

As they had in Bountiful, the two women sat up late and talked by the stove that night. They had a lot of territory to cover. Linnea had to tell all about Mrs. Goff's confinement, and the boxcar Mr. Goff let them use, and their ride in the parlor car, and how she had given him Beauty, the calf. Her heart ached for the little thing, she said, she'd got so attached to it—and listen to Bonnie mooing in the coal shed. She must miss her calf awfully. There wasn't a law or anything about disturbing the peace right downtown like this in Ogden, was there? Oh, no, there wasn't. Almost everybody had a cow.

Mrs. Sterling had heard from Brother Bell again, she confided to Linnea. Wasn't that the darnedest thing? Coming into Olaf's shop and seeing her and getting so dead set on her like that?

They brewed more coffee and put their feet up on the oven door and drank it, Linnea beginning to blossom like a rose in what she thought of as "human companionship" again. Mrs. Sterling blossomed, too. For some reason she got twice as pretty as ever when she thought of Brother Bell being after her like that. Wasn't it a scream? In fact, Mrs. Sterling had had not one or two but *several* letters from him. You know what he was just as well as offering her? A half a house up on South Temple. Him! that had never been known to part with a dime, Linnea said marveling, except maybe for tithing and things like that. Couldn't love stand you on your head though?

"It's not like he'd pay the rent exactly, from what I can make out," Mrs. Sterling said, as though to apologize for the poor man and say he wasn't *that* crazy. "He's got a mortgage on the place, or the bank has got a mortgage on the place and he owns the bank, or something. So it wouldn't be what you might say coming out of his pocket, although from what I can make out he'd even . . ." she paused in embarrassment. "We could eat. Only he doesn't come right out and say *that*. He more hints it, like."

"Well, there's no fool like an old fool," Linnea said comfortably. "Will wonders never cease."

"I don't know whether I'd ought to say anything to John about it or not," Mrs. Sterling said. "I've been thinking. He might get mad. He might think I led Brother Bell *on* or something." Her right eye veering off prettily to the side, she squinted the other and pursed her lips. Linnea saw her in the Princess of Sweden costume listening to the "Book of Ether."

"I don't know either. You can size him up," Linnea offered. "If you think he'll laugh about it—it's just human nature, after all—why, show him. If you think he'll get mad, why, don't."

Mrs. Sterling took the hairpins out of her dark hair and let it fall about her shoulders. She ran her fingers through her short bangs. "To tell you the truth, my husband is *very jealous* of me," she said, in rather a pleased tone. "I think maybe I must of mentioned it. When we was engaged, if I even so much as looked at anybody else, he just had a fit."

"Well, you can decide later whether to mention it or not. It ought to make him laugh. It's just human nature. It ain't as if there was anything mysterious about it. There hasn't been no *harm* in it, sure."

It was very warm and cozy in the room and they were both growing sleepy.

"There's some people that's naturally jealous," Linnea mused. "Any little thing and they flare right up. Me, now. I wouldn't say I was of a jealous disposition exactly, but at the same time like I was saying to the Goffs the other day, if it'd been me, instead of Sigrid, and Olaf had come to *me* and asked me if he could marry somebody else eight years younger, I'd of said no. I know very well I'd of said no, Church or no Church, Prophet or no Prophet. Like I said, I don't know what possessed Sigrid . . . she keeps such a close watch on the purse strings and she ain't one of these what you might call *fanatics* about religion like some of Brigham's wives was for instance, and she's as jealous as all get out, over Olaf. . . . The older I get, the less I can understand how she would of consented to it for a minute. It would of been better for me, and better for the kids, if she hadn't," she added, "I get to thinking sometimes. I'd of married somebody else, maybe. I don't know what possessed me. I'd of been the only wife, like you are. The kids would of been some other little kids—"

"Not Bertha and Gertrude and Stellie and Rudie and Parley," Mrs. Sterling said, "but some other kids, not nearly so cute, maybe, not with all their ways. Why, I never saw a cuter bunch of kids in my life."

Linnea smiled sunnily with relief. "Polygamy or no polygamy, I guess I'm not so bad off, am I? With kids like them?"

"I'll say you're not so bad off," Mrs. Sterling said.

"But you can understand how I'd be mad at Olaf? Not coming near? And how a person'd want to pick up and leave Bountiful?"

"Sure I can," Mrs. Sterling said. "But it'll all blow over."

"It *is* a problem, though, you can see that? Polygamy? It didn't use to seem like it, but all of a sudden it is."

"Well, John isn't that kind that would—he wouldn't—so it hasn't come very close to home—but I think I'd maybe—I don't think I'd—" Mrs. Sterling said slowly, and then briskly, "What I think is, it'll be abolished before too long. That's what the talk is everywhere."

"But you can't abolish big families of kids," Linnea said. "There's the rub."

"That's it," Mrs. Sterling said. "But they'll work it out someway."

Linnea yawned and rose, cupping her hands about the cooling chimney. "Well, it's no skin off my nose no more," she said. "I've settled *my* end of it myself, once and for all." A sudden homesickness to see Olaf and give him a talking to, and make up with him (if he got down on his knees to her) assailed her but she shook it off.

"No, sir," Mrs. Sterling said, going back a bit, "it was always more John that was jealous, someway. I wonder how the men would like it if we come and said we wanted another husband? I wonder how John would like it if I come dragging in Brother Bell by the heels and saying I wanted to marry him too? Can you imagine what would happen?"

They went off to bed on a gale of laughter but had to hush up so as not to wake the children.

CHAPTER 16

Mrs. sterling, and Linnea, too, had a shock coming to her the next day, but at breakfast she didn't know it, or at lunch. It was at quarter past two—Linnea looked at the clock but she didn't know she had looked until later, when she remembered and it seemed important to mention to Ingeborg and Gunilla when she told the story that it was just exactly at quarter past two that he knocked at the door.

Mrs. Sterling's husband! John Sterling, missionary returned from far-off Norway. He was nice looking, but his picture flattered him a good deal, Linnea thought privately. He was more ordinary appearing than not, she decided, and surely he must have been very sick at his stomach a very short while ago for he was as white as a ghost and his lips had a bluish tinge. Mrs. Sterling mentioned it. She said, "John, you look as sick as a ghost. Did you eat something or what's the matter with you? Do you want to lay down? You'd ought to. You look like you're about to heave."

He thought he had eaten something, he said. Some of the converts on the train had bought a sack of doughnuts. Several converts had come in a party to America, to Zion, and he had accompanied them and watched over them. He did lie down, on the lounge in the parlor, and Mrs. Sterling brought a cloth wrung out in cold water and pressed it on his forehead.

Out in the kitchen Linnea said what a surprise it was for him to come home today and Mrs. Sterling said yes, wasn't it? But the children hadn't really had the joy of him yet, with him feeling so sick like that. He looked like he could hardly stand to have them pull at him and kiss him and want to hug him the way a couple of youngsters would naturally want to do with their father who had been gone on a mission for longer than two years. As a matter of fact, Johnny hardly remembered him and had to be almost forcibly brought in, batting his eyes faster than ever, and made to embrace his father, so it wasn't he that wanted to climb over him so much as Estelle who, of course, remembered him very well. They couldn't really any of them get the joy of John for the time being, Mrs. Sterling said, until his stomach kind of calmed down and his color came back. It was peculiar to see him so sick, his stomach was usually like cast iron, but maybe it really was those doughnuts the converts had bought. When he felt better, they'd have a real reunion. He had probably brought the kids some things from Norway and he would tell them all about the trip and everything.

Linnea apologized heartily for being there. She said she thought she and her family would surely be gone before the husband and father came home, they hadn't intended to stay very long. She said she noticed a sign in the window across the street that there was a room for rent and she was going to run across and take it, if the landlady had no objection to children. Mrs. Sterling said the landlady wouldn't have any objection but she, Mrs. Sterling, would. Why, husband or no husband, they were as welcome as the flowers in May. Over her protests Linnea put her shawl around her shoulders and went over and rented the room, and when she came back Mrs. Sterling said Linnea had really hurt her feelings TERRIBLY. But Linnea gave her arm a squeeze and said she knew she didn't mean that—a husband was one thing but a *sick* husband was something else, and neither one nor the other would want a strange woman and five strange children running around his house the first day he came home. How was Mr. Sterling, by the way?

Well, he was a little bit better. The sweat had gone off his upper lip and he seemed to be lying more relaxed, not like he was doubled up with cramps, but he still was as white as a sheet. It was awfully peculiar, Mrs. Sterling said. The children hadn't got a bit of joy out of their father yet. Herself, either. Him being sick like that, she said, so that he had to go off by himself and lie on the lounge in the parlor and wince if one of them even so much as walked past the door, made him seem like a stranger, sort of. It was awfully peculiar. Not a bit like she had looked forward to.

"*This* wouldn't be no time to tell him about Brother Bell," Linnea teased softly. And then, "But he'll be fine in a little while, and then everything will be as natural as can be. I think I'll start rounding the kids up and we'll go over and get settled at the rooming house."

"Not a step will you go," Mrs. Sterling said sharply, "not a step, mind you, except over my dead body, until you've had your supper. Why, you'd hurt my feelings so I'd never forgive you as long as I lived."

"All right," Linnea said, "we'd be tickled to stay to supper, but only if you promise to let me do the cooking while you spend the time with your husband."

She argued but finally Mrs. Sterling agreed to that and said she thought it was lovely of Linnea to offer to do it. She went in the parlor to have a look at her husband and said he seemed to have fallen into a doze, and he was still pale. It was a very peculiar thing, how he'd happen to come home deathly sick like that from a two-year mission in Norway.

Linnea was nursing Parley and Mrs. Sterling was sitting across the table from her. They had just said well, this was the first really nice spring day, wasn't it? and Linnea was thinking about getting the potatoes on to cook if they were going to have supper at five o'clock, when Mr. Sterling startled them both very much by standing in the doorway.

"Why, John," Mrs. Sterling said, jumping up and going to him. "Do you feel better?"

"Your color's lots better," Linnea said in the tone in which one pays a compliment. "For a little while there you sure looked like you was ready to cave in."

He was much better, he said, but he held himself oddly and carefully as if he had suffered a tumble down a flight of stairs and was trying himself out now to see how many bones were broken.

"Come on over here and sit down," his wife said, patting the chair seat beside her and then getting up and lighting the lamp on the table and turning it up bright although it was still daylight. "Linnea's going to get supper. She's such a good cook."

"Nothing to brag of," Linnea said. She smiled cordially at her host.

"She's the one I stayed with out in Bountiful, you know," Mrs. Sterling said, patting the seat again, "that I wrote and told you about. That we went to the costume ball. You know. This here's her little baby Parley. Not so little, either, for eight months old. He weighs a ton. You'd ought to lift him. He's the cutest thing you ever laid your eyes on when he sits up and starts to laugh and carry on. You want to watch him when I speak Eight Fingers and Ten Toes for him. He just goes all to pieces."

But Mr. Sterling didn't want to sit down on the chair beside her and he didn't seem to be listening to her conversation, either. He said he had to go down to the hotel.

"What do you have to go down to the hotel for?" Mrs. Sterling wanted to know, coming around and taking Parley off Linnea's lap and giving him a hug.

Well, for his trunks and things, Mr. Sterling said.

He had been gone fifteen minutes before Mrs. Sterling said, "Now isn't that the most peculiar thing. Honest to goodness, I don't seem to *know* the man any more! Now what would he want to leave his trunks and things down to the hotel? Why wouldn't he just bring them on home with him in the first place?"

"Maybe they was in among the converts' luggage," Linnea said, sifting the flour for a batch of biscuits. "Maybe that was handier or something."

Mrs. Sterling dug her nose in and planted a kiss on Parley's creased neck and waited for his tickled laugh. "You don't suppose he's gone and lost his mind, do you?" she asked. "On his mission? Too much religion or something?"

"Of course not," Linnea said practically. "He's just had a terrible upset stomach, is all. He don't feel good yet. You'll see. When he gets over it, he'll be just like he always was."

"One thing I know," Mrs. Sterling said, "it *wasn't* handier to leave his trunks down to the hotel than to bring them directly home, and I bet I'll get to the bottom of all this peculiar acting or know the reason why."

It was just when Linnea put the biscuits in the oven and Mrs. Sterling was setting the table that Mr. Sterling came back and brought the girl in behind him. Then everything dawned on them suddenly. It dawned quicker, and harder, on Mrs. Sterling than on Linnea, more like what writers write about sometimes: a bolt from the blue.

No matter what anybody says, a pretty Norwegian girl is about the prettiest thing on God's green earth, and this one was no exception to the rule. Linnea didn't do a thing but stand there with her mouth wide open until she remembered it was rudeness itself to stare, and shut it, and looked away, but looked right back again. Mrs. Sterling had her mouth open too. She was hanging on to Parley for dear life and as Linnea said afterwards, you could have knocked her eyes off with a stick.

The girl just stood there, in back and a little to one side of Mr. Sterling, and didn't do a thing, but somehow the air in the perfectly quiet room crackled. She couldn't have been more than eighteen if she was that. She had a foreign-looking knitted cap pulled down on gold and resilient hair that had the life of looped-up snakes. They kept wanting to push the cap off with their springiness, shining extremely, and the girl kept reaching up with a large childish hand to tug it more firmly down and anchor it. She had a foreign-looking coat on too, of a tight unknown but old-fashioned cut, and heavy shoes. Her skin was as thin as Parley's and at least as pink. Her eyes were big as a half a dollar and of limpid quaking blue, with long eyelashes that flared up around them like a fan. Her two front teeth were a little too large and overlapped ever so slightly but all her teeth were perfectly white and it didn't matter a bit. In fact, it made her prettier, if anything, for her short upper lip under her short nose self-consciously trying to cover what she must have considered her chief blemish, gave her a still sweeter and more heart-melting look, like Parley with a pacifier.

"This is Miss Sigrid Tolene," Mr. Sterling said. "Sister, rather. For she has been baptized."

Another Sigrid! Linnea glanced out of the corner of her eye at Mrs. Sterling but she was just hanging on to Parley and standing there.

"She is one of my converts," he said.

Oh, well, if that was all . . . a convert. Linnea began to breathe easier.

Mr. Sterling still looked very much under the weather, from the doughnuts. He was still pale and he was holding himself that careful way. "I am going to marry her," he said, "in the Church."

He stopped holding himself that way then and when he let loose he began to shake all over like he had the palsy or something—the man was scared out of his wits, Linnea decided. Well, no wonder! Out of tact, she did not glance at Mrs. Sterling again to see what she was doing. There wasn't a sound from her. Not even Parley made any of his baby noises. The girl tugged at her cap and Mr. Sterling continued to shake in that cowardly way. It was very embarrassing to stand there and not know what to say or do, whether to go or stay. The moment was as long as a sermon.

"And her sister, too," Mr. Sterling announced, breaking the silence. "I'm going to take her unto myself as wife and helpmeet, also. She happens to be two years older."

"Oh, she does, does she? Now isn't that lovely? Well, you happen to be two years crazier," Mrs. Sterling exploded then. "Two more wives! You must be completely out of your head!"

The girl began to sniffle softly. Poor little thing, Linnea concluded. One of these poor little numskulls. Pretty enough to go on the stage, too, or marry a rich miner like Tom Kearns, in short, make something of herself, but no brains. I should talk, Linnea said, I really should, I've done so well myself. . . .

"The Prophet—" Mr. Sterling began.

"The Prophet!" Mrs. Sterling raged. "You just dare to stand there and Prophet me! You just dare! I'll—I'll pick up this lamp and throw it at you!" Linnea moved then, fast, and took Parley out of her arms. "You can Prophet me just so far and no farther, and you've gone to the end of the line this time, Mr. High and Mighty! This is where you get off at!"

Linnea thought about the biscuits in the oven because they smelled as if they were burning but she would have to go around Mr. Sterling to get to them and it seemed better to let them scorch, at least for the time being. The girl still sniffled.

"Not only that," Mrs. Sterling said, "you get this—this OX out of here"—they all looked surprised at the word, even the lady herself—"or I'll Prophet you! If this—this OX isn't out of here in one minute I'll burn down the house!"

They never found out whether she would or not because at that minute, in all the fine feathers of her fury, she fainted dead away. Linnea ran and laid Parley down on the lounge in the other room—who finally let out a squall that would wake the dead—and ran back to find the Norwegian girl had dropped into a chair and was weeping bitterly with her head on the table between her two arms, with her cap nearly off, barely perched upon the alive and scintillating loops of her hair. And the children filing in from outside, hungry, utterly bewildered by the scene they saw. Linnea shooed them all out again, promising supper in no more than five minutes by the clock, and hurried to dash a dipper of cold water over her prostrate friend. Mr. Sterling, ascertaining that his wife was in no danger of expiring, went off, taking the tearful emigrant with him, to the hotel, to get the sister who happened to be two years older and bring her home too.

"This was a shock to her," Linnea said to Mr. Sterling when they were leaving, "as you might imagine. It seems to me that you could of handled it a little different, but of course that's none of my business. What I want to say is, if I was you I wouldn't come back for a couple of hours. We can get supper over then and your wife can kind of get hold of herself."

Mrs. Sterling revived and Linnea got the children in and fed, and themselves fed—Mrs. Sterling only ate a little of everything else but she pronounced the too-brown biscuits unusually good and ate three of them with honey and drank two cups of coffee—and got the dishes washed up as fast as she could, as though they were under siege.

Her hostess was going to barricade the door but Linnea said that wouldn't do any good and would just create a disturbance, for Mr. Sterling had one of these stubborn chins and very prominent jawbones and anybody that had a chin and jawbones like that wasn't one that would give in very easy. He'd break the door down as sure as fate.

"Why, I couldn't let those women in my house," Mrs. Sterling said. "He's gone stark staring crazy. Here polygamy's nearly at an end and everybody's thanking their lucky stars it is, and he's never had such a thought in the world. And then! He comes home from Norway and wants to marry two more women at the same time! Why, he's out of his head. I won't stand for it. I won't stand for it a minute."

"What are you going to do?" Linnea asked.

Mrs. Sterling was going to do a lot of things, first one thing, then another. It seemed very fresh and novel, and somehow admirable, too, when she came out suddenly with the very sensible proclamation that she was going to leave her husband and get a divorce from him!

Linnea stayed in the room with them while the man and woman discussed their troubles (the two young Norwegian ladies had been re-quested to remain in the parlor in the meanwhile), for Mrs. Sterling had asked her to do so. Linnea could not fathom Mr. Sterling at all. Whether he loved his wife or not, or had ever loved her, she could not decide. Now his wish, since she would not "be reasonable," was for her to abandon him to his own devices as soon as possible, and leave him alone to do God's will. Mrs. Sterling, hours after the big surprise, still wore a flabbergasted look, but she laid down the law to him. Mr. Sterling gave up in despair: she simply had no notion what a divine injunction signified. If God ordered a thing, he said, that was a thing that had to be done: who did puny little man think he was, to argue?

"I'm no puny little man," Mrs. Sterling said, "like some people I know, not mentioning any names, and I can argue if I want to. All I want to say is, I get my rightful property."

"Always concerned with trivialities," Mr. Sterling said sadly, "never with the big issues at stake. Well, the time's going to come when you're going to be a pretty sorry woman, a pret-ty sor-ry woman. That's all I can say."

"The time's right here now," Mrs. Sterling said, "I'm such a sorry woman I could kick my behind from here to Salt Lake that I ever laid eyes on you, and you may call my good china and my pictures and ornaments and my crocheted tablecloth, and all my linens, and half of the furniture, trivialities if you want to, but I don't. They're mine and I want them and I won't go a step out of here unless they go with me." She began to gather them together by standing on tiptoe and plucking down a picture from the wall, so brightly colored and wet-looking you could almost smell the paint, of a straw-hatted young man sitting beside a pompadoured young lady on a bank entirely made of daisies, in a walnut frame. She placed this firmly on the table and started to remove the hand-painted plates from the plate rail.

"I've worked hard to furnish this house," Mr. Sterling said. "You're not going to clean me out and leave me with nothing, I should hope!"

"That's exactly what I'm doing," his wife said, with a meaningful look at the shut door of the parlor from whence not a sound issued—the two Norwegian girls were as still as the grave—"leaving you with *nothing!*"

Remembering Miss Sigrid Tolene's great and her sister's not inconsiderable beauty, Linnea thought Mrs. Sterling went a little far, but she gave her a look of encouragement all the same. "I'm going to take anything I want," the lady went on inexorably, "and if you try to stop me, I'll—"

"I'll go to the Church authorities!" Mr. Sterling said, clutching his stomach again, for his indigestion had come back.

"You're just about thirty years too late," Mrs. Sterling taunted. "What could the Church do? Tell me to sit around and watch you get these two Scandinavians in the family way every year as regular as clockwork?

Tell me to let them crowd me out of house and home? Listen, while I tell you something," she said, "polygamy's a thing of the past: it's on its way out the window and a blamed good thing it is: and the Church hasn't got the power of life and death over me, either, even if it was nothing to get funny with when Brigham Young was alive. You go to the Church authorities and what will they tell you? They'll tell you you're right and I'm wrong and what good will that do you?"

"Plenty of good," Mr. Sterling muttered.

"Because I'll go to the Government authorities, and I'll tell *them,* and what will they do but send the agents over and where will you be but in jail and a lot of Scandinavian women you can get in the family way *there!*"

"Hah!" Mr. Sterling said.

"Hah yourself!" Mrs. Sterling said. "The only reason I'll agree to leave this house is because I can take everything that belongs to me. If I can't, I'll go straight to the Government and you know what they'll do to you."

Mr. Sterling, wounded by the unfeelingness of his wife and still suffering, by the look on his face, from the stomach cramps, stalked to the parlor door. "Crucify me," he said, turning the knob, pushing it open and walking in. "Go ahead and crucify me," he said, shutting it behind him. That meant she could take what she wanted and go.

Mrs. Sterling and Linnea looked at each other. There were tears of vexation in the former's eyes, anger, jealousy, mortification. But Linnea had a twinkle in hers and the first thing you know they were smiling and then laughing outright for, as Mrs. Sterling herself said, the whole thing was too silly for words.

Linnea whisked her own children, and Estelle and Johnny, over to the rooming house across the street, and put them to bed—the four girls, Bertha, Gertrude, Stellie and Estelle in the big brass bed, and Rudie and Johnny on the floor on quilts and pillows kindly provided by the avid landlady, shushed them and told them to go right to sleep for they were going to Salt Lake tomorrow, and then, Parley sound asleep against her shoulder, went back to Mrs. Sterling's.

Neither the dyspeptic missionary nor his blonde ladies stuck their noses out of the parlor, nor was there a peep out of them, and Mrs. Sterling and Linnea set to work packing. Parley slept like the angel he was on two chairs placed together while they got everything assembled. Linnea, sent into the parlor with the clothesbasket by her friend with orders to take the what-nots off the what-not shelf, the oversize pink seashells and four rainbow glass balls off the organ, the enlarged photographs of Mrs. Sterling's mother, grandmother and heavily bearded father off the walls, the plush tablecloth off the center table and the fuchsia out of the window, did so with feelings of reluctance, but she need not have minded so much, she thought afterwards.

For when she rapped on the door and went in—no invitation to do so was forthcoming—she found it very like, she later told Ingeborg, going into a waxworks museum. Bolt upright in the tufted chair sat Mr. Sterling without moving a muscle or uttering a word, his hands on his knees, and bolt upright on the horsehair settee sat the two Norwegian girls, still in their caps and coats, with their hands folded in their laps, without moving a muscle or uttering a word. "It give me the creeps," Linnea said. "I said, 'Pardon me, I had a little errand to do in here, I won't disturb you long,' and smiled, kind of, as nice as I could, so that it wouldn't look like we was *all* taking everything so deadly serious like the Day of Judgment or something, but do you think I got a look out of them? No, sir, not a look or a smile. It was like they was three statues sitting there as big as life and twice as natural. It sort of give me the creeps. But the girl was a beauty," she said, "as beautiful as a actress or somebody. I sized her up again out of the corner of my eye and she really was. I thought to myself, Here you go and waste it all on *nothing*. And somehow or other it made me just sick, anybody wasting her beauty like that."

Mrs. Sterling sent a neighbor boy for the same drayman who had brought Linnea's things up from town, and by eleven o'clock that night, though the man protested the hour and said the job could as well wait till morning, and it cost her more than she counted on as a consequence, the two women's possessions were on their way to the station, even Bonnie, tied on behind, mooing as if her heart would break.

The rooming-house landlady provided them with a second room for that night, greedy for news of what had taken place to cause such an upheaval as this. Mrs. Sterling obligingly told her. The landlady was startled, aghast, amazed, indignant and wrathful by turns while she listened, as a good neighbor should be, gave her solemn promise, without intending to abide by it a moment longer than sunrise, to tell *no one*, threw her arms around Mrs. Sterling, wept, made hot cocoa, peeped through the drawn curtains at the house across the way to see if the lamps were still burning, announced with horror at something after midnight that they were *not* and was as friendly and comforting as a neighbor could be. Linnea, however, was glad when sleep overcame the lady and she had to apologize and go to bed, for that gave them the chance to do the same, but Mrs. Sterling would not shut her eyes. Would not or could not. She turned and muttered long after Linnea was too drowsy to comprehend what she said any more. "She's young enough to be his daughter," she said, "but I don't care about that, you understand. I don't care how young she is. Why should I care about how *young* she is? I don't care about her looks. Why should I care that she's so beautiful, or rather that some people might say she's beautiful,— I wouldn't, myself, particularly, and I say it honestly, I wouldn't say

that she was the prettiest thing that ever drew the breath of life or anything like that—what's that to me? Nothing. Just nothing. No, what I
care about, Linnea, what galls me so—are you listening or are you
asleep?"

Linnea swam upwards from her dark pool and stuck her head out of
eddying sleep blinking and said, "No, I'm not asleep," before she sank
back downwards again to the bottom like a stone.

"What I care about," Mrs. Sterling said, "what I care about . . .
what I care about, Linnea, is honesty"—it sounded like she said honesty
but Linnea, plummeting downwards fast, could not be sure. "Do you
think it matters to me that the girl is only eighteen years old? Do you
think that hurts my feelings? Do you think I care that she's supposed to
be so everlastingly beautiful? Well, I'll tell you right here and now, I
don't. I don't care the snap of my fingers. My feelings aren't any more
hurt than yours are. Anyway, you can bet on she's the kind will age fast.
You can bet on in ten years she'll look like something the cat drug in!"
Mrs. Sterling derived comfort enough from this to be soothed to silence,
at least—Linnea thought to actual slumber, hearing no more from her—
but Mrs. Sterling denied it absolutely in the morning. She said she
never closed her eyes all night.

Ingeborg was hospitality itself, but Mrs. Sterling, when they all arrived in Salt Lake, refused to spend over a night in her house. She said
that eleven children and three women in two rooms were at least one
woman and two children too many. She and Estelle and Johnny ate
lunch there and set out from Ingeborg's to find a place to live. Linnea
saw that Ingeborg and Mrs. Sterling didn't hit it off so well and did not
try to persuade her to stay.

In the late afternoon Mrs. Sterling returned to announce triumphantly that she had found just the very thing she was looking for, four
rooms, with lots of windows and not only a front porch but a back porch
as well—one whole side of a double house up on East South Temple.
Usually no one was more self-possessed than she but she stammered over
this happy announcement. Not only stammered but flushed scarlet, and
when she came to mention the slight detail that Brother Bell was her
landlord—he had a mortgage on the place, or the Bank had a mortgage
and Brother Bell owned the Bank or something—the tune was a familiar
one and Linnea remembered that she had heard it before, in Ogden—
Mrs. Sterling could not seem to look straight at her friend at all but out
the window and up at last summer's flyspecks on the ceiling and everywhere but in Linnea's sympathetic eyes. For they were sympathetic. "She
would never," Linnea maintained forever afterwards, "never for one
instant have stepped off the straight and narrow if her husband hadn't
gone and done her that way. Imagine, coming home from a mission

with two women and telling you he's going to marry both of them—one of them eighteen years old and so pretty she'd put your eyes out, and the other twenty and nothing to sneeze at either—what would you have done?"

"It don't look to me like you're the one to talk," Ingeborg pointed out gently. "Against it, I mean. Being in polygamy yourself."

"No, but wasn't that an awful thing for a man to go and do? It's no wonder in the world she stepped off the straight and narrow, especially when Brother Bell was standing there with his mouth open waiting to catch her like somebody waiting under a tree for a big ripe apple to fall."

"That's just it," Ingeborg said. "The right kind wouldn't of *had* him dangling in the sidelines. The right kind wouldn't of *had* a man waiting for her to fall out of the tree. A decent woman don't have a man lolly-gagging around, waiting for her to drop down in his lap. No, sir, Linnea," Ingeborg said, "husband or no husband, women or no women, polygamy or no polygamy, that woman's no good and would of taken any excuse to slip off the hook, no matter what it was, so she could do just what she blame well pleased. That's *my* opinion," Ingeborg said.

"Well, you're wrong," Linnea said. "It was all her husband. She'd of been a faithful little wife keeping house for him yet if he hadn't pulled such a trick on her."

"That ain't *my* opinion," Ingeborg stated firmly. "And as long as we're on the subject, I might as well say I think you had little to do to take the kids and go up to Ogden, when you snuck off from Bountiful, to somebody like HER, instead of coming straight to Salt Lake where you belonged and coming here to ME, that's been your friend all these years. I think you had little to do, if you want to know what I think!"

"You know why I went up there. Olaf would come here the first thing —he wouldn't think I'd be in Ogden. That's why, Ingeborg."

"All I know is, you wouldn't of done such a thing as this, if that woman hadn't influenced you."

"Ingeborg, listen, will you? Mrs. Sterling never had nothing to do with me leaving Bountiful."

"I feel like giving her a piece of my mind," Ingeborg said. She paused, thinking. "That eye of hers cocked to one side so smarty."

Linnea laughed. "As if she could help her eye being cocked to one side!"

"I got a notion to tell her."

"Please don't, Ingeborg. She really ain't to blame for anything, either her troubles or mine, and she'll be gone in a little while."

She was, as Linnea had predicted. Before nightfall, Mrs. Sterling and her children were settled in the house provided by Brother Bell. Linnea, going with her to view the large freshly papered and painted rooms and array of windows, stifled a deep sigh. She would almost be willing to listen to the Gospel twice a day from Brother Bell herself for such an abode as this. When the two families came down on the train that morning there had been some talk that Linnea and Mrs. Sterling would share, at least for a time, a dwelling, but now, of course, that was out of the question and neither mentioned it. Linnea offered to help her friend unpack and get settled when her things arrived, as her own possessions, except for their clothes, would remain packed until she was permanently settled. (Even if she had wanted to unpack, which she did not, there would not have been room for a single cup and saucer in Ingeborg's crowded but meticulous two rooms . . . and the hallowed parlor was as out of the question to use, as by a true believer the thigh-bone of a saint would be, to stir a pot of soup.)

But Mrs. Sterling thanked her and said she thought she would be able to manage very well. For some reason, she threw her arms around Linnea and took a notion to cry hard against Linnea's breast, and Linnea patted her hair back as though she had been Stellie sobbing about a bruise got in a fall, but she did not explain why she wept, only why she did not. "I don't care how young she is," Mrs. Sterling said, "I don't care how beautiful she is. I don't care if John doesn't love me anymore. I wouldn't shed a tear over HER, I can tell you. I wouldn't shed a tear over HIM. Not a tear. Not one single solitary tear. Why, she can be fourteen if what she's after is to be so everlastingly young, like that was something to brag about . . . she can be as beautiful as Snow White and the Seven Dwarfs . . . do you think I care? Do you think I'd cry over something as silly as *that?*"

"Of course you wouldn't," Linnea said comfortingly.

"And not only that," Mrs. Sterling said, drying her tears and blowing her nose, "I haven't got any special influence with Brother Bell. *I* have to pay rent just like anybody else."

"In a pig's eye," Ingeborg said when she heard about it.

"I will never," Linnea said, "I will never speak to Olaf again as long as I live. We been gone from Bountiful a week today and he ain't made the slightest move to find us yet."

"How do you know?" Ingeborg said, emptying the dust pan into the stove and hanging it and the broom behind the door where it belonged.

"Why, because if he had, he would of found us, that's all! The weather's been good. He could of got out to Bountiful and discovered the house was locked up and we was gone. He could of asked around till he discovered we went up to Ogden. He could of found out we had wound up here. He could of used his head and realized right away that we was with you, and come and at least *inquired* if we was alive or dead."

"How about you inquiring if he is alive or dead? He ain't got no particular lease on life, has he? How do you know *he* ain't dead and buried, and with you disappeared off the face of the earth how could anybody even get to you, to notify you?"

Linnea's face paled. "You hadn't ought to say things like that," she faltered. "You hadn't ought to joke like that."

"Who said I was joking? Maybe it's true, for all you know."

"It ain't true, of course. Naturally."

"What difference would it make to you? You said you wouldn't speak to him ever again anyway," Ingeborg said sensibly.

"I meant if he was alive! I didn't mean if he was dead," Linnea protested.

"Oh, you'd speak to him if he was dead, is that it?"

"Don't be so onry and tease me like that," Linnea said. "You know very well what I mean."

"Something really might of happened to him," Ingeborg insisted.

Thus it was that, though it would "spoil the whole thing," as Linnea grumbled sadly, and she might just as well have not run off and gone to so much trouble, for all she accomplished by it, she finally got dressed up and went down to Olaf's tailor shop.

Her conscience, with a little prodding from Ingeborg, had got the better of her, and she decided that one of two things had happened, neither Olaf's fault: he was ill or (and she would never forgive herself) dead and buried. Or there was possibility number two: Linnea and her family had eluded him so cleverly, had disappeared from the face of the earth so completely, that in spite of trying every way to find them, he couldn't do it. Thinking how she would die of grief if the former were true, thinking how she would beg forgiveness on bended knee for causing him worry and promise never to do such a cruel thing again, if the latter were the circumstance, she made her way downtown to her husband's tailor shop. With fear and trembling she went up the steep stairs to the floor above Carter's Gun Store. Halfway up, she fancied she could smell the steam from dampened wool cloth under a scorching-hot iron, which greatly reassured her and stiffened her backbone. He was alive, and he was pressing something. She opened the door with confidence and a relieved feeling in her chest. Sure enough he was both: alive, and pressing the front of a blue serge coat.

"Olaf," she said. "I tell you I've been through something the last five minutes coming down from the Z.C.M.I., turning in here and walking up these stairs. I tell you, I'm just shaking, I'm so glad you're all right."

He put his arms out, gathered her in and kissed her lovingly, reaching backward with one hand to set the iron up for sure on end so it wouldn't take a notion to burn a hole in the garment. "All right?" he said, kissing her again. "Why wouldn't I be all right? How's Parley? How's the kids? How's Bonnie? How's the calf?"

She pushed him back with both hands. "You ain't been out there then?" she said. "You don't know?"

"Out where? Know what?" he said. "I'm coming out tomorrow afternoon, though. I was just saying to myself yesterday, yesterday I was saying to myself, Olaf, I was saying, better be in jail for polygamy than not never to see Linnea and them sweet little kids! I'm coming out tomorrow and going to stay till Sunday evening. I been so homesick to see you and Parley and all, that I just couldn't hardly stand it. But there's been so many arrests, and Sigrid said—not only Sigrid, either, but the Bishop of the Ward and different ones—that it was just foolish to go out of a person's way to get took up and arrested. And the reason I ain't wrote a line for several days is because I was going to collect money owed me and you think I could? I've had the worst trouble in the world to get it, but I'm sure to have it tomorrow, and if not that, I got more coming. I mean, I'll have money tomorrow *sure*—and I know how you need it and I just didn't have the heart to send you a letter with not a dime put in it—I kept waiting, knowing for sure I'd have what's owed me today or tomorrow—say, you're not mad, are you?" He looked at her, puzzled.

"No, I'm not mad," she said. "Why should I be mad? Why should I be mad because I took the kids a whole week ago and went to Ogden and locked up the house and threw the key away, and you ain't found it out yet? I was sick and tired of the whole thing, you included. I was dragging Bonnie through the mud and I said to myself, there's no man living can plant me out on ten acres like a tree and expect me to stay there. Not much, there ain't, I said. I should let Sigrid lord it over the universe in town right down on Fifth East like a civilized human being, while I—I should do such a thing, I said."

"Ogden?" Olaf said.

"I'm not mad," Linnea said. "If me and the kids been gone from Bountiful a week, and been up in Ogden, and could be swallowed up so that nothing was ever heard of us again, and my own husband don't even know about it, if he thinks we're still out on that God-forsaken farm with no money, no clothes, no nothing, waiting for five cents from him, and his company once a year, if he don't know whether we're dead or alive and cares less, why should I be mad? I'd be a pretty sight, wouldn't I, getting mad over something like that?"

"I'd like to know what I done, that's all. A man's got a right to know what he done."

"*You* didn't do anything. My, no. Neither did Mrs. Sterling's husband that come home from his mission bringing two Norwegian girls, neither did he, coming out flat-footed and saying he's going to marry the both of them—both, mind you—and here Mrs. Sterling, that's been married to the man going on nine years, wakes up to find herself throwed out to fend for herself like a alley cat somebody wants to get rid of, wakes up to find herself tossed into the clutches of that nasty old Brother Bell. *You* didn't do anything. My, no. No man ever does anything. Goodness me, no. Every man living is just as innocent as a bunch of lambs."

"Linnea, just give me a chance to get this straight and I'll fix everything up as good as I can," Olaf said. "What do you mean, you've left Bountiful? What did you do with the furniture? Where's the cow? Where's the calf? What do you mean, you been to Ogden? What was you doing in Ogden? What's Mrs. Sterling and a couple of Norwegians and Brother Bell got to do with it? What are you talking about? What are you doing in Salt Lake? Where's Parley? Who has got the kids?"

"If you will mind your business, I'll be glad to mind my own," Linnea said coldly.

Olaf could clatter down the stairs after her and beg her to explain and offer to make amends, if amends were what she wanted, but he could not go running after her down Main Street in broad daylight in his shirt sleeves so he had to give up, and let her go, and come back up to his shop, sorely hurt and perplexed.

It did not take him long to find out where his capricious family was, and seek them out at Ingeborg's, but there he met with rebuff indeed: not from Ingeborg—who said the whole thing was beyond her and she didn't know what the world was coming to, when a sensible woman like Linnea would take a notion to do like she done—but by the once so agreeable Linnea, now unlike herself, touchy and cantankerous, who gathered her children around her like a hen with her chickens and took them all into the holy parlor and shut the door, when she saw Olaf coming up the hill.

"I guess I've really hurt her bad all of a sudden," he said sorrowfully when Ingeborg knocked at the door and asked her and Linnea refused to come out of the parlor, refused to talk to her husband or allow the children to talk to their father. "Here we been married twelve years going on thirteen and had our little differences, but never nothing like this. Linnea ain't one to sulk. She'll come right out and say exactly what she's mad at, say this has got to be done this way and that has got to be done that way, but I never knowed of her to sulk and act like she's acting now. I must of hurt her to the bottom of her heart, and here I didn't even know it, I didn't even know what I done, I don't know now." He walked over to the shut door and tapped upon it. "Linnea," he begged, "I *couldn't* get out to Bountiful. I didn't dare. The federal men are watching everybody like hawks. You wouldn't want me to get took up again, would you, like the winter you had to sew up all them bolts of goods just to get enough to live on? You wouldn't want me put in jail?"

"Go away," she called sharply.

"Between them, they pretty near got it settled now, the Government and the Church," Olaf said. "Pretty soon everything's going to be all right. No more sneaking around. Everything's going to be fine. Couldn't I just see the kids? Couldn't their dad just give them a kiss once?"

"I'm separated from you," Linnea said. "From now on, I'll make my own way. You can find somebody else to bury out on a farm in Bountiful where she can't come to town for months on end and where she don't see her sister nor her folks nor her old friends for weeks at a time. You can leave her there and not send her a dime, though *Sigrid* ain't been going without, I'd bet my life on *that*. You can spend all you got on Sigrid, because she was the first and foremost, and your last dime on Sigrid's kids, and live there, and sleep there, and eat there, like you do anyways, and forget me and mine like we didn't amount to a hill of beans, which you don't think we do or you'd of treated us a lot different. Go on back to Sigrid. Me and the kids'll manage. We got nothing anyway, with you."

"Linnea, come out and let me talk to you."

No answer.

"I've hurt her something fierce," Olaf said over his shoulder to Ingeborg. "She's never done like this before."

"She's spoiled. You got her spoiled," Ingeborg said crossly, lifting a corner of the faded clean quilt which covered the pans of rising bread on the table, to see if they were ready to go in the oven. "When you *do* make over her, you make over her till it's a caution."

They heard Linnea shushing the children. "You could stand there a thousand years," she said then, "and it wouldn't make no more difference to me, than if you was a wooden Indian. You go your way and I'll go mine."

CHAPTER 17

LINNEA USED OFTEN to say, You show me somebody that's stubborn and I'll show you a numskull. This stand of hers however, was not to be misconstrued as having any connection with stubbornness, as she frequently told Ingeborg. The simple reason was that she had had enough of polygamy, of being one of two wives, with only half enough of what it took to get along on: attention, money, love. It was not necessary to announce that she was now separated from her husband and was making her way alone. Everybody knew the polygamists were being watched, and few men were foolhardy enough to make open visits to several households, so nobody in the community thought it strange that Olaf did not put in an appearance at her abode. The Bishop of the Ward did not have to inquire if something were amiss and offer in a fatherly way to help smooth things out. What his advice would be, Linnea knew already—resign to the Lord's will, endure, be steadfast in the Gospel, and she felt too angry and forsaken to take much comfort in or abide by it. Linnea thought for the time being it was as well not to have the word bruited about, that she and her husband had come to a parting of the ways, particularly in church. For the putting asunder of those whom God had joined together was frowned upon by the pious and if one were a member of the congregation at all it seemed the most acceptable thing to be a member in good standing.

At first, Olaf, knowing Linnea's deep good humor and her store of common sense, thought she would take him in again, for she had always been quick to forgive. But this time she was adamant, and it puzzled him, for even now he did not see why she should be so angry. "I've done worse things," he thought, " I know I've done worse things. I must have. And she never held a grudge a minute. But now! She won't look at me or listen to me and I'll be blamed if I know what to do." He talked his problem over with almost everyone he knew except Sigrid. He didn't say much to her. His friends all said his conscience should be clear, he had done the best he could: women just naturally acted up once in awhile: no man ought to blame himself when a woman acted up: it was their way. But Olaf grieved about it, for Linnea had his heart. He gave Ingeborg money to give her, but never quite enough, the times having grown so hard, and Linnea turned it down proudly. As the weeks went on, Olaf grew more and more uneasy. It looked as if Linnea meant what she said—she was going to go it alone. His logic said it was better this way, polygamy was a hardship anyway from beginning to end, he didn't make enough to support two families, two women meant trouble, but his heart yearned after her like Solomon for Bathsheba, he yearned after her with loose and yearning insides as hot as tears.

They sold Bonnie and all the children cried, when the man came to lead her off, even Parley who was only a year old, but he knew the cow, too, her frothing milk and the look of her soft eyes. Mamma sniffled about it along with the rest of them but it couldn't be helped, it wasn't practical to keep a cow in town—besides, Mamma wouldn't be able to care for her regularly once she put out her shingle as midwife and started to work.

Their house, this time, on N Street and Fourth Avenue, around two corners and across a street from their old dwelling but quite out of the old neighborhood and a part of another, was of red brick, small, ugly, in a filthy, run-down condition, but the rent was next to nothing and Linnea set about with the old enthusiasm to make it habitable. Again the formula worked—cleanliness was next to godliness. Scrub rags, buckets of hot soapy water and Linnea's strong willing arms, plus those of her daughters, Bertha and Gertrude, now considered big enough to help—even Stellie had work to do—soon transformed the hovel into a handsome abode, at least to their partial, proud and not overly critical eyes. The made-over snow-white curtains at the shining windows, their old possessions cleaned, dusted, polished, refurbished, pictures hung, dishes set up prettily in the cupboard, made a home out of it, especially when Mamma cooked the first kettle of sour-sweet beans there, and took the first batch of bread out of the oven and set the first pot of boiling coffee back on the stove.

"Ingeborg stays put all the time," she said thoughtfully, her cup held in her two hands right under her nose, her elbows on the table, "her and the kids. She wouldn't any more dare leave that house than jump off the Tabernacle—of course, owning a place might make a difference. But no matter how many times we move, give us leeway to get cleaned up and straightened around, and we got as good a home as anybody. Wherever we are, it always feels like home, don't it?" They did not know she inquired wistfully, begging reassurance, but with the usual tact of children they gave her the reassuring answers: "I'll say it does!" "You bet it does!" "Better'n anybody's," they said.

"Better'n anybody's," Gertrude repeated staunchly.

Linnea hung out her shingle and set up as midwife and in no time she had her first case. She could leave the children now, for Bertha was twelve-going-on-thirteen, and might be expected to keep house for and watch over her sisters and brothers, but the first afternoon and night and day she had to be absent Linnea was very uneasy and couldn't get home fast enough to find out if the house was still there, not burned to the ground, and the children were alive and whole. It was, and they were.

But they had a scare.

It was the first time in all their lives that Mamma had left them alone, to sleep in a house all night and wake up in the morning without her. There was a strong maternal streak in Bertha, and an aptitude for housekeeping, that made her a fine substitute for that Queen of all mothers and housekeepers Mamma, but Gertrude, Stellie and Rudie rebelled a little against her bossiness and they had frequent quarrels. However, the arrangement worked out passably well and Mamma was proud to congratulate Bertha on the state of domestic affairs when she came home. Bertha tattled a good deal, and Gertrude and Stellie hotly denied her accusations or justified their behavior, but on the whole Mamma felt satisfied with the way things worked out. A few admonitions each time, a few promises asked and received, and she would be able to leave home as often as necessary to make a living.

It wasn't so much, that first night alone, after supper was over, the dishes done and Parley rocked to sleep, that they *had* a scare as that they *made* one out of thin air by talking of burglars.

Gertrude began it. "A burgular can get in anywhere," she announced.

"Not if the house is all locked up," Bertha said, with Rudie on her lap. "The doors and windows and all."

"They can get in over the transom," Gertrude said. "A burgular can always get *in*."

They discussed it at some length, recalling to each other the ways of burglars as revealed by the few tales they knew. It was very dark outside and the house began to seem forlorn and unprotected without Mamma, a frightening place, not brightly enough lit by the lamp. The stove, set with a roaring fire for supper, had made the room too warm for the mild summer weather, even now that the fire was out, and it would have been pleasant and refreshing to open a door or window or both and let a cool sharp breeze blow through. But they felt that it was as much as their lives were worth to do so and preferred to swelter there in the airless room.

It was Stellie who asked the very sensible question. What would a burgular be after? she wondered.

That was easy. Their money, of course.

But they had no money! None at all, not even a nickel. So a burgular wouldn't be after their *money*. (He would naturally, know all about what they had and didn't have.) They began to breathe easier. Burgulars also stole sets of silverware, silver coffee-pots and teapots and the like of that. Well, he wouldn't get much in the line of *silverware*, would he? Or jewelry, diamond crowns and ruby necklaces and emerald bracelets and valuable rings. He wouldn't get much *jewelry*. They began to feel better and better until Gertrude silently pointed to Bertha's right hand still clasped across Rudie's stomach. Bertha looked down idly and gave a guilty start. She snatched it up, thrust it between Rudie's back and her own gently budding breast, and kept it hidden there.

"What's wrong with everybody?" Stellie inquired.

Gertrude put a finger to her lips, looked craftily from one window to the other (all the blinds were pulled down) and glanced at the high transom. She said shhhh.

Stellie was bewildered, then frightened, then angry. She began to cry, and Rudie joined her in a sleepy whimper. "You kids are just trying to scare me," she said. "What are you acting so silly about? You're just trying to scare a person."

"I should think you'd have sense enough to catch on to something once in awhile," Gertrude said softly and despairingly, "instead of always being such a numskull and never catching on to anything." Now she spoke with exaggerated lip movements as one speaks to the totally deaf, with painful enunciation but still not raising her voice much above a whisper. "Dumbhead," she said. "Can't you see? Haven't you got eyes? *Bertha's got a ring on*."

Bertha had indeed a ring on, the only jewelry they had in the house, a small gold band with scalloped edges and some halfhearted tracings of leaves and blossoms across the front. Papa had given it to her on her last birthday. It must be worth a pretty penny though diamonds and other gems might have added somewhat to its value. Stellie saw at once that there was indeed a point of danger here, a threat, and she stopped crying on the instant and grew very serious, as did Rudie.

"Next time, I'll get Mamma to take it with her," Bertha promised, her face paling.

"Next time is all very well," Gertrude said, still in that soft despairing way, "but what about *this* time?"

"What do you mean this time?" Bertha demanded.

"What about *this* time, I mean. A burgular could look right in through the keyhole and see it any time he wanted to."

Bertha pulled her hand out, gazed swiftly at the dangerous prize and thrust it back in hiding. "Oh, Gertrude," she said. "You just go into things something terrible."

But the matter was serious enough for them to have a lengthy discussion upon it and they finally came to the sensible decision that they would hide the ring. The question was, Where? Bertha thought a can of spice, either turmeric or cinnamon, might prove a good place of concealment; Stellie suggested the spot under the carpet—foolishly; Rudie didn't suggest anywhere being too frightened and at the same time too sleepy, a peculiar condition, like a form of intoxication. His head had got very heavy a time or two and he dropped it upon Bertha's sturdy little shoulder, but so far he had saved himself from that nonsense by rousing and shifting his position before it was too late. Gertrude admitted that the suggestion she was about to make was not wholly original with her. She had heard it from somebody or other, somewhere, at some time. She made it. It was so clever that the others saw at once her recommendation was worth acting on, and the three girls and muddle-headed boy (who would be sound asleep before the project was accomplished) at once set about to do it.

They hid the little gold ring in the mattress!

Not Mamma's feather bed, you understand—they would never have dared to fool around with that, no matter what the emergency was—but the straw mattress. They slit it with the scissors, poked the ring into the dryly crackling insides, felt it slide away out of reach of their fingers, carefully sewed up the slash—and breathed a sigh of relief. It would take some burgular to find *their* precious possessions. None did. They slept at first fitfully, uneasily, but gradually they fell into that deep but airy-breasted slumber on which childhood alone has the copyright.

Mamma thought they were very silly to scare themselves like that and was a little cross that they had slit the good mattress ticking. By the time they recovered the ring it was slit a good deal further, for first one and then the other thrust a hand in and groped after it—the hand going in at times up to the shoulder—and this lengthened the gash. It was found finally by Bertha, who had the longest arm, not two inches from the original opening. Gertrude was given the job of repairing the damage with needle and thread as she had been the prime mover. Mamma laughed at them. She said that was one of the blessings of being not so well off. You might have a lot of things to worry about but there was very little danger you'd be robbed. For some reason this nipped their fear in the bud and they were never nervous again about staying in the house without Mamma.

The Ecklunds, mother and children, settled down in their modest house and took the neighborhood to their hearts, as it took them.

The handsomest edifice in the block belonged to Mrs. Monteith. As everyone said, Mrs. Monteith's husband, old Monteith, could afford it. He was rich enough. He must have five thousand dollars in the bank if he had a cent, and not only was this house clear but he also owned the house down on State Street where he lived, except for occasional

brief visits, with his first wife, old Mrs. Monteith; for he was a polygamist.

The lady at the corner was called Young Mrs. Monteith.

She was about thirty-five and had been married at the age of twenty
to Monteith. She had two sons—Gerald, fourteen, and Raymond, twelve.
Now she was in the family way again, to her intense surprise and sorrow
and the surprise of her husband. The whole vicinity was stirred up about
it. They had almost forgotten the circumstances of her marriage after
so many years but now—she mentioned it herself, half ruefully, half
apprehensively—they recalled it, and those newcomers who didn't know,
were amply informed of it. It made an interesting state of affairs and
people in the neighborhood and far beyond its boundaries began to
await the outcome with much the same interest as is usually evinced to
a presidential election or a heavyweight championship fight. There
were even whispers that bets had been made. Young Mrs. Monteith, at
the time the Ecklunds moved into the neighborhood, still had three
months to go. Linnea soon heard the story from others and from the
lady herself, a friendly untidy creature with reddish hair and fair skin
splashed all over with pale large freckles of a golden tint, even on her
stomach, she said, where the sun had never shone in her life.

Linnea got a foothold in the legend herself, for what did Young Mrs.
Monteith do, having taken a fancy to her, but ask her to officiate at the
birth. Linnea was impressed with the honor of this, for it was being
spoken of everywhere, and would be more and more on people's lips
as the time of the confinement grew closer.

Fifteen years before, when Monteith, then a successful baker of fifty,
had come to old Mrs. Monteith, his childless wife of forty-eight, and said
he wanted to marry a young girl of twenty, old Mrs. Monteith asked
leave to think about it. Monteith considered this fair enough. She
thought about it for two weeks and then she said that wasn't quite
enough. She said she would think about it two more weeks. She did,
and at the end of the month she came to her husband with her answer.
He could marry this young woman, she said, on two conditions. Condition number one: that she would never have to have a thing in the
world to do with the lady, even to be introduced. Condition number
two: that the first girl-child born of the union should be hers, the first
wife's, and hers alone. She had always wanted a girl, she said. She
thought in this manner things would be evened up between her and the
second wife.

There were those who were so unkind as to say that Young Mrs.
Monteith, or the young lady's Scotch-Irish-English parents, had been
eager to make the match: for she was a poor girl and he was a man of
affluence who ran his own business. Not knowing at the time, young
Mrs. Monteith later excused herself, how it felt to be a mother, she was

at first more amused than not at the promise extracted of her. She even signed a paper to the effect that old Mrs. Monteith, wife number one, was to have the first child of female sex born to her. Before Gerald made his appearance she was quite uneasy, but even then, of course, not knowing what a rush of love, as she said, ran through a person holding her new-born baby in her arms, she did not worry too much. She had meant to stick by her bargain, of course. By the time Gerald was six months old she began waking up in a cold sweat, like the knight in the old tale who crossed on horseback at nighttime the mighty Lake Constance, frozen over, unaware of what he did, and upon reaching the other side and discovering it, had fallen down dead with fright. She trembled with terror at the danger she had missed. For she turned out to be more than a fond mother: she became a doting one, whose whole existence revolved around that of her offspring.

When her second child was on the way she took to her bed with a panic that turned to a kind of sickness . . . she cried half her waking hours, shook like a leaf if a person so much as spoke to her and turned a yellowish color that was alarming to see. It was said that her bile had flooded its banks and was on the rampage, working havoc all through her body. Whatever it was, it wouldn't have surprised anyone if she had died. The baby being a boy, however, she did not die, but took a swooning ecstatic look at him, grabbed him with both arms, stuck her nipple in his face and began to recover at once. It was too close a shave, though, she confided afterwards. She never would go through *that* again. It was thought that old Mrs. Monteith, upon hearing the news, gnashed her teeth like the disappointed hobgoblin in the fairy tale, but nobody saw her do it. Old Mrs. Monteith was quite a nice woman really, a little lonely, a little stand-offish, but quite nice. Nobody knew her at all well. This talk was merely bandied about because it seemed to go with the circumstances. Young Mrs. Monteith named the second boy Raymond and settled down to enjoy, as she said, two of the loveliest sons that ever drew the breath of life, and resolutely put out of her mind the thought that one, or both, could have been girls, and what suffering would have befallen her then.

Now she was awaiting her third child, with fear and trembling, but this time her bile behaved itself and she was up and about the same as ever. The third time was the charm. Nobody who heard the story but was interested in the outcome. Strangers took to lingering in front of the house or across the street pointing at the premises. So widespread was news of the case that the government agents arrested Monteith again on charges of polygamy and put him in jail, but he by some means or other managed to get himself released and went about his affairs as usual.

At the time Linnea made young Mrs. Monteith's acquaintance the lady was six months along. To know the outcome of the affair, every-body had to wait three months and it was almost more than some of the ladies could bear.

Mrs. Sterling dropped up occasionally to see them. She liked the place down on Fourth East, she said. Estelle and Johnny liked it too. It was very handy, and Brother Bell often made a call on Sunday afternoon. He visited at other times, too, but usually when the children were in bed or in school. Mrs. Sterling never once said that Brother Bell was anything but her landlord and teacher in the Gospel, and Linnea for her part said that she for one was not going to believe anything different. "Her and me is good friends," she told Ingeborg, "and I just know if there was something going on between them two, she'd tell me. She claims she has to pay rent just like anybody else."

"Where does she get it?" Ingeborg said caustically. "Where does she get the rent to pay?"

"Why, you know, perfectly well. There's that brewery across the street and she takes in some of the single men's washing and ironing, and then she sews, too. She makes enough to get by on. She works hard and she's not rolling in money by any means," Linnea said. "Besides, good heavens, look how *old* the man is."

"Don't talk about old," Ingeborg said sharply. "They're never too old!"

"Why, sure, they are," Linnea said. "You hadn't ought to think the worst of Mrs. Sterling. She's just as good as she can be. There's not a thing in the world between her and Brother Bell. She'd of told me, I know she would. No, he's just one of these old fools."

"What's them kids of his doing about the matter?"

"Nothing, the last I heard. They got him to sign everything away, I guess, to them and their mother—that's why they don't take no interest in what he does, no more. They figure they got what really matters, I guess. Mrs. Sterling can have the rest."

"Well, she's welcome," Ingeborg said.

Mrs. Sterling told Linnea in confidence that Brother Bell was a very nice man. They were carefully going through the Voice of Warning at the present time, she said, and Parley P. Pratt was certainly a deep one when you really got started on his writings. And when Brother Bell started in on it, it was just a revelation. Mrs. Sterling had remained in the Church although threatening to leave it after her husband's perfid-ious behavior, but that was only an idle threat. After she obtained a divorce through the civil authorities she was at pains to go and straighten things out with the Church.

"The Gospel's still *true*, after all, I suppose," she said, "if it ever was. And I got to live around here."

Mrs. Sterling had a long talk with the Bishop of her Ward, a soft-hearted man lenient to all, especially to a pretty face and prettier manner. When she had given him a recitation of her grievances he quite agreed with her, and promised to take the matter up with the Stake President and those authorities still higher who alone could grant amnesty. Where Mr. Sterling had done ill, the Bishop felt, was not in wishing to take unto himself two new wives, but in not notifying Mrs. Sterling of the case beforehand, perhaps writing to her and breaking the news from Norway before he completed his mission there. Also it was usual to ask a wife's consent in such matters as this and abide by her decision—if she said yes, all right; if she said no, no new wife. That was the usual procedure, but of course, ahem, it had often been got around. Her husband had really not handled the matter right, the Bishop agreed with Mrs. Sterling, and if she divorced him, she would not be much censured. As far as the Church was concerned, he said, if she continued a good member, a staunch worker and a true believer, all was forgiven and forgotten. She promised to do so, greatly relieved. She never had said for a minute it was the *Church,* she reminded her friends and acquaintances. She had only said it was her husband, and she was glad to be back in the fold.

The Voice of Warning was a very deep book, she told Linnea. Brother Bell could start in on it and just drag on and drag on for hours, but of course it was very interesting. She had learned a lot. No longer did Mrs. Sterling joke about Brother Bell, by so much as a word or look, and Linnea gave up the habit too.

One of the men from the brewery across the street, a Mr. Brenneman, a very nice young man of about thirty-eight, a German, but with brown eyes and black hair, not the blonde German type at all, was very interested in religious matters too, Mrs. Sterling said. She did his shirts for him. He was taking up something called Theosophy. It was very interesting. This woman who started it all, this Madame Blavatsky, claimed she got these hand-written letters from the spirits. She could freeze a person in their tracks just by looking at them. She lived in India or somewhere. This Theosophy was certainly peculiar. Mr. Brenneman had such a broken accent it was a little hard to follow him all the time, he had only been in America about three years, but he was certainly interesting. Sometimes when he'd bring his bundle of soiled shirts over or stop by to pick up the clean ironed ones, they used to have a nice discussion. She would either make coffee or he would bring some beer, and they would have some bread and cheese. It didn't hurt to be nice to somebody so far from home, Mrs. Sterling said.

"He ain't so far from home," Ingeborg said when she heard about it. "The man only lives on Third East, don't he? And Mrs. Sterling lives on Fourth East. That don't sound to me like it's so far from home."

"So far from *Germany,*" Linnea explained. "She's really an awful nice friendly woman. And by the way, her taking in some washing and ironing like that *proves* there ain't nothing between her and Brother Bell. She wouldn't be such a fool as to go into something like that and work hard at the same time!"

Mrs. Sterling liked this Mr. Brenneman very much and they had some very nice talks together. She had explained to him about the platonic relationship she carried on with Brother Bell. Much of the old man's kindness toward them was for the children's sake, as Brother Bell loved children, she told Mr. Brenneman. It was true: he really did love children. If he happened to call when they were still up or when one of them was home from school with a cold, he always recited to them at great length not only whole chapters from the Book of Mormon, but from the Bible as well, so that it was an education to hear him, better than going to Sunday school. Mr. Brenneman respected this pure relationship and admired Mrs. Sterling more every day. Brother Bell seemed to have got the idea that Mrs. Sterling had taken it upon herself to convert the brewer to Mormonism and never had a word to say against the project. However, the two men, with some diplomacy on the part of Mrs. Sterling, managed to come together seldom, though holding each other in the highest esteem.

Sometimes Linnea felt very lonely (and unprotected) without Olaf even though, as she said, he was nothing to brag of as supporter and protector, but he was up there in the tailor shop and she could drop in and he would give her what money he could spare. Besides, he had a lovely disposition. She had liked him to come home and spend a night with her once in a while: it was some reason for her to clean up the house even better than usual, and put clean pillow shams on and maybe push the sanitary couch where the table was and the table where the sanitary couch was, change things around a little (when she knew he was coming). Fix herself up more, too, crimp her hair across the front, try a braid instead of a bun, and tie on one of her nice aprons. Cook something a little fancy and special, also, maybe *fattigmans-bakelser* or *köttbullar* or *risengrynsgrot*, put a handful of flowers in a glass in the middle of the table. When he didn't come home any more, there wasn't much point in taking extra pains with the house, the children and herself. She saw now that he had praised her more than she realized, made her feel proud of herself, made her do more than she might have done otherwise, to please him. Without him she did not feel so proud of herself any more and wondered what was missing from her spirits that kept them light and buoyant like a balloon blown up.

But when she fell into the error of missing him and wishing they were as they once had been, she reminded herself that he had used her shamefully, that in Bountiful she was no better than abandoned, that Sigrid had always had the best of everything, that she was a fool to go into polygamy in the first place. Then was when she could harden her heart and turn down the overtures he still made—though less often now, being himself a man of pride, who could let a woman run over him a little, quite a little, but not so it was too much of a good thing—through mutual friends of theirs.

The time was not yet, Linnea felt, for her to make an announcement of their separation or go to the church authorities with a request for a divorce. Since he could not have come to see her and the children openly in any case, with so many government spies around, no questions were asked and no one in the community knew, except a few intimates, that the Ecklunds were not going along as usual. When the polygamy problem was settled for good and the nosy investigators sent home, then it would be time enough for a showdown, time enough to ask for a divorce, to come out openly and say she was not for Olaf and Olaf was not for her. Always providing she could think of a good reason, for the one she had, such as it was, growing more ephemeral by the day, would not sound like much to the priesthood. But she had time, she would think of something.

She missed him, though, his praise and fondness, and wondered how she could possibly (since it was not as though he had been like a real husband, sharing a home with her) miss him so much, and supposed she might get over it. She considered her soft feelings traitorous, as the crippled child feels his soft muscles are traitorous to him, and hoped to toughen them by a kind of daily dozen, reiterating to herself over and over why she should not care a snap of the finger for Olaf, since he had not cared a snap of the finger for her.

But he would have liked to hear about young Mrs. Monteith and would have wanted to be informed right away about what she had got, a boy to keep or a girl to give away. And hear all the other news and gossip, the way he always did.

In a way, it was better to have Olaf even in polygamy than not to have him, and sometimes she missed him more than she would have cared to say.

It was no hardship for Linnea's three girls and two boys to be without Papa. They did not speak of it, having been told it would be buttinsky to do so and that if children minded their business, grownups would mind theirs.

The truth was, it seemed as if Mamma was quite enough. Bertha, who had the most to lose, would never have been caught dead saying it, but it was certainly no skin off *her* nose that Papa never came home any more. For she was twelve-and-a-half now and Mamma let her sit at the table at coffee time and have a cup of coffee just like a big lady, not only when Mamma was alone but when company was there and she could take part in the conversation. The other children could not do this. They could have weak coffee at mealtimes, but they could not participate in the midmorning and four o'clock ritual. At these times they were told to play outside, or in the next room, or quietly in the corner, being handed a buttered coffee bun or piece of toasted kaffe-kake, and not bother. They yearned to reach an age when they could take part in this adult activity. Papa's absence, Bertha thought but did not say, had hastened her advancement by months at least and therefore, never having been well acquainted with him in any case, she could not regret it. Especially since she now had the honor—she on one side, and Parley on the other—of sleeping with Mamma every night. Not only the honor but the comfort, for Mamma took great pride in her bed and it always had taut clean sheets, a plumped-up feather mattress and rounded pillows. There were soft and bright comforters upon it, too, and under them, with their edge of turned-back white muslin, the soft luxury of Mamma's outing-flanneled back against her front or Mamma's outing-flanneled front against her back. Bertha would not be pleased if Papa came home again, if she had to leave her warm nest beside Mamma and find herself compelled to go and crawl in with Gertrude and Stellie, to make room for him.

Her two sisters, with no axe to grind, could be more disinterested about the matter. Papa was all right. They had more things to eat when Papa was home, Sunday-like repasts, more bountiful meals served at a later hour. Of course, they had to go to bed earlier. They didn't like that. They didn't like Papa telling them to do so either, for instance. It didn't seem like Papa had the right like Mamma had, to boss them. But he brought them something once in awhile, maybe a bag of jelly beans or a big sack of coffeecake from the Idaho Bakery, and Mamma had said many a time that they should thank him for shoes or stockings or a piece of goods for a new dress. That went to show Papa wasn't really so bad. Gertrude had had the experience of hating him, when she wanted to go around and tell the neighbors about Parley being born and Papa wasn't going to allow it, but on the whole she liked him a good deal. Stellie and Rudie did, too. He was an appetizing man in the clean blonde way, affectionate and kindly. They would not be so very sorry if he came back. Parley was too little to care one way or the other.

Linnea was gone often now on cases, sometimes overnight, but the children were not afraid any more. That was one of the blessings of being poor: nobody would break in and steal from them. Sometimes Linnea thought that was the only blessing. It was harder than she had had any idea, to collect what was owed her for the confinements she went to. They'd say, could they pay her two dollars now and the rest later? Of course, she always said. Or could they pay it all later? ("What could I say?" she would ask Ingeborg. "Here the kids didn't have shoes on their feet and there wasn't enough in the pantry to put in your eye.

Could I say you got to pay me? With the whole outfit looking half-starved? Could I? Why, nobody could, that had any heart in them at all.") Later would do fine. Or pay in produce? The trouble was, what could she do with a wagonload of green corn, for instance, except share it with the neighborhood, and sugar was too high to can ten or twelve crates of berries at a time. But she got sewing work from the tithing office and she made a few dollars with midwifery and they managed to exist.

It was Lily Jensen who suggested to Gertrude they sneak off and go down on Fifth South one day to see Old Mrs. Monteith, the wicked fairy, and see what she looked like. It was a long old walk on a scorching day and they nearly got licked when they got back, they had been gone so long, and besides hadn't asked permission to go, hadn't said a word to anybody. They almost never got to see Old Mrs. Monteith. Thinking she would at least be in her front yard or on her porch taking the air they hopped and skipped back and forth in front of the house on the sidewalk hoping to catch a glimpse of her until the shadows took on the purple tinge of late afternoon and they began to get a little uneasy thinking how far it was to walk back home. Lily would have given up and departed, she was the one who had instigated it up to now, found out Old Mrs. Monteith's house number and everything, but Gertrude suddenly took command. "No, sir," she said, "we won't go home till we see Old Mrs. Monteith, after we come so far and waited so long." They hopped once more to the corner, skipped once more back.

At Old Mrs. Monteith's gate Gertrude stopped. "Come on," she said and pushed it open. She went into the yard and started up the walk. Lily, too amazed at her daring to protest, went after her, but when she saw what Gertrude intended, tried to pull her back, tried to get her to run before it was too late. In genuine alarm she reminded Gertrude with whom they had to deal. Gertrude's own knees were unsteady but resolutely she went up to the front door and knocked. They could hear the knock go clear through the house like the house was hollow. Nobody came to answer. "She'll be—so—mad," Lily chattered, "making her come to her—front—door—through her parlor. We should have gone to the back!" Even Gertrude, after a long wait, was beginning to think she had been rash and was studying how she could turn and fly without appearing inglorious and overborne when they heard the slow footsteps. Then the knob turned, and the door opened, and the lady looked out at them through a crack about six inches wide.

"What do you want?" she said.

Lily looked at Gertrude in fear and desperation.

Gertrude swallowed. "We want to get to the meeting house," she said.

"Which meeting house?" the lady asked.

"The one in this ward."

"Oh," she said. "Well, it's two blocks down, across the street, and in the middle of the next block to the left."

"Thank you, ma'am."

Very slowly they turned and left, slowly they went down the steps, slowly down the walk. Outside the gate they broke into a run and ran as hard as they could, two blocks in the wrong direction, four blocks altogether out of their way, so Old Mrs. Monteith would not suspect anything. The sun had almost set when they got all the way home and everybody was furious. It was a very silly thing to do, Mamma said, to go down on Fifth East and sneak around and try to get a look at Old Mrs. Monteith. It was a low thing. And what did they accomplish by it?

"Well, we saw her, anyway," Gertrude said lamely.

What did she look like? Stellie wanted to know. But even Mamma and Ingeborg were quiet, waiting to hear.

Gertrude drew a deep sigh. If she had been alone—but no, not even then, for too many people could have checked up on her. "She just looked like a old lady," she said sadly. "Didn't she, Lily?"

Lily said yes.

Not mean or nothing?

Not particularly. Just like any old lady with gray hair and a gingham apron on, not fat or thin. Just an ordinary old lady. Little pearl earrings on.

"You see," Mamma said accusingly.

They saw. It had been a silly thing to do.

CHAPTER 18

IT HAD BEEN the hottest week, when butter had to be kept in a bowl instead of on a plate because it was oil to pour instead of butter to spread, when you could fry an egg every day on the front sidewalk if you wanted, and the shade itself was hot. God pity those with the dead to keep, watching the ice in the tubs and buckets around the corpse that melted away like youth and beauty, melted as fast in the night as in the daytime. August heat is tiring, like a contest with somebody bigger and stronger than you are, who eventually gets you down by sheer weight. People had pale faces. All the children were cross. There wasn't anything cold enough, or thin enough, or clear enough, or crisp enough, or delicate enough, to eat. There were no clothes of sufficient gossamer to wear, no air fresh enough to breathe.

Like pain, like loss, like being forsaken, however, this ends, and rain falls upon the bone-dry weather.

The best is when it starts overhead and falls straight down, falling on the roof of the house, falling on the roof of slumber, drip, drip, in early morning, say before dawn. All the pale-faced sleepers hear it, asprawl in nightgowns or union suits, or naked, the thinnest sheets kicked off. Their limp hands and limp feet, their limp eyelids and slack mouths, their ears with the stiffness taken out, their tired salty hair with the lights unstrung, all these hear it. A shiver goes down the sleeping spine like a vine trembling in the wind. The hand goes out, gropes in a wide half-circle, finds the fallen sheet, finds more, the quilt forgotten like unforgettable love, folded over the footboard, brings first one, then the other, over the sleepy shoulder that is cool now, chilled, because the cover is warm. Oh, delicious slumber then, under the snug cover, the steep roof, the rushing bountiful rain! Do you doubt that it is raining? See it then with one eye through the window, the warp of the cloth of wet morning, line after line after line, while the other eye shuts all the tighter in soothed sleep.

Gertrude heard it and saw it in the pre-dawn and pinched Stellie to hear but Stellie was too far gone to do anything but double up her knees and stick out her behind in protest. Rain! Now it would not be hot today. It would be cool. She shivered as though the rain were dripping upon herself and cuddled close to her sister. What was so nice as to stay in the house all day while it rained outside? With the fire going! With bread baking! With coffee on! In Mamma's clean kitchen! She saw the pictures of this dimly, deliciously running across her eyes, went back to sleep, the antique thoughts of snugness and shelter like velvet curtains hung upon her mind.

It delighted them all, the rain. Rudie insisted on getting out in it after breakfast, but Mamma said no. They compromised by an agreement that he remain on the front stoop. He tried this for a little while but it bored him so much, the porch being very small, that he finally gave up and came back in the house where he sulked and sprawled underfoot until Mamma was quite desperate. She said the first thing anybody knew she was going to have to spank him. Luckily, an empty shoe box got him started on a pinny peep show which occupied him a good part of the day, although before it was completed Mamma had parted with the postcards (except five or six of the most beautiful, with padded silk, real pieces of velvet pasted on and a wealth of sand-textured glitter, that nobody in their right senses could part with) she had been saving so long. Stellie cried right out loud over this act of outrage, this mortal wound, and even Gertrude and Bertha, big as they were, almost wept with jealousy and disappointment, but Rudie hollered loudest of all and Mamma, the cards in her hand, went ahead with her barbarism and gave them to him, to cut out what he wanted and make a pinny peep show.

"I'm ashamed of you," she said severely. "Three big girls! Almost young ladies! And Rudie's just a little boy!"

"You wouldn't give them to *me*," Stellie said sullenly.

"And why wouldn't I? Because I thought you was nearly a young lady that could be allowed to *sew a doll dress on the sewing machine,* that's what I thought," Mamma said.

Stellie's face flooded with light. "Now?" she screamed.

"What about me?" "And me?" Gertrude and Bertha chorused.

"You can each one of you make a doll dress on the sewing machine, when we get done with our work. This afternoon, maybe. There!" she said. "I guess that's better than having a bunch of old postcards!"

It was. They agreed on that. But then, they had to join together to assure suspicious Rudie, who had come to the conclusion by listening to their conversation that what he had wasn't nearly as precious as he thought it was, and was ready to throw up his project for something more satisfying, that the sewing machine was *nothing* in comparison with the postcards. They'd trade with him any time, they said. And then some.

Parley, the baby, almost too fat and too big for the tall narrow high chair, sat in it like an angel and, Bertha having pulled him close to the rain-washed windowpane, entertained himself by looking through it and banging on the sticky tray with a big tin tablespoon, his favorite toy. It was the kind of rain that fell in torrents, let up and fell in torrents again, with thumping drumming thudding sounds. When it fell, it came down so hard it fairly bounced and Parley would crow with pleasure. They all liked it. No matter what they were doing, the whole day, they had time to watch the tumbling thundering rain when it took a notion to fall hardest. "Any fevers," Mamma said informatively, "will be sure to break up today. Anybody in fever ought to get as cool as a cucumber and be better now." It was nice to have this brought to mind, that hot-faced sick people would be cooling off in the cool weather, their hot pillows cooling, their hot hands growing calm and cool.

Something important was going to happen in the afternoon but none of them knew that. Linnea, especially, wouldn't have sat talking so calmly if she had had any idea. When they weren't doing something else, they sat around the stove and talked. The grate glowed a rosier red than usual, because the day was so colorless, crystal and gray-blue, and one was hopelessly drawn to it as the moth is drawn to the flame. One would pull up a chair, or tuck one's feet under one on the sanitary couch, and fix one's eyes upon the rose of fire, and there one would sit, staring, talking softly and listening. Linnea had mending to do—more than that to do—but she stared, too, sat and stared, talking, the clock ticked, and the rainy hours passed like hours in paradise.

A topic that greatly engaged them, for want of something better, was Conference, the great semi-annual church convention, in some five weeks' time. New clothes, alas, were out of the question, but each of the three girls was to have new collar and cuffs on her best merino dress, *white* cotton stockings, and her hair put up the night before in rag curls. The white lisle stockings alone were enough to make a girl languish in ecstasy, they were such a mark of elegance and distinction. Mamma had not bought them yet, but she was going to do so. The topic was good for an hour's conversation any time. For the white stockings always brought toe slippers to mind. And toe slippers . . .

If there was anything, anything in the wide world that Bertha, Gertrude and Stellie wanted more than anything else, barring nothing, it was toe slippers. Toe slippers were low-cut shoes with a strap across the instep. They were made of black kid and the strap fastened with a winking little button on the side. They had "spring" heels. To wear a pair of black spring-heeled toe slippers was as good as being an heiress or on the stage. If there was one way to climb up on top of the world, that was it. The Golightly girls had toe slippers, the Orbit girls had toe slippers. Everybody had toe slippers. For best only, of course. You couldn't be more low-down if you stood on your head than you were if you had to wear high shoes and didn't have toe slippers. Bertha said seriously it was all she could do to stand it, Gertrude said so too, and Stellie, persuaded by their intensity, was caught up in it and said so too.

But toe slippers—nice as they would be, to wear to Conference—were as out of the question as a gold watch for everybody. Mamma had been so firm that all three knew there was no chance of getting them. It was enough—even they had to agree to that—to get to wear *white* stockings, instead of black ones. As Mamma said, when it was as hard to get a fifty-cent heel of beef for Sunday, where did they think she was going to get toe slippers? Shoes, yes, good substantial high-topped shoes, yes, when they needed them, shoes she would get somehow. (They hadn't gone barefooted yet, had they?) But toe slippers they needed like they needed a pair of wings—fine, if they had them, but nothing to cry about, if they didn't—and she wasn't going to lose any sleep over them.

"As far as I'm concerned," she said, "I'm going to put some new trimming on my velvet poke." This she told them everytime they discussed Conference, and the clothes they were going to wear, but it never became tiresome, any more than the white stockings became tiresome or the reiteration that their hair was going to go up in rag curls the night before. It was lovely to hear it, like hearing a well-loved poem.

"Yes, sir," Mamma said dreamily, rocking in front of the stove, "I'm going to buy some ostrich tips and one thing and another and make a regular picture out of that hat. I can just see it in my mind."

"Blue," Gertrude offered lovingly.

"Blue," Mamma said.

Aunt Gunilla was coming to town with the whole family, she was going to stay all night. And Ingeborg and they were all going to get together afterwards and eat supper. There would be baking done the day before, the mere list of which, named over, could make the saliva run in a stream.

They talked about Conference, their clothes, the food to be prepared, while the cool rain fell and the fire felt good. The world was all outdoors and they were inside. Rudie with infinite patience and pleasure cut out figures from the postcards and made his pinny peep show on the oilcloth-covered kitchen table. Parley banged his spoon on the highchair tray or kicked his heels or crowed, or did all three together, or sat meditating as a baby will sometimes do, lost in a brown study, watching the slant of rain. Mamma and her daughters, woman-like, sat around the stove and chattered. They had work to do, but they could leave it a while, they could sit and talk. Until the knock came at the door, that is, and scattered their thoughts to the four winds for hours after, especially Mamma's, who couldn't settle down to *anything*.

It came at just the expected time for a knock, just before the pot went on for afternoon coffee.

The unexpected part of it was who stood upon the steps smiling when Bertha opened the door.

Parley had just been put down on the couch, Gertrude dragging her feet out of the way to make room for him, to finish the nap he began in his narrow chair, bolt upright, with his fat chin resting on his fat chest like an old man.

Somebody knocked, was the way it began.

"You go, Bertha," Mamma said.

Bertha obligingly went to the door and threw it open.

Olaf stood there, Linnea's banished husband. Papa stood there, looking scared, looking tickled pink, looking absurd, looking homesick and rueful and beseeching all at once.

Linnea went limp in her rocking chair with an unlooked-for sense of relief and joy, and her face got red and then white. In an unconscious motion one hand flew to her hair to feel with lightning swiftness if there were any untidy strands dangling. The other flew to her neck to smooth her collar, adjust her brooch. She was red again, and a smile broke through; white again, and it dwindled to nothing. But her eyes gave her away. Olaf, when he read them, didn't give her a chance to get up. No, sir. He made a beeline for her where she sat like a painting by the stove in the rocking chair, and swooped right down and threw his arms around her, and kissed her and kissed her. And the first thing anybody knew, her arms were around him, too, and she was up out of the chair, hugging him for all she was worth, and kissing him back. By that time, the surprised children had rallied round, and seeing the reception Mamma, who decided these matters, gave him, they gave him a fine reception, too, everybody crowding up and hugging and kissing until nobody knew who was who.

"They grown, ain't they, though?" Olaf said beamingly at Linnea, his arms around his two biggest girls, his middle held tight by Rudie's and Stellie's encircling arms.

Mamma was fixing her hair again and straightening her waist that Papa had mussed so. "Ain't they, though?" she said. "You! Coming in on us like that! If I'd of had any idea, you wouldn't of got in so slick, I can tell you that. You wouldn't of got in a-tall."

"How can you tell a big fib like that?" Olaf chaffed her. "You know you're glad to see me, and I'm so glad you ain't mad no more I could fly higher'n a kite."

"Who said I ain't mad no more?" Linnea said severely, but then she burst out laughing and tears came into her eyes and she said first, "You kids quit hanging on your father like that. Let the poor man sit down and get his breath, at least," and then, "I am glad to see you. I didn't realize how glad I'd be." Bertha and Gertrude, self-conscious from the rebuke, went and hovered over the stove, Rudie went back to his work saying, "I'm making a pinny peep show and everybody who looks in got to pay a pin, even my mother and father." Stellie sulkily dropped down beside the sleeping Parley on the lounge. "You wake him up and you'll get something," Bertha said.

"Quit bossing, Bertha," Mamma said. "Listen, kids, I got an idea."

"What I come to tell you about, was about the Manifesto," Papa said, "in case you ain't heard. Nobody's talking of nothing else. Utah's going to be a state before long, not a territory no more. Ain't that wonderful? After so many years' begging and pleading."

"Oh?" Mamma said courteously. "Well—state—territory—I guess it don't make much difference as long as people behave theirselves. Listen, kids," she said, "me and Papa got some things to discuss. We're going into the bedroom. Why don't you surprise us and get the coffee all made nice? Set the table like I set it for company. Put the *skorpar* on, and butter, and the cream and sugar—"

"For everybody?" Gertrude asked.

"What do you mean, everybody?"

"Do we all get to sit at the table, or do just you and Papa and," she swallowed, "Bertha, get to?"

"Why, all, of course," Mamma said, "today. We got to celebrate, ain't we? But you and Stellie and Rudie just get a little coffee in the bottom of your cup, filled up with hot water and milk. No taking a notion to drink big cups of strong coffee around the place all of a sudden."

"Goody, goody," Stellie said, clapping her hands.

"All right, then," Mamma said. "You kids go to work and make coffee, and get it on the table, and show me and Papa how nice you can do it. We're going in the bedroom to talk. We got a few things to talk over." She slipped her hand through Papa's arm. "You holler when you're ready, Bertha."

"Papa," Gertrude said petitioningly.

"What, Gertrude?" he said, smiling down at her. She had sidled over to a position by the door they had to pass through.

"Do you know what toe slippers is?" she asked.

By the stove, the faces of her sisters took on a look like her own, so there were three of them lighting the room like candles lit: faces of pure and tender saints, the lips tenderly supplicating, the eyes rolled upwards spiritually. "Yes, Papa," Bertha said. "Toe slippers."

"Toe slippers," Stellie echoed.

"What about them?" Papa inquired, looking from one to the other.
"They're just *beautyful*," Gertrude said. "Just beautiful, that's all."

"No begging Papa for nothing," Mamma said. "Why, the man hasn't any more than hardly got in the house let alone sat down and had even so much as a swallow of coffee, and you start in like that! I'm ashamed of you," she said, "every last one of you."

"I didn't do nothing," Rudie called. He had gone back to his project on the kitchen table.

"You get your pinny peep show off of there so the girls can get coffee on," Mamma ordered, her attention called to him.

"Where'll I put it?" he wailed. "If I move, it'll just spoil everything."

"No bawling now," Mamma said in the voice that meant no bawling, so Rudie stopped and began to gather up his things.

"What's this about toe slippers, and the girls here looking like they'd lost their last friend? All three of them," Papa said teasingly.

"If it ain't one thing, it's another. Now it's toe slippers," Mamma said. "Happens to be. Next week it'll be something else."

"Oh, no, it won't," the three girls said fervently in unison.

"We'll have to get to the bottom of this," Papa said to Gertrude but gave a smile and a big wink to her two sisters, too. "Won't we?"

They shot radiant looks at each other. Toe slippers! Papa was back. Maybe they would have toe slippers for Conference! "You get a fresh teakettle of water," Bertha said deliriously, taking the lid off the stove and poking at the fire. Without a word of protest, both the smaller girls, with Papa's eyes upon them, leaped valiantly to obey like soldiers under the eye of their commanding officer.

"Can we get up little old Parley," Papa said, catching a glimpse of his big rosy baby asleep on the lounge, "so his old man can heft him a little, huh?"

"When the girls get coffee ready. When they holler to us," Mamma said. "Then he's been asleep long enough and you can wake him up. He's the best little kid I ever seen. No trouble a-tall."

The bedroom felt so cool as to be almost chilly after the hothouse warmth of the kitchen and Linnea took her shawl off a nail and wrapped it around her shoulders. She took a seat on the side of the neatly made bed and leaned over and patted a place near the foot for Olaf. He took it, and then they looked at each other rather self-consciously in silence. The gray weather, the streams of water running down the windowpane, made the room seem colder than it was. Olaf discovered that he had got quite wet coming over, though he hadn't realized it before.

"I'd ask Ingeborg about you," Olaf said finally, "and different ones. They said you was making out. I kept worrying, though. Had you on my mind."

Linnea looked pleased at this, and shy, suddenly, as a girl is shy with her first sweetheart. "I been on several confinement cases," she said. "Bertha's big enough to watch over the kids now, and I can go and leave them. And then I got scrip for staple stuff at the Tithing Office, for sewing up shirt and flannel petticoats and one thing and another. We made out. Just," she said. "But we made out."

"You look good," he said. "Awful good. Heftier, ain't you, some? the heftier you get, the prettier you get."

"That ain't true," she said. "Say, remind me to tell you. I was on one case that about broke my heart in two. The mother and the baby got along all right—but this little two-year-old, just big enough barely to be out in the yard by himself—there was a lot of other kids in the family, and big kids, too, you'd of thought the least they could do would be to watch their little brother—well, sir, if the poor little soul didn't go and fall down in a anthill. I tell you, them ants nearly ate him up by the time somebody heard him screaming and run out and grabbed him. I never seen anybody so bit in my life. I just cried to see him, I felt so sorry for him. Well, sir, here he was screaming and bawling—he'd stretch right out as stiff as a board and then he'd double himself right up in a ball, then out he'd go again. We had a time with him. I tell you, I never seen such agony. Well, I didn't know—I thought of sal soda— and then you know what I done? I just got me some ball bluing and I mixed it with a little cold water and I plastered that poor little tyke with it till he was just covered. You never seen nothing so blue in your life! He stopped crying, too, though he sort of moaned under his breath for a long time even after he fell asleep. Well, sir, that wasn't the end of it. No, sir. He woke up then from his nap and he had one of the ragingest fevers you'd ever want to see and swelled up to twice, three times the size of him. Couldn't stand the covers. Couldn't stand nothing. A while there, I really thought he was a goner. Poor little soul, laying there all swelled and bit and suffering, with these long eyelashes of his—I bet they was a inch long—and these pretty brown eyes—my heart was just breaking in two. But I just kept plastering on the bluing, keeping it wet and thick, and by and by he cooled off and the swelling went down, and—he got better!" she said. She took a deep breath. "I don't know if ball bluing was the right thing," she added. "You never seen anybody so blue."

"It must of been the right thing," Olaf said. "I have."

"You have what?"

"Seen somebody bluer."

"What you talking about?"

"Me," Olaf said. "When you run me off that time, up at Ingeborg's. When you didn't want to see me no more."

"I meant it, too," Linnea said.

"You glad to see me now?"

"Of course I am," she said softly. "Why wouldn't I be? I was sorry about flying off the handle like that, you been as good as you know how. Of course, though, there was arguments for my side, too. For instance—"

"I know," Olaf said hastily. "But things'll be different now. The Manifesto—"

"What's this manifesto business all of a sudden?" Linnea asked.

"Why, President Woodruff," he said. "The President of the Church. Today he issued this Manifesto, see?"

"And what's that got to do with anything?"

"Why, now Utah has got a chance of getting to be a state, and not only that—"

"What is it, anyhow?"

"What is what?"

"A manifesto?"

"It means a statement. President Woodruff put it out today. We've give up polygamy."

"Who's give up polygamy?" Linnea inquired.

"The Church. President Woodruff issued this paper, see? Everybody's talking about it. You don't hear anything else on the streets, just this Manifesto, see? No more polygamy! The Church, the Church members, that is, will refrain from contracting marriages forbidden by the laws of the land. That's the way it reads: refrain from contracting marriages forbidden by the laws of the land. I read a copy of it myself."

"What about," Linnea said, "plural wives? Me, for instance?"

"All the arrangments ain't made yet," Olaf said, "but the President ain't so dumb. He's got something up his sleeve, all right. There won't be no new plural marriages, like he says, but he'll fix it up so all the old marriages can go right on without no more trouble and persecution, and if he does that, he's done something."

"What's the members supposed to do?"

"Why, nothing," Olaf said. "Only, from today on, a Latter-Day Saint can't only marry one wife, like a Catholic or Methodist or anybody."

"Oh," Linnea said.

"But all plural marriages that's already gone through with, the people get to go right on with them as though nothing had happened. At least, that's the way the rumor goes. That's the kind of a deal President Woodruff made with the Governor. That's what people say. It'll all come out eventually: he'll make a speech about it in Tabernacle. It'll all turn out all right. I'm tickled pink it's over."

"What's over?"

"Why, all this sneaking around. Going against the Government and everything. I was in prison for six months, you want to remember. Now there won't be any more such things—spies, and government agents, and soldiers camped up at Fort Douglas to maybe take a notion to fight us, like the North fought the South. No more arrests, and trouble and dissension, and being throwed in jail. Just peace and quiet, like we *should* of been having all these years, instead of being so stubborn, when the hand of every living person in the United States was against us because of what we believed."

"We still believe—what we did believe, don't we?" Linnea asked slowly.

"Just think, Linnea! Now we can live like human beings again! All the deputies will go back where they come from," Olaf said. "It'll be peaceful and nice around here, like any other town. People will be let alone. They can do what they want. No more sneaking around. No more gumshoes back of every bush. And Utah can get to be a state. . . . It'll be wonderful!" Olaf said.

"To save me, I can't get all worked up over Utah being a state," Linnea said. "I can't seem to bring my mind to bear on the matter someway. You're awful excited and tickled. I'm tickled, too. It'll be nice not to figure we're going to have to fight the soldiers up at Fort Douglas that was put there to keep a eye on us, and to think maybe they'll be sent home. And to be able to come and go as natural as you please. And no more deputies and U.S. Marshals and government agents and I don't know who all, swarming around. But you know I was born in the Church," she said.

"What's that got to do with it?"

"My folks was converted in the old country, in Norköping, Sweden, where they come from. They was converted, and come to America, and then I was born. I was born in the Church. You was converted—you and Sigrid both—you might of been awful young, but you was converted."

"What's that got to do with it?" Olaf repeated.

"Well, my folks believe every word of the Gospel. I was born in it. I believe it, too."

"I do, too. Since when didn't I believe the Gospel? Do you got to be born in the Church to believe the Gospel?"

Linnea put her hand up to hush him. "I want to know something," she said. "Why did the Church take up with all this polygamy business in the first place?"

"Why, because—"

"Because the Prophet Joseph Smith told them to. He said it was the right thing to do. Why did he say that?"

"Why, because—"

"Because God give Joseph Smith a revelation. Didn't he? Said, Joseph, I want polygamy, I want every good Latter-Day Saint to marry more than one wife, and multiply and replenish the earth. Ain't that what God said? According to the Prophet?" she asked.

"Yes. But what—"

"Well," Linnea said, "it looks to me like if a revelation comes from God Himself, it had ought to be took in earnest. I took it in earnest. God ain't talking through His hat, you know. When he passes down a revelation to a Prophet or somebody, he means it. Don't he mean it?"

"Sure, he does. But, Linnea, let's talk about—" Olaf laid one of his hands over his wife's and found it to be cold. "You're cold," he said. "Let's go back in by the fire."

"Don't he mean it? God, I mean?"

"Sure, he does."

"Well, then!" she said triumphantly. "Who does President Woodruff think he is all of a sudden, writing this paper of his, this Manifesto? Saying polygamy ain't no good and saying the Church ain't going to follow it no more?"

A gentle rap came at the door. "The coffee's all ready," Bertha called.

"Just a minute, darling," Linnea answered. "We'll be out in a minute."

Olaf stood up.

"No, sit down," she said, "sit down here a minute. I want to ask you . . ."

He sat back down. "Well, I don't know," he said, "I never really thought of it. But I imagine President Woodruff had some kind of a revelation, too. Or something."

"What kind of a revelation?"

"Why, from God, you know."

"Saying what?"

"Why, saying—probably saying that President Woodruff should stop what Joseph started."

"Yes, but God told Joseph to start it. Deliberately. Didn't he?"

"He was supposed to of."

"Now he tells President Woodruff to stop it. You know what I think?"

"No, what do you think, my dearie?"

"I think," Linnea mused, "that's a pretty no-account way for God to do. Change his mind like that. After all the trouble everybody went to, to please him," she said bitterly. "And the misery they went through. Why, people was *killed* on account of polygamy! People was drove out! They suffered, they really suffered. Everybody was against them, everybody. And it ain't been no fun, polygamy ain't, don't let anybody spoof you. It's the worst-feeling, jealousest, onryest thing that ever was invented, polygamy is. And what was the good of it all? All these kids running around all over creation that shouldn't ought to even been born, by rights. God wanted it, and then he don't want it no more. Took a notion not to want it no more," she said, "like a doggoned spoiled young one that hollers for something and his idiot of a mother gives it to him and when he gets it, why, he throws it right away. God's got little to do,

that's all *I* can say. President Woodruff's got little to do! The Counsellors
got little to do! All you no-good busybody no-account men got little to
do! Every last one of you!" she stormed. "I'm blamed mad, if you want
to know!"

"What you mad for? I mean, *mad*, necessarily?"

Bertha tapped at the door again. Linnea said, "Put the coffee back
on the stove and stay in there nice till we come in. We'll be through
talking in a minute. Now, what was I saying?" she said.

"Saying you was blamed mad. But let's not—"

"And I am, too. I'm mad enough to chew nails. It makes perfect fools
out of all us women that trotted right along doing the doggoned men's
bidding like we didn't have sense enough to come in out of the rain.
Sometimes I'd like to tell the whole kit and kaboodle of you to go and
jump in the river! That includes the Almighty, too the Lord God Himself, if you want to know!"

Olaf laughed at her fury. "Wouldn't that be a fine thing to do? Aw,
come on Linnea, smile, why don't you? It ain't so deadly serious as all
that. Don't you love me? Ain't you glad I come home again? Why, gosh,
Linnea, we're going to start fresh, you and me—"

Her face softened and she began to smile. "Oh, well," she said, and
shrugged her shoulders. She put a hand up to her hair. "We better go
in and get the coffee. The girls have probably showed off to beat the
band."

Olaf beamed at her. "The leaders'll fix it all up. The President and
his Counsellors. You'll see. Say, Linnea," he said, "shall I come home
every other night? Or should I spend a week with you, and the following week with—" he broke off. "And then the next week with you
again? I was thinking about it on my way up here, in case you didn't
hold a grudge. That's the way Brother Romney does and it works out
fine. Brother Ivins, too, only he's got five, and that way he only gets
around to each woman every fifth—"

The smile faded from Linnea's face. The resentment came back that
felt like an iron corset cover three sizes too tight, the anger that burned
hotter than a mustard plaster on bare skin. "I want you to get a divorce
from Sigrid, and just have me," she said wickedly. "I guess that'd ought
to put a stop to a lot of craziness. Once and for all," she said.

Olaf had been jocular. He was going to have his sweetheart back, his
plump delicious Linnea with her talent for comfort and skill in living.
He was going to spend half his time with her. She flew off the handle,
yes, but only when she had provocation. She had pride that flared up
like a dried-out Christmas tree accidentally set on fire, but that was
good. You couldn't hold pride against a woman. Mostly she was warmth
and delight itself. She sang, she laughed, she cooked, she talked. Whatever she told, she told inimitably, interestingly. Her friends worshiped

her. She was the color of a May morning. She was an incomparable mother, willing, busy, selfless. Somebody to have back, if lost, Linnea was! Somebody to go to a lot of trouble for, chase after, want. And the kids were cute, well-behaved, beautiful. He'd like to have all five of them strung out in a line along the street, and him holding them by the hand. "Whose kids? Whose nice kids?" different ones would ask, "Mine," he'd say, "and I got two more. These kids, and two more," "Well, you're not so slow," they'd say. Now he didn't feel so jocular. He felt uneasy, and heavyhearted, like something was wrong. He didn't want anything to be wrong, now that Linnea hadn't held a grudge, and had taken him back, and they had made up again, just as he had hoped. He wanted everything to be all right. And now here she came out with this talk about divorcing Sigrid. She was just hurt, that's all. That crackling pride of hers had had a match set to it. Well, poor girl . . . no wonder . . .

"Listen," he said gently, "let's don't us talk about this now. We been all over it before. Let's us go in and get our coffee, and we'll wake up Parley and I'll jounce him on my lap a while. We'll let the girls tell me about them toe slippers they was talking about like they was discussing the jawbone of Jesus. Huh, Linnea?" He slid over close to her and put an arm around her shoulders.

She drew back. "This time I really mean it," she said.

"Why, I couldn't get no divorce from Sigrid," Olaf said. "I wouldn't have a leg to stand on. Not a leg in the world. Why, she'd fight it to the last breath."

"What if she did?" Linnea said, hard-faced.

"Linnea, listen, my dearie. It wouldn't do a bit of good. Not a bit of good in the world. And not only that, we might be ousted from the Church!"

"What if we was?"

"Don't you believe nothing no more?" Olaf said desperately. "I don't seem to know what's got into you all of a sudden."

"We'd get along," Linnea said. "The Church ain't all outdoors, you want to remember."

"Our roots is here!" Olaf said.

"Mamma," Bertha called, tapping again.

"We'll be out in a minute!" Linnea reassured her. "Just you kids be nice and sit and wait a minute, and we'll be out."

"Our friends is here," he went on. "Everybody we know."

"There's other friends in the world. We could go to Oregon or some-place, start over. We'd do all right."

"And leave all we got? My business? Why, I been fifteen years building up my business. Property? Leave all we—"

"Property?" Linnea said. "I got nothing. Just a handful of furniture, and the kids. Not even a whole set of dishes since Rudie pulled the cupboard down on top of him. Have you?"

"Have I what?"

"You said property. What property is that?"

"Why—" he said, swallowing. "Why—"

"Have you got property?" Linnea asked gently. "What you might say property?"

"Well, I—" he said.

"Have you?"

"Well, my God, Linnea, I was paying rent anyway! It don't amount to much more. The house was eight hundred dollars—"

Linnea looked at him with tragic eyes. She didn't say anything.

"Half of it's paid. I was going—"

"He didn't tell me," she said softly to herself. "While I went without, he buys a house for Sigrid. A HOUSE, mind you. He don't buy no house for me. Why should he? Who am I? Nothing, nobody, the mother of five children that the Lord and President Woodruff get their heads together and decide they should never of been born." She was too shocked, too stricken, to cry. "Me, that's been on the move like a gypsy, that nobody ever loved home better. Me, that's wanted a roof over my head and my kids's heads, worse than anybody that ever drew the breath of life, that's prayed—"

"I didn't say nothing about it. I knew you'd be mad if I told you," Olaf said miserably, "but what I had it up my sleeve to do was, pay for this house of Sigrid's, see, and then go ahead and get a house for you. Surprise you with it. Honest, dearie, I—"

"And how long was that going to take?" Linnea asked. "If I may make so bold."

"Why, a—year or so, a couple of years. And then I was going to get a house for you." He took out his handkerchief and patted his face, for in spite of the way the weather had cooled off he was sweating.

"Now *that*," Linnea said, "is the kindest and nicest and besthearted thing a man ever said. The most considerate."

"Oh, Linnea, why don't you listen—"

"Sigrid got her house first. Like she knowed she would. Like anybody with half-sense would of knowed she would." She stated this to nobody in particular, unless to the falling rain, for she was staring out upon it through the window. "If I'd of used my noodle, which I never did, not once since I been born, so whatever happens, serves me right for being a numskull, why, I would of realized when the time come for somebody to get a house, it'd be Sigrid. Not me. I'd of realized it. But no, it never so much as entered my mind. I knowed she was the one to be thought of first, always. I knowed she got and I went without, I knowed her kids had and my kids hadn't—"

"If anybody could of divided more fair," Olaf protested, "than I done, I'd like to see who it would be. Or tried harder to do right."

"—but when it come to a HOUSE," Linnea went on, as though he had not spoken, "I never thought, I never, never thought—that anybody —could do anything so mean, so onry, so sneaky—" She bent over, crying bitterly. Olaf tried desperately to embrace her but she pushed him off. "Don't you dare come near me," she said.

"Linnea, listen, please, my dearie," Olaf pleaded. "I want to make up so bad with you. I want to see you. I love you. I always loved you. Since the first minute I seen you come walking in to choir practice with Ingeborg in that little cape with the stand-up collar, I been wild for you. Always was, and always will be. Why, your eyes is so pretty—your mouth is so pretty—your hair is so pretty. Listen, my dearie," he said, "why, you got no idea how Sigrid was after me every day of the world from morning till night. Buy me this house, she says. Then you done your duty to me and mine, she says. After that you can get a house for Linnea. But I come first, she says. I was married to you first and I'm the oldest and I'd ought to be provided for, she says. Buy me this house, she says. It's only eight hundred and I know how we can manage it, she says. We pay rent money anyway, rent money that just goes up the chimney like smoke. We might as well be getting something for our money, should of, long ago, she says. Well, sir, Linnea, she dings at me and she dongs at me till I didn't know whether I was coming or going. I—"

Now Linnea, from behind her tears, spoke directly to Olaf. "You know," she said, "every other time we got in a tiff or had a little argument, even the last time, up at Ingeborg's, when I was so mad because you left us so long out to Bountiful, and neglected—"

"I didn't," Olaf broke in. "I couldn't help it if the U.S. Marshals was on everybody's trail!"

"Why, every other time," Linnea went on, "when I said I was done with you once and for all, when I said I was through with you and never wanted to see you no more, why, I didn't really mean it, Olaf. Deep in my heart I didn't really mean it. But this time, *this* time," she paused to seek out words, "I'm as done with you as a woman's done with *work* for good and all when she's laid in her coffin. I'm so done with you, I couldn't be any more done with you if I was Mrs. Orson Pratt and you was a pipe of opium. I'm so sick of you, so finished with you, I can't even see you no more, like I was stone-blind. I can't hear you no more, like I was stone-deaf. This time I don't mean nothing, down deep inside, except I never want to see you again as long as I live!"

The girls cried about Papa going out like that, so pale. Taking his hat and going out, saying, "Good-bye, children, be good. Come down to the shop when Mamma lets you."

"Ain't you going to drink coffee?" Gertrude wailed. "I run clear up to the graveyard to get flowers for the table. In all the rain. I got all wet. So the table'd look pretty."

"It does," Papa said, "it does. Only I got to go. I can't stay. . . ."

Gertrude had got a handful of overblown pink roses and a few insect-nibbled buds too tightly rolled ever to unfurl, and placed them in a blue china sugar bowl with only one handle. This was in the exact center of the oilcloth-covered table. The cups and saucers, six of them, were as precisely arranged around the edge of it as 12, 2, 4, 6, 8, 10 around the face of the clock. The *skorpar* was piled upon the hand-painted plate like a fort built of log upon log, two this way, two that way, two this way, two that way, with no roof on top. Somebody had been at the butter (still soft) and gathered up all its loose flowing scalloped edges and piled them on top. A drill team on the Fourth of July couldn't march in better array than the silverware upon the table.

Mamma, at least, admired their handiwork. She came out of the bedroom with red eyes, blowing her nose, and when she found the girls all crying, said, "What in the world's the matter out here? Has the roof fell in or something?"

"Papa wouldn't even look!" Bertha sobbed. "He wouldn't even *look*, and we worked so hard to make the table look nice!"

"Well, I'll look," Mamma said. "I want the bawling to stop." She blew her nose again, standing by the table and carefully inspected its beauty. "If that ain't one of the prettiest set tables I ever seen in my life!" she said.

"But Papa's gone," Gertrude whimpered, "and what good is it now? It was all for Papa!"

"Don't say things like that to Mamma," Bertha reproached her. "It don't sound nice. And anyway, we love Mamma lots the best. We don't care *nothing* for Papa, in comparison."

"Hush," Mamma said. "It ain't right for you to talk that way. You're supposed to love your Mamma and your Papa both alike."

"We don't, though," Bertha said stubbornly.

"We *did*," Stellie confessed, "when we thought he was going to buy us toe slippers. That would of been a good idea, for Papa to buy us toe slippers. Wouldn't it?"

"Wouldn't it, though?" Gertrude said wistfully.

They had their coffee anyway; even Rudie, for the first time, got to sit up to the table with the ladies and have afternoon coffee. His pinny peep show, however, being nearly completed (all he had to cut out and paste in, he said, was two more stars and a tree) he felt too busy to leave it for long and soon disengaged himself from the fair company to go back to his work. Parley was awake now, and on Mamma's lap, but he was not the curb to female conversation that a male usually was, being little more than a baby.

Mamma had told all the girls at one time or another, as they became old enough to inquire, about the institution of polygamy. Since it was the only condition they knew, and since Mamma had given her sanction and esteem to it, they took it for granted that it was a very excellent state of affairs. But Mamma made it clear from the beginning that polygamy was all right for her and for everybody who had so far embraced it, but it would never do for a minute for them. They were not even to consider it, she told them. She managed to give them the feeling that it would be more old-fashioned and out of style than anything else, like wearing their grandmother's iron hoops, to go into polygamy. It was as well they got this notion from Mamma, half respect and half disparagement, for now, of course, with President Woodruff's Manifesto, polygamy was declared null and void and would indeed soon be considered unfashionable by all the best people. Mamma being through with Papa, however, it didn't make much difference whether polygamy was "in" or "out." They could speak of it academically. One thing they knew for certain: Papa had done a horrid thing. He had bought a house for Aunt Sigrid (as they called her) and her children, and had not bought one for Mamma and them.

"Papa has seen fit to buy Aunt Sigrid a house," Mamma told them, "and he ain't seen fit to buy us one. But that ain't the special reason why me and your papa can't make a go of it," she added hastily. "We just—had our differences, the way a couple will do sometimes, and now we're done for good and all."

Tears gathered in first one pair of eyes and then in another. Mamma looked at the three woebegone faces in surprise. "We been alone so much," she said, "the deputies being around everywhere since Gertrude was born, and before, so your father couldn't really come and go as he'd of liked, and in fact wasn't hardly ever home a-tall, that I can't see what's all the bawling about. It ain't as if I wasn't going to come home no more, that's been with you since you was born."

"Well, Papa promised," Stellie began.

"He didn't promise!" Bertha put in.

"Not outright *promise*," Gertrude said.

"—that he would buy us each a pair of toe slippers!" Stellie said. "And now he's gone! And ain't coming home no more! And we'll never get 'em now. Never, never get 'em. As long as we live." The teardrops bounced out and down her cheeks as brightly as the rain streamed down the windowpane.

Bertha cried, too, but not so extravagantly. Gertrude held her tears back, but looked as though she stood on the very edge of doom.

"Well, I never!" Mamma exploded. "Just caring for a man for what you can get out of him! Not paying no attention whether he lives or dies, just so you get your toe slippers! Is *that* the kind of girls I got? Is *that* the kind of kids I raise?"

They all denied it, dried their tears and by one means or another got back on Mamma's good side as fast as they could. But it was not easy to stay there. Today she was as variable as the evangelical wind that bloweth where it listeth. One minute they rubbed her the right way and the next minute they didn't.

"Well, I ain't going to miss Papa such an awful lot," Bertha said later on. "He never come home hardly ever, and he never give us much."

"He come home whenever he could," Mamma said sharply. "How would you feel, with a bunch of deputies after you every minute? You couldn't move around so easy, could you? You wouldn't be so smarty then, would you? If they was going to throw you in jail? Why, men was beat up, and shot, even, for going to see their families! No," she said, "you can't blame Papa for not coming *home*. And as far as *giving* was concerned, why, he divided about as fair and square as a man could divide. When Sigrid got a stove, I got a stove, when Sigrid got a parlor carpet, I got a—but no, I didn't happen to need a parlor carpet at the time. I got them fancy gilt curtain poles and the lace curtain, and I think the parlor lamp, at the time. And ain't he give me a five, and a ten, and a five, and a ten, any time he could, so it amounts to as much as Sigrid and her family's had, through the years? No," she said, "you can't blame Papa for not *giving!*"

"Well, he bought the house for Aunt Sigrid and he didn't buy the house for us," Bertha said argumentatively. "You said so yourself. That ain't so fair and square."

"Is that anybody's business? A busybody little girl's business? Like you?" she said, and Gertrude and Stellie were glad they had kept still. "Since when did Papa have to ask your consent when he wants to do something? He got a bargain on that house of Sigrid's," she said, smoothing Parley's hair back while he watched in the most earnest way her lips move, scarcely blinking. He cuddled closer to her breast but still kept his eyes fixed on her. "He couldn't afford *not* to take it. Why, it was dirt cheap. And anyway, it ain't all paid out yet. He was going to buy us a house next. So there, Miss Smarty." Papa would have been surprised if he had hefted Parley, what a chunk of boy he was, she thought, hoisting him from one side of her lap to the other. It was kind of mean not to let a man heft his little boy. But he had brought it all on himself. Inside, she still felt that cold rage like the tide coming in.

Bertha sighed in exasperation. "Well, my gosh," she said, "I thought you was *mad* at Papa. I thought you didn't *like* him no more."

"I never said I was mad at Papa, and I never said I didn't like him no more," Mamma said severely. "No man ever tried harder, that *you'll* ever lay eyes on, to do what was fair and square, than him. There's no better, kinder, honester man walking around on two legs than him," she said, "if you want to know."

It was a relief when they got occupied with the exciting business of sewing on the machine. Mamma made them take turns. How eagerly each awaited hers, to sit down with a little scrap of material and put her two feet on the treadle. How the wheels spun! How the belt went round! How the needle glittered and dug into the cloth with little short jabs, up down, up, down, stitch, stitch, click, whir, making a long row ------------- of perfect stitches, a row so firm it would hold till Doomsday, a fact they found out to their sorrow when a seam was crooked and Mamma set them to work picking it out. *That* was a bother, you may be sure. What a noise the sewing machine made, modern, whirring, gyromancical, predictive, like the noise of a later century when everything, men and women as well, would be as efficient as this. Rudie left his pinny peep show, a finished work of art now and one less alluring, therefore, to its creator than when in the making, and joined, too, in the fun.

"This is not going to be any regular thing," Mamma said, "sewing on my good sewing machine. I want you to get that through your heads. Why, with a bunch of kids tromping on it and jerking on it and banging on it, this machine wouldn't be worth giving to the junkman inside of a week!" But in the goodness of her heart, even Rudie was allowed to sit at it and treadle, though he had to stretch mightily to do it. He objected to Mamma's close watch over him though, claiming that the girls had more leeway, but Mamma didn't let up. She was afraid he would run the needle through his finger. "I knowed a lady once," she said, "that run a needle through her finger. It went through the nail and clear through the bone. She couldn't budge it. She was trapped there, with the needle through her finger, pinned down to the machine. She was all alone in the house, too, so she had nobody to help her. She tried hollering, but nobody come. Luckily she was sitting right by a window, so finally, when one of the neighbor boys come by from school, she could rap hard on the window with her thimble and get help. When he went for the neighbors and they started coming in, she fainted dead away, keeled right over. She'd set there with that needle through her finger for nearly two solid hours, pinned down to that machine. They had a time, I tell you, to get it out. I guess they just next to never done it. They even had to call a doctor. Just in case you ever take a notion to get fresh," she said, "sewing on the machine when I ain't here. I give you fair warning, is all."

So with the coffee, and the sewing machine, and supper later on, in the freshness of the first cool day and evening for many a week, and paying a pin each and looking one by one in Rudie's pinny peep show,

the hours passed pleasantly, in spite of the episode with Papa, and
Mamma's subsequent capriciousness of mood. They got to stay up an
hour later than usual but to pay for this privilege they had to get down
on their knees and say their prayers. Sometimes Mamma let them say
their prayers in bed; in fact, most times, not liking the idea of drafty
cold floors, except on very important occasions, when they all had to
pray for somebody that was sick or to avert some national calamity.
While they prayed, silently, Rudie by the couch in the kitchen, Gertrude and Stellie shoulder to shoulder by their bed and Bertha kneeling
down by the big bed, Mamma got Parley slipped under the covers without waking him for he had, as usual, fallen asleep in her arms. Kissing
his cheek where his long eyelashes rested she thought with a pang like a
stab wound that he didn't have a father any more. Then she reminded
herself sensibly that he had done without one practically the whole
time, and could go on doing without. It hadn't hurt him yet. . . .

By some mysterious means the prayers were all finished at the same
instant, and with great bouncing and zest the children hopped into bed,
still bouncing after they got into it, so that all the bedsprings squeaked
shrilly. "Now that," Mamma said teasingly, braiding her hair, "is the
way you'd ought to get *up* in the morning, so full of life you can't hardly
hold yourselfs, instead of going to bed like that. And at night, you'd
ought to go to bed like you get up in the morning, yawning and scratch-
ing and moaning and stumbling around here asking me where's this and
where's that like you was blind as bats and no more woke up than a
lizard. That would be the way to go to bed," she said, "if you ask me. I
bet I knowed what you prayed for," she added, "as sure as God made
little apples."

Three little giggles rippled down to a river of laughter. "What?"
"What?" "What?"

"Toe slippers," Mamma said.

"I didn't!" Rudie shouted from the lounge in the kitchen, upon which
he had stopped bouncing so he could hear the conversation better. "I just
said now I lay me and all the blesses."

"That was a very nice boy," Mamma called. "Now you go to sleep,
won't you?"

The giggles rippled down again. "How did you know, Mamma?"

"You'd ought to be ashamed wasting God's time like that, asking for
such things. If you're going to ask for something it looks to me like you'd
ask for something that would do people some good—"

"Toe slippers would do us some good," Gertrude said softly.

"—like good crops for the farmers, or that all the sick people would get
well, or that there wouldn't be no more wars or something. Why, when
I was your age, Bertha's age, that is, and I said my prayers," she said,
"you know what I prayed for?"

"No more wars!" they said.

She dimpled. "I didn't have a bit more sense than you got. Only, I happened to have my sights a little higher. I prayed for a Faustina Polonaise."

"What's *that?*" they said.

"A kind of dress. There was a lady in Conference had one. Somebody said that was what it was. I wanted one just like it, dark green velvet trimmed with old-gold satin. That was one of the prettiest ladies, by the way, I ever laid my eyes on. She was one of the younger bunch of Missus Grants, one of the last women the old man married. She didn't live long. Died of galloping consumption, I think was what they said it was. She had this red hair, you know, with kind of a pinkish cast to it, and she had this milky white skin. I felt awful bad when I heard she was gone, for some reason, I don't know why. Maybe because she was such a sight for sore eyes. Anyway, about this dress. I prayed for weeks for a Faustina Polonaise," she said. "I couldn't think of nothing else. Green velvet with old-gold satin. I could imagine it so plain I could just fairly taste it."

"Did you get it?" the girls asked interestedly. They were all sitting up in bed with their arms hooked around their knees.

Mamma went over to the lamp and got ready to blow it out. They all lay down and pulled the covers up around their chins in expectation. "No," Mamma said, "I didn't. I can't say that I did. And it was just as well, for I knowed later I wouldn't of looked so good in green or so good in that style. That's the way it is with lots of things we pray for—we don't get them, but then we find out later that they wouldn't of done for us a-tall. It looks like God's got a knack for knowing them things—what to give and what to hold back. No," she said, "instead, about six months later, I got a Eudocia Basque."

"What was that?" they asked, delighted.

"China-blue flannel. It looked lovely on me," Mamma said, and took a deep breath and blew out the light. She went over and pulled up the blind. The rain had stopped and there was moonlight shining down on the wet leaves and grass and shiny black sidewalks. It was so quiet that one realized with surprise that the rain had been noisier than one thought, raising more of a hullabaloo.

"But what *was* it?"

"A Eudocia Basque?" Gertrude added.

"Why, a basque, of course. That was the name of it. Now I want you kids to go to sleep," Mamma said, climbing into bed beside Bertha, "and not another peep out of you."

The loud knock that came on the kitchen door nearly scared them out of their skins. "Maybe it's Papa!" Bertha sat up and said hopefully, thinking again of the toe slippers and of prayers being answered. "Oh, maybe it is!" she said. She hopped out of bed and flew into the kitchen.

Mamma got up and found a match and lit the lamp. "If it is," she called, "if it's your father—you tell him I meant what I said! Tell him I wouldn't any more have anything to do with him than I would marry Brother Bell! You tell him that!" she said. "If he thinks he can get in here after that onry underhanded thing he done—"

"But you said you didn't hate him," Gertrude said bewilderedly, blinking in the lamplight. "You said he was so nice and good. And you said—"

"You never mind what I said," Mamma said crossly. "The thing for you to do, is to go to sleep. You mind what I say!" she shouted to Bertha.

Her eldest daughter had the door open now and they could hear who it was.

It was Young Mrs. Monteith's son Raymond. He had come to get Mrs. Ecklund, the midwife. He had come to say his mother needed her very very bad.

CHAPTER 19

YOUNG MRS. MONTEITH's house was nothing to be ashamed of. Not only was it capacious, stylish and well-built, but it was so clean it made you sit up and take notice.

"I seen it happen time after time," Linnea said, comfortably seated in the kitchen, the clock striking one. Young Mrs. Monteith had had a few pains that nearly sent her through the ceiling, but now they had "toned down some," as she said. Linnea set her to pacing the floor, for that was the usual course. It was thought to speed things up and calm the mother.

"It seems so long since I had a baby, I kind of forget how to act," Young Mrs. Monteith said, smiling. She had a clean plisse wrapper on, run through with ribbons, and her hair hung down her back to her tailbone in one thick loose braid. She was paler than she had any reason to be.

Linnea, cocking her head on one side and slightly squinting, noted her contours expertly as she strolled up and down. "If she don't have a girl," she thought, "I'll miss my guess. She ain't shaped right for a boy. She's too low down." Aloud she said, "Yes, sir, I seen it happen time after time. A woman'll clean her house like crazy just before her labor comes on her. Not because she thinks her time is nearly here and she wants a clean house for it, necessarily. No, she just take a notion to tear in and clean. Something makes her do it. I've done it myself, nearly every time. I bet there's been more attics turned out, and steps scrubbed, and carpets beat, and windows washed, the day before a baby starts coming that night, than you can shake a stick at."

"I done that," Young Mrs. Monteith admitted, "cleaned my head off yesterday and today. Took a notion, like you say. Most women really *do* that, come to think of it. I've heard it said before."

"Well, it sure shows," Linnea said admiringly. "I never been in a nicer, cleaner house in my life. It's as pretty as a picture, too," she added.

"Maybe you'd ought to set down now, and rest a spell. You look kind of white-faced."

"Maybe a woman feels extra good or something, the day before," Young Mrs. Monteith said. "Sometimes people gets those spells of feeling so wonderful and strong and like they could lick the world just before they die, too. I've heard. Ain't you heard that?" Young Mrs. Monteith dropped down in a straight chair, a pain came and went, while she shut her eyes tight and hung onto the arms of it. Then she folded her hands in her lap. "I don't think I'm going to be able to stand it if it's a girl," she said suddenly. "It's got so it bothers me all the time now. I ain't been sleeping very well. I think about it. I can't get it out of my mind. I'm—kind of foolish over my kids," she said, "awful set on them, you know. Maybe a little too much." Linnea searched for a word of cheer and comfort. Before she came out with more than "Well, you got to remember—" Young Mrs. Monteith added, "But I'm as sure as I'm setting here," she said, "that it's going to be a boy. You know why?"

"No, why?" Linnea asked gently, thinking again that from the shape of her she was going to have a girl as sure as the grass grows round the stump.

"Well, for one thing," she said. "I've had a dream, over and over, see, that I got a toothache. That tooth aches just as bad as anything ever ached. Well, sir, I wake up. It's gone! I got no more toothache than the man in the moon. Now, don't that seem funny to you?"

"It does seem sort of funny."

"Old Aunt Hallie—my aunt, over on First North, that broke her hip last spring—told me that meant a boy sure. I've had other dreams too. There's this maypole, see, set out in the middle of a big piece of lawn, all hung with flowers, and I've got this streamer in my hands and I'm dancing around it. I've dreamt that several times."

"For goodness sakes," Linnea said, stifling a yawn.

"But that ain't all! Not by a long shot," Young Mrs. Monteith added eagerly. She winced and waited for a pain to go by. "I've had this craving for different things. Old Aunt Hallie says she can tell every time whether a baby's going to be a girl or a boy by the things the mother craves. I took this notion for baloney, see. I couldn't get enough baloney. I'd send the kids down to the Salt Lake Meat Market as they got the only kind I like. Well, I et baloney till it was coming out of my ears. Then I wanted cranberries. Well, sir, there ain't no cranberries this time of year. I just about went out of my mind wanting cranberries. Then oysters! Then rhubarb! Old Aunt Hallie says them things mean a boy for sure."

"Let's hope so," Linnea said soothingly.

"And sick! Why, I've turned deathly sick," Young Mrs. Monteith said, "at the most lot of things! The smell of coffee, for instance. I smell coffee

and I just want to throw up my heels. Or the sight of lamb," she shuddered, "or mincemeat, or a piece of paisley goods, or orange color—anything orange color—and there's one particular woman at church . . . I
know you won't say nothing. Mrs. Pingree. You know she's got one of
these big faces with no eyebrows and no eyelashes and this big bald forehead, and her skin always looks so red and shiny, like she's been scalded
—well, sir, all I have to do is lay eyes on Mrs. Pingree and I'm done for,
I'm ready to gag. Now what could that mean," she demanded, "but what
I got a boy coming?"

"I can't imagine," Linnea said, "unless it means you got a girl coming." She laughed a little to show she was only joking.

Young Mrs. Monteith remained in dead earnest.

"Old Aunt Hallie says not. I try and get up to see her once a week,
poor old soul, flat on her back like that." She paused. "Besides, I just
happened to think of something else I forgot to tell you. One day—it was
about a month ago—I took a notion I smelled cigar smoke. Well, sir, no
matter which room I was in, no matter where I went or what I done, I
smelled this cigar smoke. I—"

"I got a friend," Linnea said, "from Ogden originally, but she lives
here now. She loves the smell of cigar smoke. Just to show you—she's
all alone, got no men folks in the house, but just to show you—" A pain
came and Linnea watched her patient with sympathetic eyes, silently,
waiting for it to pass. "Just to show you," she resumed, when Young Mrs.
Monteith's hands had stopped gripping the arms of the chair and were
relaxed in her lap. "She'll crumble up a few leaves of a good cigar and
burn them on top of the stove, so there'll be the smell of a cigar in the
house, she likes it so well. It gives her a cozy feeling, she says, the smell
of it."

"I never told you about the day the clock stopped, did I?" Young Mrs.
Monteith had worn a look of polite attentiveness while Linnea was
speaking, but now she was anxious to go on with her story. "Aunt
Hallie says the clock stopping was the most important of all."

"You don't say," Linnea said. "No, you didn't tell me."

"Well, sir, the clock took a notion to stop one day! It was July 25, to
be exact. I remember because it was the day after Pioneer Day. The boys
was both cross and laying around the house because they et too much
the day before. I let them go on a picnic with their Sunday-school class
out to Cottonwood Canyon. Anyhow," she said, "it was in the forenoon,
and here the clock was ticking along as nice as you please, and all of a
sudden it stopped. I had my eyes on it the very minute the pendulum
stopped swinging. It give me a kind of a shock, someway. It's a clock
that always runs. I've never knew it to stop. I keep it wound, and—it just
always runs, that's all. Well, it was wound up then. It didn't have no
call to stop. Well, sir, I joggled it and I fooled with it, and finally I set

it back up on the shelf there," she pointed, and Linnea observed that it was now five after two in the morning. "And can you imagine!" she said. "A couple of hours later, here it started to run again! All by itself! And has been working fine ever since. Don't that seem like a kind of *message* or something? Like the smell of cigar smoke? Don't that seem like a message too?"

"It seems—" Linnea began.

"Anyway, with all that," Young Mrs. Monteith interrupted her, "I'm just sure I got nothing to worry about. Old Aunt Hallie says so and she's not the only one. I'm sure I'll get a boy!" The pain that came now was severe enough to bring a groan from her.

Linnea got up from her chair and went over and took her gently by the shoulder. "Well, I guess we're soon going to find out. It's time you got in bed," she said.

But they didn't find out so soon. It got to be six the next morning by the clock that had mysteriously stopped and started again—eight-thirty, eleven, noon. Everybody and his brother had been at the door to inquire. A lady from around the corner and down the street, Mrs. Hyde, did nothing but answer the door and say "No, it ain't here yet. No, she's still in the midst." Most of the neighbor ladies had come and offered to help, but Young Mrs. Monteith, in pain, between grunts and squeals, begged of Linnea that nobody should be allowed in. When the inquirers became too many, however, for Linnea, she consented to allow a woman in as doorkeeper. Raymond was dispatched for the neighbor chosen, Mrs. Hyde, the only woman, it seemed, for blocks around, who had not already been there to offer assistance. She came willingly enough, but she let Linnea know that she had had plenty to keep her busy at home. Her disinterest seemed to be her main virtue. She had a bad-dispositioned face and a hoarse voice. But she could keep people out, and she proved to be much jollier than she looked.

Gertrude and Stellie ran over even before they had their breakfast. Did Bertha have the mush on? Linnea wanted to know. Yes, they said. They would eat when they got back. What was the baby? A boy or a girl? What O what? Neither one. It wasn't born yet. Young Mrs. Monteith was still in the midst. Their faces fell.

"I tell you what," Mamma said, "I don't want you to keep coming here bothering Mrs. Hyde, and bothering me, either, because I may be awful busy in a little while. I tell you what I'll do to let you know. The front parlor has got two windows, side by side, with the blinds pulled down. You notice when you go around the house. Now, listen, if the baby's a boy," she said, "I'll raise up *one* blind. If it's a girl, I'll raise up *both* blinds. Then you don't got to come in. All you got to do is walk past and look at the blinds. One for a boy. Two for a girl."

"Mamma, let me ask you something private," Gertrude said. She had used Mamma's big comb this morning: the wide teeth marks could be seen in her slightly dampened hair. Stellie had only given hers a lick and a promise.

It came to Linnea like a heartache looking down at them that they were really awfully nice little girls. Willing little girls. Good and pretty little girls. Being somewhere else, not home, and having them come to her, like today, hand in hand, asking about Young Mrs. Monteith's baby, made her realize how terribly much they meant to her. How much all the kids meant. She could spare one about like she could spare her liver or her heart. "What do you want to ask me, that's so private?" she said indulgently. She bent her head down, to hear.

Gertrude put her face close and spoke in her ear. "Does Young Mrs. Monteith *really* got to give the baby away, if it's a girl? Really and truly? Or is that just made up?"

Mamma glanced down the hall and at the half-shut bedroom door. "You heard the story," she answered softly. "Just the same as me. Your guess is as good as mine."

She brought it up to Young Mrs. Monteith an hour or so later, when she had made her check to see how things were progressing. She stood at the foot of the bed, having just thrown the light coverlet back over it, and spread the perspiration-dampened sheet over the humped-up knees of Young Mrs. Monteith. "If you don't mind my asking," she said. "Tell me—do you really intend to give your baby away to your husband's first wife, if it's a girl? You don't really intend to, do you?"

If anybody ever looked like she was being drug through a knothole, as Linnea told Ingeborg afterwards, it was Young Mrs. Monteith. She was putty-colored, with big dark circles under her eyes. All around her face her reddish hair was plastered down, dark with sweat, the color vanished from it, the sparkle gone. She panted when she breathed. The pains came so often that she never really had time to recover from one onslaught before another was upon her. This had gone on all night and half the morning. She was so tired she was dazed. She moaned automatically, as though she didn't really mean it, just moaned and moaned, even in the moments between pains. "The reason I asked her," Linnea said later, "even when it didn't seem to be no time for it and it seemed cruel, was because I thought maybe she'd pop out with something that would put her mind at rest. She was troubled in her mind, if ever I seen a woman troubled. I thought it was holding things up. She just wasn't making no headway. . . ."

Mrs. Monteith wet her pale swollen lips with her tongue. "I got to," she said. "I signed that paper when my husband married me."

"That don't mean nothing!" Linnea burst out. "It ain't as if it was the *law*. Why, you was only—what was you? Eighteen?"

"Seventeen."

"A seventeen-year-old girl shouldn't ought to be held to no paper she signed." Linnea sponged off the sweating face, brought a glass of water and gave her a drink.

"Why, I got to! It was a agreement."

"No, you don't," Linnea said staunchly. "You'll have a easier time of it if you make up your mind now that, boy or girl, you ain't going to give it away to nobody. I think that's what's holding things up. You ain't coming along like you'd ought to. The first thing you know, I may have to call a doctor or somebody. You got to let go. You got to go to work and get this here thing over. You don't want to lay here and suffer till the middle of next Christmas, do you?" She spoke softly, comfortingly. "Why don't you just say you ain't going to give the baby away and put a stop to all such foolishness? Old Mrs. Monteith must be off her base or something."

The poor untidy head tossed back and forth on the crumpled pillow. "I got to, I got to. . . ." she whispered. "But I wish I didn't. I need— I want—"

"You don't got to! That paper don't mean nothing. Why, it's just a *Church* paper. It ain't as if it was the law or nothing. And even in the Church, I don't know how Old Mrs. Monteith ever got away with such a thing."

"She did. We all three went to the Endowment Office. She—"

"Why, if you was to go to the President of the Church, President Wilford Woodruff himself, or any of the high officials," Linnea said, "and told them all about the whole thing, why, I bet they'd put a stop to all this foolishness before you could turn around. *They* wouldn't let Old Mrs. Monteith get to the first turn in the road, with such a thing as that. The Church may done a lot of things, but I don't believe they'd ever in the world separate a mother and her baby."

"It's going to be a boy!"

"Sure, it's going to be a boy. Only, supposing it ain't? That's why you're having such a hard time. That's why you're hanging on like grim death to a nigger's heel. You're scared out of your wits it'll be a girl."

"I—ain't afraid."

"Well, you don't have to be. Because even if it *is* a girl, you'll get to keep her, she's yours—don't you understand, Young Mrs. Monteith? *You* don't got to give no little girl away, not on your life you don't, not in the state of America. Why, if the worst comes to the worst, we'll call out the whole Union Army," Linnea said lightly. "We'll—"

"You better quit that kind of talk. Not let the Lord hear you. . . ." Young Mrs. Monteith brought out harshly. Then she bit her lips and shut her eyes tight. Her hands went over her head and crawled upwards, grasping the brass poles of the headboard of her stylish bed. She squealed like a stuck pig, then lay very still, breathing heavily.

Linnea looked at her with compassion, sighed, and did what little she could do. "There, there," she said, "I was trying to help you. I didn't want to rile you all up. You just go ahead and have your baby. . . . Everything's going to turn out just like you want it to. Whatever you want, you'll get. Whatever you want to have happen, will happen, you'll see, you'll see. . . ." It was a hot day today, though the rain yesterday would seem to have promised a spell of cool weather. Linnea went over and lowered a blind on the eastern window where the sun blazed in. She wished she could open the window a little and let some air in, but Young Mrs. Monteith was in a lather of perspiration and she was afraid of a draft upon her.

"You don't understand," Young Mrs. Monteith said thickly, like a woman who talked in her sleep. "The law's got nothing to do with it! It was a promise to God!"

A seventeen-year-old girl's got no business going around making such promises to God, Linnea thought to herself but did not say as Young Mrs. Monteith was in no condition to be argued with. "*He* don't want any such promises. God ain't no dummy, you know. He probably thinks such things are just as silly as I do," she said aloud.

"It was a promise to God," the thick-sounding voice went on, coming from the dry lips. Linnea bent and moistened them again, with the corner of a linen napkin dipped in cold water. "Do you think I'd dare go back on a promise to *God?* You know what he could do?"

"No, what?" Linnea said gently.

"Why, anything, that's all! He could cause me to go blind, he could send me crazy so I'd have to be took to a asylum, he could make my heart stop so I'd fall over dead. But I don't care about *that*," she said, "what he'd do to me wouldn't make any difference. God knows that. He knows every little thing about a person. That's what makes it so bad—"

"And so good," Linnea said.

But Young Mrs. Monteith would not be interrupted. "So bad," she repeated. "He knows how I feel about my—my boys," she said, "Raymond and Gerald. Raymond's fourteen, Gerald's twelve. He'd strike at me through them. Say for instance I'd have a girl and I'd keep her, I wouldn't stick to my bargain. All right. The law can't make me give her up. The police can't come and take her away—"

"Your darn tooten they can't," Linnea said. "You just remember that."

"—but I made a promise to God, see. I owe him something, just like if you borrow money, you got to pay it back. Only more so."

"God ain't no pawnbroker; he ain't no banker, with a mortgage on somebody's farm; he ain't no snoop from a collecting agency. He's *God*, in case you got your wires crossed somewhere."

"So I got to keep my promise," Young Mrs. Monteith went on wearily, slobbering a little at the corners of her lips, her eyes glazed-looking with fatigue. "He'd strike at me through them, see? All of a sudden, something would happen to Raymond. Something terrible, like drownding. Or something would happen to Gerald. Something awful, like a train running over him. And—"

"What God would that be," Linnea asked, "you're talking about?"

" 'I am a jealous God,' " Young Mrs. Monteith said, " 'saith the Lord.' Or something like that, in the Bible. You know. 'The Lord is a jealous God.' Something like that. I got to keep my promise. . . ."

"That must be some other fella," Linnea said. "It ain't the one I'm acquainted with, not on your tintype it ain't."

Mrs. Hyde was kept busy answering the door. "No, it ain't here yet" —"No, she's still in the midst." "No, Young Mrs. Monteith don't want anybody in there with her only just the midwife. The midwife's Mrs. Ecklund." "No, it would be better if you didn't come in." "What's all the big excitement? What's all the gawking about? Ain't a woman never had a baby before?" "No company wanted, begging your pardon. You can come when it's all over and Young Mrs. Monteith is having visitors."

The whole neighborhood and half the town seemed to know that Young Mrs. Monteith was "in the midst." There were a great many people on the sidewalks, lingering in front of the house. Housewives, mostly standing gossiping together, with a child or two at their skirts and a baby clutched in their arms, old women, giggling girls in pairs, their arms twined around each other's waists. The men and boys must have been better occupied for there did not seem to be any, only a slow old man or two, dawdling down the sunny street with a cane. "It looks like people would have something else to do than gawk around all day," she said crossly. She had made a hurried trip out to see if there was still plenty of water on the stove and if it was still bubbling, and was on her way back to her patient. She had stopped and was looking through the dining room windows which faced the street.

"It looks like it, don't it?" Mrs. Hyde said. "What I do," she went on, "when I open the door, is not to look any too pleased. That shows people what I think."

The crowd worried Linnea. It was the first time she had ever officiated at a birth in which the public took an interest. Usually, an obscure little mother gave birth to an obscure little baby—nobody cared a pin. But this time there were a lot of eyes on her. People by the hundreds were concerned—or seemed to be concerned—about Young Mrs. Monteith having a baby. Only she wasn't having it very fast. My goodness, Linnea thought, wouldn't it be a fine thing if Young Mrs. Monteith would take a notion to die all of a sudden? Or the baby would die or something? With everybody's eyes on us like this? Why, nobody'd have me for NOTHING no more, let alone deliver a baby. I'd have to maybe sew for a living from now on and there ain't anything I hate worse. Why, I never felt so watched in my life. I feel like I was trying to do my business in front of the Z.C.M.I. during Conference. No, sir, she thought, if she don't start making some progress pretty soon, I'm going to have to call somebody. I can't handle it all alone. I'm going to have to send out for a doctor. . . .

But she delayed and delayed in professional pride, the hours ticked away and she got more and more nervous. Eventually however, Young Mrs. Monteith started to make some progress. Delighted and relieved, suddenly able to breathe freely, Linnea made a hasty examination, the stench of worn-out Young Mrs. Monteith's sweat in her nostrils, thinking, When this is over I'm going to let some air in here the first thing. "Hang on to your hat, Young Mrs. Monteith!" she said, "I think we're on our way!"

She said afterwards it just showed what you could do when you had to. Well, everybody's eyes were on her, she just had to measure up, she said. There was no time now to send for anybody. And what should that idiot of a baby do but present its behind first "right in my face," Linnea told Ingeborg, "here come the behind, as big as life!" Something like that would happen, to complicate things, "just when I would of give my eye teeth to have everything go smooth." The sweat running off her face with the effort, only by manipulation and with no instruments, she managed to turn the baby around so that its head came first.

"Hold back," she said sharply to Young Mrs. Monteith. "Now's the time to hold back! Breathe with your mouth open, slow easy breaths." But Young Mrs. Monteith wouldn't, or couldn't. Linnea made propping damming motions but here came the baby like a greased pig shooting out of the arms of a boy at the county fair. As big as a house, here it was, and it tore its mother all to pieces. "Oh, you should of held back, if you could," she said.

"What is it? What is it?" the mother barely whispered. Soaking and exhausted, her eyes were shut and if she was pale before, the pallor seemed like a pink rose blooming, to what she was now. Linnea covered her and kept glancing at her but for a little while she was sorely occupied with the baby. It took a tiny breath, another, another. She cut the cord that bound it to its mother and watched the blue color vanish, the angry healthy scarlet replace it. Now it was on its own, an awesome, a thrilling moment. A separate life. All by itself. All by its lonesome, me and myself and I. Like history, like an episode of important history. Taking tiny breaths.

But did it breathe? Her heart stopping, she bent down to it, listened, then picked it up, swung it downwards in an arc, gathered it up against her shoulder slapped the little fat arm hard. She heard the caught breath, the gasp. Now . . . it let out a long furious cry. Now it was all right, it could cruise under its own power, it was married to life, till death do us part. Linnea sighing with relief, suddenly remembered all the people outside. She had forgotten them. What would they think of her if she'd let the baby die . . . ?

Too tired to speak, Young Mrs. Monteith yet did. "A girl?" she begged pitifully.

What was better, to lie now? Or to tell the truth? Linnea finished sponging the baby off over the dishpan of warm water, got its first pants on, its shirt, its kimono tied in front with blue ribbons.

"Please . . . I don't care . . . so much. . . ." the mother said.

Linnea got it put down in its basket, snug, safe, well-covered, out of the light, to sleep as though nothing had happened, as though it were back where it started from. Now she turned her attention to Young Mrs. Monteith, felt her small dim pulse that fluttered like a bird's wing.

"You rest," she said, "go on and take a nap. You done all anybody could ask of anybody today. And more too."

"Please."

"It's a girl, Young Mrs. Monteith. But don't you worry none. We'll fix things. She's a beauty, Young Mrs. Monteith. I bet she weighs ten pounds if she weighs a ounce."

But Young Mrs. Monteith was not listening now. Her head had fallen back, her mouth gone slovenly.

"Now what!" Linnea said, her heart jumping. But Young Mrs. Monteith had not died or fainted, she had only seemed to do both. Linnea wrung a cloth out of cold water and placed it on her forehead. Then she stood looking down at her, rubbing her wrists.

Mrs. Hyde poked her head in at the door. "Girl?" she said.

Linnea nodded.

"All in?"

"Yes," Linnea said. "All in."

"There's a bottle of brandy in the cupboard. Shall I bring it?"

"I'm going to get her some coffee and pour it down her."

"Brandy would be better. More snap."

"I never do give stimulants," Linnea said. "Just a little hot coffee."

"Nothing can beat brandy."

"All right," Linnea said.

They fed it to Young Mrs. Monteith by spoonfuls, let it dribble down her throat. Linnea heated the flatirons, too, for the ice-cold feet. There was no sweat now. Young Mrs. Monteith was as cold as the angel on a tombstone. Linnea poured hot water from the teakettle into two-quart fruit jars, screwed the caps on tight and placed them around her, covered her well with quilts and sponged off her blank white face.

There was quite a lot too much blood, all the torn-up clean white rags piled high in the clothesbasket were soaked and stained. "That's what come of the baby taking a notion to come out pell-mell like that," Linnea said worriedly. "Now, if she keeps on bleeding, it's just going to be too bad." She didn't, though. She stopped. She opened her eyes, too, quaveringly. Linnea kept feeding her brandy by half-teaspoonfuls. The secundines were so long in coming that Linnea got quite anxious and was just ready to give up and send one of the boys hotfooting it for a doctor. And then, a grunt, a groan, a squeal so weak that it was like the squeak of a mouse, and that was done with, too. It was all over! Linnea took a swig of the brandy herself, in sheer relief. (She suspected that Mrs. Hyde had already done so, from the brightness of her eyes and the deepening hoarseness of her voice which geniality made still more dreadful.)

Then she set to work and cleaned things up, the floor, the bed, her limp and dreamy patient, whose lips had the color coming back into them again. She put the bloody rags to soak in a tub of clean water in the spare-room closet where the boys would not happen to run across them, although there was not much danger of this as they had gone to spend the night with their grandmother whose stiff joints kept her close to home. They would be washed and boiled tomorrow, for nobody ever threw away good linen rags, but they had to be kept out of sight of children. When she pulled the blinds down and tiptoed out, leaving the mother and baby wrapped in profound silence and darkness, she happened to remember that she had promised to tell Gertrude and Stellie whether it was a boy or a girl.

She went into the shadowy parlor and across to the pair of windows. She let first one blind up halfway, then reached over and let the other one up. A girl. This was the sign that Mrs. Monteith had had a girl. There were not so many people on the street now. They seemed to have gone home.

"It's suppertime," Mrs. Hyde announced. "That's why they ain't so many gawkers, I guess. They gone home to eat supper."

"I guess so," Linnea said, stretching tiredly. "Well, I guess I'll go wash," she said, "and get me some coffee. I ain't had any, come to think of it. My, we was busier'n cranberry merchants in there for a little while, wasn't we?"

"You was busy," Mrs. Hyde said hoarsely.

"You helped fine," Linnea said. "I don't know what we would of done without you around here today. That brandy sure wasn't a bad idea. It brought her right around."

"I got supper on the table. All you got to do is go set down and eat it," the old lady said.

Tears swam in Linnea's fatigued eyes. "Well, say—" she said. "If that ain't nice of you."

"Girl, huh?"

"Yes. Girl," she said. She blinked the moisture away. "Ain't she a beauty? Fat as a little pig."

"Think Old Mrs. Monteith'll be fool enough to take it?"

"God knows. She probably will."

"Don't it beat all?"

"Don't it?" Linnea said.

At first Mrs. Hyde said she didn't want anything but then she decided she did and sat down across from Linnea, first brewing herself a pot of tea, which Linnea graciously told her she herself wouldn't touch with a ten-foot pole, but it was every man to suit his own taste, wasn't it? Mrs. Hyde had to get up and answer the front door twice and the back door three times but she said she didn't mind people's curiosity. "It shows what they got in their heads," she said. "Nothing."

Young Mrs. Monteith and her baby daughter never said boo. Their bedroom was as still as the grave.

Mr. Monteith came in right after supper, a handsome burly man with thick hair graying like a silver fox and dark eyebrows that grew together across the bridge of his nose. He had a good color, tan streaked with rose. All his front teeth were good, hard and bright, but his side teeth were pulled out, at least the upper side teeth, the ones that showed. He had overalls on, and a checkered shirt. He was sixty-five and looked twenty years younger. "Well, it ain't such a mystery," Linnea thought, "Young Mrs. Monteith marrying him. And he was well fixed besides. Promised her this nice house. Give her money to live on. No wonder she signed that paper."

She said softly to Mrs. Hyde after she had ushered him into the bedroom, carrying in the lamp and setting it down on Young Mrs. Monteith's marble-topped bureau, and had come back out into the kitchen where Mrs. Hyde was washing the dishes, that it wasn't any of her business but she for one was going to ask Mr. Monteith just exactly what was what. By the looks he had given her, by the way he stooped over and kissed her lips and patted her hand, Mr. Monteith set great store by his second wife. He wouldn't stand for anything that was going to tear the heart right out of her bosom. Why, the whole thing was just too silly for words. Mr. Monteith wouldn't stand for it a minute.

But he would. Linnea almost fell over backwards, she said when she told the story to Ingeborg, to hear that he took the affair just as seriously as Young Mrs. Monteith did. It wasn't reasonable, it wasn't like modern times, it wasn't like in the free country of America: It was Noah's Ark days, Solomon days, Bible days of ignorance, blindness and obstinacy. "You heard of that saying a eye for a eye and a tooth for a tooth,"

Linnea said. "Well, you'd of thought Mr. Monteith was the guy that invented it. He was just deadly in earnest. Mr. Monteith, I says, could I have a word with you? Yes, he says. We was in the hallway, outside his wife's door. I pushed open the parlor door and motioned him to come in after me. He did, and I shut the door. Mr. Monteith, I says, what's all this nonsense about Young Mrs. Monteith having to give her baby away?"

Mr. Monteith hemmed and hawed, Linnea said. He ran his hands through his hair, walked over to the center table, stared down unseeingly at the fancy glass paperweight which weighted down nothing, being only used as an ornament next to the big carven untouched Bible, walked back, cleared his throat and said, "Well, you see, Mrs. Ecklund, she signed this paper fifteen years ago. My wife—my first wife, you understand—well, that was the agreement she fixed up and wanted signed. Fannie—that's this girl—why, she signed it. We couldn't of got married so easy otherwise."

"Well?" Linnea said coolly, looking him straight in the eye.

His gaze wavered, fell. "She signed that there paper," he repeated. "Fifteen years ago. My wife—my first wife, you understand—has still got it."

"I don't care whether it was fifteen years ago or fifteen minutes ago," Linnea said. "It's the most crazy tomfoolishness I ever heard tell of. Why, your wife won't hold Young Mrs. Monteith to it, will she? Old Mrs. Monteith won't? It'll just the next thing to kill her, is all."

"I'm afraid so," the man said weakly. "I guess she's counting on it. We never had no children. I guess she's always kind of counted on a girl."

"How old is she?" Linnea asked.

"Sixty-three. No, sixty-four."

"You scared of her or something? Put your foot down. Tell her it was crazy tomfoolishness and that she had better tear up that paper! Where do you think we're living at? Some foreign country or something?"

Mr. Monteith was silent.

"You ain't actually going to do it? Allow it? Are you?" Linnea said.

He swallowed. "Why—" he said, "she signed that paper, you know. I don't hardly see what I can do."

Linnea let out a little groan. "Oh, you don't hardly see what you can do, huh?" she said. "You might start acting like somebody that's got a little good sense, for one thing. Or you could start with taking a dive head first in a patch of poison ivy!"

He didn't fire her. So far as she could find out, he did not even mention the conversation to Young Mrs. Monteith, at least not while Linnea was still in the house.

In the forenoon of the next day she went down to see Old Mrs.
Monteith, leaving Mrs. Hyde, now very much interested in the whole
affair, in charge at Young Mrs. Monteith's. She had got several hours
refreshing slumber on the slick horsehair lounge in the parlor across
from her patient's door and the following morning was greatly restored.
Such was not the case with Young Mrs. Monteith, however. She seemed
to have shrunk to half her size, her nose had got high-bridged and
sharp, her cheeks hollow. She was of a yellowish tinge and her eyes had
no more shine to them than a rock.

Early that morning when Linnea tiptoed in, she spoke softly from the
bed. "I want you to take the baby out of here. Put her basket in the
kitchen or some place. I don't want her in here no more."

"You wouldn't hardly look at her last evening," Linnea said reproachfully. "You don't know how cute she is. Just as cute as a bug's ear. One
of them fat good-natured cuddly kids. Going to be your coloring, too
—why, she's going to be one of the cutest little girls that ever asked her
Mamma for a piece of dough to make a little loaf of bread with!"

"I want you to take her down to Old Mrs. Monteith." This was said
firmly, through stiff lips. Young Mrs. Monteith was looking at the ceiling for all she was worth, with her tearless eyes. She wasn't looking to
left nor to right.

"Today?"

"This morning."

"Ain't that kind of hasty?"

"If you don't take her, I'll get up and take her myself."

"You wouldn't get far," Linnea said sternly.

She moved the baby out into the kitchen where she slept in her basket
by the stove while the two women, Linnea and Mrs. Hyde, had breakfast.

"My appetite's kind of spoiled," Linnea said, looking thoughtfully
toward the sleeping child. "I think I'll just have a piece of bread and
butter and a cup of coffee."

"Mine ain't," Mrs. Hyde said. "It's all such everlasting silliness I
ain't even going to bother my head with it."

"It's everlasting silliness all right," Linnea said, "but even if it is,
they're all going ahead and going through with it, all three of them,
Young Mrs. Monteith and Old Mrs. Monteith and him."

"Him?"

"Mr. Monteith. And Young Mrs. Monteith is going to lose her baby
just as sure as if it *wasn't* silliness. Just as sure as if it was all as sensible
as coming in out of the rain."

"Well," Mrs. Hyde said, "people will act like goofs and there's no
getting around it. It'd take more than that for me to lose my appetite."
She dished up two fried eggs, reached for the bread and began to eat.

Linnea sipped her coffee. "A skinny person has always got such a good appetite," she said, "nine times out of ten, I've noticed. Eat to beat the band. Now it ain't that way with a fat person. Sometimes a fat person won't eat enough to keep a bird alive."

Mrs. Hyde chewed reflectively, stirring sugar into her tea. "No, and sometimes they'll eat enough to flounder a horse. It all depends," she said. "Nice little baby, ain't it? Lays there just as good as gold."

Linnea got up from the table and went over and looked down at her. The arms and hands were pressed in close, the fingers curled inwards, like salal flowers shut up, the petals of the eyelids shut, not wanting to open. The cheeks, the lashes, the scrawny hair, were limp and soft. "I think I'll go have a talk with Old Mrs. Monteith," she announced. "Maybe the whole thing was just a joke to make Young Mrs. Monteith sit up and take notice, to scare her. Why, the woman can't think a mother would deliver a baby to her lock, stock and barrel, under any such circumstances as them. I'm sure she don't want the baby. She just wants something to hold over her husband and Young Mrs. Monteith. Something to throw up to them every once in awhile. I'll go talk to her. I bet I'll have the whole thing straightened out in no time. You keep an eye on things here, will you?"

But Old Mrs. Monteith turned out to be no very easy nut to crack. She was as dead in earnest as the other two. Linnea almost had to pinch herself to believe it, but it was true. The situation gave the woman a feeling of power, let her steer the boat, gave her the reins. Either she was not used to it, and it intoxicated her, like one swallow of brandy could make Linnea dizzy, or she was used to it and couldn't get enough of it, like a miser can't get enough silver dollars. Linnea could not decide. "It's me that's cracking the whip," Old Mrs. Monteith said, "now." She did not ask her caller to sit down although she received her in the parlor. "No, I tell you," she said, "it's nothing so out of the ordinary. It ain't nothing that couldn't of been done in Bible days."

"Well, that's just it," Linnea said. "Ain't we took any steps forward since Bible days? Why, them was ignorant people. They never even so much as boiled their clothes or had knives and forks!"

"Ignorant people!" Old Mrs. Monteith repeated her words with what was meant to be fine irony.

"Listen," Linnea said, "it ain't normal, it ain't natural; none of it ain't normal and natural. You're just fooling, ain't you, Old Mrs.—rather, Mrs. Monteith? You don't mean to take a mother's baby away from her that she wants and loves, just because she signed some tomfool paper when she was seventeen? You don't really mean to do it, do you?"

"My husband tells me it is a very nice little girl."

Linnea rushed on unheedingly. "Listen," she said, "I know you wouldn't any more do such a mean cruel onry thing than stand on your head in Tabernacle. I know you wouldn't. I tell you what. Why don't you come with me and see her?" she asked eagerly. "She had such a hard time. Why, she layed there and suffered a whole night and a whole day. The sweat run off her in buckets. If ever a woman went through something, it was her."

"My husband tells me she's doing fine."

"Sure, she's doing fine. Only she's so heartsick over this craziness that she's just ready to die."

"Oh, she won't die," Old Mrs. Monteith said.

"Why don't you come with me and see her?" Linnea repeated. "If you want to make somebody so tickled they'll just get down on their knees and kiss the ground you walk on, you come with me to Young Mrs. Monteith's, and go in the bedroom where she's laying like she don't care whether she lives or dies, and walk right up to the bed and tell her you don't want her brand-new baby. Tell her it was all a joke. Tell her you never any more intended her to go through with it, than fly to the moon. You'd have the paper with you, see," Linnea said seductively, "you'd have it in your purse or in your pocket. Her eyes would be on you not knowing whether it was a trick or what it was, just watching and staring. Well, sir, you'd pull this paper out. Remember this name signed here, you'd say, holding it up for her to read. Yes, she'd say. Is that your name, you'd say, in your handwriting? It is, she'd say. Well, I'm tearing it up, you'd say, I never any more meant to keep you to it than fly to the moon. And you'd tear it up, and throw the pieces in the chamber pot, and tears would be running down the face of Young Mrs. Monteith like City Creek used to stream through Brigham's land, and she'd be laughing at the same time. . . . I tell you, the Lord would just fairly beam if he looked down from heaven and seen you doing a stunt like that! Why, I bet when you got up yonder you'd have stars in your crown so big and so bright they would put your eyes out." She took time to breathe. "Won't you?" she said. "Won't you come with me? Tear up that paper? Why, that idiot of a Young Mrs. Monteith thinks you *mean* it. Imagine. And she's just as serious as a Judge about it too, Old Mrs. Monteith. She's going to go *through* with it, if you don't tell her you was only fooling. Which you are, you must be, you must of been, if you got any sense to you, any heart to you a-tall. Wasn't you fooling, Old Mrs.—rather, Mrs. Monteith?"

"I always wanted a little girl," the woman stated flatly. Gertrude and Lily described her aptly: she was neither more nor less than a gray-haired woman with glasses in a cotton waist and rep skirt, with an apron tied around her waist.

"You're too old," Linnea said brutally, "to start in now and raise a child. When you ain't never had one."

"Maybe I am and maybe I ain't."

"You could adopt some child that ain't got any mother. Take some orphan to raise or something, if you got to have one all of a sudden. Which you managed to get along all these years without one, I notice," she said.

"I'll thank you to walk out of my house," Old Mrs. Monteith said. "Who are you to be butting in, by the way? Into other people's private affairs?"

Linnea bit her lip. "Anybody with any decency and any heart to them, would try to butt in. Not that I got any more than my share, I don't mean to say," Linnea said.

"I never had any children," Old Mrs. Monteith announced mincingly.

"There's a saying in Swedish," Linnea said. "It don't sound so good in English. But it goes like this: The Lord never give a mooly cow horns, knowing full well that if he did, she would always be poking and jabbing all the rest of the cows! The reason you ain't had any children," Linnea said unfairly, letting her anger run away with her, "is probably because the Lord knew you would of been such a no-account mother!"

"That ain't true!" Old Mrs. Monteith said fiercely. "I could of had—I didn't want—I just didn't happen to *want* any children until—"

"Until a woman's life's blood goes with it," Linnea said, "then you want one! When her heart is tore right out of her breast, and goes along, why, that's the baby for you! I tell you, Old Mrs. Monteith, somebody's going to fix your wagon for you someday, like it ain't never been fixed before!"

Usually the soul of tact, Linnea had done everything wrong today. "But there wasn't no rubbing her the right way," she said later. "No matter what anybody said she would of gone right on being just as stubborn. She's dead set after that baby, that's all there is to it."

Mrs. Hyde had two things to report to her when she returned. First, Young Mrs. Monteith had discovered that Linnea was absent and Mrs. Hyde had told her where she went and for what purpose. "Well, sir, it brought back some zip into her, you can bet!" Mrs. Hyde said proudly. "Why, she colored up and she laughed and she cried, just too excited for words. It was all I could do to keep her from getting out of bed. She's setting up in bed now, as big as life. Can't hardly hold herself. She said you could maybe talk the old lady into letting her out of her bargain. She never thought of doing that, she said. It never entered her head. She said if you was to get that old lady to give up taking her baby away from her, why, she was going to do handsprings all around the block. Nothing would do but I had to bring the baby in for her to see. She's holding it now, holding it and looking at it and admiring it, like it was the first baby that ever blinked its eyes at the light. She says she's going to name it Rosebud and its middle name after you. Why, honestly, you'd ought to take a peek in there at her. It'd tickle the life out of you."

"Oh, God," Linnea groaned. "I didn't want her to know nothing about it. Not get her hopes all up—"

"You didn't say I shouldn't tell her. I didn't know. Didn't you—get nowhere?"

"Nowhere," Linnea said despairingly. "It's just no earthly use. You seen mules, ain't you? Well, that'll give you some idea. That Old Mrs. Monteith is just a regular mule."

"Oh, no," Mrs. Hyde said, with a woebegone face. "Poor thing! I don't know who's going to have the heart to tell her!"

"Me, I suppose," Linnea said, "because I'm the one done the damage. And I tell you, I'd just rather be shot."

The second thing was, Mrs. Hyde said, that a reporter had come from the newspaper, not the church paper, the *Deseret News*, but the powerful *Salt Lake Tribune*. They heard there was something funny going on up here in regard to a baby. What was behind it all? they wanted to know.

"What did you tell him?" Linnea asked idly, wondering what she could say to Young Mrs. Monteith and how to say it.

"I told him there wasn't anything funny going on in regard to a baby or anything else. I told him to go away and mind his own business."

"Did he go?"

"Yes. But he said he'd be back."

When Linnea pushed open the bedroom door, Young Mrs. Monteith was lying on her elbow looking at the baby on the blanket beside her. With a gentle forefinger she was smoothing the unsubstantial eyebrows and eyelashes, the cheeks as soft as mucosae, the mink-like hair growing low on the forehead. The dove speaks as she spoke, saying the same words, leaning toward her child.

"Young Mrs. Monteith," Linnea cleared her throat and said from the doorway.

The woman gave a jump and sat up with a hasty frightened motion, pulling her knees up. With one hand, as though to hide it, she lifted up and dropped a corner of the blanket over her baby, placed her hand lightly upon it, kept it there, shielding. "Oh, it's you," she said, "Mrs. Ecklund! I couldn't hardly lay here, I was so excited—Mrs. Hyde said you picked up and went down to—oh, what did she say, Mrs. Ecklund? Did she—"

Linnea advanced to the foot of the bed, laid her two hands around the brass knob of the bed post which she rubbed uneasily. She drew a deep breath. "Listen," she said. "Young Mrs. Monteith. I might as well tell you right out. I went down to Old Mrs. Monteith's to see if I could get her to let you out of your bargain. Well, it didn't do no good. She's just as crazy idiotic as you and your husband are, if you'll pardon my English. She said no. She said she expects to take the baby. She's counting on it. I might as well tell you."

While Linnea spoke Young Mrs. Monteith went through a sea change of bloom to decay, she shivered, grew small and dark again who had been large and lighted, turned as nobody as the rose with petals stripped off in a sharp wind. She had been iridescent, opaline, with hope and happiness, now she was gathered, plucked, strewn, her eye as bright as the shot pheasant's. She took her hand off her baby, put her two hands carefully together.

"She can have her," she said, "any time."

"Do you mean to tell me," Linnea demanded with indignation, "that without a word you would turn your own little baby over to a woman that will be about the kind of a mother I would be a tightrope walker in the circus? If as good? Do you mean to lay there and tell me?"

The mother said nothing.

"A baby's like a engine," Linnea said, "it's got to have some power behind it, to run on. The power behind a baby is its mother's love and its mother's good warm milk. A little baby has a pretty hard old time getting up steam without its mother behind it, I can tell you. Sometimes they just naturally don't make it!"

"I said she was to have the first girl. I signed the agreement."

Linnea talked like a Dutch uncle, she said afterwards. She tried ridicule, reasonableness, anger, cajolery, reproach, gentleness, sharpness, common sense, astonishing herself with her fervor. "To save my soul," she told Ingeborg later, "I don't know why I let myself get so worked up over it. I just got so boiling mad at all that everlasting ignorance, and bullheadedness and stupidity, that I could of flew off the handle at anybody. I was just as mad as a hornet that such a thing would be allowed to happen in a country like America. It wasn't none of my business and I should of kept my nose out of it, I guess, but the stubborner they was, the madder I got till I could of fought a buzz saw." (Ingeborg, somewhat to Linnea's surprise, agreed with her all through . . . keeping a person's word was one thing, she said, a mother and her baby quite another.) "But at the same time, it tore my heart out, to see poor Young Mrs. Monteith, laying there suffering the way a man would suffer if you took a notion to chop off his leg," Linnea said, "and me saying all them mean cutting things. But I had to. I said it was up to her. I said all she had to do was refuse to give Old Mrs. Monteith the baby and that would be the end of the whole business—if she was guided by good common sense instead of by ignorance and superstition. Did she believe in goblins and witches on broomsticks? I said. I wouldn't put it past her. Such dumbheadedness! Such superstition! I said."

Her tongue-lashing did no good, however. Young Mrs. Monteith lay there and took it, and suffered, and the madder Linnea got, the more her heart went out to the poor little mother.

"Well, I guess I've said my say," Linnea said. "Tell me just one thing, and that's all I want to know. Do you want your baby or don't you want your baby?"

Young Mrs. Monteith shut her eyes. "I don't want it," she said softly.

"What was that?" Linnea said, "I didn't quite catch your remark."

"I don't want it," the mother repeated.

"All right," Linnea said. "It's just as well to know where we stand." Without speaking again she poked some of the baby's clothes in a pillowcase she hunted around and found. Then she picked the baby up and wrapped her loosely in another blanket, holding her in her right arm against her right shoulder and carrying the pillowcase in the left. "We can have Mr. Monteith take over the rest of the stuff, and the basket, and one thing and another, this evening when he comes," she said.

Young Mrs. Monteith's eyes flew open. She sat up, put back the covers and went to swing her feet out on the floor, but didn't after all. She only clutched at her heart to keep it from leaping out and following. "Now?" she said quaveringly. "So soon?"

"There's no time like the present," Linnea said. Her face was cold. "Unless, of course, you put a stop to all this craziness and let me lay the baby back down by you again, where she belongs. It's all up to you. All you got to say is, Wait, stop, don't go. And all your troubles is over."

The room was silent then. The mother did not speak. She swallowed. She blinked. Tears ran swiftly down her cheeks. Her face crumpled like a mashed cupcake. Her breast heaved.

Linnea went out the door, leaving her there keeping her foolish promise to God.

Her daughter was out on the sidewalk when she went out and down the walk and out through the gate. Because it was noon and dinnertime the streets were almost deserted, but Linnea saw many a lace curtain twitched and knew she was spied upon all along the route. "What are you doing here?" she asked Gertrude. "Why ain't you home to dinner?"

"We ate already," Gertrude said. "Oh, Mamma—you ain't giving away the baby to that mean Old Mrs. Monteith, are you? Is it really true that Young Mrs. Monteith has got to, like everybody says? Oh, Mamma, don't do it. Take the baby back. Please, Mamma, please—" In an agony, sympathetic Gertrude was hopping up and down and she kept up beside her mother, like a little girl who has urgently to go to the toilet.

"You go on back home," Mamma said, "I'll attend to this end of the business. I don't need your assistance." Again it came to her like a pain, as she looked at her that her child was very agreeable and very pretty, and she spoke a little more sharply than she meant as a consequence. "How have you kids been getting along?" she asked, changing her tone to a gentle one.

"Bertha's awful bossy," Gertrude said. She stopped hopping now, and merely walked. "She won't let us kids go over to Young Mrs. Monteith's. She won't let us go up to Ingeborg's. She won't let us do nothing."

"Don't tattle. What did you kids do last night?"

"We told stories and got the kids to sleep. Then me and Stellie and Bertha played like we each had a pair of toe slippers. We practised how we'd walk and everything. But say, Mamma, can't I see the baby or nothing? You're going so fast, Mamma. I can't hardly keep up with you!"

"You ain't supposed to keep up with me," Mamma said, slightly panting, her round face red under her clamped-down hat. "You run on home. I got business to attend to!"

"You ain't *really* going to give the little baby away, are you, Mamma? Oh, please, Mamma, no!" Gertrude wailed.

"What does it look like I'm going to do?"

"It looks like you're going to!" Gertrude said, hopping up and down again, with alarm.

"When you deal with bullheadedness and ignorance and people that believes in goblins and witches, it's like trying to swim in water that ain't water, it's molasses. You make just about as much headway." The baby started to whimper then and Mamma handed Gertrude the pillowcase while she patted her gently and made her stop. "A little new-born baby," she said, "that never was there anything so no-account and helpless, being throwed out like this. It makes a person sick. Especially when the mother would cut her right arm off for it any day, yes, and pluck the heart right out of her breast, too. Like she done today!"

By keeping up and making the right replies and carrying the pillowcase, Gertrude was allowed to accompany her mother on the historic journey. She did not go inside, however. For that matter, neither did Mamma. She merely knocked, and when Old Mrs. Monteith came to the door, handed her the baby. Then she took the pillowcase out of Gertrude's hand, gave it to the surprised old woman, and turned and left, without saying a word. Gertrude ran after her, and kept on running, or half running, until they were at the corner of the next block. "Mamma, she took it. Mamma, she kept it," she panted. "Young Mrs. Monteith won't never get it back now! Oh, ain't that terrible?" she said. "It really happened! Like everybody said!"

When Mamma took her by the hand and caught the streetcar instead of walking back up to Young Mrs. Monteith's, Gertrude knew something was in the wind, something was about to happen, Mamma had something up her sleeve, Mamma had an axe to grind. She had that certain look on her face, that cheered Gertrude up immensely. "I shouldn't take you," Mamma said. "You ain't dressed up enough." Gertrude looked back at her with large eyes and an extraordinarily solemn face while she inspected her, her heart beating fast. "Your dress is clean, though. Your shoes don't look so bad." Gertrude stuck her feet out in front of her. "Let me see your hands." The hands were stuck out too, then hands and feet dropped back where they belonged. Gertrude wiggled on the slick straw-bottomed seat with excitement. "Your hands is clean. Your hair is combed. Let me see your face." Gertrude poked it a few inches closer, jutting her chin far out in her eagerness to oblige. Mamma pushed the chin in gently. "Your face is clean, only right here." She moistened the corner of her handkerchief with saliva and rubbed briskly. "There!" she said.

"Where we going?" Gertrude asked eagerly. "To Papa's shop?"

That was so ill-advised a question that Gertrude came very nearly being set ignominiously outside and told to make for home, but her quickly indrawn breath and instant contrition saved her, and Mamma let it pass with no serious consequences. All she said was, "A lot different place than that, I can tell you! A whole lot different!"

In her wildest imaginings Gertrude could never have imagined where they were headed. Little ignoramus that she was, she didn't even know where it was after they got there. All she knew was, it was all so very solemn, it was like a funeral and a death, and going to the dentist, and going through a museum, all at once. Their destination was a big gray building a stone's throw from the nearly completed Temple. While they were going up the broad front steps she knew how serious it all was, by the way Mamma's hand tightened over hers, the way Mamma seemed to stiffen, and pale, the way Mamma spoke and didn't sound a bit like herself. On the top step, before the impressive double doors, Gertrude stopped dead still. "I'm scared, Mamma," she whimpered. "I'm scared! I want to go home!"

Her fright made Mamma turn natural again, took the stiffness and paleness and terrifying peculiarity out of her. She leaned over and shook Gertrude, but not hard, and smiled, and drew a deep breath. "Why, gosh almighty," she said, "here you're so lucky to get to come with me—why, you can tell your grandchildren about coming here today —and here you go and bawl and act like a little tiny kid four or five years old. I'm ashamed of you."

Gertrude stopped whimpering and felt better, now that Mamma was Mamma again, and felt ashamed that she had got scared and wanted to go home, a big girl like her, eleven years old. "What we going to do?" she asked.

"We come to see somebody."

"Who?"

She found out inside, when they had gone down a wide corridor, turned to the left, went through a polished door with a brass plate on it that said something Gertrude did not take the trouble to read, and into a wide carpeted room with long velvet-draped windows. There was a polished railing, a fence, as Gertrude said afterward, that came up to Mamma's waist, and behind it was a roll-top desk with a swivel chair in front of it. A young man was in the swivel chair. He got up and came over to the railing. He was extremely tall and slender, with an overly small head. He wore a skin-tight suit and a large, flowing cravat of sober black. His eyes were about as blue as snow or skim milk but not much bluer. "What can I do for you?" he asked precisely. He smiled. Gertrude looked for his teeth and discovered they were small and pointed.

"I want to see President Woodruff," Mamma said.

Gertrude's head snapped back. Her mouth fell open. PRESIDENT WOODRUFF! The President! The President of the whole Church of Jesus Christ of Latter-Day Saints! No wonder Mamma had gone stiff and pale and didn't sound natural. Well, no wonder! The President himself! She shivered, or at least something that felt like a shiver, or a dipperful of cold water, went running in little ripples down her back. Why, Mamma was the bravest woman that ever lived.

The young man pulled at his tie and looked at a large bald-faced clock with an oversized pendulum that hung on the wall over the door they had entered. It was one o'clock sharp. "Do you have an appointment?" he inquired.

"No," Linnea said, "I just come in the door. Naturally. I didn't know I was going to be compelled to go and see the President. I never dreamed of such a thing. It was the last thought that would of ever entered my mind when I got up this morning. So how could I have an appointment? I just want to go in and see him. It won't take me long."

"How about the Bishop of your ward? You could state your business to him and he—"

"I know all that," Linnea said, "but this is something out of the ordinary."

"How about the President of your stake? These things generally go through channels—"

"What do you mean these things?" Linnea said. "You don't know what I'm here for. It's something out of the ordinary, I can tell you that. It's a matter of life and death. Or anyway the next thing to it. I got to see him," Linnea said. "Who are you anyway? If I may make so bold."

"I'm his secretary," the young man said haughtily. "And I must inform you that the President does not see people without an appointment. You must go to the Bishop of your ward."

"Listen—" Linnea began angrily, but she was interrupted.

"What does the good sister want?" the rather high voice of an old man said, and there, in a doorway to the left, stood the hallowed and familiar figure of the highest priest of the Priesthood, the supreme, the sole, the President of the Church of Jesus Christ of Latter-Day Saints. President Woodruff himself! Almost close enough to touch! Right across the room! Who had not seen him in his omnipresent all-pervading glory? Who had not heard him in the Tabernacle, speak to the multitudes? For him to speak to oneself personally, for him to stand only an arm's length away—it was enough to weaken the knees and make the head spin. Not only that, he was rich!

"Why, she wants to come in and see you," the young man said, "and she has not got an appointment. And you never see anybody for an hour after din—or rather, lunch." He chose the more fashionable term.

"What is it, Sister?" the President said.

Linnea raised her voice a little, in case, being very old, he might not be able to hear so well. "It's something out of the ordinary," Linnea said, "or I wouldn't of come. I lived here a good long time and I ain't never needed to bother you before, and plenty of things has happened, too, so you may imagine it's kind of serious."

"Come in," the President said, throwing the door wide open and making a very slight bow that Mamma would never forget if she lived to be a hundred and fifty.

"You sit down and wait out here till I come out," Mamma instructed Gertrude swiftly. She went to give her a pat on the shoulder but quite missed her, swinging just to the side. Then she went blindly through the small gate the secretary held open and made for the President's door.

Gertrude, utterly flabbergasted by the day's happenings, went and took a seat where she could keep an eye on the tiny-headed young man. He sat down again in his swivel chair, which squeaked and bent far backwards before it came forward and settled into position, like a rose sat upon by an oversized beetle. He picked up a pen and began scratchingly to write, dipping it with great frequency into the inkwell.

Linnea did not expect her heart to beat so hard, her hands to grow so cold, her mouth to grow so dry, her cheeks so hot, her vision so wavering, as she took the few steps to the President's office.

He said, "Will you take a chair, please?" and she sat in the one he pushed forward. "Excuse me, please, for a moment," he said, and went through a door in back of his desk to a smaller room beyond. He shut it after him.

Linnea, glad of a moment to collect her scattered wits, held her right hand up and looked at it. It was shaking like a leaf. She dropped it hastily and held her left hand up. It was shaking like a leaf, too. It made her mad that her heart was pounding and she was shaking like that. She tried to look carefully at the room, but could not do it. The broad windows, velvet draperies, high ceilings, polished wood, elegant carpet, the three large portraits on the wall, of Joseph Smith's familiar hatchet-face, protruding eyes and high white stock in the usual profile portrait, Hyrum Smith, his brother, not of the same caliber, and Brigham Young, built foursquare like a Mormon temple, all went together to make a room of unspeakable impressiveness.

It was not until much later that she could enumerate and evaluate the separate items of the room, and could view them with detachment.

Two things brought her back to herself. A handsome clock ticking upon the wall with two filigreed hands that said seven past one, and a growl from her stomach. Now I suppose my stomach will take a notion to growl, she thought to herself. That made her smile. She could imagine herself telling the story: how she sat in the office talking away to President Woodruff as big as life, and how her stomach growled "till I could of fell through the floor," she would say. "But I hadn't ate a bite since eight o'clock that morning," she would say: "so no wonder. I was so hungry I could of ate up that pin-headed secretary as he called himself." That seemed to fix things, thinking of that. Her hands stopped shaking and her heart beat slowly and softly and she felt like herself again. After all, the President is just a plain human being, she thought. It ain't as if it was God or something. Probably got stuff the matter with him, like you or me or anybody. Maybe can't stand to climb up on the third step of a step ladder, maybe turns the air blue when he hits his thumb with the hammer. Probably loved some girl once upon a time and nothing come of it. Maybe she died and he never got over it. Maybe he's got a pretty sore spot in his heart, over that or over something else, if he's the President of the Church or not. Maybe he breaks out easy, can't eat a dish of strawberries but what he'll be all over big red welts. Maybe he has running-off of the bowels when he gets nervous. It was comforting to think all this. It made her feel right at home.

Until he came back in and said, "All right now, Sister, what seems to be your problem? What's troubling you?" and sat down facing her across the wide polished desk. Then the fright or whatever it was came back on her for a minute and she forgot all her flimsy excuses for being at ease, and she grew quite dry-throated again and she could feel the shakiness of her hands. Position, authority, exaltation, wealth, possessions and renown, were not something to talk away. They were there like the Wasatch Mountains: you couldn't say the Wasatch Mountains didn't exist even if they were out of sight. His many years were against him, though, and when President Woodruff put his hand up to scratch his whiskered cheek, Linnea saw the sad brown spots of old age, and was comforted. Mean or mighty, small or great, what could he do but die like anybody else?

Quietly then, but with a more careful enunciation than usual for she was somehow under the impression that he couldn't hear very well, she told him the whole story from beginning to end. She was gratified to observe that it amazed him.

"Can this be possible?" he said. "Do you mean to tell me a first wife required a subsequent wife to sign a paper saying she would give up her first female child, before the first wife would give her husband permission to marry the other woman? Incredible!"

"She was only seventeen, too," Linnea said. "A nice little thing but a numskull. As you can imagine."

"Did the proper authorities know of this?" He meant church authorities.

"I don't know. I should imagine so," Linnea said. "Anyway, Old Mrs. Monteith kept the paper all these years. They say. I never seen it myself. The thing is, Young Mrs. Monteith will stick to her bargain without even seeing the paper. In fact, *has* stuck to it. I just took the baby over and give it to the old lady myself. Young Mrs. Monteith is fit to be tied. But she give it up without a aye, yes or no."

"Why?"

"What do you mean why?" Linnea asked in her ordinary manner. "Why, because she's afraid the Lord will take her two boys away from her, to punish her, if she don't keep her promise. Or get revenge on her some other way. Talked herself in to craziness like that. Imagine."

"Well, what can be done?" the old man asked.

Linnea leaned forward. "I'll tell you," she said. "If you go down there and tell Old Mrs. Monteith you want that paper, and you tear it up—if you demand the baby back—if you take her over and put her in Young Mrs. Monteith's arms—if you tell Young Mrs. Monteith that the Lord ain't a bit in sympathy with any such doings as them—that the Lord sent you to straighten the whole thing out—why, I tell you, President Woodruff, everything will be all fixed up like nothing had ever happened."

"Well, you see," he said, "I never personally—"

"It'll be one of the best stunts you ever done in your life," Linnea said. "I don't dare think about that silly Young Mrs. Monteith. I just don't dare think about her if we don't straighten this thing out."

"Wouldn't the Bishop do as well? He's the one that ought—you see, I'm quite busy, I never personally—"

"If you come," Linnea said solemnly, "it'll be just like God himself coming down. They'll do your bidding just like that." She snapped her fingers. "Anybody'll do your bidding!" She was going to add "Anybody in the Church, that is," remembering the United States Army and that other President, the one in the White House, but she thought better of it. "It'll be just like God himself coming down to take hold," she said.

"Sister, Sister, you flatter me," the old man said, but he was not displeased.

"Besides, the *Salt Lake Tribune* sent down a reporter and he'll write up the story, and it would be pretty silly to have such a story as that printed in the papers. Any Gentile that hears about it will think the biggest part of us is out of our heads or something. It ain't nothing to be very proud of, you know. In this day and age."

"No, indeed it is not!" the President said, looking suddenly uneasy. "No, indeed. A story of that kind getting around. Maybe printed in other papers throughout the land. Such ignorance and folly within our Church. No, you are right. It would be most harmful." He pulled at his lower lip. "It must be stopped. But I've got business this afternoon, a meeting—wouldn't the Stake President do? Or I tell you what—one of my Counsellors is coming in here in a little while. Would he—"

"Nobody will do," Linnea said, "but you. You can speak and people will jump. You can say do this, and they'll do it. You can say do that, and they'll do it. You can wind people around your little finger. You only need to—"

He liked it but he cut her short. "Sister, Sister," he said. Then he pushed back his chair and stood up. "I'll have Ralph send for a carriage," he said.

For some reason, in her happiness and excitement, all Linnea could think of was the unspeakable whiteness of his shirt front, his collar and cuffs. "I've seen some white shirts in my time," she would say to Ingeborg, to Gunilla, to dozens of others, "but I never seen anything to equal that. That was the whitest blame shirt a man ever got into."

In the carriage itself, in that unlooked-for moment when she and her child Gertrude were actually riding in the carriage with President Wilford Woodruff, she observed other things, too, with an eye to telling and retelling the story. His broadcloth suit was bound around the lapels with grosgrain ribbon, there was a lot of black satin to his vest, his large puffy tie, more wrapped than knotted, was black with thin stripes of alternating white and bottle-green. There was a diamond in his stick-pin, small, it is true, but a perfectly genuine diamond set in the center of a sailor's knot of gold. His hat was a fine one with a napped surface, not new but in good shape. As Linnea said, Somebody had took it on theirself to take blame good care of that hat. In the sunlight, more of those brown spots could be discovered, on the side of his neck, on his cheek toward his ear through the glistening white whiskers. His eye's clear light color could be adjudged with accuracy, and other observations could be made, such as, that the pale skin of his nose had a pinhead of moisture in each pore, and that the delicate pearly hair brushed back from his ears was of much coarser texture than it looked.

Gertrude would be able to shut her eyes and see him in her mind as long as she lived. He said the usual idle adult things, What is your name? How old are you? Do you go to school? and she answered as well as she could, Gertrude Ecklund, eleven years old, yes. But then he did not pursue the conversation, and she did not venture to speak again without being spoken to, and thus displayed her good manners. She knew this day, this hour, this ride, was something so extraordinary that nothing like it could ever happen again if she lived to be a thousand. She had a sense of history. She knew she was taking part in what would have to be described and passed down, like signing the Declaration of Independence or seeing the Golden Plates from the Hill Cumorah. So she did not open her mouth. She just looked at him so as never to forget him as long as she lived (she remembered everything forever but his face)—she saw every hair, every pore, his buttons, his watch chain, his soft kid shoes with elastic sides, the ridges of his yellowing fingernails. In a large dazing dream of pure epic she never took her eyes off him or said boo.

He did not offer to say much to Mamma—this, if the truth were known, was his hour for a nap, and the motion of the carriage made him so sleepy that he had trouble keeping his eyes open. Mamma's trouble, she said afterward, was the way her stomach kept wanting to rumble and carry on. "Even though by that time," as she said later, "I couldn't even so much as think of nothing to eat, I was that stirred up!"

And well she might be. Even her worst enemy would have to admit it. To go right up to the President's office single-handed and get the President to do exactly what she wanted—that was something to blow about, crow about, tell and tell over again till the story was as old as the hills. Walk right in there as big as life and twice as natural and tell the President of the Church of Jesus Christ of Latter-Day Saints that she wanted him to go out and do something and have him do it! Have him order out his carriage and go ahead and do it! Take her along with him, let her ride along on the carriage seat beside him! That was a tale that made a person want to pinch herself, even to hear it, wondering if her ears deceived her.

They arrived in Old Mrs. Monteith's neighborhood and Mamma started pointing out the house a half a block away. The driver stopped before it. "This is the place," she said. "As Brigham put it, huh?" She laughed nervously and colored as she reconsidered her words and decided that they had sounded a little fresh. She hopped down from the carriage lightly, for all her size, and quite naturally offered to help the President who was climbing down after her, slowly, for his bony old knees were stiff and rheumatic. "I'll do that, Sister," said the carriage driver who hurried around the side of the vehicle, and took possession of the trembling old arm. "There you are, Sir," he said, "all safe and sound."

"Thank you, Sister," the President said kindly, ignoring the man, which made Mamma color up still more. Another gem for memory's store!

"This is the place," Mamma repeated apologetically. "The way Brigham said. It's got to be kind of a saying." She wanted to let him know she meant no disrespect.

"I know," he said. "Well, come along, Sister."

"You stay there till we come out," Mamma tossed upwards over her shoulder to staring Gertrude. "And not a peep out of you, either."

The President was a little stooped but he made a fetish of thrusting back his shoulders as far as they would go every little while. This motion would throw him slightly off balance so that he tottered somewhat, taking a small step off to one side, before he got back in line. Linnea, going up the walk, had to be careful not to collide with him. It seemed odd to be a good deal taller than he, as though he were just any old man.

They went up on the porch and knocked on the door. There was a baby wailing inside, from the kitchen, it sounded like, far away. It was so dim a squall that the President could not hear it, he said when Linnea mentioned it. "That's the baby crying now," she said triumphantly, "Young Mrs. Monteith's baby! Listen to it. Crying like its heart would break. I told you." What a good thing it was bawling like that, not taking a notion to snooze which you couldn't put past a new-born baby! That helped somehow. It was sort of proof, you might say, to the truth of the whole story. She was pleased.

Old Mrs. Monteith opened the door. "You again," she said.

"Yes, me again," Linnea said. "Only this time I got somebody with me." She turned to the man at her side. "President Wilford Woodruff, the President of the Church of Jesus Christ of Latter-Day Saints. That's who this is. President Woodruff," she turned to him, "make you acquainted with Old Mrs. Monteith."

"How do you do, Sister," the old man said, tipping his hat and thrusting back his shoulders which sagged again on the instant. "I want a word with you."

She pushed open the door falteringly, turning a pale pale green like the last trace of a black and blue mark. "Come—" she began.

"I want an earnest word with you about this disgraceful— Why, what's the matter with Old Mrs. Monteith?" he inquired in amazement.

Linnea caught her as she pitched forward.

"She fainted," she said. "That's all." The carriage driver who had been watching, came running up the walk, Gertrude scrambled down from the high back seat and came dashing after him. "You scoot," Mamma said sharply, catching sight of her. "You get right back in that carriage and you stay there." Gertrude went back, crestfallen.

They got the woman in and on the lounge in the parlor. Linnea got a dipperful of water from the bucket in the kitchen, stopping an instant to drop a swift kiss on the fiery wrinkled forehead of the screaming baby in the clothesbasket on two chairs and say, "There, there, honey, it'll soon all be over," before she ran back in the parlor with it. She was going to throw it over Old Mrs. Monteith's face but that seemed kind of mean. It would spot the patchwork silk pillows on the couch and wet and spoil her nicely ironed collar. Instead Linnea squeezed her handkerchief out in the water and patted it over the woman's face. "Here," she said to the carriage driver, "you pat this on her forehead, will you?" She gave him the handkerchief and the dipper. "Do like I done."

She ran back to the kitchen and took up the yelling baby, with such a feeling of gladness and relief that she could have stood right there and bawled herself. She pressed the little hot sweating screaming thing against her shoulder and whispered "There, there, it's all over now, all our troubles is over now," patting her back and whispering and cooing against the steaming head, and jiggling her up and down in the immemorial way. The crying stopped . . . changed to belching, changed to silence, with a clock ticking. . . . And here Linnea had had her eyes on the clock for five minutes or more, jiggling and patting and saying there, there, before she saw that it said two o'clock, straight up, on the dot.

She ran back to the living room with the baby in her arms.

"—and I want that paper, Sister," the President was saying severely, "and no more said about this whole shameful affair."

Old Mrs. Monteith reached in her apron pocket and brought it out. Silently she handed it to him.

"Do you think God inspired this?" he asked.

She shook her head.

"Do you know who did?"

Again she shook her head.

"Well, I'll tell you," he said. "The Devil."

Linnea swayed back and forth, patting the cooling baby.

The President took the paper, opened his coat and put it inside his vest pocket. "All right," he said, "now that's the end of the whole business, isn't it?"

Old Mrs. Monteith was sitting on the edge of the lounge. With nervous shaking hands she was tucking in stray locks of her hair in an absent-minded way and moving a hairpin or two. She did not reply, lost in thought.

"Isn't it?" he said.

"Oh," she said, "excuse me, was you talking to me?"

"I want your word that you won't cause any trouble."

"I won't," she said.

After they got out to the carriage, Linnea remembered the pillowcase with the baby's things and ran around to the back and through the back door for it. She left the child in the carriage in the awestruck arms, under the dumbfounded mouth and hopelessly dazzled eyes, of Gertrude. "Don't you dare drop her," she said.

That was how she happened to have another word with Old Mrs. Monteith. She was taking her hair down, preparatory to doing it over.

When Linnea came in, Old Mrs. Monteith made a snorting sound. "Listen," she said, "Mrs. High and Mighty! I want to tell you something that might take you down a notch or two. *I DIDN'T WANT THE BABY ANYWAY. I WAS GOING TO SEND MY HUSBAND BACK WITH THE BAWLING THING AS SOON AS HE COME HOME FROM WORK.* So you're not so smart after all! Are you?"

For some reason, Linnea knew that she was speaking the truth. "No, I'm not," she said with great dignity. "I'm sorry to say."

"Thought you was cutting such a shine!" Old Mrs. Monteith taunted. "Thought you was such a slick one! And here I was going to give the baby back anyway. Bawling thing."

"Why didn't you tell the President that?"

"I did tell him. While you was out in the kitchen with the baby."

"What did he say?"

"Nothing. He just went on with what he was saying."

"I guess he didn't believe you," Linnea said reflectively. "Or didn't hear you. I believe you," she added.

The pillowcase was in the corner. She went over and picked it up and went back to the door. "You know, Old Mrs. Monteith," she said pausing there. She turned around. "I wouldn't want you to hold no grudge," she said.

Old Mrs. Monteith snorted again but it was less a snort than a sniff.

Linnea's face was sober and thoughtful. "Because you ain't been a mean woman. Nobody can stand up on their hind legs and say you been a mean woman. Here your husband's had Young Mrs. Monteith for fifteen years and you had lots of chance to do some damage if you wanted to, and you ain't done any. You ain't caused her no trouble. She's had about what she wanted."

Old Mrs. Monteith's lower lip began to shake.

"It was just this stunt with the baby. Otherwise, you ain't been a bit mean. You got to give the devil his due, as the saying goes. I wanted to tell you. I don't want you to hold no grudge against me for the way I butted in. I was—thinking all this—when you was laying in there fainted dead away. That's why I was careful with the water, didn't wet your good pillows or nothing. Polygamy ain't such a easy proposition. I know. I'm in it. Something will come up, and instead of acting nice, here a person will act so mean and onry—somebody that ain't mean and onry a-tall—just because of polygamy—that it'll surprise them."

The last thing in the world Old Mrs. Monteith expected was sympathy and understanding. It was almost too much for her. Her lower lip still trembling, she fished for her handkerchief. "Well, my," she said, crying, "I didn't intend nothing like—but it got too big for me—I couldn't give in. I could give the baby *back*, but I couldn't give in and not take it! There's a big difference. Don't you see?"

"I do see," Linnea said.

"I don't know what got into me," the old woman said humbly, still crying very hard, with her handkerchief up to her eyes.

Linnea looked at her with deep compassion. "Why, gosh, almighty, you're human, ain't you? You got a right to act human? Are you expected to go around like you was wearing wings or something?"

"Of course it did bawl, and I ain't used to children, and I suppose the bawling would of made me nervous. I'm a good deal older now. It might of been a different story if it'd been fifteen years ago," Old Mrs. Monteith said. "Maybe I really would of kept it . . . maybe I really would. . . . I don't know. Maybe I could of been that mean. . . . Maybe I would of kept it." Her conscience spoke out. Her wet eyes begged to be reassured, absolved.

"Not on your tintype," Linnea said comfortingly. "You would of done the right thing!"

"I don't know what got into me," the old woman repeated. She had put her handkerchief back in her pocket and she wiped her eyes with her fingers.

Impulsively Linnea came across the room and put her arms around her. "I ain't going to forget you," she said, her own eyes moist. "I learned a lesson I needed awful bad."

As she went running out to the carriage, rubbing the tears from her eyes she thought, oh, dear me, I've left President Woodruff out in the hot sun! She hurried as fast as she could and climbed up beside him. The driver lifted the reins and they started out. Only then she noticed all the people, standing in their yards and on their porches, gathered in knots out on the sidewalk, watching them like they were spirits from the beyond.

She had thought she would mention Old Mrs. Monteith's metamorphosis, and how little their interference had influenced the course of events, but the sight of the silent staring awe-struck people decided her against it. A President could never be ineffectual, impotent, useless. If he directed something, it happened because he directed it so. It never could have happened, the same results could never have come about, by itself. A glance at his set beatific face made Linnea understand that this was true, and saved her from rushing headlong into folly.

"The Sister was made to come to her senses," the old man said placidly.

Linnea looked at him a little longer, thinking her surprised thoughts, not smiling, but then she smiled. She turned a big smile upon him, like a chandelier lit up. "You done wonders!" she said. "There ain't a living being could of done nothing but you!" She reached over and took the baby out of Gertrude's arms. "No, sir," she said, "I never seen a woman so knocked off her perch in my life, as she was. Well, who wouldn't be?" she said.

The President at her side nodded kindly. He took a snow-white handkerchief out of his pocket and rubbed it between his hands, then he nodded again.

The minute she opened Young Mrs. Monteith's front door and beckoned President Woodruff to come after her, she knew there was something going on in Young Mrs. Monteith's bedroom. There was a scuffle of some sort. Somebody was saying, Oh, no, you don't, young lady, and somebody else was saying, Oh, yes, I do! Somebody was kicking and scuffling. Somebody was the next thing to screaming. "Here," Linnea said and handed President Woodruff the baby. She hurried down the hall and pushed open the bedroom door. "What in the world!" she said.

Young Mrs. Monteith, looking like a ghost, worse than any ghost that ever took wings and flew, had her clothes on! Young Mrs. Monteith was all ready to go out! Mrs. Hyde was trying to prevent it, Mrs. Hyde was trying to get the clothes off her and get her back to bed. Her tumbled hair and scratched cheek, the way she was gasping and panting with the effort, showed plainly that it had been easier to say than do! Young Mrs. Monteith did not look much better, but her hair was still up and her hat was still firmly pinned on. When Linnea flung open the door the two women stopped struggling. They stopped and stood trembling, breathing heavily. "What in the world!" Linnea repeated. She reached over and jerked Young Mrs. Monteith's hat off forgetting the hatpin, and pulling out a long wisp of reddish hair at the same time. Young Mrs. Monteith did not even wince, but kept on staring defiantly at Mrs. Hyde.

"She got dressed!" Mrs. Hyde panted. "Imagine! The next day after a confinement! And she was going to go and get—"

"Hush," Linnea said sharply. She took Young Mrs. Monteith by the arm and pushed her down onto the bed, scooped up her legs, rolled her in and pulled the covers up before she knew what was happening to her.

"She's got her shoes on. They'll dirty the—" Mrs. Hyde began.

"Hush," Linnea repeated. "Now you lay there," she said to Young Mrs. Monteith. "And don't you open your mouth. If you so much as speak one word I'll brain you. I mean it too." Young Mrs. Monteith, pale and sick-looking, the covers up around her chin, stared at her with terrified eyes. "Somebody's coming," Linnea said. "You hush."

Mrs. Hyde was silent, too, staring at her in amazement.

Somebody was coming, all right. Somebody was here.

Gertrude pushed the door open for him and he walked in, carrying the baby, taking time on his way to the bed to thrust back his shoulders, slightly over-balance, totter, take his little running sidestep. Young Mrs. Monteith saw what he had—a baby. She saw instantly. It was all she saw. Her baby! Linnea had as well tried to stop a rocket. She threw back the covers, jumped out of bed, ran to him, grabbed it, kissed it, cried, said—

Mrs. Hyde was the one who recognized him. "Why, God Almighty," she said, "Saint Peter and the Holy Ghost. It's President Woodruff. It's the President of the Church!" She sank into a chair.

Then Young Mrs. Montieth saw him too. She looked up and saw who it was. Linnea knew what the greenish tinge meant. She grabbed the baby and pushed the mother backwards on the bed. "Throw some water on her," she told bug-eyed Gertrude. "Step!" Gertrude stepped, Mrs. Hyde helping her by flipping her finger against the china water pitcher on the table beside her chair. Gertrude poured out a glassful with a shaking hand and carried it splashing to the prostrate woman.

"Throw it on her," Mamma said. "I'll change the sheets and pillowcases anyway. We got time for all that."

Gertrude threw. There was a shudder and a gasp, and then Young Mrs. Montieth was shaking her wet head and blinking away the drops and saying, "Who—where am I—what's happening—"

"Don't talk any more. Don't move," Linnea said. The young woman obeyed, staring upward as though bewitched. Linnea made a beckoning gesture with her free hand. "President Woodruff," she said, "if you would, please. If you don't mind, please."

He did not mind, he advanced a step, he came and stood beside the bed. He looked down benignantly, and reached in his pocket and took out a paper. "This is an agreement," he said. "I think you signed your name to it many years ago. An agreement to give away your first female child. This child, I believe," he said, nodding toward the baby in Linnea's arms.

"Yes," Young Mrs. Monteith whispered, "but I was going to go and get—I changed my mi—"

"Hush," Linnea said.

"This paper is now invalidated. I declare it so," the President went on. "It is the work, not of the Lord, but of Lucifer, the Fallen Angel, in other words, my dear Sister, the Devil. I tear it up." He was as good as his word. He tore it across, put the pieces together, tore them across, tore them again, tore them again. It was very dramatic. He looked

around for a place to throw them. Linnea shoved the chamber pot
farther in under the bed with her foot and pointed out the washbasin.
The pieces fluttered into it. . . .

At the side of the President's carriage, she said, "You done wonders!
Absolute wonders! I knowed you would! There wasn't a living soul
could of done it but you!"

"My word," the old man said, "they both fainted!" It obviously
pleased him. President or not, he was marveling over this. He shook his
head, smiling. "First one of the women, then the other. I guess they
should have had a word of warning." She wondered if, like a lesser man,
he was considering how he would tell the story to his family and friends.

"Well, who wouldn't?" she said. "Who wouldn't faint?"

The President did not offer to shake hands. More graciously, he took
his hat off and gave her another one of his unforgettable little bows.
Then he got in his carriage and drove away.

Mrs. Hyde, still sitting limply by the washstand, was speculating how
Linnea was going to undress Young Mrs. Monteith, if Young Mrs.
Monteith was going to clutch her baby in her arms like that. But Linnea
threw back the covers and went at it in so practical a way that one knew
that, baby or not, she would have Young Mrs. Monteith back in her
nightgown and tucked in bed, with clean sheets and pillowcases on,
before you could say Orson Pratt.

"Why, do you know," Mrs. Hyde said, "what this crazy Young Mrs.
Monteith was going to do? There I was, out in the kitchen, never
dreaming—"

"I'm sorry I give you such a scratch," Young Mrs. Monteith said. "I'll
make it up to you, you see if I don't."

"I don't even know I got a scratch," Mrs. Hyde said forgivingly.
"Never dreaming," she repeated "of such a thing. She's laying there
crying, you see. I goes in there when I hear her crying so terrible hard
after you left, Mrs. Ecklund, but she orders me out of the room. Get
out, she says, leave me alone. I'm busy answering the door and one thing
and another and quite a long time goes by and I don't hear her crying no
more, so I think she's fell asleep. But then I hear a noise, so I tiptoe to
the door and throw it open—and here's Young Mrs. Monteith—all
dressed, imagine, and she's swearing she's—"

"—going to get my baby back!" Young Mrs. Monteith finished triumphantly.

"Paper or no paper," Mrs. Hyde added.

"I knowed it," Linnea said. "The minute I come in and seen them
clothes on your back I knowed it!" she said.

"Yes, sir," Mrs. Monteith said, "I was going right down there and tell

Old Mrs. Monteith she could stick the paper up her—you know what—and I was going to—get—my—baby—back!" She meant what she said. "I got to thinking about it, and when once I got thinking about it, why, I couldn't stand it another minute. I was on my way." "I knowed it," Linnea said. "That's why I hushed you up so fast. Why, I wouldn't of had you let on to President Woodruff for anything in the world! You can't fool around with Presidents like they was just anybody, you know. You can't say you need them and then not have any more use for them than you got for a old shoe!"

"You bet you can't," Mrs. Hyde said. "Not on your life you can't. I should think not. You go fooling around with a President and you might find yourself in some pretty hot water all of a sudden, some pret-ty hot water."

"All I know," Linnea said, "is that it would of spoiled everything, if he'd of knew. He'd of been disappointed, just like anybody. A President's got to be the whole cheese or bust."

"The funny part of it is," Linnea said, when she was gathering up the wet bed linen to take out and hang on the line, "that Old Mrs. Monteith was going to give the baby back anyway!"

"No!" Mrs. Hyde said. "You don't say."

"I don't believe it," Young Mrs. Monteith said coldly.

"You can take my word for it. It's true," Linnea said. She looked around the room, the bedding bundled up in her arms. It was in perfect order now, and the mother in the smooth clean bed in the clean nightgown was still holding her baby in her arms.

"Well, no wonder," Young Mrs. Monteith said, "if the *President* come to her house and told her she had to give it back! Who wouldn't?"

"The President didn't have nothing to do with it," she said. "She was going to give it back anyway. Why, she had it all bundled up ready to come when we got there!" she lied.

"You don't say," Mrs. Hyde said wonderingly. "One woman going after it. One woman bringing it back. The President in the middle. For heaven's sake." It had been well worth the trouble to drop everything and come to Young Mrs. Monteith's. It was better than the Salt Lake Theatre any day.

"Why?" the young mother faltered.

"Why what?" Linnea asked.

"Would she be bringing her back?"

"Why, because she's a lot nicer woman than you ever give her any credit for being, that's why," Linnea said. "She's somebody you'd ought to take the trouble to be nice to, I can tell you. She was going to bring the baby back, not because she didn't want it, not because she didn't think it was the cutest baby she ever saw in her life—no, Young Mrs. Monteith—she was bringing it back because she felt sorry for all she ever done to hurt you or anybody else, she was sorry about the paper, she was sorry about everything. She wants you should forgive her."

There was a silence.

"Oh, I do," Young Mrs. Monteith whispered, shamefaced. "I never thought of nothing like all that. I most certainly surely do. . . ."

The reporter from the *Salt Lake Tribune* bothered and bothered but he never could get enough of a story out of the Monteith affair to put in his eye let alone print in the paper. "You doggone Mormons," he said, "stick together like leeches, shut up like a bunch of clams." But he had a friendly smile.

Linnea handed him out a piece of coffeecake and a cup of coffee. He sat down on the back steps with it. He was a very young man. His hat had a long elastic to it, fastened to his lapel—in case it should take a notion to blow off in a high wind. She felt well acquainted with him by now. She said good-naturedly, "You've hung around here for three days, mister. You can see there ain't a thing in the world!"

The day Linnea left Young Mrs. Monteith's—oh, she was glad to get back home and oh, the children were glad to have her—she got praises and compliments that left her head swimming.

"Why, to go right up to the biggest office of the CHURCH," Young Mrs. Monteith said, "and get the PRESIDENT, and bring him down here to straighten things out, well, I tell you something, Mrs. Ecklund, I don't think there was another woman in the whole town would of done it. Not one!"

"He didn't do no good," Linnea pointed out.

"But he COULD of," Young Mrs. Monteith said, "if me and Old Mrs. Monteith had kept on being stubborn. He was the only one could of, under them circumstances. You want to remember that!"

"That's what I thought," Linnea said. "Well, anyway, it worked out fine all around. Everybody had a hand in it. The Lord too, I guess."

"Now how much did you say you charge, for a confinement case, Mrs. Ecklund?"

As usual, Linnea blushed when she heard the question. "I charge eight dollars," she said. She always blushed scarlet when somebody asked her how much they owed and paid her for something.

Young Mrs. Monteith gave her her pay in a sealed envelope. "Don't open it till you get home," she said. "I can tell you one thing. I never enjoyed paying a bill so much in my life."

At home, when Mamma opened the envelope, while Bertha begged her to look, really look, at the cake (now balanced on a plate on her hand) she had baked for the occasion, and Rudie wanted to climb up on her lap, big as he was, and Parley grabbed a fistful of hair in his delight at having her back and she had to disengage his fingers from it, and Gertrude and Stellie both wanted to tell her the same story at once . . . when she opened it . . . Young Mrs. Monteith's envelope . . . and saw . . . FIFTY DOLLARS . . . why, then it was her turn to faint! She didn't, though. She just gave a yell that was cut off short almost before she got it out . . . and took the bills out, and looked at them: five ten-dollar bills . . . like she was seeing the ghost of her grandmother. The children looked like they were seeing the ghost of their grandmother, too.

She put on her hat and ran right back there, her face as red as a beet with embarrassment and excitement, but Young Mrs. Monteith said there wasn't any mistake. She said if Mrs. Ecklund wanted to slap her in the face, and tromp all over her, and stick a knife in her heart, why, all she had to do was try to give one cent of that money back. All she had to do was try. Young Mrs. Monteith had the baby, named Rosebud, that was her name, in her arms. (Long after Rosebud could walk, the neighbors were still going to see that silly mother carrying that great big lug of a three-year-old kid around in her arms, like a woman that didn't have the sense she was born with, as they said.) She gave Rosebud a squeeze. She beamed. "No, Mrs. Ecklund, that money's yours and more than yours, and if you want to have an enemy on your hands, you just try some funny stuff like not keeping every cent of it. You just try it!" she said. "Imagine. Getting the President down here! Doing I don't know what all! No, sir," she said. "Why, there ain't money enough in the world to pay for all you done!"

That was how it came about that the girls stopped mourning for Papa. In fact, they just as good as forgot him from then on.

For the next day—the very next day, mind you—Mamma took them down, took all five of them down (but Rudie and Parley got something quite different), like it was the most natural thing in the world—to the Z.C.M.I. and there she lined them all up and bought

Bertha . . .

        and Gertrude . . .

                and Stellie . . .

                        (like it was the most natural thing in the world)

TOE SLIPPERS.

‒››› ‹‹‹‒

CHAPTER 20

‒››› ‹‹‹‒

IT WAS CONFERENCE TIME in Salt Lake City, when the faithful gathered from all the Mormon counties to hold their meetings in the Tabernacle. Conferences are held on the sixth of April, the anniversary of the organization of the Church, and the sixth of October. There is a lot to decide and do at these gatherings, problems to settle, testimonies to read, prayers to say and other important business. Invariably the people vote with uplifted hands to sustain all the presiding authorities. One of the apostles rises on the platform and moves that the President be "sustained" as "President of the Church of Jesus Christ of Latter-Day Saints," and as "prophet, seer and revelator." The motion is seconded, the show of hands is called for and the vote is unanimous. All the other officials are reelected in the same manner. A negative vote is called for, but no hand is ever lifted in opposition. However, all this does not concern us. Suffice it to say that Conference time came, and comes yet, as sure as May Day and Christmas come, twice a year.

The children especially looked forward to it for this was when relatives arrived, and friends walked in, children by the dozens showed up to play with and sleep with five in a bed, maybe—not lengthwise, crosswise. There was lots more to eat than usual, too. The house was cleaned until it fairly hollered, and nobody could find anything for a week, it being all rearranged.

Today was the fifth of October, a yellow day, as ripe as a plum or a peach, with a hot side and a cool side, like a muskmelon that's half hot from sticking out in the sun and half cold from hiding in cold leaves against the cold ground. Where the weather stuck out in the sun, it was ripe and warm; where the day hid beneath shade it was cool.

Everybody had to pitch in with the housecleaning, for another confinement case after Young Mrs. Monteith's made Mamma very late with it. Even Rudie had to crawl under the tables and dust them, and dust the chairs. It was the day before Conference and Aunt Gunilla with her family was expected: she would come before nightfall. In anticipation there was food baked for an army. The clothes everybody would wear were ready, against the wall or on top of the dresser, the girls' white stockings handled so much that they were slightly soiled though Mamma had told them and told them to leave things alone. She had to get downright threatening about the toe slippers, in order to preserve them in their bandbox newness for over a month. The rule of the past two weeks had been: the shoes could be looked at *once a day,* no oftener, take their choice as to time. Usually the girls held out all day and looked at them just before going to bed, but on one or two occasions Gertrude needed to show them to somebody and so had used up her turn during the day. Those nights, when Bertha and Stellie did their looking and gloating, and she did not, she nearly died of envy. Tomorrow they were going to wear the toe slippers uptown to the meeting in the Tabernacle. They were actually going to wear them! Victoria, going to wear her crown for the first time the next day, could not have been more excited.

Mamma was just throwing the last bucket of scrubwater out the back door, and Bertha was deciding where to stand a pitcher of ragged asters —as though it were not going to rest inevitably in the middle of the table—when Gertrude, her work performed to Mamma's satisfaction, took a notion to meander out through the front door, thinking she might take a little stroll around the block. She pushed open the screen and the first thing that met her eyes was a big blue granite-iron soup kettle piled high with brown country eggs, on the top step. Beside it sat a little blonde girl of three, quietly and quaintly, with a three-cornered shawl pinned around her shoulders and an old-fashioned lace-and-cambric bonnet on her head.

"Bernice!" Gertrude screamed, for it was Aunt Gunilla's youngest daughter. The granite-iron kettle was hers. Aunt Gunilla had brought the eggs. They were here! They were out in front! Torn between grabbing up the greatly adored little cousin Bernice and running pell-mell down the walk to the gate where the big farm wagon was stopped and the old brown horse stood and Aunt Gunilla and the kids were unloading things, Gertrude compromised by grabbing her up and kissing her and running with her (as well as she could, for she was no lightweight and Gertrude was soon puffing and blowing and red-faced) down the steps and down the walk and out to the wagon.

Mamma heard the commotion and now, rolling down her sleeves and buttoning her cuffs with her pink puffy shriveled fingers—her hands had been in water for hours,—twisting up stray wisps of hair and wiping off sweat, she came to the screen door and looked out. She saw the beautiful sight of the brown eggs, too, in the blue granite-iron kettle, and *she* gave a scream of happiness and came running. . . . Bertha heard it, Stellie, Rudie, Parley . . . they all came screaming and running, good-humored spraddle-legged Parley like he knew what he was hollering about (he didn't, until Aunt Gunilla stooped down and said, "Oh, if ever there was a doll baby it's this one," and kissed him, and then he knew, knowing Aunt Gunilla well, and hollered louder than ever, clapping his hands together like a bantam flapping its wings).

The wagon was being unloaded, children were clambering up and clambering down, all were carrying something—Helga was almost buried under an armload of patchwork quilts, Thurval had several feather pillows hugged tight, Oscar had a bulging old straw suitcase tied around the middle with a long torn strip of calico, that was so heavy it bore him over to the right and nearly carried him downwards, Alfred had a heaped-up clothesbasket with a clean tablecloth spread over and tucked in at the sides, Aunt Gunilla carried a stone crock in one arm and had a pile of starched petticoats in the other. Everybody was so glad to see everybody else that they almost knocked everybody down. Bertha, Gertrude, Stellie, Rudie and Parley, between kisses, laughing and exclamations, all got something to carry, too, and everybody started up the walk to the house at once, bumping and banging in to everybody, being given a hand or lending a hand, until the whole family, the two sisters and their children were finally in the house and the wagon unloaded.

The two sisters had to unpack what Gunilla had brought, they had to set the table and the whole family had to sit up to it and eat as if it was Thanksgiving Day itself. Then they had to clear up and wash the dishes, the girls helping, put things away, get Parley and Bernice (who was almost too big, now, to allow it) down for a nap and shoo everybody else out to "blow the stink off them" before they really had time to settle down for a good talk.

It had been too long since they saw each other, but farm work, a spell or two of sickness and one thing and another had kept Gunilla confined to the farm all summer. Gunilla's husband Frank, the stone-cutter, was gone most of the summer with the horse and wagon, traveling down through southern Utah and even down into Arizona and Nevada, or up north to the Sweetwater, to Idaho and Wyoming. He sold tombstones or traded them for produce and supplies, a wagon-load of potatoes, damson plums, or a bolt of Mormon "factory," a sturdy cotton made in the church mills, of no particular whiteness but of lasting quality. Nobody could accuse him of being handsome, but Frank was a good man and a good provider. He was a stonecutter who knew his business. If he carved out an angel with outspread wings or a lamb or a child, or both, or a baby asleep, or a girl leaning her cheek on her hand with her eyes downcast on an open book, it was beautiful, just like what a real sculptor would make. And oh, how wonderfully he could cut out letters: Our Mother, Charlie, Gone Home, Over in the

Summer Land, No Night There . . . just like a professional, as everybody said. But then, of course, he was a professional, a stonecutter, that was his business.

Gunilla seemed to can more fruits and vegetables than anybody else because she always had these wagonloads that Frank traded his headstones for, to save. That was why she could almost never leave the place in summer, besides not having the horse and wagon. She had a cow to look after, too. Frank was home these three days, looking after things. It was a promise he always had to make, to let her go and take the kids to Conference, not so much for the meetings as to see Linnea. She could go along just so long, she used to say, and then she had to make tracks for her sister's. Linnea felt the same way. They could go along just so long, the two of them, separated by ten miles (Gunilla lived out over Jordan), not writing a line, never thinking of writing a line unless heaven only knows what happened, not even thinking of each other very often perhaps, but then! All of a sudden a day came when one or the other or the two together couldn't stand it for another minute. Gunilla had to see Linnea. Linnea had to see Gunilla. They had heartaches over it. If anything intervened they sat down and cried like big boobies. If they couldn't have got there any other way they would have crawled every step of the way on their hands and knees, when the longing seized them.

This late afternoon, sitting across from each other by the stove (the sunshine was yellow streaming through the windows, but a fire felt good to the bones), Linnea and Gunilla, the two fond sisters, had a lot of catching up to do on their talking. Parley and Bernice gave up and were sound asleep in the bedroom, the rest of the children were gone somewhere, wandering around, playing.

"Sometimes ain't it a relief not to have a chick nor a child around for a little while?" Linnea said, rocking comfortably.

"Ain't it?" Gunilla said, also rocking. "A person don't realize how noisy they are until they're out of the house, and then a person realizes. All of a sudden you notice you can hear every little sound, like the clock, or a cat purring or any little thing—and then you realize that they must of been making a noise that would of woke the dead."

"I wonder how it feels not to have no kids?" Linnea said musingly. "To clean up the house and have it stay clean, and then pick up your crocheting or embroidering or just sit and twiddle your thumbs and listen to the clock tick. Maybe read the newspaper or something?"

"Ugh." Gunilla shuddered. "I should think a person would go crazy, without no kids to tend to, without the commotion, with all there is to do for them. A person would go crazy, that's all. Wouldn't you imagine?"

"That's what I'd imagine," Linnea said. "But of course once in a while a little breathing spell is all right, like now. Quiet and nice like this. But *all* the time," she said, "why, naturally a person couldn't stand it, a person would go crazy like you say."

Before supper and before the kids came back they caught up on everything, though Parley and Bernice woke up after the briefest of naps and had to be provided with entertainment, dandled and seen to the rest of the time—but the two mothers were so used to their jobs, they did them without even knowing they did them, keeping right on with the conversation.

Usually Mamma did not take the children to the Tabernacle meetings except when there was going to be something good like lots of singing. "It's cruel to make little kids sit there and not even dare so much as wiggle while some old man goes on and on, the way they do. Old men don't understand them things. They got no notion how hard it is for kids. Even big people get awful wore out with them old men sometimes, going on and on." But the girls were old enough to sit there and be bored like anybody else and anyway, it would have been unthinkable for them *not* to go. Didn't they have white stockings? Didn't they have toe slippers? Wasn't their hair put up on rags until it was such a mass of corkscrew curls it was like trying to dig the Panama canal to get through them? Didn't they holler and protest? Aunt Gunilla could do it, she said, without hurting a bit. She could, too. Strangely enough, her own daughter Hilma insisted on Aunt Linnea combing out *her* curls. Mothers, it seemed, hurt a person. They pulled. Aunts, however, did not.

The two women took the children and went in the wagon. Gunilla proudly driving the polished horse (polished for the occasion, rubbed and polished as though he had been made of mahogany) uptown to the crowded Temple Square, where the domed Tabernacle stood. You had to be picnicking on the hills above town, in City Creek Canyon maybe, looking down, to see how the Tabernacle looked like nothing so much as a great big turtle with a fence around him, nibbling at tufts of waving green trees. But walking in at one of the wide-open double doors in a stream of people, it didn't look so much like a turtle. It looked perfectly awesome.

The Tabernacle was said to hold twelve thousand people and fifteen minutes after Linnea and Gunilla got in and got their brood settled, there wasn't a vacant seat left. It was such a big building that it wasn't like a building at all, it was like a locality, Saaremaa, for instance. From the floor to the highest point of the domed ceiling was a distance of eighty feet, high enough for good-sized spruces not to have to stoop to keep from bumping their heads. An oval building, no large columns were anywhere to distract the vision, only the small columns holding

up the balconies that ran all around except in from where the golden
organ was, and the choir ranged on either side of it in two spread wings.
What was smaller than a pair of toe slippers here? More insignificant?
Gertrude stuck her foot out and looked at one twinkling toe. She looked
on either side of her—Bertha was looking at her own bright important
feet—Mamma, holding Parley, was shushing Rudie. She bent her head
and looked down the row: Mamma, Rudie, Hilma, Thurval, Oscar to the
right; Bertha, Stellie, Aunt Gunilla with Bernice on her lap, and Alfred,
to the left. Then strangers only, strangers for miles, twelve thousand
faces that got smaller and smaller the farther away they were until, when
they sat on the platform or sang in the choir, they were no bigger than
your little fingernail. They were tedious, as people gathered together in
rows by many thousands are invariably tedious, and frightening because
of it, for they look alike and because they look alike they seem not to be
very smart, staring straight ahead. Even the important men on the platform just beneath the choir—the twelve apostles, the President of the
Stake and his two counsellors, the chief bishop and his counsellors, other
bishops appointed to administer the sacrament—look like peas in a pod.
Even President Woodruff looks exactly like everybody else, so that it
scarcely seems to matter that he *is* the President for he is not unique.
What is he? He has a face the size of a shirt button! His counsellors,
two of the oldest, richest and wisest men in the whole city, one on either
side of him, have habitual faces the size of shirt buttons too.

And how these men with their tiny faces and insect hands and feet,
stand up and talk, and drone and drone on, as though everything they
said was worth pure gold. How large their stunningly tedious words are
coming from their infinitesimal mouths, for something magic, inexplic-
able, in the acoustics here, enlarges them to great size, like moons
through a telescope, and there is no getting away from them. No matter
where you stand, or sit, here come these great big reverberating words.
There's nothing to do but let them bounce by to spend themselves
against the sides of the building, or pile up in front of your face (the
letter S alone for instance, pulled hissingly through the old men's teeth),
the hissed and blown letters, S, P, B, like leaves caught in a culvert or
tissue-paper strips blown around a telephone pole, let them blow and
pile up rustlingly. A choir of dolls with oversize voices for men the size
of John L. Sullivan hallooing across a canyon give out with "In Our
Lovely Deseret." Everybody knows "In Our Lovely Deseret" and stands
and sings it, any pairs of toe slippers dwindling meanwhile more and
more away into nothing. Gertrude shifts sadly, singing, in a quite
obliterated voice but singing, thinks of her slippers, wishes she could go
to the toilet for want of something better to do (will not the multi-
tudinous people catch a glimpse of her slippers if she goes down the

aisle?) but she glances up, singing, and sees Mamma's face singing, and decides against it.

The apostle who said the opening prayer ought to have got a prize, Linnea and Gunilla said afterwards. If it took him a minute less than forty-seven minutes nobody would believe it. In fact, it seemed to take a good deal longer than that (about as long as the night before the best thing that ever happened to you in your life, was going to happen the next day, and you knew it). He was old and when asked, got up, and bowed his head for a moment in silence, the way the great pianist bows his head for a moment in silence above the keys before he begins to play. Then he cut loose. Gunilla said there wasn't a setting hen, nor a gnat, nor a bug, nor a spider, nor a worm, that he missed. He covered every inch of the whole great Mormon folkland. He started out with the President, who was to be blessed in his basket and his store, whatever that might mean, for whom wives, families, flocks and herds were to be multiplied, houses and lands increased. The President was to be made, if God pleased (and why not? why wouldn't God please?) the wisest man in the world. To confound all his enemies! Has he enemies? Foes? Do they rise up against him? Do they lie in wait to seek his destruction? Let them fall into every conceivable snare! Let them reach the nether regions!

Gertrude looked upwards from under her shut eyes at Mamma looking downwards, and drew a great sigh and twisted on her seat in utterable boredom but Mamma frowned and shook her head, so Gertrude was still again, sitting very still, her eyes half shut. She held her toes surreptitiously out and looked at the twinkling shoes but the long words, the loud words, the droning words, the never-ending words, of the old apostle, took the joy out of toe slippers even, much as toothache or the pain of conscience will take the joy out of all of life.

He got through with the President and went on to his counsellors. For them he asked only a shade less of all the blessings and renown a human being may have bestowed upon him. The apostles came next— eleven of them, by name—he himself left becomingly and modestly out—for whom benefits were requested, strictly according to rank. The bishops were next in order, but there were twenty of them, in Salt Lake City alone, to say nothing of those in outlying fiefs, each with two counsellors—he scarcely knew all their names—so the favors solicited for them were very general. The Saints at large needed a good deal, he confided heavenwards. The Lord could not blame him for speaking thus frankly? First and foremost, they needed care and protection against the inroads of the Gentiles—after that, holiness, modesty, obedience, gentleness of spirit, meekness, mildness, moral virtue. Also, they should save for a rainy day—but before that, before anything else, they should pay their tithing! Some, alas, were remiss on this score. Would the Lord—er, see that they did? The apostle paused, thinking, biting on his lower lip, but there didn't seem to be much more to say. That was about the size of it. "In the name of the Father," he finished, "and the Son, and the Holy Ghost, Amen." He paused another moment, lifted up his head and opened his eyes. Then he went and sat down.

Everybody was relieved, even the doll-size men of highest authority on the platform, the highest of high priests. Oh, what a turning from right to left and from left to right, what a shifting of bottoms, what a scraping of feet, and snorting, and clearing of throats, and blowing of noses, and coughing, before twelve thousand people settled down again, first to a song by all and then to another speech. This time, it was spoken directly to them, and best of all, they had to participate by raising their hands every little while to vote I DO. Into the deadly dullness they could thrust their hands upwards, for this was the time the great ones were "sustained." The ritual was gone through every Conference time. As did the apostle's prayer, the list started out with the President.

"I move," a second apostle stood up, walked over to the pulpit and began, "that President Wilford Woodruff be sustained as President of the Church of Jesus Christ of Latter-Day Saints and as Prophet, Seer and Revelator." From somewhere the motion was seconded. A show of hands was called for. Everybody raised his hand—it was like an acre of sego lilies rising up and blowing in the wind. A negative vote? A vote against him? Why, what a notion! No hand is ever lifted in opposition. Then came the Prophet, Seer and Revelator, first Counsellor to the President. Should he be sustained? They spring upwards, wave in the air, those lilies. Does anyone vote against him? No, no, not one. Now Prophet, Seer and Revelator, second Counsellor to the President. Yes, yes, twelve thousand times yes. Now the Quorum of the Twelve Apostles, the President and member of the Quorum. Yes, indeed, oh, my, yes. The Patriarch of the Church. The President of the Stake of Zion, his two counsellors. The High Council. Shall they be sustained? Are you trying to get fresh? The President of the High Priest's Quorum, his counsellors two. The first seven Presidents of the Seventies. The members of the Seventies. All? All? Twelve thousand hands went up and settled down, rose up and fell, happy in the motion.

This was as bad as the prayer, only it was better to get to raise the hand than not, and a great relief to be able to have one's eyes open. Gertrude used hers everywhere, her hand rising and falling when everybody's rose and fell, on the tiniest polka-dot faces in the last row of the choir, then down, and steadily forward, until the polka dots became real faces the size of headhunters' trophies hung upon a limb, then apple size, then bigger, then bigger. Finally Gertrude could see warts, lines,

blood-vessel tributaries, eyelashes, a stye upon an eye. She could see
. . . But what familiar faces were these in a row to the left, the row
three seats up and to the left that made a curve, so that every face could
be looked at, recognized? (Gertrude's hand went up, came down, idly,
absentmindedly.)

Why, there were the people from Bountiful sitting in a row! Like
Browning's Last Duchess, there they were, as if alive! Gertrude gave a
wiggle and a bound, stretching her neck to look far over at them (there
they sat, as if alive), her hand going up, falling down. Mamma frowned,
and Gertrude blinked wildly and motioned over that way but Mamma
frowned again and wouldn't look. She indicated that Gertrude was
supposed to join in the "sustaining" and keep her mind on her business.
But there they were! The people from Bountiful! Come in for Conference! For instance—the two Mrs. Barneses who had run their husband
off for marrying a third Mrs. Barnes! In fine-feathered bonnets. And
Grace, the daughter, between them, without her husband, but with a
big child standing on her lap, teetering up and down, its fat arms around
her neck. The dead twin in the locked shed, the ice from Salt Lake,
rose in Gertrude's mind, and her mouth watered, thinking of the good
pieces of ice to suck in hot summer, when the Barnes boys broke it off
in chunks for them, for all the kids, before they carried it in and laid the
cold transparent blocks around the dead child. Gertrude had never seen
him, but she seemed to have, she could always imagine him lying small
and blue under the gunny-sack-and-sawdust-covered roof, behind the
locked door, over and above the shifting melting ice, in the dark shed,
waiting for his sister to die so he could be buried with her, as the sick
mother wanted. And then, of course! They had to bury him after all!
Because his twin sister didn't die, puny and sick and no-account as she
was. She lived. So they couldn't wait any longer and had to bury him.
And that, down the row, was the very living child, grown chunky,
grown beautiful, turned three, clambering on her mother's patient lap.
All you had to do was turn your head and look along that way, to see
her. . . . And there was Flossie Barnes—or was that Flossie, grown to
be such a big girl?

The President of the Elder's Quorum? Did any voice say nay? His
counsellors two? Oh, yes, oh, yes. The Presiding Bishop? His counsellors?

And there was Mr. Goff, the station agent, with his wife, his schoolteacher daughter Lila, and his small son, who had been so nice to them,
lending them a boxcar to take their things to Ogden, when Mamma got
so disgusted with farm life. The train went through her mind like a
train going past a house, then she was inside the coach and saw the
bright windows, the sharp green blinds, the red plush of the soft seats,
the polished blood-red of mahogany. She remembered . . . Bonnie,

kicking up her heels in the pink clover, and her long-lashed calf Beauty, and thought. Why, Beauty is a cow now, giving milk.

Oh, there were the Taylors—not the whole family, just Mr. Taylor with as black a beard as ever, and one of his boys. She couldn't remember the names of all his boys. She wondered if this were the one that called her Scandahoovian that day in the strawberry patch. She had told him something, that was sure! She said: I'm a Utah white girl, SO THERE.

The apostle on the platform, as unwearied and fresh as when he started, said, "I move to sustain Brethel Parrington Fitts as President of the Priest's Quorum." (Each man for the office was named in full.) The motion was seconded. The hands, called for, went up, came down, Gertrude's automatically among them. The negative vote was called. Does anyone say no? Nobody says no. Why should they? All they want to do is say yes.

The President of the Teacher's Quorum? His counsellors? Will so-and-so and so-and-so and so-and-so be sustained? Sustain them, sustain them, says the acre of sego lilies.

"—as President of the Deacon's Quorum, and his counsellors?" says the apostle. With all the rest, Gertrude's hand goes up, comes down.

"—Trustee-in-trust for the Church of Latter-Day Saints?"

Sustained, sustained.

Negative vote? Not one.

And there was the Myers family who gave them the very dishes the Ecklund family was using right this minute, the day Rudie climbed up and pulled the cupboard down on top of him and broke all Mamma's nice dishes and nearly got himself killed. The Myerses gave them a barrel of all the dishes they possibly needed but of course they weren't a matching set, they were odds and ends. That hurt Mamma, not to have a matching set, but only odds and ends, although it was the kindest thing in the world for the Myerses to have given away what they did.

"—as Architect for the Church?"

Sustained.

"—as Historian and General Church Recorder?"

Sustained.

Negative votes?

One.

How many?

One.

Why, whose in the world is that?

Gertrude's.

All that was the matter with her, she didn't have her mind on her business. Mamma jerked at her arm, pulled it down. People close enough to see, the ones who had paid any attention, tittered, they laughed quite loud. She nearly fell over dead with shame. Would the meeting stop? Would she be publicly challenged? She did not guess how small she was, how few saw her dereliction. We almost never guess how small we are. Her heart the next thing to stopped beating, she stared straight ahead, the blood pounding in her ears. She could hear the tittering, the laughing. She had done something monstrous, raised her hand and voted against. She was sick with mortification. Another apostle or somebody made a speech that she did not hear, then the doxology, then they were dismissed. The meeting in the Tabernacle was over!

Walking outside, on her twinkling toe slippers, Gertrude might have forgotten her faux pas, or at least let it dwindle down to the right size, but Bertha, Hilma and Alfred, in fact all the children, took it up in the highest glee. Even Mamma and Aunt Gunilla laughed about it.

"Gertrude voted against!"

"Gertrude held her hand up the wrong time!"

"She voted against!"

"She just didn't want old Talmadge as Historian and General Church Recorder no more, or whoever it was," Aunt Gunilla said teasingly. "I kind of lost track of the man's name."

"No, sir," said Mamma, "she been kind of tired lately of the Historian and General Church Recorder. New blood, she wants."

Gertrude broke and ran, her cheeks burning, their teasing in her ears. There was such a crowd it was hard to get through, hard to get over to the gateway and outside the Temple grounds. She pushed through as swiftly as she could, her head down, tears stinging her eyelids.

"Let her go," Mamma said behind her. "My, but we're proud and touchy, ain't we? I don't know what's going to become of us if we keep on being so proud and touchy."

She was almost through the gates now and outside on the street. Surely everybody must know who she was, that she was the numskull who had raised her hand and voted against. As she went, they would be whispering, pointing her out saying, That's the girl that voted against! Ain't she a numskull? and look, she has toe slippers on and everything. You'd think she'd know better! Hot with shame and humiliation, she made her way as well as she could through the crowd, and then, "Well, who's this?" a voice boomed, and somebody grabbed her. She looked up in terror. It was Mr. Goff, the stationmaster, and there was Flossie Barnes, and one after one almost all the Bountiful people in a bunch. "Hey! Tears?" he said. She would have been glad to welcome them, glad to dance around them merrily talking till Mamma came up, but it was not the moment for it, her poise had cracked like a watermelon dropped on the sidewalk, she didn't know how to put it together again, she didn't have a word to say or a voice to say it with. "Hey! Tears?" he said again, but she could not speak and answer him. She wrenched herself free and ran as hard as she could out through the gates.

Of course, that was almost worse than voting against. Not to be able to act like a big girl and swallow her tears and stop there to pass the time of day with the Bountiful people like somebody with manners.

When she got to the wagon she climbed into the back and threw herself down on the floor, on the quilt Aunt Gunilla had spread so they all could sit on it without dirtying their dresses, and cried as hard as she could, feeling ashamed and disgraced. How could she live this down? But then she remembered the wagon was quite open and people could walk by and see her crying like a boobie, so she sat up, and dried her tears, and began idly watching the people go by, still smarting with embarrassment. The passers-by, however, proved interesting enough so that she soon forgot herself. One old man in the most extraordinary long-tailed coat, with a beaver hat on his head, and dyed whiskers, came by with a family of at least seven grown women, all prosperously and even prettily dressed in the most modish way, accompanied by uncountable children. They made quite a parade stringing out along the sidewalk, laughing and chattering. Gertrude watched them with great interest, and when they had gone by she watched others—two women having a loud argument and a bevy of pretty girls in charming bonnets—and in no time she forgot her sense of mortification, the tears drying upon her cheeks.

Mamma and Aunt Gunilla were a great while coming, certainly. She began to look for them anxiously, for all of a sudden it seemed to her that she had never been so hungry in her whole life. Her saliva glands began to work overtime as she thought of mashed potatoes, the brown gravy, the delicious slices of juicy meat they were going to have, the rolls, the butter, the lemon pie, the cake—in short, the "company" dinner, if they managed to live through the delay and not starve to death before they got it.

A familiar face was approaching on the dead run, a head she knew was bobbing up and down, making for the wagon. She shifted her gaze quickly as though to seem to be looking on the opposite side of the street, not at him at all, not anywhere near him, as though he didn't mean any more to her than a lamppost.

Alfred clambered up into the wagon and came and threw himself panting beside her. "Mamma made me hold Bernice," he said, "or I'd of got here quicker. They stopped and talked to them people from Bountiful, where you used to live. They was all there in the meeting. Remember the Bountiful people?"

"Sure I remember," she said coldly.

"Some of them said they seen you just now. They said you was bawling and run right on past them without talking."

She winced and turned hot with shame again. Now, wasn't that a fine way to act? Wasn't that something smart? Oh, my, yes.

"But your ma explained to them that you accidentally voted against."

"Oh, she did, did she?" She glared at him.

"They all laughed, Gertrude, like if somebody does something funny, not like if somebody does something dumb. You didn't do nothing dumb, Gertrude."

Still she glared.

"Nobody cared if you voted against," he said gently. "It didn't make no difference. Everybody was just trying to josh you. It was fun, see, you voting against. Nobody cared." He looked at her fondly. "Don't cry," he said. "Don't always cry. It ain't worth crying for."

He had run ahead of the others to tell her this, knowing her feelings were hurt. Aunt Gunilla, his mother, had stopped him for a little to get him to hold Bernice, but he came after her as soon as he could. Alfred did, after all. Her ice melted, the glare went away and was replaced by a tender sorry glance. She looked at him and then down at the toe slippers. Suddenly she looked hard at the toe slippers. She had utterly forgotten them. Why, her pleasure in them was just beginning. She had days—years—ahead, of inconceivable pride and happiness, in her toe slippers. What more did she want? What else did she expect? Secure in her knowledge of them, she could afford to smile tolerantly at her own foibles, as the woman of fifty may look back and smile on the foolishness of the girl of eighteen, without anguish. "You should seen the funny old man I seen, just now," she said. "You know how many wives he had? Fourteen! I counted them and he had fourteen. He had the funniest long-tailed blue coat on and—"

"You don't know if they was all his wives."

"I do, too!"

"I sure wouldn't want fourteen wives," Alfred said, his choir-boy voice stumbling and falling flat. It crawled to its hands and knees. "I wouldn't even want *one* wife."

"Why not?" she asked, lifting her foot gracefully and ladylikely up and viewing it with what was supposed to be modesty. It didn't matter that she voted against. Really, it didn't matter. It didn't matter that she hadn't stopped and passed the time of day properly with the Bountiful people, either. For here was Alfred, talking companionably with her, and here were toe slippers upon her feet . . . why, she was a regular fashion plate . . . and the sun shining . . . and a good dinner at home . . . why, my gosh. . . . "Why not, Alfred?"

"Why, because I hate girls, that's why!"

"Well, I hate boys," she said, sticking her nose up into the air.

"I do hate boys," she repeated. But she said it amiably and he scowled amiably back.

Mamma was tickled to have seen the folks from Bountiful, even though the delay in talking to them caused everybody to be so hungry before they got home and got the dinner on that they didn't think they could stand it. Thurval and Oscar said they thought they had tapeworms and that they were gnawing at them for something to eat and if they didn't get something pretty soon, they would turn to and eat them right up, like the boy in the old legend. So Mamma, putting peeled potatoes, peeled that morning and left to soak in cold water, on the stove to cook, and fixing the damper, and sticking the meat back in the oven for one more hour's roasting, reached under the clean folded tablecloth and took a couple of brown-crusted buns off the top of the kitchen chest of drawers where they reposed in a small clothesbasket and tossed the boys one each as though they had been a couple of bouncing puppies. She laughed, her face bright pink from the roaring fire she had stirred up. "Well, a bun ought to hold your tapeworms and keep them from eating you up."

Then all the kids said *they* had tapeworms, too. So Aunt Gunilla tossed each one of them a bun, and told them all to run outside and blow the stink off them, and not hang around and bother or they'd never get their dinner. Who could put a meal on when a bunch of kids were all over the place like a bunch of wild Indians? So out they ran, going to play a game of Ante-I-Over. Stellie lingered and said she wanted butter on her bread.

"Oh, no, you don't, young lady," Mamma said. "If you're hungry enough, you'll eat bare bread." It was such a favorite and well-used saying that she could say it without having to think. She was chopping away at a huge head of cabbage for a bowlful of the most succulent coleslaw with sour-sweet dressing that anybody ever tasted. So Stellie went out with the rest, eating her bare brown roll, and her hunger was spread enough for any bread.

When they were all outside and Gunilla was setting the table, with everything, the desserts ranged down the middle like handsome floral pieces, Linnea asked her if she had noticed him.

"Who?" Gunilla asked.

"Why, Olaf," Linnea said. "I seen him and Sigrid and the kids, walking out of the Tabernacle as big as life, when we was standing there talking to the folks from Bountiful. Out of the corner of my eye. I never let on."

"No!" Gunilla said in that marveling way she had, that made her such a gratifying companion. "Did he see you?"

"I don't know," Linnea said. "And I care less. Anyway, he didn't let on either, if he did. I just went right on talking like I didn't know they was within a hundred miles."

"Do you think Olaf seen you?"

"I don't know," Linnea said, "and I care less."

"Oh, Linnea," her sister said, "are you really as mad at him as all that? Won't you never make up with him?"

"Never," Linnea said. "Not if I live to be a hundred and thirty-two."

"Well, golly," Gunilla said as though she felt quite miserable about it, as indeed she did, "you're the one that's always so broad-minded. You're the one that's always saying we'd ought to forgive and forget. Why, if I've heard you say it once I've heard you say a thousand times, that people ain't mean, they try to do the best they can, and if they get off on the wrong track sometime, why—"

"He done something I can never get over. He bought a house for Sigrid and he never told me!"

"He told you, or you wouldn't known nothing about it," Gunilla pointed out reasonably.

"Yes, but not in time," Linnea said.

"Not in time for what? To stop it?" Gunilla teased, but when she glanced over she knew by Linnea's face it was no teasing matter. "No, but *you*, Linnea," she said, "that ain't the kind a-tall for holding a grudge. It ain't like you a-tall."

"Wouldn't you be mad?" Linnea asked, looking up from the gravy she was stirring. She put the spoon up to her lips and flicked her tongue across the edge of it in the most delicate way. It needed more salt and she put in another pinch, tasting it delicately again. This time it was just right. "No," she said, "but wouldn't you? If you was the second one all these years, and she was the first, and she was the prettiest, and always seemed to have more of a claim someway? Wouldn't you? If he snuck around and bought her a house?" It really hurt her to the core. Gunilla knew that.

"Well, yes," she said, "I guess maybe I would. Only—"

"Only what?"

"Well, you'd be the next one to have a house. He's always tried to do for one what he done for the other. He's tried hard, Olaf has."

"If he gives me a ten-room house," Linnea said, "with solid gold doorknobs and a flush toilet and cupola, and a front porch and a back porch, and a double parlor, and a stained-glass window," she said, "and roses in front and vegetables behind, and a weathervane on top, he could never make up to me for the wound he's give me here!" She struck her breast with a floury fist, thud, thud, thud.

It may have been a little stagey but Gunilla did not think so. "Well, anyway, he had his nerve," she said. "That I will admit."

"Nerve!" Linnea said. "The nerve of a elephant. It'd take something to make me forget it. There ain't nothing I know of that would."

There was one thing, but she didn't know it then.

Imagine! If Linnea didn't almost let her sister leave without telling her the most important piece of news of all. She had to run like a deer down the block and stop the wagon. So that the children wouldn't know, she delivered the news in Swedish, their parents' tongue, which she and Gunilla had learned in childhood. "If I didn't almost forget the most important thing of all," she said breathlessly. "You can never imagine!"

"What? What is it? For heaven's sake?" Gunilla said, also in Swedish.

"Why, Mrs. Sterling, of course. I told you to remind me."

"What about Mrs. Sterling?"

"She's going to have a baby! She's six months along!"

"Not your friend Mrs. Sterling!" Gunilla said in amazement.

"Yes, ma'am, that's what she is."

"That's what makes me so mad," Hilma stood up in back and said. "Anytime they don't want us kids to know what they're talking about, they talk Swedish."

"You sit down and mind your business," her mother said. "Whose?" she asked Linnea in the foreign tongue.

"What do you mean, whose?"

"Why, whose baby, of course? Whose is it? Brother Bell's?"

"Why, sure," Linnea said but the question seemed to surprise her, and she frowned, mulling over it. Mrs. Sterling was such a nice woman. It was all a person could do to imagine . . .

Gunilla smiled broadly. "Will wonders never cease?" she said, picking up the reins. "His oldest girl must be forty or more. Honestly, some of them old scoots get notions that'd surprise you!"

CHAPTER 21

EITHER BECAUSE Brother Bell was considered to be so old, or because Mrs. Sterling, by never talking of it, had made her connection with him seem so pure and platonic, the news that she was in the family way came as a great surprise to everybody. Ingeborg seemed to be one of the first ones to hear of it. When she was informed of it, Linnea stoutly denied it. "The things people go around and tattle," she said, "make me sick. Why, Mrs. Sterling is one of the nicest little women and best little housekeepers that ever was. Friendly and sweet and—"

"Too friendly and sweet," Ingeborg said sourly. "That's the kind that's usually got something up their sleeve."

"You can take my word for it," Linnea took it upon herself to declare, "Mrs. Sterling ain't any more in the family way than you are, or I am. It's just mean talk and if I was you I wouldn't repeat it."

Ingeborg looked grim. "I happen to know what I'm talking about," she said. "And anyway, I've knew you longer than she has, and you and me has been friends longer than you and her has. It looks like you'd stand up for *me* once in a while, be on *my* side of the fence. But no, if it's a choice between me and that frizzle-haired cockeyed show-off of a no-good, you'll stand up for her every time." She sniffed.

Linnea laughed good-naturedly and came and put an arm around Ingeborg's shoulders. "You jealous old thing," she said, giving her a squeeze. "Just as if I'd be on Mrs. Sterling's side, against you! But what's that got to do with anything?"

Ingeborg was appeased but she still acted a little sulky. "Well, I got it on good authority and here you the next thing to call me a liar, because you hear tell your precious Mrs. Sterling ain't anywheres near the angel she makes out to be."

"Well, my goodness, she ain't robbed the tithing office or anything, or give somebody a clout over the head with a axe, has she? All that's happened is she's going to have a baby."

"All!" Ingeborg said.

"Well, that's perfectly natural, ain't it?"

"Perfectly natural!"

"Well, ain't it?"

"Honestly, Linnea," Ingeborg said, "when you talk like that I don't know what to think of you. You, that's sat and talked face to face with the President of the Church of Jesus Christ of Latter-Day Saints. You, that's rode in the carriage with him! I just don't know what to think."

The mention of the solemn and historical event sobered her, but Linnea still would not take the news too seriously. "There's such a thing as hearsay, you want to remember," she said. "And there's jealous women that love to tear somebody off their perch if they can. Maybe one of them told you the story."

"How long since you seen her?" Ingeborg demanded.

"Oh, quite a while," Linnea said. "Maybe five or six weeks. We ain't them kind of chums that you can't pry loose from each other. You know. We're just friends. Why, I see you ten times to her once."

Ingeborg knew this but it delighted her to have Linnea recall it. She almost smiled, and when she spoke it was genially. "Well," she said, "I don't know whether it's hearsay if a woman's stuck out in front this far!" She put her hand out about a foot from her stomach and made a chopping motion. "*This far,* mind you. That, I seen with my own eyes, in Auerbach's at the notion counter. I guess you'd call that hearsay! Do you think I'm blind or something?"

Linnea sat thinking, a look of amazement on her face. "Well, that old Brother Bell!" she breathed finally, more with delight than not. "Can you imagine! That sly old fox."

"Who says it's his, necessarily?"

"Why, of course it is," Linnea said in surprise. "Whose else would it be?"

"Well, there's mention of some fellow named Brenneman or something. Big handsome fellow come over from Germany. Works in the brewery across the street. From what I hear, he's in and out there all the time. She even sits down and has a glass of beer with him." Her triumphant expression said if a woman can go any lower than that you just tell me how!

"My goodness," Linnea said, "I know all about Mr. Brenneman. And all I can say is, it's impossible. He's a Theosophist."

Ingeborg squinted at her. "I guess that don't prevent him from getting ideas in his head, does it? He hasn't got his business cut off or something, has he?"

"Ingeborg!"

"Well, has he?"

"Just as if *I* knowed anything about his business! What call would I have to know about Mr. Brenneman's business, if you please?"

"Theosophist," Ingeborg muttered.

"I do know," Linnea said, "that he's got a double thumb on his right hand. His thumb looks like it's split right down the middle but it ain't —it's two thumbs. One of his feet got two big toes on it, too, the same proposition as the thumbs, the big toe looks like it's split down the middle. He happened to mention it. 'I got this one double thumb,' he says, 'and I got this double big toe,' he says. 'It kind of runs in our family,' he says. 'My sister's got *two* double thumbs and my brother's got two double toes. Me, now. I got one double thumb and one double toe,' he says, 'got a brother that ain't got anything,' he says."

"What does he mean he's got a brother that ain't got anything?"

"Nothing double, I guess he meant, no double thumbs or toes or nothing."

"Well, what's all that got to do with him and your fine Mrs. Sterling? Has he got a double business or something?"

Linnea had to burst out laughing at that but she said, "It seems to me you're dwelling pretty strong on the men's businesses all of a sudden. How would I know whether it's double or not, or *what* it is!"

"Theosophist," Ingeborg muttered. "I can imagine."

"Listen," Linnea said, "I'm as surprised as anybody about Mrs. Sterling, but I can tell you this much: if she's going to have a baby, she's going to have Brother Bell's baby, *that* I can tell you."

"How do you know?" Ingeborg asked.

"Well, she's divorced from Mr. Sterling, ain't she?"

"Yes."

"And Mr. Brenneman ain't married, is he?"

"Not that anybody knows of."

"He ain't, I'm positive. Anyway, what I mean to say is, if there'd been anything betwixt him and Mrs. Sterling, they'd of been married long ago. He's that kind of man and she's that kind of woman. Oh, no," Linnea said, "Mr. Brenneman don't enter into the picture at all. It's Brother Bell and nobody *but* Brother Bell."

"Well, she can't marry him!"

"Why not?"

"Well, President Woodruff signed that Manifesto. There ain't going to be any more polygamy. No more polygamous marriages. So she naturally can't marry *him*."

"Polygamous marriages ain't the only kind, you want to remember. You got married and it wasn't polygamous. For that matter, a couple can go to a Justice of the Peace and get married, too—all legal and the Church having no say in the matter."

"But he's married already!"

"He could get a divorce."

"I'd see him," Ingeborg scoffed, "why, everybody knows he's so scared of that family he shakes in his shoes. He don't dare call his soul his own."

"They let him be friends with Mrs. Sterling," Linnea pointed out. "Maybe he's got more gumption than people give him credit for."

"And why do they?" Ingeborg asked. "Because he signed away the biggest part of everything he had in the world to that family, to Mrs. Bell and them three kids. *Then* they let him roam. Why wouldn't they? They had plucked him clean! Let him roam if he wanted to. When you've got the banana et, what do you want with the skin?"

"You'll see," Linnea prophesied. "Mrs. Bell ain't the kind of a woman to let her reputation be tore in shreds. There'll be a wedding as sure as I'm knee-high to a grasshopper."

Linnea was right. There was a wedding, and that in the not so distant future.

Mrs. Sterling sent over for her friend a day or two after the conversation with Ingeborg. Linnea kept feeling in her bones that she would and sure enough, one morning, Mrs. Sterling sent Estelle over before school to ask if Linnea would come and see her. Linnea said of course she would and when she got her own lunches packed and her own children off to school, she spruced herself up and spruced up Parley (the only child left at home now) and away she went to Mrs. Sterling's to find out what Mrs. Sterling wanted and exactly what was what.

The first and foremost thing Mrs. Sterling wanted, it seemed, was a shoulder to cry on, a sisterly bosom on which to rest her frizzled bangs and have a good cry. She hollered "Come in," when Linnea knocked at the door, and when Linnea pushed it open to let Parley in to run whooping with joy straight for the canary in its cage, and came in herself and shut the door behind her, Mrs. Sterling, from across the broad sunlit room by the china closet, fiddling there with a dustcloth, dropped it, and came on the fly straight into Linnea's surprised arms. She didn't say aye, yes, or no. She just dug her nose in the shirring across Linnea's breast and cried like her heart would break.

"There, there," Linnea said, patting the heaving shoulders with her right hand and taking her hatpin out, sticking it in her hat ribbon and removing her hat with her left hand. There was no place near at hand so she gave it a little toss into the air and it sailed off as nice as you please and landed right on the cushion in the Boston rocker. "There's nothing so bad it can't be mended," she said. "Many a trouble comes to us as a blessing in disguise. There's no road without a turning. There ain't no storm but what the sun shines sooner or later."

"Oh, Linnea!"

Linnea kept on patting her shoulder and knew that Mrs. Sterling's wet face must be scarlet with blushes, for the back of her neck was as red as a beet. Then she maneuvered her over to the rocker, taking her hat up and tossing it this time upon the pretty red-and-green chenille tablecloth. "You set down here," she said and pushed her gently into it. "I'll set here." Linnea brought up another rocker and sat down, tactfully not looking at her disheveled friend, who had got her handkerchief out of her apron pocket and was wiping her eyes and blowing her nose and smoothing and repinning her mussed dark hair. "When Parley gets with that bird, it's all he wants," Linnea said. "He'll set there and watch it till he's green in the face." She motioned over to where he sat back on his heels in the window seat looking upwards at the chartreuse canary hopping about and twittering in his ornate gilt cage, sending down a shower of seeds.

Mrs. Sterling could be looked at now. "Linnea," she said, "what I got you over here for, I got you over here to talk about a wedding."

"Well, my," Linnea said, beaming. "What do you know! A wedding!"

"Long overdue," Mrs. Sterling said.

"Better late than never," Linnea said cheerfully.

"It's not been no snap," Mrs. Sterling began. "Brother Bell has been as fair and true as a man could be, but he's had something on his hands with that family of his. It's all settled now though," she said, "everything's settled. Everything's been worked out fine."

"Good!" Linnea said. "If ever I was glad to hear a piece of news I'm glad to hear that!" (She would tell Ingeborg a thing or two, she thought. What was meaner than a mean lot of gossip?)

"No," Mrs. Sterling said, "it's not been no snap. I told you what an onry family he had, didn't I? When I come out and stayed with you in Bountiful because they come and threatened me and all, and I was so nervous about them? Remember? And that's when me and Brother Bell was just *friends,* before we ever—before we—before we even—"

"I remember," Linnea broke in with great tact. "I well remember."

"Well, then when they seen they could get him to sign away nearly everything he had, not everything, but nearly everything, why, then they didn't care so much. In fact, I will say this for them. After that, they let him be, more or less. They let him come and go as he pleased. Then," she said, "after you and me come down here to Salt Lake from Ogden, and I got this place from Brother Bell—what else could I do at the time, I want to know?—"

"Nothing," Linnea said staunchly.

"—why then, he had freedom to come and go as he pleased, and I was here in this house of his, and the first thing you know we—him and me —we—"

"So there's going to be a wedding!" Linnea put in. "Well, I tell you something, he might be old, and he might not be no beauty, and he might be a little too fanatic with his religion, and he might of give away the biggest percentage of everything he owns in the world, but I tell you something, Mrs. Sterling," she said, "he's got almost all his own teeth and he don't seem to let the long hair grow out of his nose like some men. Also, he don't smoke and he don't drink! I tell you, Mrs. Sterling," she finished earnestly, so that her friend would take heart, "you could go a lot farther and fare a lot worse."

"Well, anyhow, Linnea—"

"A lot worse," Linnea repeated with emphasis. "Even if we did make fun of him, you and me. We didn't mean it."

"Of course we didn't mean it. But anyhow, Linnea," Mrs. Sterling said, "if you want to hear this. I come here and lived in Brother Bell's house, see." She glanced around the pleasant sun-filled room. "I didn't know what else to do. And the children was so happy here—"

"It's a lovely place," Linnea said, "a lovely place. Anybody'd be happy here. And then, you got it fixed up so cute and keep house so nice."

"It's a double house, you know. The other side is just like this, the same rooms and porches and everything."

What I wouldn't give to be out of that piddling little house and into a nice big place like this! Linnea thought but of course did not say, afraid of seeming envious.

"I don't care very much for the people that's got the other side," Mrs. Sterling said. "The woman thinks she's smart. I'd be glad if I had new neighbors."

"Well, it's lovely," Linnea repeated, looking around. "Just lovely."

"If there's anything I enjoy, it's keeping house," Mrs. Sterling said.

"Me, too. Housecleaning and then sitting back and listening to the clock tick," Linnea said, "looking around at all you done."

"Clean curtains, starched and ironed."

"A scrubbed floor."

"Clean cupboard paper."

The two women drew happy sighs.

"But to continue," Mrs. Sterling said. "Brother Bell likes me very, very much. That I will admit. He was over here an awful lot. And then, Linnea, the first thing I know, we—him and me, that is—we—well, we—" She swallowed, unable to go on for embarrassment.

Linnea stepped into the breach. "I'm sure glad to hear it's all worked out so fine," she said, "wedding coming up and everything. Why, that's wonderful."

"You know about President Woodruff signing the Manifesto?" Mrs. Sterling asked, rocking back and forth, relieved not to have to divulge any more intimate details.

"Do I know about President Woodruff signing the Manifesto? Why, my dear lady, I've rode in the *carriage* with President Woodruff. I ought to know! I've sat and talked to him like you and me are setting here talking. Why, my dear lady, I know the man *personally*." This was said not boastfully but gaily, to instil confidence, the way one tells a child with a cut thumb, "You just leave it to me! Why, I can handle a cut like this better than a doctor!"

"I know," Mrs. Sterling said, "you told me. I heard it from others too. I don't know how you could be so brave. After we get through talking I want you to tell me again."

"Oh, it didn't amount to much," Linnea said modestly. "The way it happened was, you know I told you about Young Mrs. Monteith? Well, she—"

"I sure want you to tell me," Mrs. Sterling said. "Honestly, the whole thing was just wonderful. But anyhow to get back to me and Brother Bell—"

Linnea understood her nervous impatience. "My, yes," she said soothingly. "We got plenty of time to go on about me and the President. The important thing now is your *wedding*."

"Well, when I found out I was in the—in the fam—" She looked down and then up guiltily. "Like this," she said. "I went to Brother Bell and I—"

"Who else?" Linnea said triumphantly. She would tell Ingeborg a thing or two, always believing the worst of anybody.

"I went to Brother Bell," Mrs. Sterling said, "and I said to him 'Brother Bell'—I don't know, I always call him Brother Bell for some reason, I can't seem to bring it over my lips to call him Preserved—which his first name is—'Brother Bell'—I think if we knew each other for fifty years I'd still call him Brother Bell—'Brother Bell,' I said, 'I'm in the—in the fam—like this,' I said." Again she looked guiltily down and guiltily away. "He was very surprised. But pleased. I'd say he was quite tickled. I'd be inclined to say."

"I should just guess he was!" Linnea said.

"Well, anyway, he said, 'You'll never want for anything, Lenora,' he said. 'Anything I can do for you,' he said, 'I'll do for you.' 'The main thing I want you to do for me,' I said, 'is marry me. Naturally. I've got kids, remember. I've got my good name to think of, and my reputation to think of, for them if for nothing else! So I want you to marry me,' I says."

"You certainly have," Linnea said.

"So he says to me—you won't breathe a word of this to anybody, will you?"

"Not a word. Wild horses couldn't make me," Linnea said.

"Because I'd rather die than have it get around. Anyway, he says to me, 'Lenora,' he says, 'you know President Woodruff signed that Manifesto. The Church don't recognize polygamy no more. A man can't have but one wife any more,' he says. 'What's that got to do with you and me?' I says. 'Why, because I can't marry you,' he says, 'much as I think of you. No more polygamy.' 'Listen,' I says, 'you asked me a long time ago to marry you in polygamy and be your second wife and what did I say?' 'You should of took me up on it, shouldn't you, Lenora?' he says. 'And what did I say?' I says. 'Why, I says no, Brother Bell, I do not wish to marry you in polygamy.' 'Call me Preserved,' he says. 'It's so hard for me for some reason or other,' I says. 'Ain't it too bad we didn't do it while we had the chance?' he says."

"Do what?" Linnea asked.

"Why, get married, in polygamy."

"I thought his kids and his wife would of flew off the handle and the next thing to called out the militia if you'd of got married."

"They wouldn't of cared, after they got what they wanted out of him, all he had, or nearly all he had. They wouldn't of cared about him marrying me, in *polygamy*. All they was afraid of, at the time was that I might get a measly dime out of the old—out of Brother Bell."

"So then what happened?" Linnea asked. Parley, tired of watching the bird, was now quietly staring out the window, his nose pressed flat against the glass, his two hands spread out at his temples so that from behind his small boy's head silhouetted against the pane looked as if it had a couple of oversize petaled ears like starfish.

"So then I says, 'Brother Bell, I guess things have come to a pass where you'll *have* to marry me!' 'Well, but, my dear Lenora,' he says, 'I can't. The President has signed that Manifesto and the Church does no longer recognize polygamous marriages.' 'I don't care what the Church recognizes,' I says, 'and anyway I wasn't talking about polygamy. I'm talking about regular marriage. I want you to get a divorce and marry me,' I says. 'From Asenath?' he says. Brother Bell's wife is named Asenath. Ain't that an onry name? It sounds just like her. 'From Asenath,' I says. 'Why, she'll throw me out on my ear, Lenora,' he says. 'I don't know *what* Asenath will do if I come to her with a proposition like that.' 'You find out,' I says, 'or you'll wish you had.' I hated to be so bossy and demanding with him, but I had to, I got my kids to think of, I got my reputation!"

"Sure you have," Linnea said.

"Well, sir, he went right home and he put it up to Asenath, to his wife. He asked her for a divorce so he could marry me."

"And she surprised him and didn't raise a bit of fuss?" Linnea said eagerly. "She said yes, huh? Well, after all, what they really wanted was his money and property. Once they had that sewed up, I guess she nor the kids didn't care whether he got out or got a divorce or married again or what he done! Like Ingeborg says, once the banana's ate up, who

wants the skin?" Linnea smiled broadly, thinking of the happy ending
to come.

"She told him flatly no," Mrs. Sterling said. "Then she called the kids
in and put the proposition up to them. They told him flatly no."

"No?" Linnea said. "But how about the—ain't you—"

"I think I told you about them three kids of his," Mrs. Sterling said,
"when I come out to stay with you in Bountiful that winter."

"You told me, but—"

"The girl's going on for forty. The boys is a little younger. You talk
about old Brother Bell being fanatic. You ought to see them three, they
live, breathe, eat and sleep nothing but church. She's built like a man,
mannish-looking, you know, big husky girl. The boys is a couple of
sissies, like young ladies dressed up in men's clothes. It gives a person
the creeps. Soft white hands, no beards—"

"I remember you telling me."

"And just as onry as a nest of rattlesnakes. Why, when they come to
me that time, they scared me so I couldn't get out of town fast enough.
When they thought I was after their father's money. You know, when I
first met Brother Bell up in Olaf's office."

"But when they got everything signed over to them," Linnea said
anxiously, "they let up, didn't they? They didn't care no more?"

Mrs. Sterling nodded. "Until this come up, they didn't *seem* to care.
But when their mother called them and told them about it, I guess they
all three just about went through the roof. Well, Asenath made out she
fainted and had to have smelling salts and everything. They was just
wild! And anyway, I honestly think they got criminal minds, them kids
has, they ain't normal."

"I hope *your* baby—" Linnea began, and then broke off in some
confusion.

"My baby? Oh, my baby'll be normal, all right," Mrs. Sterling said
matter-of-factly. "But anyhow, they just simply went through the roof.
Why, they threatened everything under the sun. A divorce would bring
disgrace to them, they said, and bring disgrace to the mother, and they
was too high up in the Church to have anything like *that* happen, they
said. 'Not while we can prevent it,' they says. Why, they threatened
downright murder—and they meant it, too. If you ever had the three of
them crowd you up in the corner of a room and surround you, you'd
know they meant it. Why, I tell you, it would of been as much as
Brother Bell's life was worth, to marry me. It would of been as much as
my life was worth, to marry him. Why, he come to me and he was
shaking and trembling like he was scared out of his senses. 'Lenora,' he
says, 'they've got the very old demons in them,' he says. 'Honestly,' he
says, 'I swear if we go on with this, they'll do away with the both of us!' "

"But it finally got all ironed out, huh?" Linnea said nervously.

"Everything was all fixed up? There's going to be a wedding? Like you said?"

"Sure, there's going to be a wedding," Mrs. Sterling said.

"Maybe that will take them down a notch or two, to see that their father can stand up to them, defy them and demand his rights like a man! Lots of times, a bunch like that just has to be stood up to, and they'll back right down like cowards! I'm *proud* of Brother Bell," Linnea said.

"Oh, they didn't back down," Mrs. Sterling said.

"Well, didn't he try it again? Didn't he stand up for his rights?"

"Oh, my, no," Mrs. Sterling said. "He wouldn't any more dare go back and face that outfit and bring the subject up again, than he would stand up to a bunch of grizzly bears!"

"But how did he work things out then?" Linnea asked, bewildered. "You just got me on pins and needles. How did he get Asenath to divorce him so he could marry you?"

"Oh, he didn't," Mrs. Sterling said, "that's what I'm trying to tell you."

"But you said you was going to get married!" Linnea's eyes told her alarm.

"I *am* going to get married. I'd be a pretty sight not getting married, wouldn't I? In a fix like this?" She blushed like a girl of sixteen. "But I don't know where you got the idea I was going to marry Brother Bell! My, no," she said. "I'm going to marry Mr. Brenneman."

Linnea opened her mouth like a goldfish, closed it. "Mr. Brenneman?" she said, opening it again.

Mrs. Sterling spoke swiftly now, her eyes downcast. "Mr. Brenneman is a good friend of mine," she said. "He's asked me a time or two to marry him. I was—tied up with Brother Bell, though, and I couldn't. Not that he thinks there's anything between me and Brother Bell! He'd have a fit if he thought that. No, he thinks me and Brother Bell are just kind of studying religion together."

"And Brother Bell thinks you and Mr. Brenneman are kind of studying religion together," Linnea said, trying to get the whole thing straight in her mind.

"Well, of course, we are," Mrs. Sterling said, not looking at Linnea. "Mr. Brenneman and me are just good friends but he's—well, he's fell in love with me and wants to marry me—and so, since things worked out the way they did with Brother Bell, I accepted him, I took him up on it. I'm wild about—I mean, I like him quite a lot, and he's very nice to the kids and has a steady job and makes good wages. So next Sunday we're going to be married. Just a few friends are invited. The Bishop is going to marry us. Mr. Brenneman's going to give up Theosophy."

"But what about this baby of Brother Bell's? I mean, what about you having a baby in a few months? Ain't Mr. Brenneman going to be pretty upset about that? And do you mean to tell me he don't even know you're in the family way?" Linnea was perfectly bewildered by the complications of all this.

"Oh, he don't pay no attention. He's one of these readers and studiers," Mrs. Sterling explained. "Always got his nose buried in a book when he ain't working."

"Well, but—"

"Do you want to know what Brother Bell thinks of it?"

"Yes, what?" Linnea said.

"First of all, I'd better tell you the main thing," Mrs. Sterling said. "You promise not to tell."

"Over my dead body," Linnea said.

"Well, he didn't sign away *all* his property, even if the kids thought so. He had two or three different pieces left. This house, for instance. He owns this house. And you know what he offered to do when he seen *absolutely* his family wouldn't let him marry me?"

"What did he do?" Linnea asked.

"Why, he offered to sign this place over to me. And give me a thousand dollars in the bank to boot, if I'd relinquish all claims to him."

"This house!" Linnea said, looking around in awe, her mouth slack. "This lovely double house, on this big lot, in this fine location. Oh, my."

"It's worth eighteen hundred dollars," Mrs. Sterling said. "And then, mind you, he offered to put a thousand dollars in the bank for me if I would relinquish all claims."

"A thousand dollars," Linnea said weakly.

"I said I would, naturally," Mrs. Sterling said.

"Naturally. I should think so."

"After we got it all arranged, and he give me the deed to the house and the money in the bank, I told him I was going to marry Mr. Brenneman!"

"I bet he felt *terrible*," Linnea said. "I bet he just practically set down and bawled. A man who could do that much for a woman must be nearly frantic over her."

"Oh, no, he didn't, not so terrible," Mrs. Sterling said. "Oh, he liked me awfully well and all that, but he was anxious to save his own skin. And to tell you the truth I think he was very glad to get out of it. He had been kind of nervous about the baby and everything. I think he was kind of glad to be done with it all."

"But what did he think about you marrying Mr. Brenneman?"

"Well, like I say, I think he was kind of relieved. And now I won't be seeing him no more."

"And you got this property and a thousand dollars," Linnea said marvelling. "And you get to marry that nice young handsome Mr. Brenneman, which anybody in their right senses would naturally rather marry than old Brother Bell. Honestly, I never heard of anything so wonderful!"

"Oh, I could of married Mr. Brenneman quite a while ago but I had to wait and see what I could get out of—I mean, I had to see what arrangements I could make with Brother Bell—"

"You had to first see if the baby's *father* wouldn't marry you, before you married a man that *wasn't* the baby's father. Naturally," Linnea said helpfully. "That's perfectly clear."

"So anyway me and Mr. Brenneman are going to be married next Sunday afternoon," Mrs. Sterling said, getting up and starting for the pump to pump water for coffee, "and I want you to be sure and come."

Linnea looked after her with dazed eyes. A great big beautiful double house like this on a great big lot—worth eighteen hundred dollars—and a thousand dollars in the bank. If it was me, she thought to herself, I'd pinch myself till I was black and blue. Imagine. And going to marry that nice Mr. Brenneman, that even dropped Theosophy and took up Mormonism, to boot. Honestly, it's one of the most wonderful things that ever happened.

Usually astute in the ways of human behavior, her fondness for Mrs. Sterling made her a little thick-skulled, and it was not until a long time later that things, as she said, "sort of dawned" on her. In the meantime, since she had given her promise, she did not even discuss the situation with Ingeborg. She just said Mrs. Sterling was going to marry Mr. Brenneman and let the chips fall where they may. Ingeborg accused her of holding something back, she begged and teased, but Linnea wouldn't reveal a single confidence. Finally, Ingeborg got quite huffy and said Well, if Linnea thought more of Mrs. Sterling than she thought of *her*, she could just *have* Mrs. Sterling. Linnea had a hard time to cajole her back into good humor and could only do so by promising faithfully when the time was ripe, to tell Ingeborg the whole story.

Mrs. Sterling's sister from Ogden was there for the wedding, Mr. Brenneman, his landlady, an old tottering woman with partial cataracts that made her bump into everything, wearing a pheasant-feather toque of twice the usual height and a wine-colored waist, Linnea and Parley (she left the rest of the children at home) and the bishop who did the marrying. It was a pleasant and rather lengthy ceremony, the bishop saying a long benediction over the couple. The bishop had always been a little partial to Mrs. Sterling, as most men were, and he was so delighted that Mr. Brenneman had seen his error, dropped Theosophism and was leaning toward the true gospel, the true religion of Christ on earth, that he mentioned it several times in the prayer, asking special benefits for the bridegroom because of his enlightened state of mind. Mr. Brenneman looked very nice, in a tight brown suit and a striped shirt, with a broad bow tie. He was lobster-colored, uncomfortable and much in love with Mrs. Sterling. He wouldn't let her out of his sight.

Mrs. Sterling wore a soft gray dotted silk, so cleverly contrived that nobody would ever guess that she was *enceinte*. It had a white lace collar and cuffs, and she wore a rose-colored velvet ribbon in her hair. It had never made any difference that one of her dark eyes was slightly cocked, it only gave her prettiness a piquancy that other pretty women seemed not to have.

Her house plants were the only floral decoration for the occasion but they were enough, for, having a green thumb, she had a multitude of them on tiers in the large window, either blooming or so brightly and beautifully foliaged that their leaves were as good as flowers. Her restless canary sang what wedding music there was with thrilling force. "I'd think he'd bust a blood vessel," Linnea said. "Listen to him hollering his head off. Ain't that cute?"

For refreshments Mrs. Sterling, now Mrs. Brenneman, served a big pink cake, but it had boiled icing and somehow or other she had not let the syrup cook long enough, so that it didn't hold up very well. It seemed to want to spread and run, but everybody pronounced the cake perfectly delicious. She served it on hand-painted china.

The bride's sister Peterina, from Ogden, sat by Linnea on the lounge while they ate their cake and drank their coffee. She said Mr. Sterling married the two Norwegians—and they were all living together in the same little house. How did they get along? Linnea wanted to know. Like a charm, Peterina said. The gossip was, that they were even better housekeepers than her sister, now Mrs. Brenneman. When they washed woodwork, they had to make a mark, or they would never know where they had been. They were also very saving. They did not speak much English. The oldest wife had two babies already and was well on her way to having a third, but the youngest wife, the beauty, had not conceived yet. The talk was, that she couldn't for some reason or other. Mr. Sterling was very partial to the beauty, however, and that made the only friction in the household. However, the oldest girl had the babies and that seemed to reconcile her a little. The talk was, she was inclined to be sulky with Mr. Sterling and she used to go for days sometimes without speaking to her sister, but otherwise the household was a happy one. All three were known for their piety.

"I'll never forget your sister's face," Linnea said, "when Mr. Sterling come in with that one Norwegian girl, and then went back and got the other, and stood there as big as life and said he was going to marry them both. That was the start of everything." She looked over at the newly wedded couple, eating a slice of cake off the same plate. "If Mr. Sterling hadn't done what he done, Mrs. Sterling would of been up there in her little house in Ogden to this day, keeping house."

"I guess she would," Peterina said. "But of course Brother Bell was already after her, writing her letters and all. He might of persuaded her to leave her husband anyway. He was very set on her at the time. I don't know, sometimes I think Lenora's a case where still water runs deep."

"She would of been up there in Ogden to this day, keeping house," Linnea repeated loyally.

"I guess Brother Bell's gone by the board now, huh?" Peterina asked, laughing. "Well, if it was me I wouldn't shed any tears."

"If it was me, either," Linnea said. She wondered if Peterina knew about the baby and decided she didn't.

"Well, I'm glad they're married," the woman said. "She'll make as good a wife as a man can get, but she ain't no good alone."

"That goes for a lot of people," Linnea said.

Three months later, on the last day of January, at high noon, Mrs. Sterling's baby was born. Linnea got there too late to assist with the actual birth, though Estelle had run as hard as she could down to get her and was so out of breath and panting so hard when she arrived that she could scarcely make herself understood. "Mamma wants you *quick*," she panted, and Linnea got her hat and coat on and grabbed her midwife's case, and away she hurried. But she was too late. The neighbor next door, the one Mrs. Sterling didn't care particularly for, had already delivered the baby. That was a disappointment to Linnea but she at once took charge, explaining that she was the midwife who had been sent for. "So I'll go ahead here now, if you don't mind," she said courteously.

"Mind!" the woman said. "Why would I mind? *I'm* certainly not a midwife!"

"Well, you did a fine job here," Linnea said. "Maybe you missed your calling."

The woman had large cold blue eyes and narrow lips. Linnea could see why Mrs. Sterling was not overly fond of her and wished she would move. "Mr. Brenneman sent for me. He had to go back to work," she said. "He said I should keep my eye on Mrs. Sterling. I mean Mrs. Brenneman. Could I help it if the baby was born?"

"Goodness, I wasn't blaming you. You did a fine job. That's what I'm saying," Linnea said.

"It wasn't *my* fault," the woman said crossly. "When the baby was coming, what else could I do? Did you want me to hold everything up till you got here?"

"No, indeed," Linnea said. "You did exactly the right thing."

She breathed more freely when the woman, who claimed to have had a nice lamb stew ruined by her absence from home, took her leave. "She did fine," Linnea said to Mrs. Brenneman, "but the onry way she has with her takes the joy out of everything." She eyed her patient earnestly. "Did you have a hard time?" she asked.

Mrs. Brenneman did not look much the worse for wear. "Why, no, not very," she said. "It come so fast, though. That was the only trouble. I didn't hardly have time to turn around before here it was." She was pale, of course, and spoke weakly, and seemed to be so tired she could scarcely keep her eyes open, but otherwise she was just fine.

Linnea set out the things to bathe the little newcomer. The winter sun came in so brilliantly that she had to pull the blind down part way, to keep out the glare. She shut her eyes tight as she did so for the dripping icicles hanging down outside the window and the diamond-crusted snow on the ground sent out such dazzling shafts they stabbed the eyeballs like knives. "You take a little snooze," she said, coming back across the room. The woman in the bed was already doing so, it seemed. Her eyes were shut. Linnea glanced at her admiringly. She was very pretty, lying there against the white pillow shams, her dark hair mussed. She didn't begin to look thirty-eight years old.

Well, it was all over now. The little fellow was here. She turned her attention to him, not any too soon, for he himself took a notion to demand it at just that moment, letting out a sharp cry. "There, there," she murmured, rocking him back and forth in her arms. He liked the motion and stopped. She set about bathing him then and dressing him, spreading her knees apart to make the widest possible lap, deftly dipping the soft linen washcloth in the dishpan with her right hand and squeezing it out so it wouldn't be too wet, while she supported the baby's limber neck and soft head with her left. "Well, you're a little beauty," she confided to him, "if ever I seen one. Look at all the hair you got—why, I bet it's two inches long."

"What color is it?" His mother called anxiously from the bed.

"It's dark," Linnea said, "but you never can go on what color a baby's hair is when it's born. This'll all come out anyway and new hair come in." She smoothed it back with the damp washrag. "It looks like he's going to have a cowlick here in front."

"Does it?"

"It sure does. I should think Brother Bell would be nearly dead with curiosity to see him, when he finds out he's here," she said.

Mrs. Brenneman did not say anything. There was an uncomfortable moment of silence. Linnea caught on right away. Mrs. Brenneman did not wish to speak of Brother Bell again. Let the dead past bury its dead. From now on, it was to be as though Brother Bell had never existed. "He's got blue eyes," Linnea said hastily. "Bluish, that is. Only of course all babies have bluish eyes. They'll probably turn out to be brown, like yours." Mr. Brenneman also had brown eyes, didn't he? That made it handy. And what color were Brother Bell's? She couldn't for the life of her remember. Were they brown, too?

"How much do you think he weighs?" Mrs. Brenneman asked.

"Oh, seven or eight pounds at least," Linnea said. "He's a perfect beauty." It was then she turned back the blanket all the way and saw his extremities. She gave a little gasp. "Oh, my," she said.

"What is it? For heaven's sake, what is it?" the mother asked, alarmed.

"Nothing," Linnea said, "nothing at all. I just said that because the little rascal is so strong, he just about jumped out of my lap." She did not add that he also had six toes on his left foot and six toes on his right foot,—in other words, a double big toe on each foot. Otherwise he was, as she had said, a perfect beauty.

While she finished washing and dressing him, she was in a quandary. Should she mention it to Mrs. Brenneman? *How* embarrassed she would be! She decided not to say a word and let Mrs. Brenneman find out for herself and then mention it if she wanted to.

Mrs. Brenneman found out, but she never said a word about it. Not a word, ever, to Linnea. Linnea never said a word to her about it, either. Yet it did not spoil their friendship, it was no obstacle between them. They merely seemed to have made a pact of silence. "I guess I'd of kept just as mum," Linnea had occasion to say afterwards. "Who wouldn't, under the same circumstances?"

It could not be laid at her door that she was the one who had spread the news around that Mrs. Brenneman's baby was no more related to Brother Bell than to the Man in the Moon. He was the spitting image of Mr. Brenneman. Not only did he have an identical cowlick but he had the Brenneman double toes. It was the neighbor lady, the one who thought she was smart and who had delivered the baby before Linnea could get there, who whispered the news around.

That was how it came to Ingeborg's ears. She came triumphantly to Linnea. "Your fine Mrs. Sterling," she taunted. "I thought it was Brother Bell's baby!"

"Who says it ain't?"

"It's got a cowlick and double toes, just like Mr. Brenneman. So there."

"Well, what of it?" Linnea asked crossly.

"What of it! Why, it's been Mr. Brenneman's right along, that's what of it. BUT," she added ominously.

"BUT. Brother Bell must of had pretty good reasons for imagining it was *his* baby, or he wouldn't of deeded her the property and give her all that money!" Ingeborg went on accusingly.

"How did you find out about it?"

"No thanks to you," Ingeborg sniffed. "I found it out about it, though. There's loopholes for them things to get around. Murder will out, you want to remember," she said. "It just goes to show you what I said all the time about Mrs. Sterling. But no, you wouldn't pay a bit of attention to me. She ain't no better than she should be, I said—I said it from the start, the minute I laid eyes on her—and," jubilantly, "this proves I was right. She ain't."

Linnea sat staring off into space, thinking. She did not seem to hear Ingeborg. "Honestly to goodness, if that wasn't the slickest thing," she mused softly.

"You ain't going to be friends with her no more now, are you?" Ingeborg asked.

"I don't know why not," Linnea said.

"Well, I should think you *would* know. Because she ain't no good, that's why!"

"It all depends on what you call no good." She was still staring off into space. "Me, now," she said. "What I happen to call no good is somebody that's mean to somebody that can't defend theirself. Or somebody that's stingy, that won't give nobody nothing, even if it was a matter of life and death. Or somebody that says mean things that cuts somebody to the quick when they ain't got no comeback. That's what *I* happen to call no good."

"You know very well that's got nothing in the world to do with what I'm talking about. What I'm talking about is something entirely different. I'm talking about *no good*, and you know very well what I mean."

"I'm talking about no good, too," Linnea said gently. "That's what I just got through telling you."

"Well, how about a no-good slut of a woman," Ingeborg, exasperated, burst out, "that lives with two men till she don't know *what* kind of a baby she's going to have or who it belongs to!"

"Oh, she knows who it belongs to all right!"

"She knows it belongs to Mr. Brenneman when it should by rights be Brother Bell's, that's what she knows!"

"What are you so mad about it for?" Linnea asked. "It ain't no skin off your nose. It ain't got nothing to do with you."

"It just makes me mad, is all, burning mad."

"I guess it's up to nature," Linnea said. "Whose it ought to be." She had to laugh a little, thinking of the whole affair.

"And that old Brenneman ain't even a member of the Church," Ingeborg said accusingly. "Yet."

"I don't know why you'd call him old. He's three or four years younger than she is." Linnea hummed softly for a moment. "She sure maneuvered that as slick as a whistle," she said. "She's really well fixed now. Mind you, a woman that started out like she started out—kicked out of house and home, throwed out on the world, with two children— as good as didn't have a dime—didn't know which way to turn—"

"She knowed where to turn all right. I didn't notice her wasting any time."

"Mind you, she didn't have *nothing* when she started. And now she's sitting on top of the world. She's really got property. Why, that house she's got is worth eighteen hundred dollars. She's got a thousand dollars in the bank. And I guess Mr. Brenneman makes good money. She nor her children ain't going to want for anything. No, sir. One thing's sure and certain: she ain't going to be anybody to sneeze at."

Ingeborg had not thought of this, but it was true. Even she was convinced of that. Mrs. Sterling was really well fixed now. All the censure in the world wasn't going to do much damage to a woman as well heeled as she was. Nobody was really going to think much the less of her in the long run, if she behaved herself from now on, which she gave every evidence of doing. Ingeborg had never in her life said that it hurt anybody to have a few acquaintances that had a little something. Also, she remembered belatedly that Jesus had said something about somebody casting the first stone. It never hurt anybody to be on friendly terms with a wealthy woman: a person never knew when such an acquaintance was going to come in handy. She sighed and then she shrugged her shoulders. "Well, it ain't *me* that's been against her particularly!" she said. "*I* don't care what she does: Why should I? Like you say, it ain't no skin off *my* nose." She looked at Linnea and laughed. "Does Brother Bell know about it having six toes? That would sure cinch it, if he did. I guess it'd be something he'd never get over as long as he lives— after giving her all he gave her, all that money and that nice piece of property!"

"Who knows?" Linnea said, laughing heartily too. "You ain't seen him with his shoes off, have you? Maybe he's got six toes himself!"

CHAPTER 22

⇢⇢ ⇠⇠

It had been a cold and rainy spring but it turned warm enough that Saturday night to throw off some of the extra covers. Parley, up with the birds, shook Mamma awake in bright sunshine. She yawned and blinked her eyes and looked at the clock. It said only ten minutes to five. "Parley!" she said, "you naughty boy!" But then she saw what a beautiful day it was going to be and forgave him. Gently she said, "Go and get back in bed with Rudie! It's still the middle of the night," and smiled, shutting her eyes to the golden light. "You naughty boy," she repeated, like a compliment. It was going to be a hot and beautiful day.

"Breakfast?" he asked winningly, leaning on his two fat elbows on the side of the bed, like the model for a cherub. He had had a bath, as everybody else had, the night before, and he looked fine-spun and rosy, like a confection to gobble down, in his little white union suit. "Oh, Parley," Mamma said, "what made you get up so early? It's Sunday. Sunday mornings everybody gets to sleep later. I tell you, why don't you crawl in here with me?" she asked, giving dead-to-the-world Bertha a boost with her behind so she would move over and make room for him, "and we'll shut our eyes and take a nice little snooze together. What do you say?"

Agreeably he climbed in and snuggled down beside her, she pulled the sheet up so it kept the sun out of both her own and his eyes, and they lay there perfectly still. Sleep claimed her again, or rather a half-sleep for she seemed to be floating along on a wide comfortable dark stream and yet was aware of her little boy's head on her arm. "Go to sleep," she whispered, gently patting his plump chest, "take a little snooze with Mamma." Drowsily she opened her eyes and peeked at him. His eyes were wide open and blue as sapphires in the whitish gloom under the sheet. His face was full of irrepressible laughter. He was as wide awake as a rabbit in a pea patch. "Oh, Parley," she said, "you're wide awake!"

He giggled heartily, letting both his arms and his legs fly outwards and giving the rest of himself a wiggle.

"You didn't even intend to go back to sleep, did you?" she accused him, wide awake herself now, giving him a hug and planting a kiss on his silky topknot.

"Well," she said, while she was getting breakfast, "the time's going to come when I'll get to sleep on Sunday mornings and when it does, I'm sure going to make the most of it."

"It's the first real day of summer," Gertrude announced, coming in from outside with a bucket of water. "It's even going to be hot."

"That's what I noticed," Mamma said, expertly flipping over a pancake, "when Parley woke me up, although it wasn't hardly daylight. You know what we'd ought to do this afternoon? Come on, get up to the table now, all of you. There's enough pancakes for you to get started on. You know what we'd ought to do?"

They all made a rush for their places, Parley climbing into his high chair. He was too big for it, the wooden tray that swung up over the back of it and down and fitted over the front like a convenient little table, wedged him in too tightly but he didn't seem to mind. He got into it and Bertha pulled the tray down in place. Mamma said one of these days he was going to have to sit up to the table like the rest of the kids, but so far he could still squeeze into the high chair, and there every mealtime, he squeezed, but Mamma felt it was just a matter of days.

"No, what had we ought to do?" Bertha said, Gertrude, Stellie and Rudie echoing her.

Mamma began putting butter and syrup on the pancakes—she fixed them for all the children. She had always done it and they said they tasted better that way than if they fixed them themselves. "Why, I tell you," she said, "this afternoon, after we eat dinner, we'll all get dressed up and go for a nice long walk and get some visiting done. I promised everybody for I don't know how long."

"Me, too?" Parley, delighted with the suggestion, inquired.

"You?" Mamma said, blinking her eyes teasingly at him. "Of course not! What an idea! You'll have to stay home and paint the fence!"

Parley nearly collapsed laughing at the humor of this and so infectious was his merriment that they all had to join with him in it.

That afternoon, at about two-thirty, Mamma and her family set out on the enjoyable business of paying a round of Sunday visits. It having turned really hot, as she predicted, they were clad in their best summertime garments. Rudie's and Parley's suits were of heavy wool, and they sweated in them, but as Mamma said, it was different with boys than with girls and they only had the one good suit apiece which had to be worn winter and summer, for Best, until it was outgrown and another replaced it, equally hot. They did not complain, however, but trudged along in stiffly starched blouses and round straw hats as though they were the most fortunate boys in the world. Mamma and the girls, in white dimity, under sturdy black cotton umbrellas, looked a good deal cooler, but their great amount of underclothes and petticoats made them merely look so. They perspired too.

They made their first brief call on Young Mrs. Monteith because she was right in the neighborhood. "Now I want to warn you," Mamma said at the gate. "You had your breakfast, and you had a good substantial dinner at one o'clock with heel of beef, and I know you ain't hungry. So listen here to me. Parley, you listen, too—you're big enough. If anybody offers you anything to eat, you politely shake your head and say no thanks. Do you get that straight?"

"We're supposed to say no thanks," they said in a chorus.

"Well, just remember that, is all. I don't want to tell you again."

To Mamma's pleased surprise, who should be sitting in the parlor when Young Mrs. Monteith hospitably ushered them into it, sitting there holding the sleeping Rosebud—now a husky girl of nine months—and gently rocking back and forth, but Old Mrs. Monteith. She made frequent visits now, and the two wives had become good friends. She smiled when the Ecklunds came in and apologized for not getting up. "Rosebud weighs a ton," she said.

Young Mrs. Monteith offered them cake, pie, cookies. She begged that they would accept something.

"No, thank you," they all said. "We just got done eating."

Stellie spoke up softly. "I could maybe eat a cookie," she said, not looking in her mother's direction.

"Oh, *could* you?" Young Mrs. Monteith said, overjoyed. She put a stack of three puffy soft molasses cookies in her hand.

"Thank you very much," Stellie said and politely ate them, being careful of crumbs upon the floor. Mamma tried to catch her eye, but it did no good.

Outside, Mamma said, "You all done fine, except Stellie here. Stellie, the next time somebody offers you something you say no, thanks. Why, we had a big breakfast and a big dinner. I ain't taking my kids around visiting on a Sunday to eat everybody out of house and home!"

At Mrs. Golightly's, they were offered custard pie. "No, thank you," they said, though Mrs. Golightly insisted almost with tears in her eyes that they all have a piece. Except Stellie, that is. She did not say she would actually be willing to eat some custard pie. She merely did not join in the refusal.

"How about you, Stellie?" Mrs. Golightly asked gladly, ready to cut a generous wedge. "You won't turn down custard pie, will you?"

"Well—" Stellie said, not looking at Mamma.

"Oh, she *couldn't*," Mamma said. "She couldn't possibly. Why, she's as full as a tick."

But Stellie could. Politely she took the proffered piece and politely she ate it.

Outside, when Mamma rebuked her, she wailed, "But Mamma, she *made* me."

"Oh, no, she didn't, young lady," Mamma said. "From now on either you mind me or you go home."

But at Mrs. Orbit's they all weakened and all succumbed, for Guinevere had baked a towering coconut cake and was so proud of it that she would have been mortally wounded if they had not accepted at least a "sample."

Mrs. Orbit was the Novel Reader of old—indeed, she laid an open book titled *Marion Gray, or The Heiress of Redstone Hall* face downwards on the seat of the rocking chair on the front porch when she got up to welcome delightedly the six guests who came trooping up the front walk. Her eyes were red-rimmed. It was a *very* interesting book, and *very* small print, she said. She had had her nose buried in it for hours. For some reason, Mrs. Orbit was not the untidy woman she once had been. To her visitors' surprise they saw that her hair was neatly combed, her skirt unspotted, her waist starched and clean. It didn't take Mamma long to see what was behind it all. The Orbit daughters, Guinevere, now fourteen, Rosabella, now twelve, and Juanita, now ten, had wrought the change. The eldest daughter, Gloriana, had died in the diphtheria epidemic, the winter of the Snow, Mrs. Orbit bearing up under the blow almost notoriously well, being Christian Scientist. She also bore up under the loss of two other infant children, one after another, carried off by disease.

"It only goes to show you," Linnea said afterwards. "Sometimes it ain't training at all. Why, except for cleaning the parlor that time she invited me and the kids for Christmas, I don't think Mrs. Orbit cleaned the house from one year's end to the other. They lived in filth. Everybody knows that. Why, she never even throwed her dishwater out and God only knows what she done with the garbage . . . and never a decent meal. Them little girls had to take a slice of bread and butter and fry theirselves a couple of eggs from the time they could walk, if they wanted anything to eat. And Mrs. Orbit going to the library and coming home loaded down with them stacks of novels and reading till she was green in the face. You'd think the girls would of grew up just like her, but instead of that, look at them. Just look at them. Honestly, it seems like training ain't got a thing in the world to do with how people is going to be!"

For the past two years Guinevere, with the help of her two younger sisters, had taken complete charge of the house, and no fanatical Scandanavian housewife could have had more to show for her efforts. The Orbit children abhorred reading the way the children of a drunkard will sometimes shun liquor, and by never tasting a drop of it sidestep the fate of their unfortunate parent. They did not attend school (an education being something a female could take or leave alone) and since they did not have to go out to work, their father making enough to support the household, they were much at home. This was the joy of their lives. Their mother, whom they adored and pampered, they kept coifed and neat appearing. They let her loll and read as she pleased, so long as she kept out from underfoot. For her part, she let them take complete charge and had never a word to say about anything they did, except to offer extravagant praise which spurred them on to still greater efforts. Their father, lauding them to the skies, was so appreciative that tears would come into his eyes when he spoke of their accomplishments, and for him they worked like beavers. They housecleaned, they learned to cook, they learned to wash and iron. In fact, nobody in the whole city had brought up three girls to equal them as housekeepers. The Orbits now lived in a house as neat as a pin, glittering with cleanliness. The smell of soapsuds and furniture polish was never out of it. They sat down to delicious meals served at regular hours on spotless tablecloths. Mr. Orbit would be all broken up when he told people about it.

"It's a mystery to me," Linnea said, "when you consider the way them poor little girls was brought up."

Guinevere had baked the huge snowy cake, frosted with white and strewn liberally with curly shreds of coconut. They did not have a great deal of company and she grew flustered with a kind of choking pride when they did. Her hand shook a little as, with the knife poised over the mountainous cake, she said eagerly, "Please. Oh, please. You just *got* to sample it. It might taste kind of flat. You could tell me if you think it tastes kind of flat. . . ."

Even the youngest of the visitors knew it meant a great deal to the little housewife, and they all looked at each other, and saw that Mamma was going to weaken, and started to say, "Oh, we couldn't—" but changed it to, "Well, maybe a *little* piece."

"Oh, please," Guinevere said, a spot of color burning in each of her cheeks. "But of course it might not be nothing to brag of. It might taste kind of flat."

Mrs. Orbit, on her way into the house, had picked up her book, and taken it along with her, although of course she had no intention of reading it for the time being, and was hugging it, still open, against her bosom. "I'd bet my eye teeth it ain't flat," she said. "Anyway, you'll have to give it a try or she'll never get over it."

"Well—" they said politely. It did look so wonderfully good. "Just a little *piece*."

Guinevere, exultant, cut huge slices and passed them beamingly around.

Nothing was offered them at the Castletons. Old Mr. Castleton met them totteringly at the front gate and said with an embarrassed face that Ma had drifted off to sleep in her chair and he didn't like to wake her as she didn't sleep so good at nights. However, in about half an hour. . . .

"We didn't really intend to more'n come in and just say hello," Mamma said. "And we hardly have time to do that because we've got several places to go to, so you just tell Mrs. Castleton we stopped by and hope she's well. Is she?" she asked.

The only thing that had really got very old with Mr. Castleton were his eyes. They had that blurred rather wild look that old eyes have, with sharp pupils in the center of hazy rings like the blue tinge on glassware. Otherwise he looked about the same. His voice may have been a little higher and more querulous. "She's fine. Losing flesh, though. Ain't any bigger than a minute now. Don't sleep so good. But otherwise she's fine. Sassy as ever. Only, once in a while she gets a notion Villa's still alive. 'Villa,' she'll say, 'bring your lesson books over here and set here by me,' she'll say. Villa was the girl borned to us when my wife was forty years old, after both our two boys was grown. She died when she was eight or nine, I forget which. Caught on fire out in the back yard. The boys had built a big bonfire and it was a windy day—"

"I know," Linnea said, "she told me."

"Well, sir, her dress flared up in flames, and little gump that she was, instead of standing still, she run screaming out into the stubble field, in all that wind—"

"I know," Linnea said swallowing.

"—and naturally she was burned to a cinder. My wife caught her, though. She beat out the flames. She was burned herself pretty bad. The little thing didn't die right away. It was either two or three days later, I forget which. All I can say is, it was awful sad."

"Sad!" Linnea said. "It'd be enough to send a person completely out of their mind. I should think it was sad!"

"She still talks about you not taking Villa's little clothes that time she offered them to you," the old man said.

"I knowed they meant a good deal to her," Linnea said. "And I couldn't of made them over and let my kids run around in them right under her nose—why, we was living right next door. It would of broke her heart."

"For years she didn't hardly ever look at them, but now she looks at them almost every day. Handles them," Mr. Castleton cleared his throat and blinked his eyes. "She gets to imagining Villa's just come home from school, or that they're fixing to go to town together like they used to do. She comes to herself, though, in a little while, and gets a kind of bashful look and says, My goodness, for a minute there it almost seemed like Villa was here. I guess I got to imagining things. . . .'"

"I sure remember that pretty hat you give me when I was little," Gertrude spoke up.

"What hat was that?" the old man asked.

"Why, that pretty hat! Don't you remember? I dropped my hat down the toilet!"

"You fished it out," Linnea said, "with your long rake. We was fixing to go to the Seely wedding. Gertrude dropped the hat she was going to wear down the toilet and when you got it out it was all spoiled. So I was going to make her wear her old hat—"

"—but you called me over," Gertrude broke in eagerly, "and Mrs. Castleton went in the bedroom and got *that beautiful hat* and give it to me, and I got to wear that. Don't you remember?"

The old man tried hard, but he could not recall it to save his life. He squeezed his face all up together in the middle. He shut his eyes. He even removed his old-fashioned hat and scratched the top of his head with his gnarled forefinger, but nothing helped.

"I don't see how you could forget *that*," Gertrude said, in disbelief.

"Why, the children talk about it to this day," Mamma said. "It was a fine straw and it had—"

"No, sir," the old man said. "I'll be blamed if I can remember it."

Gertrude said, when they got out of earshot, "Imagine. He couldn't even remember that hat!"

"That's because he's so old," Mamma said.

"I hope *I* never get that old!"

"You better knock on wood to show you don't mean it, Gertrude," Mamma said. "The time's going to come when you'll change your tune."

Gertrude, laughing, reached out and rapped with her knuckles on a wooden gatepost. "Just the same, that would be terrible," she said. "Not even to remember a *hat!*"

They paid their last and lengthiest visit to their old friend Ingeborg. It was past four when they got there. The children at once begged to be allowed to run up to the cemetery and play and the two women were happy to give their permission, but at five o'clock when Ingeborg set out a small feast—Linnea begged her not to but while they carried on a conversation she went ahead and did it anyway—set coffee buns, and butter, and cheese, and sardines, and peach preserves, and squares of feathery gingerbread and heaven knows what all out upon the table— they all came whooping back. "You run right on out again," Linnea told her brood. "There's nothing here for you. You'll get your supper when we get home."

"I'm hungry," Stellie announced brazenly. Her mother and sisters and brothers stared at her with something very like fascination.

Bertha had had Parley in tow but now he broke away from her and came and scrambled up on his mother's lap. He was fairly steaming in his tight wool suit. She smoothed his damp forehead. "Hungry!" she said to Stellie. "I don't see how you got the gall even to think the word, let alone say it."

"Well, I am, just the same," Stellie didn't look anybody in the eye.

"You kids run right on out again while Ingeborg feeds her kids," Mamma said. "Her and me are going to have our coffee, and then I'll call you, and we'll go home, and I'll fix some supper for you."

"I'm hungry," Parley said confidentially.

"How about you kids?" Ingeborg asked Bertha and Gertrude. They blushed and did not answer. "And Rudie here?" Rudie shook his head manfully but he had a wistful look on his face, and he *was* sizing up what was on the table. "They're hungry," she said triumphantly. "What do you want to wait till you get home for, when I've got supper all ready here? Why in the world not feed them? Then you won't have to bother when you get home."

"But they couldn't be," Linnea protested. "They couldn't *possibly* be!" She glared at Stellie who had started it all. "I know a young lady that's going to be left entirely at home next time we go visiting!"

Stellie tossed her head.

"All kids are hungry," Ingeborg said. "There ain't any time when they can't eat."

"There comes a limit," Mamma said. "Not a one of my kids wants a bite to eat. I *know* they don't. Especially Stellie, that I don't for the life of me know what's got into the girl."

"Well, mine do," Ingeborg said, and soon all the nine children were having, though not regularly set down to the table, a piece of this, and a slice of that, and a serving of something else, laughing and chattering and having the time of their lives. Mamma found herself eating, too. She had her eye on Stellie (who had a serious reckoning in store for her) but Stellie didn't once return her glance. She ate at least one coffee bun with cheese and at least one with sardines, and possibly one with peach preserves. She certainly had at least one huge square of gingerbread. "I hope she gets her fill," Mamma's expression said grimly, "because there's going to be a reckoning. *That* I know."

She decided to use the method of icy disdain upon her, since Stellie was now nearly ten years old and really too big a girl to be licked, but she seemed to be impervious to it. When they were at home and Linnea was beginning to put the boys to bed, her patience snapped.

"Golly," Stellie whined, "are you going to make us kids go to bed without our *supper?*"

Linnea turned on her in fury. "Without your *supper?*" she said. "How you got the nerve to stand there and say such a thing is a mystery to me. Why, you've ate from the time you got up this morning until this very minute! I told you, I give you strict orders, to be polite and not take what people offered you, since I don't want to take my kids visiting and have people say we come in on them like a lot of hungry locusts! I fed you good, and I give you strict orders, and what did you do?"

"She ate all the time," Bertha said, admiringly.

"She never turned down nothing," Gertrude added, fascinated. "Not one single solitary thing."

Stellie glared sullenly. "Well, I don't care," she said. "I really *am* hungry. So there."

Mamma looked at her for a long moment, considering what to do. Then she went over to the breadbox and took out a loaf of bread. She cut three large slices. Sternly she cut the three slices into small cubes. There was quite a pile of them. She went over to the cupboard and got a big vegetable bowl, came back and dumped the bread cubes into it. None of the children, nor Stellie, all of them watching, said anything. She pushed open the back door and got a pan of milk out of the screened-in cooler nailed on the wall outside. Grimly she skimmed off some of the thick leatherly cream into a pitcher, left large islands of it still floating around and around on the milk. She lifted the pan and tipped it, sloshing out milk and clots of cream on to the high-piled bread. She set the pan down.

"Sugar?" she asked ominously.

"Yes," Stellie said defiantly.

"All right." Mamma reached up in the cupboard again, bringing down the squat china sugar bowl with the moss roses on the side. All the children were watching with wide eyes, not saying a word. Mamma shook one heaping teaspoonful of sugar over the bread and milk, reached in and scooped out another, scattered it over. "Another?" she asked.

"Yes," Stellie said, "please."

Mamma set her up to the table with the huge bowl before her. "Now you eat," she said. "You eat every crumb. If you leave one crumb of bread or one drop of milk, I swear I'll blister you till you can't set down for a week."

Stellie's cheeks were very red, her guilty eyes very bright, but she sat there and ate every bite of bread and milk.

It was when Mamma, Bertha and Gertrude got ready to go to bed an hour or two later that they noticed there was something wrong with her. She had been as quiet as a gorged cat after she ate, her cheeks staying red, and after a little she had climbed up into the far corner of the lounge and there she dozed off, curled into a ball, her head between her two bent elbows, her face hidden. Mamma had glanced her way a time or two. "I wonder what it was that got into Stellie," she said. "I never seen anything to equal her."

When Bertha, bidden to do so, had shook her sister gently by the shoulder, to make her get up and get undressed and get ready for bed, Stellie woke with a start. Her eyes looked oddly glazed, her cheeks still redder. She stared at them all for a moment and then she started passionately to cry. Mamma was by her side in an instant. "There, there, darling," she said soothingly. "What is it? What is it? Mamma's not mad at you. Nobody's mad at you. Don't cry."

Stellie cried still harder. "I'm so sick, I'm so sick, I'm so sick," she said, shuddering.

Mamma told Gertrude, who was closest, to get the slop jar out from under the bed in the bedroom *quick,* and bring it, and Gertrude scrambled for it and got it and brought it as quick as she possibly could. Not a moment too soon, however, for agonized Stellie, rolling her eyes in terror, let fly, spewing up her heels. Between torrents, while Mamma held her head and said it would soon all be over and Bertha hovered near by with a dipper of water, she said, moaning with nausea and shivering and shaking, "Oh, Mamma, I'll never eat again. I promise. I'll never, never eat again. . . ."

After she stopped vomiting and Mamma got her to bed, she still kept saying it, reminding herself . . . ginger cookies . . . custard pie . . . coconut cake . . . strawberry shortcake . . . all . . . that . . . gooey . . . ishy . . . nasty . . . horrible . . . stuff. . . . "I'll never eat another bite as long as I live," she kept repeating. She was so cold she could never get warm, her teeth chattered, she shook like a leaf. Then she was so hot she threw all the covers off. She couldn't breathe, she said, she was so hot. She was smothering. At first Mamma was just going to sit by her a little while and watch until she started to feel better, but Bertha and Gertrude had been long asleep and she was still sitting there. "I'll never . . . never . . . never . . . eat again. I promise, Mamma. I give my solemn promise. . . ." Stellie spoke very softly now, hardly above a whisper.

"Of course you won't," Mamma said comfortingly, reaching out and taking one of her small hands and patting it. "Naturally you won't." My, she was hot. Her hands was as hot as fire. She reached out and felt Stellie's face . . . it was burning so that by comparison her own fingers felt ice-cold. Her fever must be a hundred and five. But then, children often flared up with a high, high temperature and it didn't mean a thing. Anyway, all she could do was sit here and watch till morning. She heard the clock strike three, and the little ding! that meant three-thirty, but she didn't hear it strike four. At quarter after she woke up with a start, feeling cold and stiff. She blinked her eyes, rubbed them, leaned closer. Why, what was this? She pulled back the covers hastily, lifted up Stellie's nightgown. The child was covered from head to foot with a fiery red rash, her face, neck, arms, every part of her. She was all broken out. Linnea give a little sigh of relief and sat down weakly in her chair. "Measles," she breathed happily "all it is is measles."

And that's all it was.

Gertrude and Rudie did not catch it for some reason, but Bertha and Parley did.

"My," Mamma said happily, doing the thousand and one things she had to do with three children sick in bed, "I'm so relieved it ain't something *serious*. I don't mind the extra work. Just so long as it ain't *serious*."

It wasn't. It didn't seem to be. Stellie started to get better. She always thought that overeating had brought the measles on. She did not keep her promise never to eat again, but was hungry in a day or two. However, her unexampled appetite and exceptional gluttony of the Sunday before must have been a pre-disease phenomenon for it never returned. "A good thing, too," Mamma said teasingly, "or I'd of had some fun trying to keep her filled up. Not only that, she'd of growed to such a size that by next summer she couldn't squeeze into the Tabernacle!"

Bertha and Parley seemed to have the disease lightly. Though she had come down with it two days after Stellie, Bertha recovered at almost the same time. Parley didn't have much of a case either. Mamma was in high spirits over the way everything turned out. She never lost her patience once, but hummed at her work, and was pleased and gay. "They could of really *had* something," she said, "something serious. I tell you, when I was sitting by Stellie that night I didn't know *what* we might be up against."

Parley wasn't very sick . . . not very . . . but the disease didn't quite act the same with him. It acted a little different. When the girls got over it, they got over it. When the fever stopped, it stopped. It was different with him. He had fever, then he was cool and free of fever, for one day, two days—and then here he was feverish again!

It baffled Linnea. He had got over his fever! The spots were all gone! What was the big idea of him flaring up with a temperature again? She hovered over him uneasily. "What's the matter with Mamma's big kid?" she said. "What's the matter, Parley? Parley?"

He whimpered and whimpered. It wasn't like him to whimper. He was the best little boy that ever lived. She told him so a hundred times. "What's the matter?" she asked over and over again. "What's got into the best little boy that ever lived?"

He had no way of telling her. He just got hotter and hotter while she watched him and felt her bones turn to water with fear and apprehension and something wring out her heart like you wring out a dish-rag. He drank water. He'd drink all the water she would pour down him and ask for more, but he wouldn't eat anything, gruel, soup, custard or bread pudding made especially for him. "Please, darling, please take just one little spoonful," she'd beg him, but he wouldn't. He'd push the spoon away. He'd whimper. She tried over and over to give him milk but he'd push the cup away. "No, no, no," he'd say.

What was it? What ailed him? She couldn't stand to be away from his side for more than a few minutes at a time and was always hanging over him, searching his face, looking into his eyes, saying, "What's the matter, darling? Tell me." She didn't sleep. She hung over him.

He began pulling at his ear, whimpering and fretting and pulling at his left ear.

"Earache, darling?" she asked.

"Hurts," he whimpered, "hurts."

It was an earache, then! Again she breathed a sigh of relief. It wasn't anything mysterious or terrifying! All it was was an earache. "Gathered ear," she told herself happily. "All it is, is a gathered ear. Lots of kids has gathered ears. That ain't nothing to be scared of."

It wasn't anything to be scared of, but after she had done everything she could think of for him, and more, too, he kept on whimpering. Sometimes he would take a restless nap, rolling his head uneasily from side to side on the pillow. The worst was when he would sharply cry outright like someone sustaining a blow. Then Linnea didn't know what else to do but would take him up out of bed and walk with him as though he had been six months old. He was big and heavy, but she would walk with him in her arms, back and forth, back and forth. He seemed to get lighter, though. It seemed to soothe him to be walked with, he'd stop sobbing, would only faintly draw his breath in a sob at intervals. Sometimes Linnea would think, now he's going to be better, his ear's going to bust and start mattering . . . but he didn't, it didn't. When she gently bent over and laid him down, he would start whimper-ing again. Sometimes she stood for hours, her eyes fixed on him, her chest feeling like it was being too tightly hugged and squeezed, jig-gling the footboard which gave a little rocking motion to the mattress and made him more contented. Or that would not help and nothing would help. It would be late at night with all the children sound asleep. Then she would gather him up in her arms again and start walk-ing back and forth, her love for him making her knees weak, her head swim. To lose him! Her three-year-old! Her good boy! She saw him in his tight wool suit, his little round straw hat, trudging along behind her as he had done last Sunday, such a long walk—maybe it was too long a walk—but he never said boo—never said boo—and he was hot and tired—best little kid. You know how much I'd give? Fifty dollars if he'd laugh his hearty laugh. . . . "Ain't we never going to get over that mean old earache?" Sometimes she'd think she couldn't stand her love for him the way you feel you can't stand a pain in your side, another minute . . . she couldn't swallow, or breathe, and she'd walk with him, saying loving words, humming or murmuring. He'd cry, or he'd draw his breath in, in great sighs. Sometimes he'd be lulled. Sometimes she'd think he'd be asleep but he'd reach up and give her cheek a pat with his fat hand. He'd reach up again and give her a pat and her cheek would be wet.

It was only an earache, a gathered ear or something simple like that. But shouldn't it ought to of broke and run? she began to think. Shouldn't it of ought to of started to matter long before this? It didn't, though. Neither did he stop crying nor the fever go away. Linnea did not have a family physician. She was the family physician. So far they had never once needed any other. But now the time had come. She would have to call in somebody else.

It was Mrs. Golightly who recommended Dr. Queen. He was a fine young gentleman, she said, very clever and well trained, who had even been known to do an operation for appendicitis. It was some man down on State Street, and imagine, *he had lived*. He was said to swear, as naturally he would, by Dr. Queen. Mrs. Golightly's own cousin had been cured of gallstones by the doctor. He gave her some kind of a tonic that dissolved the gallstones—it just literally pulverized them and they passed right out of her system. In her urine or somehow. He was good with everything. He was said to have pulled one of the bishop's counsellors through double pneumonia. That showed he wasn't anybody to sneeze at. Linnea sent Gertrude after him.

He came in a nice buggy, drawn by a shiny black horse. He had one of the handsomest buggy whips ever seen, stuck in a holder in the side. He wore nice clothes and had a pearl-gray hat. But he was not merely a dandy and nothing else. No, he took his hat off, and before he was through he took his coat off and rolled up his shirt sleeves. He didn't care how he looked while he examined Parley from one end to the other. His eyes were so serious and his mouth was so serious when he got through that Linnea started to shake, and her heart jumped, and beat fast, and almost stopped, and quivered in the most sickening way, then jumped again and pounded. Her teeth seemed to want to chatter too, and she dug her nails into her palms.

"What is it, Doctor?" she said. "What's the matter with him?"

The doctor smiled, to cheer her, but then his face went serious again, though when he spoke it was with a light tone. "Oh, *he'll* be all right. But the ear's bad. It's really an awfully bad ear, you might as well know."

"I know," she said. "I know, that's what's been bothering him."

"He'll have to be operated on, I'm afraid."

"Operated on?" she said, as though unbelieving.

"He'll have to be taken to the hospital."

"The hospital?"

"I guess I'd better tell you. So far as I can see, it's his only chance."

She stood thinking, or not thinking, but quiet enough to be thinking. "Then he'll have to go," she said.

"We'll take him right now," Dr. Queen said. He stood up and rolled his shirt sleeves down, reached for his coat.

She was embarrassed to speak of it, for the talk of money is always embarrassing to the poor. They have little, or none, yet it is required of them on occasion and they have to clear their throats and say, Idiot, dolt that I am, I don't have any . . . I am temporarily out of funds . . . temporarily broke. They are embarrassed the way they would be if they were accidentally knocked down in the street, and when carried to a strange bed, were found to be wearing underwear made of flour sacks . . . what can they say? How can they explain their shame and indignity? Linnea cleared her throat and said, "I'm kind of short of cash right at the moment. What will you charge? What will everything cost? I only ask—not because I want to dicker—" her cheeks colored—"but because I'm kind of short of cash, you know, right at the moment. I couldn't pay you right away. I'd have to pay you a little as I went along. I wouldn't want you to think you was going to be paid in full, the way I'd like to get my purse out right this minute and pay you, and then me not settle up a-tall." She couldn't look him in the eyes for immemorial shame.

"That doesn't make any difference," the young doctor said. He was buttoning his coat now. "You bundle the child up and we'll take him right now."

She didn't cry. Parley was going to be operated on and he was going to be all right. He was going to get better, just like the man down on State Street got better, only he had appendicitis and Parley had something wrong with his ear and with the back of his head. He had to get better—there wasn't any question about it. He couldn't—of course not—God in heaven, no, no, of course not—do anything else. She would tell him this when he was a grown young man, would sit reminiscing with him, "So then this doctor said we must take you to the hospital and he would operate on you, you can imagine how scared I was. . . ." She would go on and tell him the whole story. He would have heard it many and many a time by then. Not crying she hurried and got herself ready. It didn't take her five minutes. She gave quiet directions to the staring children. No running through the house—no fighting—no leaving and running off somewhere—no piecing between meals—in case I don't get home for dinner, why, go ahead and eat and wash up the

dishes—in case I don't get home in time for supper—why, fix supper.
There was the boiled beef to slice, for one thing. Parley would be well
over his operation by evening, she would think. Then she could come
home at least for a little while. ("I was just about worried out of my
senses," she would tell him later, "when I got you ready to go to that
hospital. . . .")

"This is the first time any of my folks ever been to a hospital," she
told the doctor, as they drove along First Avenue.

"That so?" he said.

"I ain't only been in it a time or two, to visit."

"That so?"

"Anybody that's not used to a hospital, it kind of scares them, you
know. The thought of it."

"You don't want to be scared of a *hospital*," he told her kindly.

"It's just—the thought of it," she said, trying to smile. "Anybody that's
not used to it." It was midmorning and hot, but she carefully pulled
the blanket up over Parley's shoulder and the side of his head, in case
he should get chilled. His head lay in the crook of her left arm, his legs
hung over the right side of her lap. The doctor said not to dress him,
so she just put a little clean union suit on him, thinking with a pang
how he wasn't so fat now, how his ribs almost showed, how he could
slide right in his beloved high chair without a bit of trouble now. . . .
She put stockings on him and bundled him up in the blanket. Dr.
Queen wanted to take him but she said no, she said thank you very
much but she could carry him herself, she was so used to it. So used
to it, after the days and nights . . . so terribly fond . . . and used to
it . . . so heartbreakingly, idiotically fond . . .

("So then we took you to the hospital. I tell you, that was one of the
worst mornings I ever spent!")

Even when she carried on a conversation with the doctor, she kept
thinking of Parley . . . not so much thinking of him as seeing picture
after picture . . . of him as a baby and right on through every day . . .
his laughter sounding beneath, like a brook running . . . fatty . . .
you big old fatty . . . say Mamma . . . say Rudie . . . where's
your eyes? . . . where's your nose? . . . where's Bertha? . . . where's
Mamma's own kid? . . . now he takes the first long step, and at least
three jerky steps after, into Gertrude's arms . . . he splashes the bath
water . . . hollers bloody murder . . . kisses the whole family . . .
sticky kisses, jam-face, honey-face . . . fixes his gaze on a bird . . .
lunges after a butterfly . . . there never was a little kid had more fun,
anything that tickled the family, tickled him too, from the time he was
born . . . he crawls into bed with his mother . . . his face is so bright,
his eyes are so bright . . . he is so full of light and life he can hardly
stand it . . . so full of laughter. . . .

"You sure got a nice horse there," Linnea draws a deep breath and says to the doctor. "Where did you say you was from? Do you like Salt Lake?" All the usual polite things to say in conversation. But thinking of Parley underneath . . . who is very sick . . . and lies against her breast perfectly still . . . but his eyes are open . . . he looks up and sideways . . . his blue eyes look into her own, knowing her well. She tightens her hold on him. She was never so used to anything in her life as the feel of him in her arms, his weight, his warmth. Nor weight, no warmth, no feel, could ever take the place of his. Her insides turned liquid with fear and grief. She holds him tighter. "No," she said, "once you get used to the climate, you'll like it all right. Hot in summer, cold in winter."

The doctor said something about the altitude and she nodded, thinking that if Parley . . . if Parley . . . if he . . . if he . . .

It was the big hospital, the Holy Cross Hospital, with the long corridors, the high, high windows, the far-off ceilings. She held on to Parley until the very last minute, until the room was picked out and the bed was turned down and the nurse put her arms out. Then Linnea put him down in the bed, telling him brightly he would sure have something to brag about when he got home, telling him there wasn't one kid in five hundred that got to go to a *hospital*. He lay right down, he lay right down in the midst of the pillow. It didn't make much difference to him . . . he whimpered faintly . . . but he was sleepy and shut his eyes . . . he opened them quickly, though, to see where Mamma was. If Mamma was there, it was all right. If Mamma wasn't—he opened his eyes wider, searching . . . but she was. She was sitting right beside him, as close as she could get. She even had hold of his hand. He let his eyelids flutter, droop. "He's awful tired. He ain't slept."

The nurse had on the habit of a nun, or some kind of a sister. The Holy Cross Hospital was a Catholic Hospital. In the corridors there were niches for statues of various saints, and Mary in a Norwegian blue robe and Jesus with biscuit-brown hair and sparkling red gashes in the center of his corded hands and feet where the nails went through, and there was the flickering light of candles burning, though the halls were lit with a brighter shriller light than they and the candles were not in plain sight. Maybe candles did not burn at all but it seemed as though they did.

("And here I had you in this hospital," she would tell Parley, "and if ever I was scared to death in my life . . .")

Linnea said to the nurse that there was something about a hospital that scared a person that wasn't used to it. "Why, there ain't a one of my folks ever been in a hospital before!" she said. "That's why it seems so funny. Not being used to it. Why, I haven't only *visited* in a hospital a time or two, let alone anything else." How small Parley looked, lying there in the bed . . . ("You sure looked little laying there in that big high bed. . . .") my God, my God . . . how small . . . she had a feeling as if her heart would break with love for him and bent closer. "Shall I take his stockings off? Shall I do something for him?" Can I give—my life—for his own? What have I got I can give?

It was another nurse, in the same holy habit, with a capacious white apron over it, who came to the door with a sort of cart. "It's ready now." What's ready now? "I'll take him now."

("Oh, Parley, if ever you seen anybody shake in their shoes . . . when she come for you. . . .")

"Let me—let me lift him—let me take him—" Linnea begs.

The complexion looks yellow or unhealthily red against the punishing white of the neckpiece, the coif. This woman has a yellow face and the hairs of her eyebrows are so long that they straggle and trail downwards, but she smiles gently and is kind. "I'll take him. We'll get along just fine."

"Oh, he might be scared—he's not used—he might be scared of your dress, you know—a little—he's not used, you know . . . them wings out to the side of your face—"

Gently, gently. "We'll get along just fine."

"Oh, you'd better let me go with you."

("So then I tried to get her to let me go to the operating room, Parley, and she wouldn't let me.")

"He's, you know, he's only three—he's not very used—he's been awful sick, you know, with his ear, ever since last Wednesday—"

"Mamma, Mamma—" Parley wheedles almost in the old way.

"Oh, please let me take him."

("I tried to get her to let me take you . . .")

"Please. I won't be no bother. He's so used to me, see. He don't hardly know what to do without me. You know how you'll get so attached to the baby of the family? Well, he's the baby of the family. You see— listen, please—listen, really—"

"You can just leave everything to me," the holy nurse says. "We'll get along fine."

"Mamma, Mamma—"

("You kept saying Mamma, Mamma. . . . I tell you, Parley, if ever my heart was tore in two for a minute there . . ." She would tell him all about it, for the hundredth time, when he was a grown young man.)

"Please. Oh, please!"

She can hear him whimpering *Mamma* down the hall, wanting her. Then he cries it outright. *Mamma,* he cries. She stiffens. She will have to run after him, get him, take him, hold him, hug him, comfort him, take him home. Oh, God. Oh, God. What *is* all this anyway all of a sudden? All this stuff, all this being in the Holy Cross Hospital and

Parley screaming for her down the hall, going to be operated on, going to—going to—Parley—sick. Baby—sick. For the first time, she lets out a kind of bellow of grief. Where's her handkerchief? Where is it? She buries her face in her two hands, the tears running between her fingers. His crying is carried farther and farther away. ("I heard you growing dimmer and dimmer . . .") She can't go after him. She has to stay here and wait. Right—here—and—wait.

At first, she tiptoes outside in the quiet corridor, to the very end, past the shut and open and half-open doors, to find a clock and find out what time it was, but she only did that once. The rest of the time, the long time, she stayed in the room, sitting by the scarcely disturbed bed where Parley had lain and where they would put him when they brought him back. Sometimes she walked over and looked out the window at the poison-green lawn. How shady, how well-kept it was, under the green trees, a spray of glistening water drops whirling here, and here, and there, to keep it damp and glittering. She did not cry now. She just strained her ears to hear a sound from Parley—one little sound —maybe when they brought him back. And waited. ("All I could do was stand there and wait. . . .")

She should have brought Gertrude with her perhaps, the only one of the girls who didn't come down with the measles. Gertrude would have been quite a lot of comfort. It was hard to stay alone, waiting. ("I tell you, Parley, I never thought time could go so slow as it did, when you was in that operating room and I was there not knowing whether you was going to live or going to . . .") She thought she might go out and tiptoe down to the end of the hall and see what time it was again . . . it must be lots later, lots later . . . she decided not to. There was a big built-in desk down that way and a hawk-nosed old nun that looked at a person inquiringly so that a person felt uneasy. She put her hand out and patted the pillow where his head had lain, where it would again lie. Oh, how good she would be to him. From nowhere, his last birthday cake drifted before her eyes . . . three candles burning. . . . "Make a wish, Parley." "He don't know what a wish is!" "Sure, he does! Go ahead and make a wish." "Say: I wish I had a thousand dollars." "Silly! Don't make him wish that! Make him wish something could come true!" "What could come true?" "Why, anything. But not a thousand dollars!" "All right, Parley, make a wish. Say *I wish I had a Shetland pony.*" "So all you kids could ride! I know you! It wouldn't be Parley's a-tall." "Sure it would." Parley then, gleefully—"I wish I had a Shetland pony." "Now blow!" "Blow hard!" "Blow, Parley!" He got so excited, he got so red, he blew so hard. "Parley gets his wish!" "Parley blew out all the candles?" Three years old—three—three —three—laughing his head off, clapping his hands, best little kid that ever lived, that ever . . .

She heard their footsteps coming down the hall. She thought she heard the cart too. She hurried and stood up, turned the covers back. They would put him to bed. Why, nothing ever *really* happened to the children. ("So then, Parley . . .") A person would get pretty scared, and worry, but somehow or other, the Lord must have had his eye on them, for everything always turned out all right. Everything always did. Always. Always. ("So then, Parley . . .")

Doctor Queen had a long white coat on. It looked just like a duster. With him was the same nurse, the nun, the sister, with the yellowish complexion and the straggling eyebrows. Linnea smoothed the pillow where her baby's bandaged head would lie, not knowing what else to do.

The doctor walked right up to her. "Mrs. Ecklund," he said, "please sit down."

"Sit down here in this chair," the nurse said.

("They told me to sit down." She would tell him the whole story time after time.)

It seemed like she was pushed into the chair but maybe her legs gave way and she sat down in it herself.

"I have sad news for you." "Prepare yourself for sad news." "Sad news." "Sad news." She heard it echoing down her mind.

("They told me you were . . .")

Oh, God, what a thing to tell a person—a lie like that—a brazen bald-faced LIE!

CHAPTER 23

IT SEEMED so good and kind that Ingeborg was there, Mrs. Golightly was there, Mrs. Kittio, Young Mrs. Monteith, Mrs. Orbit, everybody was there at one time or another all day long. Linnea didn't know how they knew about it so fast. How did the news travel so fast? The sad news? The sad news? She was home now. One thing—she couldn't brag about being very brave. She hadn't been very brave all day. The scalped, the operated on, the injured, the terribly battered and beaten, the cut, slashed, wounded, the amputee, they have the look in their eyes that she had—dazed, glazed, hazy, amazed, not full of tears. She did not mind that she had not been very brave, sagging into unconsciousness, frothing at the mouth, and it had been she making those hideous sounds, too, those cat-like growlings and mewings of grief. She was still making them. It wasn't anybody's business that she hadn't been brave. Whose business was it? That she was making those growling mewing sounds of woe?

Everybody was there at one time or another all afternoon and evening and half the night. It was Bertha who was the little mother, though, who lined up the kids and saw that they got fed. Gertrude cried so hard that now, at twilight, she had a headache and buzzing in her ears and a puffy swollen face. Her intention had been, to cry forever, for Parley had been her great pet. She could look ahead and see herself as an old lady still crying about the death of her little brother. Nobody paid any attention to her. The doctor brought Mamma home and that was terrible to see: the big and beautiful tree chopped down, the mountain flattened, the Tabernacle smashed and stomped on, this was her. She did not look at any of them. She was weak. Big, strong Mamma that was so wonderful, that was up to anything and everything always, was now weak, and torn, and trampled, and not worth a cent. She had an odd unfamiliar face, of a different tint than it had been, not pretty to look at. Gertrude, crying hard and swallowing air and hiccoughing with grief, had hoped Mamma on her way past, who had never done anything else, would stop to comfort her, but she did not and Gertrude was left alone. The violence of her unsolaced weeping began to frighten her a little and she stopped to speculate on it, consider it, as one observes the behavior of a strange animal in a cage.

They put Mamma in the bedroom where she lay down in her clothes, with her shoes off. She said to Bertha, "Take his high chair—put it away—I can't stand to see it."

"In the coal shed, Mamma?" Bertha asked anxiously. The tears trickled out of her eyes, but she knew, being the eldest child, that she was next in command—if Mamma stayed in the bedroom, then she was, as the saying goes, Chief Cook and Bottle Washer. Sad as she was, she liked the idea of a position of authority in front of all the ladies who were coming and going.

Mamma made sounds of crying that were even a little bit like laughing if you didn't know. "No, I couldn't stand that," she said, "his high chair out in the coal shed. It'd be like . . . oh, my, oh, my, but I can't stand to see it in the kitchen either."

"How about me giving it to somebody?"

"Do that, Bertha. Give it to somebody."

"Who?"

"Somebody that needs it, but not where a person would be running in to it every minute, every time they went to see somebody. . . ."

Bertha knew Mamma's way well enough—the first thing she did was to make coffee. By that time Ingeborg was there, and Mrs. Golightly and other neighborhood women going in and out. They had already started to bring food, too, as was customary, and a bowl of bread pudding and a large loaf of fresh bread stood upon the table. The tragedy had caught the ladies unaware. They had nothing special prepared. By tomorrow they would have had time to have baked something they "needn't be ashamed of."

Bertha said she would take the coffee in to Mamma, though Ingeborg wanted to. Ingeborg had a saucerless cup in her own hand and was sipping from it as she walked uneasily around. Gertrude and Stellie, crying quietly now on the lounge, and diverted more than they would have cared to admit by the ladies coming in, and later, by the dishtowel-and-napkin-covered bowls or plates of this or that were carried in and placed on the table ("It's only soup, but I thought maybe a little hot soup—" or, "They ain't really *fresh* cinnamon rolls but tomorrow—" or, "It's only applesauce," the ladies apologized as though they had been guilty of serious crimes), wanted to go into the bedroom, too, but Bertha told them to stay where they were and they minded.

Mamma said she didn't want the coffee and could not drink it. She was lying prone with one arm up over her head.

"You drink it," Ingeborg said sternly, taking a sip from her own cup.

"Grief is one thing but we don't any of us want to go crazy while we're at it."

"It won't do no good to get rid of the high chair," Mamma said numbly over her shoulder to Bertha who was putting the cup and saucer down on a straight chair drawn up to the bed. "I been thinking. Everything will remind a person. There ain't any place a person could look, where they wouldn't be reminded. All over the house . . . he's played and been everywhere . . . and then, his suit, and his little hat, his . . . shoes he wears . . . he wore, I mean . . . for every day . . ."

"There's families lost three kids in *one night* with diphtheria," Ingeborg reminded her, still in her stern voice. "Don't you remember the Whiteheads? Him going up to the cemetery in a snow storm with three of his kids dead in the back of the wagon? What if it'd of been not just Parley, but Stellie and Rudie as well, or Bertha and Gertrude? What would you do *then?*"

"Oh, Ingeborg . . ." Mamma whispered brokenly. But she turned over on her side and tasted the coffee.

"Don't you think *I* know what it is to lose a baby? Ain't I lost one? You don't want to get the notion in your head that you're the only one that's ever been through something, you know. There's other people been through something, too. There's lots of people besides you going through terrible things right this minute, besides you, you want to remember." Ingeborg sounded mad and quarrelsome, but it was just that she felt so bad for Linnea and felt so bad about Parley being dead. She had held him on her lap many a time, and fed him, and wiped his nose, and brushed his hair, and she had given his round cheek many a dry peck. He came about as near being a favorite as Ingeborg could have a favorite and whenever she wasn't scolding or snapping at the grieving mother she was shedding tears in the kitchen or pantry, wherever she happened to be, so that soon her eyes were redder and more swollen than anybody's.

Mrs. Brenneman left her baby son with his father and her daughter Estelle (when nursing time rolled around she would go home and feed him and then come back) and came bringing a jar of canned peaches and a jar of canned pears. She didn't cry so hard when she went in the bedroom but she went all to pieces when she came out. "If that ain't the most terrible thing that ever happened," she said, "why, I tell you I thought I was going to keel over in a faint when I heard about it. I couldn't believe my ears. I said to my husband—he was on his way back to work—he's on the night shift now—I said to him, Parley's dead, Linnea's little Parley. Imagine, I said. Why, that will just about kill Linnea, I said." She stood by the stove, crying. "Imagine. And here the poor little thing never had nothing but measles and a gathered ear. Honestly, it scares a person to think of it. If it'd been something *serious!*"

"He died on the operating table," Ingeborg said.

"I know, but what did he die of? Was the doctor lancing his ear or what was he doing?"

"He was just being operated on, that's all I know."

Gertrude cleared her throat. "Bertha said the doctor was going to take a piece of bone out of the back of his head and let the pus out. Bertha said Mamma said."

"He died on the operating table," Ingeborg repeated. "That's all. Never knew what hit him."

"Poor little kid. Imagine," Mrs. Brenneman kept drying her eyes but the tears kept coming back.

He came home, Parley did, who had never been away alone before, not running up the walk, clambering and banging up the stairs, making a beeline for his high chair at suppertime, but high off the ground like a doll delivered in a box from the Z.C.M.I., a doll with real hair and eyelashes and china hands and feet. It could not say Mamma. Mrs. Kittio and Mrs. Orbit and Young Mrs. Monteith dressed the doll in the parlor by lamplight. Parley, its name was, with fine soft human hair and real eyelashes. In fact, it all looked so real it would fool you. It was wearing Parley's best and only suit, the one for Best. And what was this occasion if not requiring his uttermost Best? The women did not light candles, they never did, but they brought in another lamp and turned both the wicks down as low as they would go. Lamplight served. They spoke in that whisper that the touchy sleep of death requires—no working man who has to work by night and sleep by day asks you to be quieter. It can scarcely stand a voice above a whisper. It can scarcely stand a footfall. Oh, how silent it asks you to be. Mrs. Kittio said they would have to watch carefully and not let any cats in by mistake. Cats would get in, in spite of you, if there was a corpse in the house, she said. But they kept watch and ward, and none did.

Linnea knew Parley was home and in the parlor. He would not whimper now. She could take as long a nap as she wanted to. She would too, she really would—it had been days and nights since she slept—only she had got in an accident somehow, been cruelly injured. There were bleeding stumps where her arms had been, bleeding stumps where her breasts had been, and they bled and ached, oozing and draining away her life. Take the weight and warmth and feel of Parley away from her arms and bosom and you hacked and chopped them off, you destroyed them.

She lay face down on the pillow, not moving. She could take a nap if she wanted to. Parley wouldn't make a sound, not with the pain of earache, not because he woke up like a bird before five o'clock on Sunday, not a sound, not a peep out of him. She could sleep. . . .

It is more than grief, more terrible, what it is that runs along the hollow center of the bones, that rises upwards from the pelvis, aerating, effervescing, in long lines of bursting bubbles. The heavy heart floats upon it, tossing and tumbling. . . . It would sink but the rising flood pushes it up and up, too high against the ribs, too high in the throat, drowning it. . . . Linnea breathes through her open mouth, thinking she too will die, clutching the quilt she lies upon with ice-cold fictitious hands. A call she had forgotten comes, and she rises, for it is urgent and ancient, and she saves her life for a minute by sitting upon the slop jar, seeing all the room as though somebody in the right-hand corner, high up, nearly to the ceiling, were pulling the whole thing upwards and to the right with invisible ropes, stretching everything out of shape upwards and to that one corner, while she relieves herself by urinating copiously, an oddly cool torrent. She puts the lid back on and pushes the slop jar out of sight, falling upon the bed again, mostly because she can not stand and see the room all being pulled and gathered up into one corner. It is unnerving to stand up when everything is distorted like that, so she lies down, this time on her side. Maybe that will stop that terrible rising liquid thing that is worse than grief . . . it starts with that running in the hollow bones . . . then, from the pelvis, rising upwards in the breaking bubbles . . . they wash the terrified heart up too high . . . crowd it against the shoulder blade, the throat, too high. . . . She does not cry now but sits up, running a freezing and trembling hand over her cold lips—she wipes off the beads of perspiration that cling in a mustache line, wipes her wet forehead.

When Ingeborg brought the lighted lamp in and set it on the bureau, she said, "A little light on the subject won't hurt you. There's no sense laying here in the dark."

Linnea wanted to tell her. She was lying again on her side, but she raised herself up on her elbow and half sat up. "Ingeborg," she said, "did you ever—" but she broke off. It would be too hard to describe it.

"Ever what?"

"Well, it's such a funny feeling, you know. So funny. So peculiar. I can't explain. I bet anything—I don't know how to tell you—but it feels like—I bet it's exactly like dying, Ingeborg."

"You ain't dying," Ingeborg said shortly.

"I know, but it's so funny. You know in the middle of your bones? Well, it's like water running. I don't know how to explain it exactly. It's so peculiar. And then the room—" she rubbed her tender swollen eyes, blinked them rapidly, and then looked here and there as though to test them out.

"What about the room?"

"Well, it seems like everything's being gathered up in one corner, right over there in that right hand corner, like it was all tied with ropes and somebody's perched up there pulling and hauling it all upwards."

Ingeborg stared down at her sympathetically. "You're not going to take a notion to go out of your head, are you?" she asked gently.

"What kind of talk is that?" Linnea said. "No, what I mean is, everything looks like it's a little out of shape, being pulled over that way." She blinked her eyes again. "So funny. You'd ought to see what I mean."

"You're hungry, is all."

"Oh, I couldn't eat a mouthful of food for nobody."

But for politeness' sake she ate half of a bowl of soup for Mrs. Brenneman and some bread pudding for Young Mrs. Monteith. It seemed incumbent upon her to apologize for keeping to the bedroom. A bereft mother would lie down, but in a little while she would get up and be out in the rest of the house where everybody was, not hiding like a coward, as though sorrow were something she couldn't handle. "I seem to feel so—peculiar," she said, ashamed, to Young Mrs. Monteith, and to Mrs. Brenneman. "Honestly to—goodness, it's the funniest thing but everything seems to look out of shape, kind of, and being pulled over that way. It makes a person kind of dizzy and sick to their stomach, a little. I seem to do better with my eyes shut."

"Bed's the place for you," they said. (Don't come out, stay where you are, while Mrs. Kittio and Mrs. Orbit finish dressing and fiddling with the life-size doll in the parlor.)

She talked to whoever came in and out, keeping her eyes closed, apologizing always, or lay very quietly in the room all alone. She had stopped thinking a long time ago. Every once in a while, that thing she had not been able to describe to Ingeborg would come upon her, that horrifying thing made of ocean, made of bubbles of air, but she would survive. She had been so occupied with the uncommon and alarming feeling that she had not wept. Not thinking, she had mourned in the dry-eyed way, as painful as a dry birth. Very tired, she was too wide awake to sleep, as though after too many cups of strong coffee. There didn't seem to be a chance in the world of sleeping or crying or letting loose. She was wound up too tight, overwound, like a clock. She was strung taut as a clothesline. But then she could seem to hear the light sweet childish voice of Bertha, or Gertrude, reciting for Parley in the high chair, "Baby said when she smelled the rose . . . O what a pity, only one nose!"—hear her saying for him while he sat listening rapt and shining-faced, "Baby said when she smelled the snuff . . . Dear me! One nose is enough!" Linnea whispered it herself, whispered and heard it, she stepped upon the little poem as on a little safe raft and floated out of harm's way to rest.

Ten fingers and ten toes!
Two eyes, and one nose!

Baby said, when she smelled the rose—
O what a pity! Only one nose!

Twelve teeth all even and white,
Lots of dimples, but one nose!
Baby said, when she smelled the snuff—
Dear me! One nose is enough!

Enough . . . enough . . . one life is enough . . . so full of good
things that you thought O what a pity, *only one life* . . . so full of bad
things, terrible things, that you thought Dear me! *One life is enough*
. . . but it wasn't, it wasn't nearly enough . . . it was, it was too much
. . . it wasn't . . . it was . . . Linnea's tears gathered and fell, gathered and fell, wetting her pillow and she noticed that the more there
were, the cooler they were . . . and something that had been squeezing her to death, let loose, and dropped her like a hot potato, the spring
unwound with a snap, the clothesline sagged . . . while she thought of
this and cooly abundantly wept . . . one nose is enough . . . one nose
is enough . . . one life is enough . . . O what a pity, only one nose
. . . Dear me! one life . . . Dear me! one rose . . . one child . . .
one death . . . one God . . . one sleep . . . one reason . . . one
purpose. . . . When Olaf came at eleven that night, having only just
heard the news, Ingeborg peeked in, but Linnea was sound asleep and
so Ingeborg went in and covered her tenderly up and carried the lamp
out and said softly, "She's asleep, poor thing, so you can't go in. She's
been through something today, I can tell you."

Olaf went quietly in and looked at the dead boy who seemed quite
real only of the wrong color, and then he came back out to the kitchen.
Hot as it had been that afternoon, it was cold now and the women had a
fire going. Olaf picked up the coal bucket and took it out to the coal shed
and filled it, and brought it back and set it down by the stove. Then,
as he could, among so many milling ladies (there were not many, only
three now, but in all the rooms passing backwards and forwards in
rustling skirts like small trees being dragged upon their swishing leaves
down a forest path, doubled and tripled with motion and sound), he
began his own long vigil of regretful grief, the only man among them,
keeping what dignity he could. He left at a little after six in the morning and said he would be back before noon, as he had some things to
attend to.

Bertha wouldn't go up and stay at Ingeborg's all night, but the rest of
the children did, Gertrude, Stellie and Rudie. Ingeborg told them to
remain there until she came home, but they didn't mind her. By seven
o'clock the next morning they were home, having been wakened much
earlier by the bright summer sun and their busy blood. Ingeborg's children trouped along with them. The minute their mother got her eye on

them, though, she sent them packing. "Make for home," she said, "and see that you stay home. What do you think this is anyway? A circus?" She wanted to send Linnea's children back, too, but they flatly refused to go. That is, Gertrude and Stellie refused to go. Rudie, who had begun to construct with Chucken, Ingeborg's only son, a doghouse for a non-existent dog the night before, was not averse to going back and finishing it. When the Jensen brood made their way ignominiously home, their mother's scolding tirade in their ears, he went with them.

Mrs. Golightly appeared, to help cook breakfast. Bertha and Gertrude, not quarreling, united to fix Mamma a lovely and appetizing tray. It did not matter that it was only their largest baking pan with the narrow rim around it. They prepared it daintily with a pineapple-lace-edged doily and picked and chose the prettiest dishes and brightest knife, fork and spoon.

They tapped at the door, and then they went in the bedroom, Gertrude first to make way, Bertha proudly with the breakfast, and Stellie bringing up at the rear. Mamma woke up from a sound sleep and when she saw them advancing to her in the room bright with sunshine she had a feeling of holiday, of wonderful well-being, not a cloud in the sky. It took her an instant to remember.

It happens that way. The grief is there, to hang around the neck like a millstone. Though but a night old, it is the most familiar thing, like being of a repudiated color for twenty-five years or having a fire-mole across the cheek or lying in a cell waiting for execution. But for one instant, the disallowed, the marred, the man about to be hanged for murder, forgets. Maybe he blinks his eyes only once before remembering but this is euphoric instant, regeneration and excursion, whale's elbowroom and saint's immunity, the power and the glory. Then! back it comes, here it is, the heavy landslide upon the defenceless head, the water coiling to suck down and drown, the house burning upon the smothered inhabitant, the blemish, the noose, the pain, the grief, the agony, the loss. It happens that way, every morning, to somebody.

Mamma looked at them walking carefully. Oh, their three faces of beauty and light . . . the dead face of their brother small and helpless carried off to die crying her name of mother . . . their bright heads of warm flickering hair, their light bright glistening eyes. This is too much for her to see and she crumples with sorrow. It is unspeakably too much for her to see, the three faces of her daughters. . . .

They all come to her, not knowing what else to do. Bertha says brokenly, "We brought your breakfast, you know, on a tray."

"Not really a tray," Gertrude says sobbing, "because we didn't have one, but a pan—"

"—just as good," Bertha sobs.

"We didn't have a regular tray," weeps Stellie.

For them, the sight of them, Mamma is torn apart. If she was carefully glued together like a smashed figurine during her night of sleep, now she was dropped and shattered to pieces again. Her cries, though muffled by her pillow, are shrill and wild. This is desperate bright morning, this is inconsolable sorrow, selfish, self-centered, bitterly boiling and roiling.

It touches off dreadfully the same wild grief in them. She hears the clamor of it around her. She grows very silent, listening. Then she opens her eyes and looks at them. Look what she has done to their beauty! They weep, they are ugly with fright and grief. How with shame, she reaches out and takes Bertha by the shoulder, then Gertrude, then Stellie, giving them one after the other a hard shake. "Stop it," she says. "Stop it this very instant! Bawling's not going to help anything, bawling and blubbering ain't going to bring nobody back! Why, you keep on like that and one of these fine days you'll have softening of the brain or something."

They look up, astonished. Her safe hand again! Her sure face once more! It is too much to hope for. "You was bawling," Bertha says uncertainly.

"I know I was bawling, but I'm going to put a stop to it now. . . ." She waits for the fright to go out of their eyes, and sees it go, sees it vanish, as the puddle melts beneath the sun's rays.

"We're not sissies, you know," she said, forbidding her tears to gather. "We're not a bunch of boobies. If the Lord gives us a trial to bear, why, we can bear it."

Bertha's overjoyed face said she would be oh, so glad to give the reins back in to Mamma's hands. It wasn't much fun to take charge when Mamma was bested, laid low. Gertrude and Stellie looked as if they had something to hang onto again. They were hanging on, too, for dear life. All three girls had wet eyes but they were drying fast.

"No, siree," Mamma said, looking at each one closely to see that she had not done any real damage, unsettled them, foolishly impaired them in a way she would give her eye teeth not to have done. "We might be a lot of things but we ain't a bunch of boobies. Anything we got to stand, we can stand. Since when couldn't we stand anything I'd like to know?" she said. She took a deep quivering breath and smiled. "What's on the tray?" she asked tenderly.

"Oh, coffee. If it ain't hot enough, I'll go get more!"

"Oh, eggs, Mamma."

"Oh, toast."

"Oh, jam."

"The best doily."

"The prettiest dishes."

"Well, what do you know about that! Did anybody ever see such a sight?" Mamma said. "Have you kids ate? You can eat some of this—it's away too much for me—"

"It ain't, either."

She made herself smile and then she didn't have to make herself. She made herself eat and then she didn't have to make herself. She made herself pick up her burden and cheerfully carry it, for it was imposed on her by Somebody wiser than Brigham Young or Joseph Smith or anybody that ever lived, and all of a sudden she seemed to know it, and seemed to know . . . that pretty soon she wouldn't have to make herself carry her hardship but would do it easily and cheerfully, not saying boo, and that . . . the burden seen as the will and the way of God was the too-heavy load of wet wash dried out by sunshine to the easy armful of light warm linen . . . resignation the verbena scent and attar of damask roses to everlastingly sweeten it. . . .

She smiled upon her daughters, and ate, and drank her coffee.

"Don't you feel bad no more, about Parley?" Stellie ventured to ask. Bertha and Gertrude glared at her.

"Sure I feel bad," she said quietly. "Only I ain't going to act like a booby over it. *That* ain't no way to act." With a feeling of great relief she noticed that everything looked the way it ought to now. There was no more of that funny distortion of walls and furniture that made one feel so squeamish. She considered peacefully her bones and her insides that now felt ordinary and natural. Also, she once more had hands, arms, breasts, to gather her four children in with, and lay their heads upon. These seemed to have grown back in the night.

Sorrow for Parley would lie in wait, to give her a scratch or a claw or a gash or a thump sometimes when she least expected it, when she went inadvertently past its hiding place, but for the most part it would be docile enough, only mournfully crying at night sometimes far beneath her dreams . . . Mamma, Mamma . . . imitating with sly facility Parley's last voice.

She got dressed and washed her hands and face and combed her hair, and came out of the bedroom. Ingeborg, Mrs. Brenneman and Young Mrs. Monteith were in the kitchen sitting around the table. There was the feeling that there were a great many people in the house but only Mrs. Orbit and Mrs. Hector were in the Parlor with the body now "lying in state," a term often and affectionately used—that is, now ready to be viewed by whatever callers came and wanted to see it. They were both going home soon to get their work done up and then they were coming back this evening. Young Mrs. Monteith was going home, too.

Ingeborg stayed. She said she wasn't going to step a foot out the door until the funeral was over and everything that could be done, both for Linnea and Parley, was done. She said it was little enough to do for the best friend she had in the world. Mrs. Brenneman said she would have to go and come as she had a man to cook for. Linnea told her she didn't really need to, but she said she wouldn't hear of anything else. None of the ladies mentioned it but they were all proud of Linnea for getting up and coming out of the bedroom. They looked at each other with the proud looks that said, *She's* not one to break. Bend, yes, maybe, her own eyes proudly said, but not break . . . not even yesterday . . . bend, yes, bend double . . . but not break. . . .

They led her in and had her look at her dead son. Yesterday when they consulted her, she had told them what to get: the white casket, the white shoes and stockings, the little white cashmere suit, so she knew what she was going to see. She had planned, with suggestions from this one and that one, the funeral, too—who should speak, who should say the prayer, who should sing "Your Dear Little Rosebud has Left You," and "Beautiful Isle of Somewhere." The blinds were decently pulled down and the room was decently dim. The lamps were blown out, but this morning the smell still hovered on the air of the wicks turned too low, guttering, sputtering, smoking, all night. She knew her friends were nervous and anxious about the way they had dressed him, if he looked all right, if they did a good job, if she was pleased or if she thought they could have done better. Critically she looked: his blouse looked fine. It was a very pretty blouse. He never in the world had one so nice. Besides, his best cambric was in the wash, it wasn't even washed and ironed. What waist was this? She stood looking down at it and suddenly she remembered. One of the rich ladies Ingeborg did the cleaning for gave it to her. Ingeborg set great store by it, not only for the exquisite handwork (it had belonged to the spoiled son of the house) but because it was said to have been made in Paris, France. She was always going to let Chucken wear it some day when the occasion arose, but none did, none great enough, and Chucken outgrew even the possibility of the honor. However, his mother kept it, not for use, but as a work of art. She often showed it, when she showed her embroidery and crocheting, as something to be preciously examined. Linnea looked at the delicate collar turned down over the pure white jacket. A child all dressed in white looked like the child of a nobleman. He . . . looked like a little Earl, this one did. It was a thought to bring tears to the eyes, his look of nobility, but she merely stared reflectively at it. When she wept after what seemed a long time, it was not considered as weakness. Nobody thought so. A mother can be brave but she doesn't necessarily need to be made out of cast iron. There's got to be a little leeway. Dimly through her tears she traced the delicate leaves and buds across the blouse, and thought how uncommon he looked, like somebody of royal blood. Then she looked up and caught Ingeborg's eyes worriedly upon her . . . she tried to say wordlessly, Oh, Ingeborg, not the waist you was always so proud of, every stitch made by hand . . . honestly, I wouldn't want you to give that up to him. Ingeborg's look said back, It's the least thing I can do and don't you even mention it. . . . Don't you even mention it or I'll never speak to you again! Oh, how cross and angry Ingeborg looked crying for Parley.

Linnea brushed her fingers across her eyelids, looked scrupulously again upon the ladies' handiwork. The small hands were neatly laid across the chest and the right one held a tiny nosegay. The hair was parted right. She glanced up as though to say, He looks just beautiful, you did such a nice job. Then her eyes faltered and looked down again . . . not at the blouse, or suit, or casket, or what the ladies had done . . . but at Parley, PARLEY, mind you. That's who this was, that's who this was, yellowish, bluish around his curves and hollows, cooled and hardened, killed, destroyed, ruined, dead, gone, finished, done with, that's who this was. It was so ghastly she wanted to throw back her head and yell. She wanted to scream at God, holler at Him, moan and yell. She couldn't do that. She ran into her helplessness like a shut door she thought was wide open. She banged into it and down she went upon the floor in a heap.

Nobody blamed her, though. As they all said, a mother can bear up but that doesn't mean she has to necessarily be made out of cast iron. A mother has a perfect right to faint if she wants to. There's no law against it, they said.

They revived her, feeling sorry and sympathetic.

Soon she was all right, as good as all right. She went back out in the kitchen. She didn't have to go to bed in the bedroom.

Everybody was gone, but they would straggle back as soon as they could when their work was done. Only Ingeborg stayed. It was time for midmorning coffee and she made it. The two women sat up to the table and drank it, just the same as always.

"Mr. Orbit is going to kill a chicken and bring it over this afternoon," Ingeborg said.

"He is? He shouldn't do that."

"Why not, I'd like to know?"

"Oh, because."

"Well, he is, that's the way people do when there's trouble."

There was a silence then.

"I kind of got better acquainted with Mrs. Sterling—Mrs. Brenneman, I mean—last night," Ingeborg offered. "Her and me set up together the biggest part of the time."

"You must be tired," Linnea said. "Why don't you go lay down? Take a little nap?"

"What would I want a nap for? I ain't tired. No," Ingeborg said. "As

I was saying, me and Mrs. Brenneman got better acquainted than usual last night."

"Good," Linnea said. "I'm glad to hear it."

"She ain't so bad, I came to the conclusion. Anyway, nobody seems to want to hold nothing against her so why should I? Besides, a person's got to admit, she ain't trash, exactly." Her property wasn't anything to sniff at, Ingeborg meant, and besides, didn't she have money in the bank? "She told me not to mention it to you right at this time," she went on. "She said you wouldn't be in the mood to fall in with anything like that."

"Mention what?" Linnea said. "Fall in with what?"

"She said after the funeral would be plenty of time to tell you and see what you thought of the idea."

"Tell me what? Think of what?"

"Well, she don't like the idea of that woman that's got the other side of her house, so she's give her notice, and July first she's going to move out. Mrs. Brenneman wants you to take her flat."

Linnea gave a little gasp. She would have been more than human if, when she thought of those spacious rooms, those handsome windows, the front porch, back porch and *faucet in the kitchen,* her heart, even in the midst of all its tribulations, had not given a jerk and a jump for something amazingly like joy. She always liked to move anyway. Even if the place she was leaving was better than the place she was going into, she liked to move: I'll fix it up, she'd say; in a month, you won't know the place. If, on the other hand, the new abode were superior to the old, then there was no holding her. In spite of herself, then, thinking of taking possession of that fine, comfortable, five-room apartment, with a tried and true friend as her landlady, of moving out of these tiny rooms full of painful memory, a crack of light shone in her darkness. "Oh, but this house is so cheap," she said. "Mrs. Brenneman gets twice the rent. I couldn't pay any such price."

"She said it would be the same as this place. That's what she told me," Ingeborg said. "Only she said she wasn't going to broach the subject until—after. Only I thought I'd tell you." I know you so well, her eyes said. If there's one thing on God's green earth that will make you feel a little better, it's the prospect of moving.

"But how could she afford to take half the rent, for heaven's sake?" Linnea asked with something very near excitement in her voice.

"Afford? With a thousand dollars in the bank?" Ingeborg scoffed.

"Well, I mean, why in the world *would* she?" In spite of herself she could see the whole happiness: moving day—a fair day, a bright day— everything packed and ready: then going there to the empty echoing rooms (so much better than the old, always) the sound of her footsteps and the scurrying children's going through them, their voices airily bouncing in the emptiness: the stove put up first thing, the coffee put on, the unspeakable deliciousness of that first cup of coffee: the bed put up, the wonderful flattening out in it that first night for the sweetest deepest tiredest sleep of the whole year: the waking in sun-flooded chaos, the beautiful, the wonderful, the satisfying Herculean labor ahead. Last of all the "touches"—paper fans opened and tacked to the wall, fluted antimacassars, red ribbon rosettes . . . a thousand embellishments she would imagine and extemporize. In spite of herself, she could see the parlor ready for company on Sunday, smell the stove- and furniture-polish, hear the crackle of the Sunday fire, feel the elegant coolness being thawed out, see herself saying *This is the parlor, won't you sit down and make yourself at home?* "How could she? Take half the rent?" Linnea said, blinking the picture away.

"Well, she's going to broach the subject. The way she figures is this, and she's right, for like she says she's got a man now that earns the living. She figures if you pay her what you pay here and then do a little sewing for her on the side and a little looking after her baby when her and Mr. Brenneman goes to *Turnverein* or want to take in a show at the Salt Lake Theatre or something, why, you can more than make up the difference. It ain't such a bad idea, if she didn't take a notion to overdo it and have you sewing up rent for six houses and one thing and another."

"Oh, she wouldn't overdo it. She ain't one to do that! Just the opposite! Her kind, she'd never ask me to do all I'd ought, and I'd have to go ahead and do for her as I seen fit. I know *her*."

"Well, you and her could work it out. You'd more than make up for it—she wouldn't be handing out something for nothing, that's one thing sure. It ain't such a bad idea, though. When the funeral—when all this is over," Ingeborg said, "you can consider it. I just thought I'd mention it."

"Well, I won't even think of it for the time being."

"Why not?" Ingeborg asked.

"This ain't no time to think of *pleasure*." The reproach was more for herself than anybody.

"Nobody said it was," her old friend said. "Only, between times, I thought maybe you could kind of mull it over in your mind."

"Between what times?"

"Between mourning and grieving."

"There ain't no between times," Linnea said slowly.

"Not yet, there ain't," Ingeborg said. "But by July you'll surprise yourself. I surprised myself, and you know how bad I felt over Jensen and the baby—why, I like to bawled my eyes out. And a week later my mouth was watering for potato dumplings! So that just goes to show you."

The ladies were here again, Mrs. Golightly and Mrs. Orbit, when Olaf returned to the house. He came in at the back door. They knew that there had been an estrangement of several months' standing between Linnea and her husband and did not know where to look, they were so embarrassed and uneasy. They did not know what the couple would say or do. But Linnea rose from the table like a queen and greeted Olaf. She said to the ladies, "Me and him are going into the bedroom to talk a little while. Will you excuse us please?" And the ladies, put at ease by this, nodded, murmuring, "Sure we will," "Sure we'll excuse you," "Most certainly," "Take your time." She turned and went into the bedroom and he followed her.

"The first thing I want to say," she said, when she shut the door and stood with her back against it looking gravely at him looking gravely at her, with his hat going round and round in his hands, "is how sorry I am that I . . . never let you heft him . . . that last time you was here. That's been nagging at me like toothache. He was asleep and you wanted to wake him up. 'Let me heft him,' you says. 'No,' I says, 'let him take a nap till you and me get done talking.' Well, then you and me come in here and got talking, and the first thing you know we got mad at each other—"

"You might of got mad at me," Olaf said. "I never got mad at you."

"And then," Linnea went on carefully, "you left, and he was still asleep, for we had never woke him up, and you never got to heft him like you wanted to, to see how big he had got to be. So you never knowed . . . and now he's dead . . . and you can never heft him again. You, that was his pa, and had a perfect right." She broke off, "It's been nagging at me like toothache. I—"

"Linnea, oh, my poor, poor girl," Olaf said brokenly. He threw his hat on the bed and stretched out his arms. "Oh, don't be mad at me no more, Linnea," he whispered, "when death can come like it comes, and lay waste, and a person can stand on his head but a person can never stop it, and you a woman all alone, Linnea, my poor girl, my dearie, as helpless as a little baby chick. . . ."

"Olaf," she said, her face starting to crumple, "the kids had the measles, see—how could I think? and then Parley come down with this earache, see—how could I think? how could I imagine?—and I was up nights with him, and he didn't get better, but I thought he would, he was bound to, it was a gathered ear, see—first thing you know it would bust and the matter would run all out and then he'd start to get better— how could I even imagine?—" She was coming gradually toward him like a sleepwalker, her mouth pulled all out of shape, the hooks of grief caught in the corners and yanking it grotesquely down. "He was so good —he cried a little right along—sometimes he'd cry hard, it hurt him so, but he was good, Olaf. He was the best little kid you ever seen in your life. I'd walk with him, see, Olaf, holding him like this," she showed him how, cradling her empty arms and swaying back and forth, "maybe half the night, and maybe he'd stop crying and I'd look down and here he'd be looking right up at me,"—she seemed to not want to cry and the effort made her face as ugly as a mud fence—"and he'd reach up and give my face a pat. Pat my cheek, he would. . . ."

"Oh, poor little boy. And poor girl that you was, all soul alone," Olaf said, weeping so that his face was soaking wet. "Come here, come here."

She went toward his arms with blind glazed eyes. "And anyway Mrs. Golightly told me about this Doctor Queen. He operated on a man down on State Street and the man got along all right, so naturally, why, naturally—"

"It was Parley's time to go," Olaf said. "It was just his time, that's all." He took a step to meet her.

"And anyway they carried him out, this nun, see. All the nurses are Catholic sisters up there at the hospital. They're nice, though. I wanted to take him—he was afraid, you can imagine—but she said it would be better if she took him—to the operating room—and the last word he ever said—"

"Come, dearie, come," Olaf whispered.

"—was—calling me, you know, calling—my name. And died, you know, Olaf, died right there, never come to, and only a little past three years old, too. The last word he ever said in his life was—calling—me. But naturally he would."

(Sitting quietly in the outhouse, Gertrude shed a tear for Parley. A hard-backed gold and blue-green bug came walking down a slit of sunshine, and she watched him waveringly. She took a corner of her dress and wiped her eyes out so that she could see better and scrutinized him, drumming her heels on the floor. She thought a deep thought: that this bug would die as Parley had died, for everything and everybody died. Then she thought another deeper thought: that before death, came life, and before life, came death. Then she thought the deepest thought of all: that blonde hair hanging down in ringlets was twice as pretty as blonde hair braided in skimpy braids. She wondered if Mamma would possibly consider letting them wear curls to the funeral and decided that, if she and Bertha went at it right, she probably would.)

At the moment he took her in his arms, the flood broke loose and the torrent of tears came down, and he held her, crying. They both cried, clinging together. . . . It took quite awhile for them to get back on dry land, with a firm footing under them, but they did, little by little, and then they sat on the bed talking. Linnea said, "I never thought I'd forgive you. I really never thought I would, I got so mad."

"The minute I heard about Parley—Mrs. Sterling's husband Mr. Brenneman come down and told me, and waited while I got my clothes on and brought me up here—night shift, he says he's on, and just got off work—why, the minute I heard about Parley—first, I felt so terrible I couldn't think, and then I could think, and I knowed this was the one thing that'd make you take me back, no matter how mad you had been and saying you'd never have nothing to do with me again. Like that day up at the Tabernacle—"

"Conference before last," Linnea said.

"—you wouldn't even look my way."

"Well—" she began defensively.

"But I knowed this was the one thing that'd fix things between us."

"Death, you mean," Linnea said. Her face, though damaged by tears, was beautiful again now, looking at him beautifully. "I never thought—I never dreamed—it clamped down on other people all the time, but it didn't seem like it could strike so close to home. Anybody that was mad at anybody else would *have* to make up, it looks like, when death comes along and shows so plain . . ."

"Us, especially," Olaf said.

". . . how little our lives is, how we ain't any bigger than a minute and die like flies. Only what do you mean, us?" she said. "Especially?"

"Why, I say us especially because *we* would naturally have to make up, you and me," he said. "It stands to reason. Under the circumstances we couldn't do nothing else."

She looked at him, puzzled. "That's what I been saying, that death brings people together. But what do you mean? Saying *we'd* have to make up, you and me? We are made up, and wanted to, but we didn't *have* to necessarily."

"Oh, yes, we did. Sure, we did," he said.

"Why? What are you talking about?"

"Well," he said, not looking at her. "It was you and me *had* Parley in the first place, wasn't it?"

"Yes," she said.

"Well, then, it will have to be you and me have another boy to take his place, won't we? Or a girl as the case may be? That's all the answer I can see. What else can we do?" He stated a logical fact, there was no arguing against it, it was the most sensible declaration in the world. "That's why I knowed we would make up. There wouldn't be anything else we *could* do, the way I figure."

"No, there wouldn't be," Linnea said, slowly after she had thought about it for a moment. "I guess there wouldn't be at that."

"So I wasn't talking through my hat when I said that under the circumstance we couldn't do nothing else but make up and get over our differences. Was I?"

"No, you wasn't," she said.

Gently he reached over and patted her hand.

"I'll—try—not to be so mean no more," she said.

He moved closer to her, putting his arm around her waist, and when her head drooped toward his shoulder, he pressed it firmly there, patting her soft and disarranged hair. "Why, you wasn't mean," he said. "There ain't been a mean bone in you."

"Jealous," she said, large comforting tears beginning to gather and fall, "and mean. As onry over Sigrid as a woman could be."

"You was not!"

"I was, too! I ain't going to be that way no more. I'm going to be nice from now on."

"Maybe I'm getting a little ahead of myself," he said, "maybe this ain't no time to mention such a thing, but, Linnea, listen, I got my feelers out for a house for you!"

"A house," she repeated. "Imagine. If things don't fall down in a person's lap! Why, I think I got a chance to move into the other side of Mrs. Sterling's house in July."

"I know. She mentioned it to me last night," he said. "And that would be all right. You and the kids could live there till I put this deal over I got in mind."

"What kind of a deal?" She did not look at him, for she knew her eyes were shining all out of reason.

"Oh, a deal I got in mind. It may take a while. But I thought I'd mention it. You ain't going to be *many* years older," he said, "till you got your own house. That I would be willing to bet on. I'd eat my hat."

"Olaf," she said, "I just don't know what to say."

"Fifty by a hundred, six-room house, eight hundred dollars—"

She drew a deep breath. It would cost as much as Sigrid's!

"But you could move to Mrs. Sterling's first, and that would give me time to put this through, and then you could turn around and move into the new house."

So not only was there the delicious prospect of moving once, but of moving twice! "Olaf, I just don't know what to *say*," she repeated. "I just simply don't know."

She had been as good as dead, and now she was alive again. Alive and breathing and warm, she sat against her husband's side, and he held her, gently patting her arm. She could hardly bear to feel so much happiness and unhappiness at the same time—the ladies were here in the house and murmuring together behind the door, the parlor smelled sweet with carnations, for a terrible reason, and death in a white coffin wore embroidery from Paris, France, and had a bouquet of withering flowers in its tiny hand—and so she thought as quickly as she could of moving, of Mrs. Sterling's flat and then of this house Olaf was talking about.

"Where?" she said.

"Where what?"

"Where would the house be located?" She rubbed her cheek against his shoulder. From now on, she thought, she wouldn't be so hard to suit any more—she had had some sense knocked into her for a change.

"Why, a couple blocks from where we are now," Olaf said. "I mean, where me and Sigrid—from Sigrid's house. I have to, see, dearie. It's the same fellow owns the property that owned Sigrid's—my—house. I'd be getting it through him, see."

Two blocks from Sigrid's house!

She sat up, the old bright light of battle in her eyes. "We ain't going to fight no more, we're not going to have any more bickering, and arguing, and all like that, but I tell you something, Olaf," she said, in the old way, "you just try to get me a house two blocks from Sigrid's *if you dare!* You just try and move me two blocks from Sigrid. You just try it! You got another think coming!"

Olaf didn't say a word. He looked at her, a twinkle in his eye.

She caught on. She stopped. She turned red. "No," she said more gently, in fact, about as gently as a woman can speak unless she wants to take a notion to coo like a pigeon, "but I really mean it. I wouldn't any more live two blocks from Sigrid's than I'd fly to the moon!"